WANTED

THE CHASE RYDER SERIES, BOOK 1

JO HO

This book is dedicated to my other half, Matt, who is quite possibly, the sweetest guy there ever was. He has shown me what unconditional love is and brings joy and silliness to every day. I don't even mind that my cats love him more than me now.
(I do, really).

I also want to thank Dawn for sticking with me since we were seven years old, showing she had great taste, even then! She has been the biggest cheerleader in my life and I wouldn't have written this book, or made this giant leap without her support.

SIGN UP TO JO'S NEWSLETTER!

Be the first to hear Jo's news, book releases, and giveaways.
Apply for her ARC teams (she has one for ebooks AND one for
audiobooks) to get free, advanced copies of her books to read/listen to
and review.

Plus, you'll get a free book as a thank you for signing up! What's not
to like?

Sign up and join all the cool kids at
www.johoscribe.com

1

———

PROLOGUE

EW YORK CITY, NY

He had been running now for days.

The hot asphalt stung his cracked soles and the burning sun pounded onto his thinning frame, but he knew he couldn't stop. He had to get away.

A battered blue truck thundered past, and he flinched. No matter how often it happened, he still wasn't prepared for the rush of sound that roared into his ears. Where he was from, there were no cars. No vehicles of any kind.

He lifted his nose to the wind and welcomed the heady sensation of another new smell to add to his collection. Juicy, with a hint of smoke. He licked his lips, mouth watering in anticipation. Crossing onto the sidewalk, he moved towards the aroma, to where an overweight man in a greasy apron cooked on a stand. Meat patties sizzled on the grill.

He hadn't eaten since the escape, and now his stomach protested painfully. He padded up to the man and gave him a hopeful look, but clapping eyes on him, the vendor grabbed a broom and started shaking it in warning.

"Get lost, you filthy beast!"

Red from the heat of the flames, perspiration slid down his wobbly chin and landed with a plop an inch away from the meat. When his target failed to move, he glared down at the optimistic hopeful and—

WHAAM! Steel-capped boots lashed out onto his rump.

The sharp stabbing pain shocked the brown and white dog who had never felt anything like it in his life.

He blinked back tears and howled.

2
___

THE CEO

The CEO wasn't pleased.

Though considered an attractive man by many, The CEO had an eerie way of smiling that never reached his blue-gray eyes. Of slim build, he took great pains with his appearance, which showed in the Saville Row tailored suits he'd had shipped in from London. Custom made, a single suit could feed a starving African nation for a week — not that he ever would, abhorring charity as he did.

Deceptively soft-spoken, The CEO's calm exterior masked a ruthless streak that terrified men twice his size. Any who failed to do his bidding had a way of vanishing, never to be seen again.

The CEO stood by his desk in the glass office overlooking The Facility. Pouring himself a glass of Cognac, he sipped at the drink, letting the warmth of the liquid slide down his throat.

For all intents and purposes, The Facility was a high-tech laboratory where secretive experiments were being conducted on a daily basis. White-coated scientists rushed around below conducting wide-ranging research, but few knew the real reason for The Facility's existence. Only The CEO's most trusted advisors had the key to that secret, which essentially included only two people: the muscle, and Dr. Elora Robins, the brain.

After years of research, they had finally created the perfect specimen, only for him to escape. The CEO frowned, remembering the ineptitude of the staff member who was ultimately responsible. His name was Julio, and he was one of the night janitors.

Julio had worked at The Facility for close to twenty years when its number one focus was genetic engineering and DNA splicing. An illegal immigrant, The CEO had hired him specifically (as he had done with all low-level staff) as he knew Julio couldn't afford NOT to keep quiet about what went on in the lab. As an added bonus, Julio also worked for below minimum wage. The CEO had never understood anyone who paid higher rates to such low dwellers unless they liked flushing company profits down the drain.

On the night of the escape, Julio had been suffering from a bout of food poisoning. It seemed he'd left out some food at home that had been visited by houseflies. On his fourth trip to the toilets, when nausea and diarrhea had almost forced its way out, Julio had left a security gate unlocked.

This was all the opportunity that the resourceful dog had needed. Sticking to the air shafts and lesser used walkways, the dog had snuck out of The Facility before the alarm was even raised.

Needless to say, when it was discovered that Julio was to blame, The CEO had had him disposed of. His family is still searching for him to this day.

The CEO fingered his sleeve now as he waited for the call to be patched through. *The Mercenary wouldn't let him down. He knew what was at risk.* They had lost the dog for a few days, but a new sighting had pinpointed him in New York City. Feeling the beginnings of a headache, The CEO took another sip of his drink, a three-hundred-year-old brand of Cognac that cost the same as a small car.

Finally, Suzanne, his assistant, spoke through the intercom.

"Sir, he's on one."

The CEO activated the speakerphone and spoke one quiet word. *"Well?"*

The Mercenary's voice was strained.

"Alpha escaped."

The glass slid out of his hand, smashing onto the granite floor. Shards of glass flew in every direction. Almost immediately, the office door flung open and Suzanne bustled inside. In her forties, she was his right hand and prepared for every eventuality. Including this, it seemed. Suzanne had entered carrying paper towels, which she now used to mop up the spilled liquid. He watched her in silence before issuing The Mercenary's next command in a voice loaded with threat.

"Find him, or don't bother coming back."

3
___

CHASE

G REENWICH, FAIRFIELD COUNTY
Everyone loved sunsets. Everyone, that is, but me, Chase
Ryder, to whom sunsets signaled that yet another hard night was
approaching.

In the leafy upmarket park surrounding a man-made lake,
wealthy couples strolled hand-in-hand admiring the mottled orange
sky. I stirred, waking from my nap beneath a towering oak. Oaks
were best as they provided plenty of foliage to protect against sudden
showers and prying eyes. There was also the added bonus of load-
bearing lower branches that someone nimble could scramble onto
should trouble come calling... and you should know, trouble had me
on speed-dial.

I stared at my reflection in the water. The face that stared back at
me was fourteen but looked younger. A button nose and blue eyes
gave the illusion of innocence. My mouth was plump; a little bigger
than I'd like, but at least I'd never need collagen. The shoulder
length hair would be a glossy chestnut if it weren't hanging in one
big, greasy streak. Despite my current condition, I knew I was above
average, but I'm not exactly what you'd call vain, usually choosing to
hide my face rather than show it.

My stomach emitted a low rumble. I slipped a hand into a pocket and retrieved the last of my money, a hundred bucks or so. All that's left of my stash. It might seem like a good amount, but I'd already been on the road for eight months. In that time, I learned to only spend when I absolutely had to. *If only I was rich, I wouldn't be in this mess.*

I looked around at my surroundings. Yummy mommies with Pilate's-honed bodies bouncing designer-clad babies on tanned knees. The only hunger they knew was self-inflicted. I compared my figure to that of a passing cyclist, frowning when I realized that the only difference between us was our ages.

Originally from "The Paper City" Holyoke in Hampden County — one of the poorest cities in Massachusetts — I'd come here thinking I would receive more charity in affluent Greenwich, which had seen Mel Gibson and Meryl Streep among its wealthy residents, but these people, so caught up in their self-made dramas, barely noticed me. I'd totaled less here than if I'd stayed home.

I frowned as a shadow fell over the water, obscuring my face. *Strange.* The shadow didn't encompass the whole park, just me. Too late, the danger signs came into my head as a hand clamped down on my shoulder. The nails were ripped and blackened with dirt. I noticed the smell next, pungent, like raw sewage mixed with a brewery.

"Spare some change?"

I spun around to find myself gripped, vice-like, in the arms of a guy who was maybe seventeen. His glazed eyes focused on the money in my hands. I looked at his arms — yup, mottled with needle tracks. I scanned the area quickly, searching for help, but help wasn't coming. *Note to self: if trees are leafy enough to shield you from prying eyes, they'll also shield the nasty druggie who has you in his grasp.*

I froze in terror.

The druggie eyeballed the money in my hand and snatched it from me. He hesitated then, doubt clouding his eyes, but when he realized we were isolated from the rest of the park, they narrowed shrewdly.

"That it, or you holding out on me?"

Without waiting for an answer, his hands started patting me down. Here's something you should know about me: no one, but no one touches me without my consent. Instantly, a surge of white-hot fury broke through the fear. I screamed into his face.

"Don't you touch me!" and struggled like a wildcat. He was startled but much stronger than he seemed and moved like I was nothing but a mild annoyance. As he reached into my pockets, I saw my opportunity and plunged two fingers into his windpipe, slamming the palm of my other hand under his nose, snapping the weak cartilage there. Eyes wide with shock, he released me instantly.

Groaning in pain, he sank to the ground, hands around his now bloody nose. Fallen, he looked much younger. Not much bigger than me and nothing like the terrifying beast I'd thought he was. I swooped in and snatched my money back.

Shooting a quick prayer to the YouTube gods of Krav Maga, I grabbed my backpack and got the hell out of Dodge.

4

———

SULLY

E *LLINGTON, CONNECTICUT*
      I tossed aside the thin sheet that covered my body and glanced at the bedside clock's digital display: 1:47. Those seemingly innocuous numbers filled me with a sudden, though expected, weariness. I stared up at the ceiling and sighed.

Every night, the same goddamn thing.

As I rolled over to stare out of the window, a stray beam of moonlight caught the wedding band on my finger. The ring glinted, a tiny spark in the inky blackness, but I ignored it, the same way I ignored the framed picture that was currently lying face down on the vanity table. I didn't need to see it to know what it contained; the image was seared into my brain.

Taking care not to disturb the empty side of the bed, I picked up my watch, absently running my fingers over the engraved inscription on the back. "To Sully, with love and thanks from the Bauer family". The watch was a gift from a grateful family whose beloved cat I had saved. Although my actual name is Jake Sullivan, no one but my father calls me that, and anything that helped distance myself from that tool was a good thing in my mind. I slipped on the watch, grabbed a pair of tracksuit bottoms from the floor, and tugged them on.

Moments later, I jogged out into the dark. With my mussed brown hair, week's facial growth, and sweat encrusted gym clothes, I knew I wasn't quite the poster boy this prestigious neighborhood insisted upon, but to hell with it. There were extenuating circumstances.

The barren streets were silent, but in their own way, welcoming. Out here, in the dark, I could let the full range of my emotions run riot.

And tonight it was anger.

They say grief comes in seven stages, but for me, they alternated each night. Days were tough, especially the sunny ones that taunted me with how life could have been. On those occasions, I stayed away from parks and beaches, anywhere that might prove too nostalgic. The memories would flash up, stabbing like a knife in the chest even now, almost a full year later.

Things were changing, though. I was beginning to find the odd moment to be grateful for: the scent of freshly cut flowers, a traffic-free Route 83 during an emergency callout. Little by little, I was learning to cope... but as soon as my head hit the pillow, the demons would come.

Placing one foot in front of the other, I stared up at the stars and wondered how much longer it would be before I would get used to sleeping alone.

5
———

CHASE

The sun had barely risen, but I was already on the hunt for breakfast. Like they say, it's the most important meal of the day.

It had taken me all night to shake off the druggie incident. I knew I was lucky this time, but I couldn't afford another slip-up. In the future, I would stay away from trees, bushy or otherwise.

From experience, I knew Monday mornings were the most fruitful, with restaurants tossing whatever hadn't sold from the week before. It was with this promise of delectable treasure that I jogged into the back end of a strip of restaurants and climbed into the dumpster behind The Blessed Palace, a popular Asian establishment. The place was kinda tacky looking, covered with gold and red dragons that looked more like a distorted fish than those epic mythological characters, but they do a weekend buffet that never failed to impress, judging by the length of the waiting line that curved around the block on a regular basis.

Sadly for me, Lady Luck hadn't just left the building, she'd taken a slow boat to China, as a deep dumpster dive only delivered some decomposed fish heads *(seriously gross)*, half a fortune cookie *(semi-gross, and empty, so no good fortune for me — figures)* and something I'd prefer not to examine in closer detail. All you need to know is it looked like Swamp Thing's illegitimate lovechild with a roach.

Enough said.

I sighed with irritation. *Damn greedy staff must have taken the left-overs home with them.* That's the problem with Asians. Never waste a thing.

Shoving the cookie into my mouth, I picked my way over the remaining mess of empty cartons and boxes. As I grabbed hold of the skip to haul myself out, I heard a sound and froze. Someone had just yelped. Loudly. In a that-really-hurt kind of way.

I raised my head and peeked over the edge of the dumpster. A mangy dog, some kind of collie mix, was backing away from a man. There was a bone in his mouth, but the guy had one hand on it. He wore the uniform of The Blessed Palace and struck repeatedly at the dog with a wet dishtowel.

THWACK! The towel made a whipping sound as it connected with the collie's flank. The dog whimpered but didn't let go. He didn't attack either, just kept backing away. It's like the thing didn't know he had two rows of sharp teeth.

My eyes narrowed into slits. From the collie's thin frame, I could tell he was starving, maybe even more so than me. It could have been my own lack of food or the injustice of it all, but I felt a sudden rage building.

Stealthily, I crawled out of the dumpster and dropped silently, landing behind the guy in my Kmart sneakers. He twirled the towel, readying another strike. Neither of them had noticed me yet, so I took full advantage of the situation. I reached for the nearest trash-can, snatched the lid off, and HURLED it at the guy's head. The dull sound it made on contact made us all wince. He dropped like a hot spring roll. I looked at the dog. "RUN MUTT!"

And took off. I only glanced back when I reached the end of the block, so it was a shock to see the dog panting right behind me.

"Shoo! Scram!" I waved my hands at him, but he just cocked his head at me. Seeing that we were alone, I slowed my running to a jog.

Clearly Angry Chinese Man wasn't after us. Which, come to think of it, was weird.

I suddenly stopped. What if I'd hit him too hard? Heads are pretty soft and not the best defense against steel. What if I'd... *killed* him? My life didn't flash in front of my eyes so much as my mugshot.

Muttface suddenly dropped his bone. That alone was shocking enough, but then he clamped his jaws around my wrist and started tugging.

"Hey, dufus! I just saved you! What kind of gratitude is that?"

And then I heard it. Furious shouts. Furious *foreign* shouts. I glanced back and saw Angry Chinese Man was not dead after all, but alive and kicking — and he had brought friends. *With cleavers.* The dog and I stared at each other, the same expression mirrored in our eyes... holy crap.

Muttface tore off, stopping a few yards ahead of me. He looked at me and barked once before tearing off again. Didn't need a membership to Mensa to figure out what he meant. Having no Plan B, I sprinted after him.

The dog ran fast, but never in a straight line. It was like he had experience evading capture. Already light-headed, I was becoming dizzy with all the twists and turns we were taking. *I* had no idea where we were any more, so Angry Chinese Man and chums had no chance. I followed Muttface down a side street.

And suddenly I collapsed.

One minute I was running, the next I tasted tarmac. I felt a wet, sandpapery tongue on my face.

And then there was darkness.

6
―――――

SULLY

Staring moodily into a mug of black coffee, I stifled a yawn. I sat at a kitchen table, eyes staring blankly at a newspaper open in front of me. My next client was due any second, but I found it difficult to care. While the late-night workout sessions meant my body was in its prime, my mind felt groggy, and I wished I could sleep the day away. But duty called.

"Your eleven thirty canceled," came a shout from the next room.

Or maybe not. It was Florence, my elderly, no-nonsense receptionist-come-assistant. This was a small practice that didn't require much staff, so multi-tasking Florence was a Godsend, though her domineering attitude wore me thin on occasion. Her long floral dress made slapping sounds against her legs now as she marched into the kitchen. An image of Florence doing a Hitler salute flashed into my mind before I shook it guiltily away. When I caught the determined look on her face, however, I steeled myself, ready for trouble.

"Since there's nothing in the diary until three, now would be a good time for you to do some spring cleaning. Clear out anything you don't need," she suggested. She gestured upstairs at my house above the practice. Her eyes bored into me, but I refused to take the bait, lowering my gaze to the paper.

"Another time. I'm busy."

She glared at me, but not without some sympathy. It was quite the feat and a Florence special. With a sigh of impatience, she snatched the paper away, grabbed my chin, and raised it to meet her gaze. But when she spoke again, it was unnervingly soft.

"It's unhealthy, dear."

I swallowed. I knew she was right, but just the thought of clearing *her* things away caused my chest to constrict. Experience meant I knew Florence wouldn't be dropping this anytime soon, however. With no energy for a fight, I nodded meekly.

"I'll make a start," I conceded and made my way slowly up the stairs.

At the top of the stairs, I shut the door that separated work from home and walked into the living area. The room was decorated eclectically, the result of many happy weekends perusing the local flea market, but right now, it seemed as if a tornado had left its devastation in its wake, with empty microwave trays and beer cans littering the floor. I stepped over them and turned the television on, finding comfort in the inane infomercial chatter. Tossing a crusty pizza box from the sofa, I lay down and shut my eyes. I'd get to it, but first I needed a snooze...

CHASE

I don't know how long I was out for, but it was the smell that woke me. My mouth was as dry as parchment, and my eyes felt like they were stapled shut, but I forced them open. I had to see what was causing the delicious aroma wafting towards me.

There was a something on the ground. It took a second for my vision to clear, but when it did, I thought I must still be in La La Land. There, in front of me, lay a carton of STEAMING DUMPLINGS! I blinked. The dog sat next to them patiently, as if waiting for me to react. When I gaped stupidly, he nudged the carton towards me and *grinned*. I spotted the Blessed Palace logo on the side of the box and pulled what can only be described as a comical double take.

No way...

I forced myself into a sitting position, dusted the street scum from my face, and reached for the food. My fingers closed around the edge of the box.

It felt real enough?

Muttface woofed and pawed the ground as if to say get a move on. I needed no further urging and shoved a dumpling into my mouth. Holy taste bud explosions! Turns out, those lines were onto something! I inhaled the box of deliciousness, even giving a few pieces to my new best furry friend, surprised to see how delicately he ate them. Clearly, I could learn a thing or two. Together, we *woofed* them down. In no time at all, the carton was empty. I tipped it upside down, just in case there was another sucker hiding in there, but nada. C'est finito. I looked at the dog.

"That was the best meal I've had in... just the longest time. If only we had some fritters too, huh? I could die and go to foodie heaven." Muttface cocked his head like he was actually considering my words, then suddenly took off without a backward glance. I felt a pang of crushing disappointment. "Thought we had something going here," I called after him — but I was talking to thin air. Littlest Hobo was long gone. Feeling kinda bereft, I thought about how I was humanizing the dog. Me. Miss. Anti-Dolittle. Eight months on the streets could sure change a person.

As a kid, the only pet I'd ever had was a baby duck, and that lasted for all of a week. One day, as a treat, I decided to let him swim in the gutter (The Paper City = Poor = No Paddling Pool for Ducky), only he got swept away by the current and into a drain. I'd lain on the sidewalk, ear pressed to the drain, listening to his cries until they were all but swallowed by the gushing water. I cried for months after. OK, I was five, but still.

Back to my present situation. Muttface is just a dumb animal. So, somehow, he brought me food from the same restaurant we ran away from. Ironic, but hardly rocket science. Maybe he'd already stashed them some place when Angry Chinese Man caught him. And while I was having my tarmac nap, he'd fetched provisions. It made sense. Kind of.

I could stay here waiting for Big Trouble in Little China to happen, or I could move on and find a bed for the night. It was a no-brainer. I staggered to my feet, swaying a bit, my blood sugar still low despite the recent meal. I'm one of those annoying girls who can eat whatever she wants without putting on a pound, but that also meant my high metabolism required more sustenance than the average girl of my size, which, being homeless, sucks big time.

I made my way back onto the main street and spotted a bus shelter on the other side of the road. It wasn't great, but it might do. I just needed to check if it was watertight — nothing worse than waking up to a mouthful of rain.

Expensive cars roared past, not in the least concerned by my bedraggled state. Car-jacking was low in this part of town, but these guys weren't going to risk a higher insurance premium just to test out that statistic, especially for pungent moi. I wasn't counting, but it had been at least five days since my body had seen any water, and that was even before the dumpster dive. I waited for a break in the traffic.

"Woof."

The sound came from behind. I took an involuntary gasp and spun around — but a bit *too* fast. Balance and co-ordination fled me as my foot slipped from the curb. I caught a brief glimpse of my furry best friend before I felt myself tumbling backward into the sea of cars.

Time slowed to a crawl.

When you're about to die, adrenaline pounds through your body and details fly out at you in what can only be described as supersonic vision. Like Muttface's eyes, which I only just noticed were an emerald green with gold flecks. And the see-through plastic tub he gripped in his mouth containing banana fritters, covered in sesame seeds that formed the initials BP.

While I was in slo-mo, the dog, conversely, seemed to be moving at super speed. In one quick motion, he dropped the fritters and lunged for my chest, snagging a mouthful of T-shirt. I hung there, suspended over the road, just inches away from my demise, anchored only by this animal's teeth and a prayer that the cheap polyester fabric wouldn't give out. A car horn blared to tell us to quit messing around. As if.

And then the dog pulled me to safety.

I sank to my knees, shaken, gasping for the breath I hadn't known

I was holding. I couldn't believe it. I wasn't dead. I was alive. The dog had saved me.

Muttface tapped his paw on the tub of fritters, which had landed unscathed on the sidewalk, and chuffed softly like he was inordinately pleased with himself.

My jaw hit the floor.

8
____

CHASE

I admit I was freaked.

Too much was happening, and I wasn't prepared for any of it. A million questions swam through my already taxed brain. I found myself eyeballing the dog constantly. There was no other logical explanation than the conclusion I'd come up with for his talents, and trust me, I'd exhausted all the possibilities in the hour since my near miss with the reaper.

Muttface was an alien disguised as man's best friend.

Which was kind of brilliant, if you think about it. What better way to spy on a different species than to camouflage yourself as the number one pet in America? Just look at him: head swiveled around, sniffing his butt like a real dog. He couldn't be more disarming. Or gross.

We'd discarded the bus shelter idea due to both our discomforts of it being so overlooked *(well, I'm assuming Muttface had objections; he was definitely restless)* and we were now camped out in a shopping mall's mother and baby room, which to me felt like The Hilton.

I was trying to ignore Muttface — who had suddenly taken a great interest in sniffing each of the toilet stalls — and turned my attention to the room instead.

There were marble walls, a glass-domed ceiling, and hanging baskets overflowing with dried flowers. Opposite the stalls stood a floor-to-ceiling mirror etched in gold, while the far wall was covered with posters of upcoming movies in steel frames. An entire area of the room was kitted out with sofas and bean bags. *I mean seriously, why would anyone put sofas in a restroom?*

I was hoping the security guards would forget to check this place so we could stay the night. I'd gotten lucky previously once or twice, though they were never as nice as this. I was pretty sure I could fit on one of those gigantic baby-changers if I rolled my legs up. Could probably fit on there *with* the dog. I figured that along with mansions and cars, rich people must have bigger babies.

Feeling uncustomarily light-hearted, I plucked a flower from a basket and tucked it behind my ear. Turning to the mirror, I meant to mock my own reflection. Instead, I was shocked at how I'd taken dirt to a whole new level. Quickly, with Muttface guarding the door, I gave myself a flannel wash (one of the things I always carried in my trusty backpack) and dried off using an air blade dryer thingy. There was even a classy hand cream dispenser—

—Which promptly disappeared into my bag. It's not like I condone stealing, but this place wasn't going to miss it. Besides, it smelled like *coconuts.* Then I turned to my furry friend, who was busying himself with his own version of a bath. I'd put things off for as long as I could, but I knew it was time to get some answers, whether I was ready for them or not. I perched on the edge of a baby changer and cleared my throat.

"Hey, dog. Could you stop that? We need to talk."

Muttface immediately ceased licking and fixed his intelligent eyes on me. Then he waited, head tilted. It was disconcerting, to tell the truth.

"I'm going to ask some questions. I'm assuming you can't actually speak?"

He barked. I heard the chastisement in his tone.

"Correction, you can speak. I just don't understand what you're saying."

He barked again and wagged his tail.

"We're going to need to establish some rules for this to work. How about I take one bark as yes and two for no?"

"Woof." His butt shook with excitement. I grinned in spite of myself, pretty sure we were making history here. Shame about the restroom though, nice as it was. Maybe, in years to come, they'll rewrite this whole event and make the setting more palatable. I heard they change things all the time.

He pranced on his feet before settling back down.

"Let's begin. Are you... an alien?" I waited expectantly, but he said nothing. I suddenly realized the possible flaw of my questioning. "You know what that is, right? Creature from outer space? Not of this Earth? Little green man? Or furry in your case?"

One bark.

"So, you're not an alien, but you know what one is." I felt the need to clarify, for my own sanity if not his.

Another bark. Hmmm.

"But clearly you're super intelligent."

The resounding "WOOF!" was obviously something he was very proud of. And who could blame him?

"Were you born that way?" The question was greeted by two barks. Our first no. I tried to decipher what else it could be. My eyes landed on one of the movie posters. Some sci-fi thing to do with DNA splicing. I felt the hairs raise on the back of my neck.

"Did someone make you like this?"

"*Woof.*"

This time, his bark was somber, like he was remembering something deeply sad. The ramifications of this hit me pretty hard. If he was made, it was for a reason, and I don't think it was to perform at Rocco's Traveling Circus. I reached out and stroked his head. He leaned into me, pink tongue hanging out in a goofy expression. Honestly, you'd think he'd never been petted before.

"Did you run away from the people who made you?"

Another bark. This one more determined. He stared at me and tensed his body as if how I responded would determine his next move. I thought about what he'd just revealed and realized we had more in common than I'd initially thought. I dropped down from my perch and cupped his face in my hands.

"Just because someone made you, doesn't mean they deserve you. If that was the case, I'd be back in Massachusetts. If you're worried I'll send you back, don't. I wouldn't do that to you."

He regarded me solemnly. Then his tail twitched suddenly, swinging from side to side in the biggest wag I'd seen to date. When I smiled, the dog leaped up, and I got my first whiff of doggy breath as he licked my nose to my forehead. Not an inch of my face escaped unscathed. It wasn't the most pleasant experience of my life.

"Stop that! Rule number 1, no licking!" I wiped my face on my sleeve, trying to rid it of any excess saliva. "So," I asked nonchalantly, "are you planning on sticking around, or is this a flying visit?"

"WOOF!"

I managed not to smile, but honestly? I felt a huge sense of relief at his answer. It kind of surprised even me.

"Then we need to call you something other than Muttface. I should warn you, Lassie and Hooch have been used to death." Several other possibilities ran through my head; Beethoven, Bruiser, and Bingo, but none of those felt right. And then I was hit with a spark of genius. And the cherry on top? It was still a B name!

"How about... Bandit? That means outlaw, in case you don't know, except you probably do, seeing as you seem to know a lot for your type..." I was babbling, suddenly nervous, surprised by how much it mattered to me what he thought of my choice.

Next thing I knew I was on the ground, the wind knocked out of me as a giant tongue slobbered over my face again.

We probably needed to run through our rules of engagement a few more times.

9

———

SULLY

The hands on the antique brass clock revealed it was a little after six in the evening. A freestanding monolith that took up the whole of one wall, it was the one luxury I kept in the practice. A little ostentatious for the simple surroundings of the workplace, but I didn't care. Besides, there was no room for it upstairs. It was a family heirloom passed down from my father and had sentimental value. That we both treasured it was the only thing we had ever agreed upon.

I sighed at the time. I had thought I'd be done with work by now. The Red Sox were playing tonight, and I had planned on watching the game, but instead, here I was, rifling through the cabinets, compiling a medicine list. Really, this fell under Florence's job description, but after our earlier altercation, I had avoided her for the rest of the day. Childish, I knew, but I was the boss. I was almost done when the doorbell rang. Irritated by the interruption, I growled down the hall.

"Unless someone's dying, we're closed. Come back tomorrow."

"Sul, it's me," a familiar voice said. "Open up."

I frowned but put down the list and unlocked the front door.

Mark Armstrong stood outside. All chiseled jaw line and broad shoulders, he was a regular hit with the ladies, though, unlike me, Mark was a player who cherished his freedom. We had been firm friends since college. Mark worked as a consultant down on Wall Street. I never really understood what his job was, only that it involved ridiculous amounts of money and offshore accounts. Mark had the kind of lifestyle most people envied. And the icing on the cake? He only worked three days a week. Today must have been a work day, as Mark was still dressed in an Armani suit in lieu of his usual shirts and slacks, and instead of a briefcase, he carried a perspex tray of lasagna.

"Figured you could do with some home cooking."

I pulled a face. "Like I haven't been through enough already."

Mark sidestepped smoothly past me, not waiting for an invitation. "Relax," he said. "I didn't say it was *my* cooking."

I closed the door as Mark made his way up the stairs. "Then I hope you gave her a good time at least. First, there's mothering, then comes the smothering. That's your saying, right?"

Mark ignored me. He stood in the living area, taking in the empty junk food wrappers and general mess. I felt some embarrassment, but I knew Mark wouldn't make this into a thing. "I keep asking to borrow your cleaner..." I cleared a space on a chair for Mark, but he shook his head.

"I'll heat this up, get some beers going. You, my friend, are heading for the shower." He moved into the open-plan kitchen. Once a safe distance away, he tossed a look back at me. "You're pretty ripe."

I sniffed under my arms and had to agree that I wasn't at my best. Mark set the dial on the oven and placed the dish inside.

"Instead of food, I'll bring you a case of Axe next time."

I grabbed a tennis ball from a shelf and aimed it at Mark's head. Anticipating a comeback, Mark side-stepped. The ball went wide, sailed over his shoulder, bounced off of the kitchen tiles and rolled into the sink.

"If you could only score like that the rest of the time," Mark quipped.

I mumbled something unintelligible as I stepped into the bathroom, slamming the door behind me.

10

—————

SULLY

When I stepped out of the bathroom fresh from my shower, dressed in a pair of jeans and a cotton shirt, I had to admit I felt almost human again. The rich aroma of the reheating lasagna caused my stomach to flip-flop. *Real food,* I thought. *Not something out of a box.* I padded barefoot into the kitchen but was surprised to find it empty. Two beers and place settings were neatly laid out on the table, but Mark was nowhere in sight. Hearing a sound across the hall, I followed it to my bedroom... where I froze in the doorway.

Having erected several removal boxes, Mark was rifling through the closets at a rack of women's clothing. He had an armload when the floorboards beneath my feet creaked, revealing my presence. Mark spun around guiltily.

"What the hell are you doing?" My eyes glittered angrily.

Mark dropped the clothes onto the bed. "You can't avoid this forever." He stepped towards me, palms held outwards, placating. "We hoped you'd arrive here yourself, but it's been ten months. You needed a push."

"We?" My breath caught as it came to me. "Florence."

"She's worried about you. We both are."

"So you thought you'd *ambush* me?"

Mark took a step back, sensing my building rage.

"Sully, come on. I only want to help. Let me help you."

A range of conflicting emotions flickered across my face. Anger, fear, and then pain. Mark made an attempt to continue when his leg knocked against the pile of clothes, sending them tumbling to the ground.

I reacted like a man possessed. Darting forward, I scrambled around, snatching the clothes from the floor as if they were made of a precious material that would disintegrate if left there a second too long.

"Sully." Mark's voice was pained, struggling to watch his friend's desperate behavior. He cleared his throat. "They won't bring her back. Nothing will."

But I was beyond hearing, now methodically sorting the clothes into a neat pile. My touch was gentle, reverent.

Mark steeled himself. Clenching his fists, he braced himself.

"Emma's gone," he said flatly. "You need to accept it."

I suddenly rounded on him.

"You think I don't know that? There isn't one second of any day where I haven't thought about her cold body lying in a box instead of with me. I can't sleep, I can barely function, but her things keep me sane. Having them here keeps her close to me." My voice cracked, raw with pain.

But Mark refused to bend.

"You're holding on when you need to let go." He slipped a business card from his wallet, offering it to me. "Look, just... call them. They're expecting you."

I didn't move. Sighing, Mark set the card onto the table. Unbidden, my eyes roamed over the typed lettering. *Dr. Philip Grass, Psychologist. Specialist in grieving.*

"Get out," I said softly.

Mark hesitated. Then placed a hand on my shoulder.

It was the wrong thing to do.

ROARING, I flew at him, shoving him back through the hallway to the top of the stairs.

"Jesus, stop!" Mark cast a startled look over his shoulder at the fast approaching steps, but my rage knew no bounds. Mark reached for the banisters, fingers closing around the sturdy wood. He held on, anchoring himself even as I continued to push.

"I want you gone! Leave us alone!"

Unable to withstand my fury and at a disadvantage beneath me, Mark stumbled down the steps, all the while pleading with me.

"Can you hear yourself? There is no more 'us'."

With a determination built of desperation, I forced him through the hallway and out of the practice. No sooner had Mark's foot landed outside than I slammed the door on him.

Mark walked slowly back to his car. I waited until he unlocked the car, then I slid open the upstairs window. The lasagna flew at Mark with unnerving aim, landing inches from him. Hitting pavement, the dish smashed into a thousand pieces. Meat sauce and glass splashed onto his pants.

"Nothing wrong with my aim now," I said.

Gritting his teeth, Mark climbed into his car and drove away.

11
———

CHASE

I woke to find dog hair in my mouth and the smelly beast stretched out by my side. At some point during the night, he must have crawled onto the baby changer with me. He must've been cold and needed the added warmth. *Note to self: Give him a blanket, or at least a towel, next time.*

I yawned and stretched. Light streamed in through high set windows, showering the bathroom in iridescent sunlight. I blinked, somewhat taken aback. The place was practically sparkly. I was entertaining the possibility of this being our nightly stay when Bandit suddenly sat up and cocked his ear.

"What is it?" I asked.

Bandit looked towards the door, gave a low warning growl, and bolted into a toilet cubicle. I scrambled after him and had just enough time to climb onto the toilet before a cleaner entered, pushing a cart. Tacky salsa blared out from her cheap headphones. I peeked through the crack in the door to see a Hispanic woman wielding a mop, dancing to her phone. Good. At least she wouldn't hear us over that racket. I waited until the cleaner entered the first cubicle and signaled Bandit to follow. Quickly, we snuck out, darted around the cart, and escaped into the mall outside.

A scattering of early morning staff was trickling in. I knew we had to get out before we were spotted - a girl and her dog would stick out like a sore thumb. Seeing a sign for the exit, we started for it, when a gorgeous smell assaulted our nostrils. Practically drooling, Bandit sighed and gave me a pleading look.

I craned my head for the source of the heavenly scent and found it just a few feet away; a pastry stand, being looked after by one lone worker with his back to us. I was figuring out how we could sneak some goods when Bandit darted ahead. I watched in amazement as Bandit slunk closer, always keeping out of sight. Within seconds he had reached the stand. He snatched three pretzels into his mouth and made it back to me before anyone had seen a thing. I beamed at him.

"You sneaky little thief!"

I swear he grinned at me.

Shoving the stolen goods into my bag, we bolted for freedom and didn't stop until we were at least two blocks away. I found a nice spot by a green and handed a whole pretzel to Bandit. His eyes went so wide with happiness I thought they would explode out of his head.

Stupid dog.

12
___

CHASE

After breakfast, we headed downtown. My newfound
companion's special abilities had got me thinking. Like me,
Bandit knew a thing or two about survival. Also, like me, he had
sticky fingers — or paws — and could lift things better than anyone.
Clearly, we could survive just taking what we needed when we
needed it, but I realized we should aim higher. Here was a goldmine
waiting to happen!

Having been broke my entire life, I had always craved money.
And right then, I considered the various ways we could utilize
Bandit's skills. Obviously, there was street performing, but that was
just one step away from begging, which I draw the line at (there was
that small matter of pride). I could enter him into a dog competition,
but that would bring too much attention to us. I doubt my mom
would care enough to find me, but Bandit's real owner, that was
another story. I knew I still needed the full lowdown from the dog,
but somehow I kept putting it off. Some sixth sense told me he or she
was way bad news.

I looked at him now, padding next to me. His tongue lolled out in
a sign of contentment, and he seemed for all the world just a normal
dumb dog, but I could see he held his posture differently to other

mutts. No matter what he was doing — goofing around, resting, or eating — Bandit was constantly aware of danger.

In my experience, there were only two types of people in the world: one's who had suffered by the hands of others, and one's who hadn't. Bandit fell into my camp.

We arrived outside a grand stone building with an ornate welcome sign that read: "Welcome to Ashdale Library."

Perfect.

I reached up and unwrapped my scarf, then tied it around Bandit's neck. He cocked his head at me in question, but I didn't elaborate. As I headed inside, I called back to him.

"Come on boy, time for some schooling."

At the word "school", Bandit pricked up his ears and bounded after me.

13

CHASE

I let out an impressed whistle.

The old stone facade disguised a thoroughly modern interior. A glass ceiling hung over the central chamber. Shelves filled with books formed a maze across the floor. I could make out some familiar-sounding titles — The Hunger Games, Harry Potter, Twilight — but I had no interest in those.[1] My gaze swept the room until I found what I was looking for... a bank of computers. Happily, there were only a few other web geeks around. I started towards them when a voice stopped me dead.

"Young lady, there are no dogs allowed in here."

This had come from a prickly looking librarian. I casually studied the name on the badge pinned to her chest. Miss. Thorne. *How apt.* I stared over Miss. Thorne's shoulder and allowed my gaze to drift to one side.

"Even guide dogs? I'm partially blind." The lie came with no effort at all.

Miss. Thorne blinked at me behind wide-rimmed glasses, her expression horrified. What a terrible faux pas she had just committed! Her face flushed an ugly red. She took a step back and stammered.

"I'm sorry... I didn't know."

I smiled sadly at thin air.

"No worries. I get it all the time. Glaucoma," I explained helpfully. Miss. Thorne took another step away from me as if to keep my eye disease at bay.

"Can I assist you with anything? Our braille texts are on the next floor up?"

So someone who couldn't see would have to stumble up a flight of stairs all on their lonesome? Whoever designed the layout of this place should be given an award. I shook my head.

"That's very kind of you, but my dog is trained to look after me."

Miss. Thorne cleared her throat.

"Excellent. Well, I'll be here if you need me. You just have to call."

I waited patiently for her to go, and after a few moments, she finally got the hint. Spinning on her heel so fast it was a miracle she didn't snap her ankle, Miss. Thorne walked stiffly to the check-out desk.

Stooping down, I clutched hold of the scarf around Bandit's neck and spoke into his ear. "Lead the way, fella." Bandit snapped to attention and — quite literally — pranced to the computers, enjoying the charade. I rolled my eyes at his antics. Someone had to teach this dog, less is more. Happily, the computers were out of Miss. Thorne's line of vision, so we wouldn't be getting any questioning looks sent our way.

The computer was already on, so I pulled up Google and searched for some money-making schemes. Windows popped up with helpful banners like: "Earn $1000 a day working from home!"; "Get paid for surveys!"; and my own personal favorite, "How to gamble your way to a fortune!" While I was pretty sure I couldn't get into a casino for that last one, the gambling thing struck a chord in my brain. Poker!

I looked at Bandit by my side, his back ramrod straight. He was taking this acting thing very seriously. If I could teach him to understand poker, he could be my spy on the inside. I could have him perched somewhere inconspicuous and he could spy on the game for me. I'd just have to teach him a few basic signals... Excitement flooded my body. This could work!

I cleared the unhelpful pop-up windows and opened YouTube. I honestly don't know what I would have done without this site. I've learned self-defense, the best techniques of dumpster diving, and even how to collage. Yes, I'm an artist. Surprised?

Although I'd drawn the short straw in most everything else, one thing I had going for me was my photographic memory. Didn't matter what I saw, heard, or read. Once it went into my brain, it would stay ingrained in there forever. Hence the glaucoma reference.

I loaded various how-to videos and hit play.

"Boy, pay attention. You're getting a quiz later."

A whine of excitement escaped his lips.

Seriously.

What a freak.

14

CHASE

We had been walking now for hours.

The day had long since disappeared, having been swallowed by the night, taking along with it the green lawns, flower displays, and coffee shops of Nicetown, Connecticut. Here, the streets were littered with trash. Run down properties were boarded up and covered with graffiti. Others fared little better, as decaying stoops and overgrown, over-junked, front yards battled for attention. Scantily clad women crawled the curb, attempting to flag down passing cars.

Yes, folks, we'd arrived in Ghettoville.

My foot lashed out at an empty Coke can. It flipped over three times before landing into a blocked gutter with a splash. Bandit had to stifle his urge to chase after it. I gave him an apologetic look.

"Sorry. Wasn't thinking."

He shot me a look — he couldn't understand the sudden need to pursue the can. The need left him uneasy.

"You're a dog. Dog's chase. Deal with it."

He woofed, and I could tell my answer displeased him. Earlier, when we'd left the library, his tail was alert and wagging; now it barely even twitched. We'd only been together a short while, but already I was starting to read his body language, and man, was he dog tired.

After Bandit had digested what seemed like every poker video under the sun, we left the library for a jaunt in Walmart[2], where we obtained our own pack of cards. Then, in a nearby park (gotta love Greenwich for the amount of square parkage), I proceeded to teach Bandit sign language, Chase Ryder style: a cocked right ear meant I should raise, both ears facing behind means I fold, and a cocked left ear, call. I knew this amounted to cheating, but you try eating days-old meat crawling with maggots then get back to me.

A couple of shady looking guys walked past. I gave them a wide berth, but they paid me zero attention. They headed towards a dive of a place where a flashing neon sign above the entrance read "McCall's". The guys strolled inside. I was about to move on when I spotted the poker chip one of the guys was tossing in his hand.

This was it, I thought to myself. *This was the place.* No fancy door-man, no dress code. No one would notice a girl and her dog... I hoped.

I waited for a few beats, and when the coast was clear, I slipped in with Bandit.

Like I figured it would be, the place was dimly lit. Tables littered the room in a haphazard fashion, where a dozen or so customers sat drinking amber colored beer. Despite the rock music emanating from a jukebox that had seen better days, the dance floor was empty. A baseball game blared from an ancient television set overlooking the bar — which was lucky really, as the sole barman had his full atten-tion on it. There was a distinct air of despair in this place, and I didn't need Bandit's nose to smell it. I felt a pang of sympathy for the drunk drowning his sorrows in the corner. He looked like how I usually felt. Beaten.

I moved quickly to a cigarette dispenser, pretending to study the brands inside. Bandit stuck close by my side, but we didn't need to be so cautious. The patrons were so deep in their alcohol-induced stupor that there wasn't even one curious glance our way.

From the central bar, two corridors lead off: one to the restrooms and the other some sort of private room. I watched as the shady guys marched up to a closed door and knocked three times. The door was opened by a man whose giant head seemed to float on a cloud of heavy cigarette smoke. When the smoke cleared, I saw the poker game that was in progress beyond. I stared down at Bandit and grinned.

"This is it. You ready?"

He pawed the ground, and his butt shook with excitement.

Despite the lack of attention thrown our way, we kept to the shadows as we crossed the bar and made our way to the closed door. I gave Bandit one last look, then before I could chicken out, I knocked three times. As before, the door opened, but this time, a guy with a patch over one eye shot us a startled look.

"This ain't no nursery. Get outta here, kid."

He turned his back on me, figuring I would heed his words, however, I shoved my foot in the door and forced my way inside. Eight grown men zeroed in on me, including the guys we had followed.

"I'm here to play." I'm sure I would have sounded more convincing if my voice hadn't wavered at the end of that sentence.

Patch grinned at me, revealing a gaping set of black teeth. I cringed and mentally affirmed I would take better care of my own molars in the future.

"This is a private game, young lady."

I gave him the best glower I could manage.

"I have money," I said. Then I pushed past and marched up to the surprised table. I gestured, and Bandit immediately took his position behind the other players. But he couldn't keep still. I think he was nervous, picking up on my vibes.

A big guy with the dealer's pin smirked at me.

"You're pretty gutsy for a kid."

"And you're pretty chirpy for a guy who's going to lose it all," I shot back. Dealer continued to smirk at me, though there was now a hardness in his eyes. Guess he didn't like being shown up.

"Alright kid. Show us what you've got or get out."

I tensed. This was it. Bandit must have sensed my sudden indecision as he stole back to my side. I reached into my backpack, withdrew my carefully saved stash, and slammed it onto the table with as much force as I could muster.

"Here." I kept my eyes level with his. *Show no fear,* I chanted to myself.

Dealer broke his gaze to take in the money I had slammed down... and burst out laughing. One by one, the men around the table joined him in laughter until the whole room was in an uproar. Except for me. I kept my face a mask of defiance, refusing to show my confusion.

"A hundred and twelve dollars?" he choked out in between laughs. "A hundred and twelve?"

Patch left his position by the door. His grin wider — and even grosser — than before.

"What's so funny?" I demanded.

Dealer leaned back against his seat and pointed to the current betting pot on the table.

"See that? That's just the starting bets for this hand. We open with fifty which means, you wouldn't even last one round." He smiled a slimey smile before continuing.

"While I do find your naivety charming, I think it's time for you and the fleabag to leave."

Patch grabbed my shoulder and started steering me to the door, but I twisted away from him, dived towards the table and grabbed my money. The other men made as if to stop me, but Dealer held them off.

"No. Let her take her hard earned cash. We are men of honor."

At that, the room erupted again. Bandit, not understanding what was happening, whined unhappily.

I shoved the money into my pockets, then tore out of there with Bandit close at my heels. To my fury, I felt tears pricking at the corners of my eyes. Determined that none of them would see me crying, I found a door marked FIRE EXIT and pushed it open. We stumbled out into a back alley.

"I can't believe those jerks!"

Bandit circled me and shoved his nose into my hand. I petted him without thinking and automatically started to feel a bit better. I remembered reading an article on how pets were great stress relievers in a copy of Reader's Digest before. I took several deep breaths and calmed down. *Oh well. Not all of my plans were winners, but at least we didn't lose our money. Could've been worse.*

Bandit bared his teeth at me and growled.

I snatched my hand back, confused by the complete change in him. And then I smelled it. Hard liquor breath.

Breathing down my neck.

I spun around to find the drunk from earlier standing behind me — only now he didn't seem so pitiful. He staggered towards me, reeking of desperation and whiskey. Bandit growled warningly again, baring his sharp white teeth.

"I don't want to hurt you, just give me the money," he pleaded.

Here's the thing you should know about me. I'd managed to make four hundred bills last eight months. You do the math. With a hundred and twelve still left, that meant I'd used roughly a dollar a day to live on, which I think you'll agree is pretty hardcore. I could go four days on what you spend on a coffee. I take nothing more seriously in life than cash. So was I going to hand it over to this drunk? You bet I wasn't.

Seeing the determination on my face, he looked almost apologetic.

"You don't understand. I need that money. It's a matter of life and death."

I almost snorted in his face.

"Welcome to my world, scumbag."

OK. Here's another thing you should know. My mouth shoots off before I even know what I'm doing. It's one of my worst traits and something I really should work on.

All niceness faded from his face, and he lunged for me. Bandit started barking like a crazed thing. I tried to run, but he snagged hold of my backpack and wouldn't let go. Then I tried to elbow him, but my bag got in the way. He must've slipped as I felt his crushing weight land on top of me. We tumbled onto a crate of empty bottles.

I managed to twist around until I was facing him. I kicked out, getting him on his side. It must have hurt as he suddenly shrieked and backhanded me across my face. My head snapped back as stars clouded my vision. There was a metallic taste in my mouth — blood — and I realized I must have bitten my cheek. His hands went for my pockets, where he must have seen me stash the money when a ball of fur suddenly flew towards him.

A scream of agony pierced the night. I watched with fascinated horror as Bandit clamped his fangs around the drunk's right hand — the hand that had hit me and was about to strike again. The drunk was frantically trying to shake him off, but Bandit wasn't letting go for no one. I felt a moment of deep pride. *Go, boy!*

I was pushing myself up when I saw the drunk reach for a bottle that had had its base smashed off. Jagged edges glinted, caught by an overhead streetlight. It took a split second to realize what his intentions were, but by then I was already too late. I flung myself forward at the same time the bottle flashed through the air and stabbed into Bandit's stomach. He yelped and dropped like a stone.

The drunk stood over him with the bottle raised high, preparing to stab again. Blood pounded in my ears as I realized Bandit wouldn't last another round. I screamed.

"Here! Take it! Leave him alone!" I threw the money at him. A cloud of paper bills rained onto the ground. He scrambled on all fours for the money. When he had taken every last bill, he disappeared down the alley without a second glance.

I bolted to Bandit's side.

15
___

CHASE

There was so much blood.

My hand pressed tightly against the deep wound, but it barely stemmed the flow. Bandit whined, his whole body trembling in pain. He panted loudly, the white of his eyes showing. Did that mean something? Was he dying? My encyclopedic brain ran through everything I'd ever learned on first aid, but it was no use - the data filed up in there applied only to people.

"Hold on, boy. You'll be OK," I choked out.

Bandit looked at me like he knew I was lying. Cold panic ripped through me. *No God, please, please let him be OK.* My heart was thumping so loudly I thought it would explode from my chest. There was a high-pitched ringing in my ears that dulled the world around me. Abruptly the ringing died down and I could hear with crystal clarity: nearby cars screeching to a halt as the drunk skidded into traffic, followed by car horns blaring, and screeching tires. In a white rage, I hoped for the resounding thump that would signal a collision, but it never came. Why do the bad guys always get away?

Unwrapping the scarf from his neck, I turned it into a tight bandage and tied it over the wound, but I'd barely finished the knots before his blood seeped through, blossoming over the thin material and staining it red. I had to get help. He wouldn't last much longer like this.

I wrapped my arms around his body and tried to lift, but he was so heavy, my legs started to buckle from the effort. A whimper escaped his lips as I tried unsuccessfully to lay him down again gently. I spun around, taking in the junk in the alley: there were multiple trash cans, some boxes, and something half hidden behind a doorway. I jogged forward a few steps and had to stop myself from bursting into tears of relief. It was a little worn, but there was no denying the Whole Foods shopping cart!

Quickly, I grabbed a box, flattened it, and shoved it inside the cart. Shrugging out of my denim jacket, I lay it on top. It wasn't much, but it was the best I could do to soften what was going to be a very bumpy ride. With a strength I didn't know I possessed, I maneuvered Bandit onto the makeshift gurney. He flopped loosely in my arms and barely made a sound. This I knew was a very bad sign. I slid a hand under his nose and felt a weak blast of hot air against my fingers. Still breathing.

"Hang on, I'm getting you help."

Seizing the handles of the cart, I thundered out of the alley.

16

CHASE

Shop fronts blurred past, but none were what we needed. I didn't stop for anyone. There was no time. Pedestrians dived out of my way, shouting insults. Did they think this was some kind of sick game? I shot another glance at Bandit and paled at the blood that was turning my jacket red. He wasn't even that big. *How could he have so much blood?* The thought briefly crossed my mind that Bandit wasn't fully grown. He was probably quite young. I shook my head and focused.

Where were we going?

Suddenly, I knew what to do. My eyes swept up and down the streets until I pinpointed a telephone booth across the road. I swung the cart so hard the wheels shrieked in protest. Then, not waiting for a gap in the traffic, I ran into the road.

Brakes screamed. Horns blared. An irate driver leaned out of the window and yelled some pretty foul things at me. I ignored them all and pushed the cart over the street. Bandit's tongue was hanging completely out of his mouth now. It was pale. Almost white. Definitely not a good sign.

Making it to the booth, relief flooded through me when I saw the phone directory hanging by a cord. I flung it open and prayed I'd find what I needed.

17

SULLY

I stared into the carton of another unappetizing takeout. Oily noodles with burned pieces of rubber that masqueraded as chicken. That home-cooked lasagna sounded mighty good right about now. Shame it was nothing but a stain on the sidewalk.

I let out a long sigh. I shouldn't have flipped like that. In the last ten months, I had systematically severed ties to all our friends — anything that reminded me of my previous life with Emma. A few had stubbornly hung on in there, but I had managed to push away every one of them until Mark was the only friend I had left. Except maybe now that bridge was burned too.

I reached for a Coors and gulped the sweetness down. Tomorrow I'd call and eat humble pie. But not tonight. Tonight was terrible-Chinese-and-get-drunk-in-front-of-the-box night. All day, Florence had spoken to me in a clipped tone of voice laced with disappointment. I had tried explaining my side, but Florence wasn't interested in anything I had to say. She was so steaming mad that — despite being her boss — I had given her a wide berth. What that woman couldn't do for Catholic guilt.

I got up from the dining table and moved to the window. Emma had always loved this view. I stared past the perfectly manicured neighborhood lawns and into the distance, where just below the horizon, the New York skyline blazed with lights. This view was the reason we had bought this place. "A little piece of heaven," she had called it.

I thought Emma had lost her mind when she first set eyes on the rundown property and declared that this would be our forever home. Its previous elderly owner had long given up on the upkeep, and time had taken its toll on the bricks and mortar. The neighborhood disliked the eyesore, but put up with it due to their love and respect for the old coot.

Like many other times in her life, Emma had seen the potential of the place and had haggled like a pro until the real estate agents — disarmed by her tenacity and charm — finally caved. I thought of the happy months we'd spent renovating the property to change it from the dump it used to be.

I closed my eyes so I could see her again. Hair piled messily on top of her head, she wore those painted-splattered dungarees she liked for decorating. She waved a loaded paint brush around — narrowly missing my face — and painted different color patches on the wall, which in fairness all looked yellow to me. Then she stood back to study them. I loved the way her nose wrinkled whenever she was thinking. When she had finally decided on a tone, I had grabbed her hand and twirled her around as we'd danced to the radio in celebration. Our marriage had been filled with silly, wonderful moments like these.

My eyes flashed open, filled with tears. *Oh Em. It should've been me.*

The familiar, crushing ache began to build inside. I grabbed my head and squeezed. My head pounded with the pain I was physically causing, but I kept up the pressure until I couldn't take it anymore. My hands dropped to my sides, relieved that the raw pain in my heart had momentarily been interrupted.

But the pounding continued.

I frowned as I slowly came to the realization that the pounding wasn't in my head anymore.

It was real.

18

CHASE

I could see the lights on the floor upstairs. So why wasn't he coming?

The sign on the window confirmed that this was the place I was looking for. Although the clinic was closed now, I knew someone lived above. I had seen his silhouette by the window.

I stabbed at the bell with a bloody finger while pounding on the door with my other hand.

"Please," I cried desperately. "We need help!"

Finally, a hazy figure appeared through the glazed glass and began moving forwards. Lights flooded on, blinding me. Then I heard the furious voice of whom I assumed was the vet.

"Why the hell are you pounding on my door? Do you know what time..."

His sentence trailed off. I could feel, rather than see, him looking over my shoulder.

"What the—?"

"You've got to help him. He's been stabbed."

19

———

SULLY

I barely registered the sight before me.

The kid — she must've been all of fifteen — was covered in blood and hysterical. A quick scan of her body revealed she wasn't harmed. However, I couldn't say the same for the dog lying in the shopping cart.

He was a tri-colored liver Border Collie. Pedigree, and very rare judging by his green eyes. He was also dying of a gaping wound in his stomach. Normally I wouldn't take house calls this time of night, but this was clearly an emergency, and if I didn't do anything, the dog was going to die.

The girl was babbling at me, but I'd already tuned her out, my professional head taking over. I grabbed the cart and wheeled it inside.

"Close the door and come with me," I commanded.

Surprisingly, the girl shut her mouth and complied.

I steered the dog into the operating theater and hoisted him onto the table. I felt for his pulse; it was weak, but it was there. A quick examination of the wound revealed a laceration deep enough that it exposed both muscle and tissue. He'd lost a lot of blood. I pursed my lips. Infection, along with possible organ failure, was a very real concern right now.

"I'll need to operate to have any chance of saving him."

"Do it," she said. "Whatever you need to do, just don't let him die!"

"Go wait in the lounge."

This time, however, she wouldn't comply, shaking her head violently. "I'm not leaving him! This only happened because of me. I was attacked. He saved me." The Girl's voice cracked as she struggled to hold back the tears. I had seen upset kids before, especially when I'd had to put down their beloved pets, but this was something else. This level of desperation reminded me of myself at the hospital, at Emma's bedside, holding onto her pale and non-responsive hand... Shaking my head to clear the unwelcome memory, I took in her battered clothing and general griminess. She was a street kid, I would bet my life on it. This dog was probably her only friend in the world.

I softened my voice.

"I'll do the best I can, but you can't be in here. He has an open wound. You could risk infecting him."

My words sliced into her panic. She looked up at me then and must have been reassured by what she saw there. She swallowed, then nodded, moving across the room. When she reached the door, she shot me a pleading look.

"You have to save him, OK? He's special."

I nodded and got to work. Reaching across the bench, I snapped on a pair of gloves then set up a donor blood bag, measuring out the correct dose of anesthetic for a dog this size.

When I looked up again, she had gone.

20

CHASE

I left the operating theater, but there was no way I could just sit there, twiddling my thumbs. Bandit's life was hanging by a thread, and I couldn't believe there was nothing I could do! Flashes of our recent travels came into my head like a movie of our best moments that was being projected directly into my mind. I could feel myself on the verge of a panic attack and had to clamp down on it. *Breathe!*

I ran my tongue over parched lips to discover how dry they were. Like someone whose brain's been lobotomized, I didn't even know how I had gotten there. All I can remember is seeing the details for this place in the directory then running the eight blocks here. For the first time, I noticed my surroundings.

I was standing in a waiting area. There was no hiding the fact I was in a veterinary clinic, but someone had given it a good try. The room was painted a cheery yellow, and a giant bulletin board wrapped around the four walls with hundreds of photographs pinned onto it. I moved in for a closer look.

They were all snapshots of healthy animals and their happy owners. Scribbled on some were messages addressed to "Sully" thanking him for his great work with Fido, Gizmo, and Dodo. I scanned the many messages and felt a tiny spark of relief at the sheer number of success stories contained on the board. I decided right then that when this was all over, there'd be one more photograph stuck on this board.

I glanced at the name again — Sully — and guessed that that must be the guy with his hands inside Bandit now. The thought of that brought a vivid image to mind that struck me with renewed terror as a wave of nausea overcame me.

I bolted into the next room, hoping it was a restroom, but found myself inside a kitchen. I ran to the sink and got there just in time for the acrid bile to fly out of my mouth. I retched until my stomach cramped and there was nothing left inside.

Afterward, I wiped my mouth on my sleeve and drank a glass of water, giving myself a few moments to recover. My forehead was clammy, and I suddenly noticed my hands were shaking. Maybe my sugar level was low. Come to think of it, I hadn't eaten since the pretzel that morning. Driven by the natural instinct to survive, I pulled open the kitchen cupboards and investigated their contents.

The first had neatly lined rows of mugs advertising different pet food brands. I marveled that someone — clearly with nothing better to do — had taken the time to face them outward and turn their handles to the right. Somehow I didn't think it was that Sully guy.

The next cupboard contained a mixture of hot drinks and powdered milk. I actually contemplated taking the milk since it was still a source of protein, but then I arrived at the final cupboard and hit the jackpot! Inside, there was a smattering of energy bars, a box of cereal, and a couple of packs of cookies. I swiped the bars and cookies and snagged a handful of cereal, which I crammed into my starving mouth. I must've swallowed half the box before I reluctantly set it aside. I'd stripped the entire cupboard in under a minute, which must've been a record.

A part of me felt bad about what I was doing. Sully was in the next room attempting to save Bandit's life, and here I was thieving, but something told me if he knew the truth, he wouldn't really have minded. Judging by what I'd found here, he could more than afford to eat. Besides, if Bandit survived, he'd need all the food I could salvage.

I fingered an energy bar, sorely tempted. Saliva flooded my mouth, and I could almost taste the sweetness, but I stopped short of tearing open the wrapper. Although my stomach churned with hunger, I decided I would save it for Bandit. It was the least I could do.

I opened the fridge. Instead of the food I expected to find, there were boxes and boxes of medical vials and syringes. As they were of no value to me, I closed the fridge and resumed my exploration of the house. Two doors lead out of the kitchen: one opened into a no-frills bathroom, the other onto the base of some carpeted stairs. I wondered if I should keep going - the stairs didn't have the same feel as the rest of the clinic. Framed certificates and memorabilia lined the walls, which weren't yellow anymore, but a pale green. I hesitated, but then I convinced myself that if I kept myself occupied, I wouldn't think about the scene next door — and the potentially devastating result.

Cocking my head, I listened for any sounds of life from upstairs, but there was nothing. I'm usually pretty stealthy, and this carpet would muffle any excess sound, even if I weren't unusually light on my feet. I headed up, telling myself I only meant to have a peek.

When I reached the top, I found myself in a living room. Huge windows looked out onto the upmarket neighborhood. I guess this was a nice place. Kinda hard to see it though, covered in trash like it was. Takeout cartons and burger wrappers littered the place. I picked up the nearest carton. Whatever it was had long died and was now a congealed green soup. Nice. I set the box down.

The room was painted in yet another cheerful color, this time a spring orange. Drooping plants with brown encrusted leaves overflowed from every window. Whoever had the green thumb hadn't cared for them in quite some time. I moved past a sofa covered with workout clothes and investigated the many framed photographs on a bookshelf. Sully had his arms around a pretty woman in every one. There they were running down a beach; sharing a dog at a Red Sox game; sipping coconut shell cocktails in an exotic far eastern place (Thailand?). I stopped on the last photograph on their wedding day. Could two people look more in love?

Would I ever experience love like that?

I carried on through the living room into a hallway, past the bathroom, and found myself in Sully's bedroom. Like the rest of the house, it was messy. *Why do people have nice homes if all they're going to do is trash them?*

Yes, I felt weird in a grown man's room. I knew I had to keep myself occupied though, so my mind wouldn't play the "what if" game. You know like, "What if Bandit doesn't make it?"

See, not good, is it?

The walk-in closet stood out, as it was the only tidy thing in here. Inside, dresses and shirts hung neatly on hangers, all arranged in the same direction, and in ascending length order. So cropped tops started on the far left, mid length shirts took up the middle section, and by the time you got to the right, the hems of full length dresses draped on the floor.

I noted Sully's wife was petite; only a size bigger than me. I hoped she wasn't one of those who starved herself to look good and thought back to the happy face in the pictures I had seen. No, she seemed much more sensible than that.

My fingers reached out, itching to feel the fabric of a beautiful white dress, but before they could make contact, I whipped them back in horror. Dried blood covered my hands.

Bandit's blood.

I spun around and staggered into the bathroom to see my gruesome reflection staring back at me. There was blood all over my top, on my face, and in my hair. How had I not noticed this before?

I blasted the tap and frantically started scrubbing.

21

SULLY

I had been working on the collie now for close to two hours.

My mind was a blur. I wasn't even sure how I'd managed it on my own. I'd set up a blood transfusion — taking blood from a healthy dog who was in for a broken paw. Putting an animal under can be tricky on even a healthy animal, but on one as injured as this, well, there's a lot of luck and prayer involved. Sometimes the animals reacted to the anesthetic and never woke up again.

I hoped that wasn't the case here.

The nasty gashes in his stomach were caused by a sharp, serrated instrument. Amazingly, no internal organs were punctured. I concluded that whatever had sliced into him hadn't penetrated his intestines. I cleaned the wound the best I could, sewed it up, and covered it with a bandage. I'd have to check on the wound regularly. The worst thing that could happen now was for it to get infected. Having done everything I could to save him, all we could do now was wait. Hopefully, he'd come around in a few hours.

After I disinfected the instruments and pulled off the rubber gloves, I took my first unhurried look at him. He really was a gorgeous thing. Glossy white coat with brown patches. Unusually, his face was white, barring the top right section, dissected in a perfect diagonal under his nose. His eyes were closed now, but I knew they were a brilliant jade green. He was worth a lot to someone. Somehow I didn't think he belonged to the girl.

Although the dog was currently malnourished, there were signs it wasn't always this way. His blood pressure was low, but that was par for the course with blood loss to this degree. The cracks on his feet were new, which was unusual in and of itself. I'd pegged him for about two years old and never had I seen soles so smooth. Almost as if he'd never stepped foot outside before.

His teeth were so pristine you'd think his owner had used whitener on them. No buildup, only slight doggy breath. I looked inside his left ear. As expected, it was spotless — also unusual for a dog that's been on the streets. Tugging gently on the dog's right ear, I looked inside to see a row of numbers and letters tattooed into his ear. It was some kind of identifying code. I jotted it onto a notepad I kept handy and made a mental note to look into this when I knew more about the dog's condition.

My neck muscles complained wearily. I reached up to massage them, surprised to find it was almost eleven at night. Suddenly my thoughts drifted to the girl, and my stomach twisted into knots. I'd let a complete stranger — and a homeless one at that — loose in my home.

Stupid, Sully. Stupid.

I ran from the operating room.

22

SULLY

I ran into the waiting room, but the girl wasn't there (not that I had really expected her to be, but sometimes, it's nice to be proven wrong).

She wasn't in the hallway or kitchen, and my office was empty, which just left *upstairs.* I swallowed as a bitterness began a party in my mouth. Taking two steps at a time, I raced upstairs...

And gave a huge sigh of relief. Everything was as I had left it. ~~We~~ *I* hadn't been burgled. The room was still a bomb site, except now, buried under my workout clothes on the sofa, the girl slept. I froze and gave what Em had fondly dubbed my bug out face.

She dressed tough, but it couldn't hide the fact she was a naturally cute kid, albeit one who'd had it rough. The bottoms of her jeans were worn, and the soles of her baseball boots, coming apart. A dirty backpack lay on the floor next to her. Even in sleep, its strap was looped tightly around her wrist.

It was that single detail that undid me. Explained a lot about her life. I wondered what horror made her run away from wherever she was from.

I didn't want to wake her, but I couldn't just hop into bed either, so

I did the next best thing. I opened the fridge and took out a loaf of bread, some butter, and a block of cheese.

Moments later, two packed grilled cheese sandwiches were toasting in a skillet. Before Em had passed, I was the cook in the house, but it had been a while since I'd wanted to do anything this domestic. If my instincts were right, I figured the girl would be hungry.

Besides, I had questions, and answers were always more forthcoming when softened with a bribe.

23

CHASE

I was dreaming.

Bandit and I were stuck in this weird Matrix style world, only instead of computer binary codes, we were surrounded by drunks hurling playing cards at us, and in the background, there was this sizzling sound, like someone was cooking a BBQ, except the meat smelled liked burned cheese.

My nose wrinkled involuntarily. It was like a magic compass and always did that when food was on the horizon. Dimly, I was aware of more noises: the scraping of plates and pots banging. My eyes flashed open, and I leaped up with a snarl, ready to fight.

Sully was standing at the sink, a tea towel over one shoulder, his mouth wide open, startled by my aggressive stance. I blinked at him, completely disoriented.

"Hi there," he said.

I didn't reply, glancing wearily around the room instead. *Well, this was pretty stupid of me. Alone. In a stranger's home.*

"You hungry? I made grilled cheese." He gestured at the dining table where the sandwiches waited with two glasses of milk.

My stomach made an involuntary sound. Something between a growl and all out shouting. I wanted nothing more than to sink my teeth into that sticky cheesiness, but there was something I had to know first.

"Bandit, my dog…" Fear constricted my throat so tightly, the words got stuck, and I couldn't finish the full sentence.

Sully's expression was grave but hopeful.

"I did what I could. He just has to rest now. If he comes out of the anesthetic, there's a good chance he'll make it."

"*If* he comes out?" I questioned.

Sully held my gaze as he spoke. "It can be hit and miss for a healthy dog and Bandit, you said?"

I nodded.

"He was cut pretty bad," he continued. "All we can do is give him time."

I flung my bag onto my shoulder and started for the stairs.

"So we should be by his side, right? What if he wakes up and no one's there? What if he's in pain?" Clearly, I had forgotten my own rules of that game. I made it to the top step when Sully stopped me.

"That much trauma, combined with the anesthetic, he'll be out for at least four hours. Plenty of time for us to eat and get to know each other."

I must've shot him a hard look, as he suddenly backed off, mortified.

"I meant that in a far less creepy way than it sounded," he said.

I hesitated, but honestly? I was growing so faint from hunger that the only thing stopping me from falling down the stairs was my hand clutching hold of the banister. Gruffly, I nodded and went across to the table. He sat opposite me.

"I'm Sully."

"Chase," I mumbled as I grabbed the sandwich nearest to me and bit into it. The taste was so overwhelmingly good, so fresh, that if I had any tears left in me, I would've cried.

Sully tried not to watch me as he started on his own. We ate quietly for a few seconds. Just two strangers enjoying a meal. He was good, I'd give him that. Not one question so far, but I knew they were coming. I braced myself. He polished off his sandwich in five or six bites while I was determined to savor mine. Who knew when I'd be eating like this again? He gulped down his milk and wiped a hand across his mouth.

"What happened?" he asked simply.

Usually, whenever a grown-up asks me anything, my first instinct is to lie. I'm not even sure why. Call it my healthy distrust of them. But this guy seemed different. After all, he could've called the cops on me the minute I turned up at his door, but instead, he'd helped Bandit and cooked me a meal. Figured I owed him the truth, if nothing else.

"A drunk attacked me, took all my money. Bandit tried to protect me, but the drunk stabbed him with a bottle." My voice was flat. I could've been reciting the weather report for all the emotion I showed.

Sully looked shocked. There was a well of sadness reflected in his eyes, but all he uttered was "Tough break."

I appreciated he didn't try to make this into a thing. I finished my sandwich, drank the milk, and pushed back my chair. The food was a nice gesture, but it didn't make us bff's. I was determined to put a little distance between us. As I stood up, there was a strange expression on Sully's face. Took me a while before I realized he was staring at my bloodstained shirt. I plucked at it self-consciously.

"There's a washer downstairs. I can take care of that?" he volunteered.

I looked down, embarrassed by his kindness.

"I don't have anything else to wear while it's in the wash."

He studied me for what seemed an indeterminable amount of time before speaking again. "Wait here." He disappeared from the room, returning moments later with a pair of jeans, a tank top, and an olive green sweater. I'd seen those clothes earlier, in the closet, but didn't want him to know I'd been snooping. He handed me the clothes.

"Probably a bit big, but... you can keep these." The words seemed to stick in his throat.

I couldn't hide my surprise.

"Won't your wife be mad?"

Pain flashed in his eyes. I knew instantly I'd said something wrong. He clenched his fists and closed his eyes. I guess he was counting in his head or something. When he spoke it again, it was barely a whisper.

"She doesn't need them anymore."

Things suddenly fell into place. The terrible mess in the nicely decorated house. The decaying plants. Sully's wife wasn't around anymore. I didn't know whether she had left or died, but I knew not to ask. The guy looked like he was hanging by a thread.

His shoulders slumped as he piled dirty plates into the sink.

"I'll wait with Bandit. You can use the bathroom if you want. Up to you."

With that, he turned and went downstairs.

I stood there, the clothes clutched in my arms. A huge part of me was thrilled at the thought of a hot shower, but this guy was still a stranger. I looked at the pretty clothes he'd given me. They smelled of lavender. There was no way I could change into them as I was. The blood in my hair had dried, giving me unwanted red low lights with a disgusting, crunchy texture. He'd said Bandit wouldn't wake for a while. What was the harm?

Still, I hadn't survived so long on the streets without learning a thing or two. I dragged a chair into the bathroom with me, locked the door, and wedged the chair up against it. If he tried to break in while I was in the shower... well, he wouldn't be able to.

I turned the water on full blast, peeled the blood-soaked clothes off my body, and stepped into the shower.

24

SULLY

I couldn't believe how I'd reacted to her simple question. I'd played it off, but the truth was, I'd needed to be alone for a while. Pretending everything was fine was exhausting, and that was on top of the long day I'd already had. I knew I would have to pull an all-nighter to watch over the dog. Usually, I'd farm that out to staff, but since I was the only one around tonight... at least I wouldn't have my nightly sleep struggle.

I checked in on Bandit. He was still out, but his color had improved somewhat. I placed my fingers on the inner side of Bandit's thigh and felt for a pulse on the femoral artery. The beat was slow and steady. Another positive sign.

The old boiler kicked into gear, the ancient pipes rattling within the confines of the walls. Chase was taking me up on the shower. Good. She'd smelled pretty foul, but I hadn't wanted to put her on edge any more than she already was.

With nothing else to do, I suddenly remembered the serial number tattooed into Bandit's ear and fetched the laptop from my office. Firing up the MacBook, I typed the numbers into a veterinary database of found animals. I hit return and waited, not really expecting to get a result.

I was wrong.

Within seconds, a warning flashed across the screen:

If you see this dog, call us immediately on the following number.
He has escaped from a medical facility and carries a contagious virus.
The virus is NOT transmittable to humans. Repeat. It is NOT
transmittable to humans. However, you should not approach him.
Please call and we will handle the extraction.
On his safe return, you will be handsomely rewarded.

The warning was followed by a picture of Bandit at full health. I was right; he was a stunning dog, and now I knew why.

He was a lab dog. A virus carrying medical experiment.

Despite the wrench in my gut and how I knew this would kill the young girl upstairs, I did what any professional in my line of work would do.

I picked up the phone and dialed.

25

SULLY

After a few rings, the call was answered by a curt female voice. "HPA, how can I be of assistance?"

"Hi," I began. "I'm calling about a warning you filed with the National Pets Registrar about a missing Tri-colored border collie."

There was a sudden silence on the line. When she spoke again, it was with barely controlled enthusiasm.

"I'm a vet with a clinic in Connecticut. A girl just arrived with an injured dog, pretty sure it's the one you're looking for."

"Could you give me your name, sir?" she asked.

"Jake Sullivan. I run Ellington Pet Care in Sudbury Park Estate."

"Thank you, sir. Now, I have a few questions for our extraction team. Have you come in close contact with the dog?"

"Yes. He was injured. I performed a basic op and sewed up the wound. He'd lost quite a bit of blood, but I performed a single transfusion."

"I see." She didn't sound pleased by my having saved his life. I got the distinct feeling the dog was nothing but an experiment to her. It made my betrayal to Chase all the harder. "And either before or during the operation, did you communicate with the dog at all?"

I paused, perplexed. *What kind of question was that?* She must have felt my hesitation as she quickly tried to cover it up.

"What I mean to say is, was the dog awake when he was brought to you?"

"Barely," I replied.

"So you didn't speak to him, he didn't respond?"

OK. This was getting weird. I frowned at her line of questioning.

"I'm sorry, what kind of medical facility is this?" I asked.

"Please hold, sir."

Cheesy elevator music piped down the line. I was stunned. I'd asked a simple question, and she'd put me on hold? Something felt wrong about this whole scenario. I held the phone in my hand, wondering how long it would be before she got back to me when the music abruptly cut out. I sat there, shocked, hearing nothing but the dead dial tone. *She'd cut me off?!* Turning around on my stool, my eyes followed the cord to the phone — and stopped dead.

Bandit sat next to the phone, awake, his paw nestled firmly in the cradle.

It was he who had cut me off.

26
—————

SULLY

The dog and I traded looks. Then slowly — slowly — Bandit lifted his paw off the cradle, planted his foot on the ground, and shot me what I could only describe as a hurt look.

Though I was puzzling over what had happened, my work instincts took over. My eyes ran over him, performing a quick check. All things considered, he was in great form. More than great if you considered he shouldn't be able to stand right now. This was one driven dog.

Bandit started sniffing the air anxiously. I wondered what he was doing before it came to me.

"She's upstairs," I informed him. "Chase. She's having a shower."

As if he understood exactly what I was saying, he stared straight up at the ceiling and cocked his head, listening for any movement above him. He must've heard something that confirmed my words because the anxiousness disappeared, replaced by a weariness he directed at me.

I wasn't sure why I was talking to him like a human, but I couldn't deny there was keen intelligence that shone from his eyes. We kept a watchful eye on each other until the door cracked open behind him, followed by the appearance of Chase. The change in Bandit was immediate. His tail wagged back and forth so vigorously that it almost threw his whole balance — he was still shaking off the effects of the anesthetic.

"Bandit!" Chase went to hug the dog, but I grabbed her arm and physically stopped her.

"Wait. There's something you need to know about him," I began. Chase turned to Bandit then, a reproachful look on her face.

"What did I say about keeping it secret? What did you do?" she demanded.

To my surprise, Bandit acted like a child being reprimanded. He lowered onto all fours (showing submission) and whined pitifully. Though he couldn't speak, his actions were clear. *It wasn't me. I didn't do anything.*

"Yeah, right," Chase chided. "Couldn't wait to show off, I'll bet."

Bandit barked twice.

"At least you're alive, though. That's what counts."

One bark. Followed by a long, relieved sigh.

I saw animals respond to their owners all the time. Florence had three cats who talked to her nonstop, even mimicked the sounds and tones of her voice. It's the highest form of compliment a pet can ever give their owner.

I love you so much I'm going to learn to speak the way you do.

But what was happening here wasn't the same. I looked questionably at Chase. She sighed too as if the game was up.

"One bark is yes, two means no."

"What?" I managed to mumble.

She turned to the dog. "Boy, are you hungry?"

One bark.

"What about a drink, you thirsty?"

One bark.

"Did you like the man who hurt you earlier?"

Two angry sounding barks.

"Am I glad you're alive?"

One joyful bark.

I watched the whole exchange with my mouth open, but Chase

didn't catch my reaction. She busied herself at the sink and gave Bandit a bowl of water, which he slurped up gratefully. To me, she asked, "Can he eat something?"

I nodded mutely and grabbed a tin of doggie chow from a shelf. Inside, my mind was racing. There was no way in hell they'd rehearsed that little charade, no way, but then... how was that possible? Was this some kind of hustle these two did? Was the dog just a distraction, and I was about to get robbed? I shook my head. No, there were plenty of richer houses in this neighborhood, and Bandit's wound could not be faked, and neither could Chase's very real concern.

My thoughts a tangled mess, and unable to make sense of it all, I focused on the one thing I could do — pouring the dog food onto a plate — but as I went towards him, Bandit bared his teeth at me. Startled by his reaction, Chase frowned.

"Sully's our friend boy."

Two barks.

"He is, he saved you."

Two barks and a worried whine. Chase looked up at me in apology.

"I'm sorry, I don't know why he has a problem with you."

"I do," I said quietly. Suddenly the phone call with "HPA" resounded in my head. One sentence in particular which hadn't made much sense at first, but now cast a whole new light on things: *did you communicate with the dog at all?* Could it be? Could this dog have the same intelligence level as a human?

"I... I think I might've made a mistake."

One loud bark.

Chase didn't understand a thing I was saying, but she was a smart girl and fear was fast sinking in. I could tell by her sudden sped up breathing.

"Oh no. Who did you tell?" she asked.

I shook my head, still unwilling to accept what my mind was starting to rationalize.

"There was a warning. They said he escaped from a medical facility. That he carried a virus."

Bandit shot two barks at me and pawed the ground, agitated. Chase was staring at me in utter horror.

"No, they were doing horrible things to him. He escaped yes, but he doesn't have a virus. They're lying!"

"But... how do you know that's true?"

Chase all but wrung her hands at me. "Just look at him! What more proof do you need?!"

The dog was pacing agitatedly, Chase matching him stride for stride. A gnawing ache appeared in my stomach.

Doubt.

"It's too late," I said. "I've already called them."

Chase flung her bag over her shoulder, cold determination on her face.

"Then we have to go."

Bandit stood up immediately, ready to leave with her when suddenly, two vehicles screeched into the drive. I ran to the nearest window and looked through a crack in the blind.

Two unmarked gray vans sat outside. The doors slid open, revealing six or so swarthy men in black combat gear. They spilled out of the vans welding tranquilizer guns and took formation on the front porch. My trained eyes recognized the darts on the guns — Ketamine — but at that dosage, it'd be enough to knock out a horse. Grimly, I remembered Ketamine could also be used on humans.

The doorbell rang.

We all froze.

A clipped baritone called in through the letter-box.

"Good evening, Mr. Sullivan. We're from HPA, and we're here for the extraction. Could you let us in?"

27

CHASE

"What're we going to do?" I whispered. *"We can't let them take him."*

Bandit chuffed softly in agreement. I flung an arm around his neck, hugging him close. Sully watched us guiltily from his position by the window.

"I'm sorry. I don't see any way out of this."

Indignant fury made me brave. "You were the one who caused this! You can't *not* help us now!"

"Legally, he's their property, and you have no idea what virus it is he's carrying. He could be dangerous," Sully said.

I threw my hands up in the air, exasperated. "They're lying to get him back, can't you see that? It's not like they can say he's super intelligent!"

Sully peeked out of the window again. Then back at us. He obviously still didn't believe the four-legged truth that was staring him in the face. "Do you know what they'll do to him if they get him back?" I pleaded. "They'll lock him in a cage, and he'll never be free again!"

My words must have struck a chord, as involuntarily, Bandit started shaking with fear. It was awful to see, but so was the resigned expression on Sully's face.

"I've done what I can..." He trailed off, unable to find the words to finish the sentence, but I already knew where he was going with this. Glaring at him, I unzipped my bag.

"Give me the meds I'll need for him. At least do that for us." I gestured at him impatiently as anger and fear flooded my body. Coming to a decision, Sully sprang into action and started tossing things inside.

"You'll need to change his bandage twice a day. Clean the wound with disinfectant and cover it up again." He shoved a bottle of pills into the bag. "He also needs one of these, three times a day, preferably with food." Sully zipped up my bag and steered me to the kitchen. "Take the back door and head right. There's a path behind the back yard that's pretty overlooked by the trees. They won't see you there."

He stopped suddenly. "Look, whatever this is about, I really am sorry."

Bandit must have decided he was being sincere as his tongue snaked out and licked Sully's hand. And in that tiny gesture, all was forgiven. Sully's eyes turned bright with something that looked suspiciously like tears, but before I could get a proper look, he took off.

"Where are you going?" I called after him.

"To buy you time," he replied.

28

SULLY

I had no idea what I was doing. I knew I should hand Bandit over to the men at the door, but I couldn't shake the doubt that had crept into my mind. Things just weren't adding up.

As I moved slowly down the hall, I ran over the things that were bothering me: like the conversation with HPA and the bizarre line of questioning that had come from the receptionist. And now the men standing on my front porch. How on Earth had they gotten here so quickly when not even an hour had passed since my call?

I stared at the silhouettes of the men outside. Virus or not, did they really need so many of them? Wasn't that overkill? They looked more like a SWAT team than the animal wranglers a lab might have. I took a deep breath and moved the last few steps towards them when THE DOOR EXPLODED INWARD.

Splintered wood flew past my face, narrowly missing my cheek. Reacting on pure instinct, I ran back into the clinic, into the waiting area. Dazed, my ears ringing, I briefly wondered how tranquilizer guns could've done that to the door. Staring down the hall, I got my first close-up look at the men and saw that a few carried not tranquilizer guns, but *shotguns*. Well, that would explain how my door was now hanging off its hinges. Realizing with a growing horror that these men weren't what they seemed, I knew I was in grave danger.

I bolted into my office, to the work desk where two phones (a landline and my cell), my wallet, and a dock for my laptop lay. I snatched up the phone intending to call the police, but instead of a dial tone, there was a scratchy whine. I dropped it back onto its cradle and snatched up the cell, flipping it open only to find that same scratchy noise.

They were blocking my phone lines!

Sounds of crashing came from the room next door. The men were storming my home now, overturning furniture and destroying everything in their path. They would be here in seconds.

Not knowing what else to do, I snatched up my wallet and started heading for the back door, through the recovery room, when one of the men pounced on me. Though I was taller, my adversary had at least thirty pounds on me. I swiveled on my feet until I faced him. The guy snarled into my face.

"Stop fighting, Doc. It'll go better for you."

I hated people telling me what to do at the best of times, but this jerk was in *my* house. Glowering at him, I stomped on his toes, then swept my foot up behind his knee, knocking him off balance. He went down like a fallen tree. I hopped over him, but the guy's hand snaked out and caught me around the ankle. I grabbed the water bowl Bandit had been using and swung it at the guy's head. *One, two, three times!* Steel smashed into his skull until the guy was out for the count.

"He's in here!" I heard someone shout.

I bolted through the recovery room towards the exit when Chase's panicked voice cried out suddenly. "Help, help!!" A cacophony of dog and cat cries blanketed the night, distressed from the attack.

They were in the kennels.

I crept towards them silently, hoping the animal calls would mask any sound I made. Plastering myself to the corner, I saw Chase gripped by two men. One had a deep scar on the left side of his face. The other had the build and stature of ex-military. He had a commanding and menacing presence and only spoke when necessary. This must be the scumbag in charge.

Scarface shook Chase roughly.

"Where's the dog, kid?"

"You're too late," Chase cried. "He's long gone."

I had to hand it to her. Nothing fazed this girl. Scarface didn't seem as impressed though as his hand lashed across her face, leaving an angry red imprint of his palm. Chase's head snapped back violently. Just seeing it made my teeth jar; I don't know what it must have felt like for Chase.

"That all you got?" she taunted, eyes flashing.

A vein in Scarface's forehead throbbed. His hand clenched into a fist as he went to punch her again. But suddenly a sea of cats and dogs spilled out of the kennels, swarming around their feet! Scarface tried to find Bandit but couldn't keep up with them.

"Boss?" he asked.

"Go," the military man instructed. "I'll deal with the girl." His hand slid into his Kevlar vest to retrieve a wicked looking syringe.

I didn't know what was in the needle this time, but I knew it couldn't be good. While the last thing I wanted was to become embroiled in whatever the heck was going on here, I couldn't in all good conscience let them hurt the girl; Emma would turn in her grave. If I was going to do anything, I had to act now.

Using the animals as cover, I stole behind Military Man and struck at his syringe-wielding hand. Not expecting the move, the needle dropped to the ground, where, stampeded by a heavy-footed Bull Mastiff, it shattered into a million pieces. Military Man roared furiously, turning his attention to me, flinging Chase to one side.

"Run!' I screamed.

Chase bolted down the hall as Military Man barreled into me, crushing the breath from my windpipe. Grabbing me in a headlock, he squeezed. I felt a wall of muscle constricting my airway, pushing down on my chest. This must be what a car feels like in a steel compactor, came my distant thought. I clawed feebly at Military Man, but he held on with vice-like arms.

As the world began to swim, and I started seeing stars, there came a chorus of ferocious barking. I felt the pressure easing slightly and twisted my face in the direction of the sound. Some escaped dogs had formed a circle and were snarling at us.

Wait, not at us. At Military Man.

Globules of thick saliva dripped out of the Bull Mastiff's mouth. Low, threatening growls reverberated in the back of his throat. Unsurprisingly, Military Man took a step back.

It was a mistake. The dogs advanced as one.

In one smooth move, Military Man released me and sprinted for the operating theater. The dogs raced past me, bounding after him.

I was in shock and stood there, gaping stupidly after them. After a few moments, I looked towards the exit to see Chase and Bandit running away. I stared back at the clinic, at the home I had made with Emma and which was now being destroyed. My heart seized in my chest. I knew it was just panic, but it felt as serious as a heart attack. Every instinct in my body screamed at me to rush upstairs and save Emma's precious things. Her smiling face on our wedding day — my favorite picture of her, and the one that I had had to place face down as the sight of it tore me apart — flashed up in my head. All I had to do was run up those stairs, and into the bedroom, and the picture would be there...

Then another image flashed up. Chase's anxious, tear-streaked face when she had first appeared on my doorstep, with Bandit, bleeding out in the shopping cart.

As I fought with myself over what to do, a gunshot blasted into my reverie, causing me to crash back down to Earth.

Tearing my gaze away from my home, I ran after them.

29

CHASE

We ran for what seemed like miles until blisters formed on my feet and my lungs were on fire.

Within a few short minutes, Sully had caught up to us and was now leading us down meandering footpaths, behind opulent backyards with swimming pools and double garages. He had obviously come this way many times before. He never hesitated, taking each turn and corner confidently, stopping just in time as we reached a road with traffic. We zig-zagged across the neighborhood until he finally took us uphill to a secluded clearing where we could see all the way down to NYC. It was here where we saw the mushroom cloud of smoke billowing into the sky. Sully squinted at the direction of the smoke, taking it all in. Pain flashed over his face.

"They're burning down my home," he'd said quietly.

And I realized he was right. We hadn't run nearly as far as I'd thought. From here, we had a perfect view of the blazing fire that consumed his clinic. Lights from neighboring houses flooded on as concerned residents gathered around. In the far off distance, the screaming sirens of an approaching fire truck blared, but I knew it was already too late. It wouldn't reach the clinic in time to save it.

It was a shock when I'd first realized he was running after us.

Back in the clinic, Sully had been so reluctant to help that I had been ready to burn the place down myself, but when they started blasting holes in his home, I understood how much danger we were in. Despite how I had some major trust issues when it came to adults, I kept my misgivings to myself. Besides, they had almost killed him. It wasn't safe for him back home anymore, even if the home were still standing.

I sank to my knees, from emotion or exhaustion, I wasn't sure. Maybe both. Bandit pressed up against me as if offering his strength. Sully tore his eyes from the fire and looked down at him.

"What was that down there?"

"The thing with the dogs? Pretty sure he got them to attack the bad guys. He probably just asked," I said.

"Woof," came Bandit's reply.

I stroked him, gratefully. "Thank you, boy. You saved us."

Bandit flopped onto his side and raised his legs in the air. I reached down and scratched the uninjured part of his stomach. Sully didn't say anything, just continued staring at the blaze in the distance, anger and pain rolling off of him in waves. It was uncomfortable to watch.

I opened my backpack, rifling through it until I came up with a pack of cookies that I fed to Bandit, conscious he still hadn't eaten yet and needed to keep up his strength. He gobbled them down so fast I thought he would take my fingers with them. I was relieved by Bandit's appetite, though. Wanting food = good. It meant he was on the road to recovery. Sully finally looked back at us and frowned at my choice of food.

"What, it's not like I have a wide menu available," I said, opening my bag to show him my stash.

Suddenly, he reacted, recognizing the contents inside. "You stole from me? While I was saving your dog? That's what you were doing in my clinic?"

My cheeks started flushing, but I felt justified in my actions. "Bandit needs to eat, and you looked like you could afford it."

Sully looked outraged by my response, but I wasn't backing

down. What else was I supposed to do? Suddenly, Sully laughed, incredulous. "You come knocking on my door, covered in blood, Bandit in your arms. I help you save him and in return, you steal from me. And now my home is gone. Everything. There's nothing left of her."

And wow, if that didn't feel like he had sucker-punched me in the stomach. It was like I could feel everything he was feeling, and I did not like it one bit. In a bid to change the subject, I forced myself up, despite my calves screaming in protest. Since my lungs didn't feel like they would burst anymore, I knew I had to make a move. If those guys were searching for us, I had to put as much distance between us as possible.

"Bandit and I need to keep moving. We're too close still. I can't risk them finding us," I said. "Boy, are you OK to move again?" I asked Bandit.

His tail wagged, and he stood up, if a little wearily. My guilt escalated another notch. "We'll rest once we're a safe distance away." He licked my hand to tell me he was OK. He understood. I turned to face Sully, biting my lip as I struggled to find the words.

"I'm sorry," was all I finally managed.

Sully didn't respond. Didn't move a muscle, in fact. Just stood there, frozen, unblinking. The thought came then that maybe he wasn't so much shell-shocked anymore, but in *physical* shock.

My mind ran through what it knew about the condition. Keep the patient warm. Well, it was pretty hot out here tonight so, check. My eyes took in the condition of his face. Was the skin clammy or just sweating from the run here? I didn't know. I was about to reach out to take his pulse when he suddenly turned and focused his dark eyes on me.

"I'm coming with you."

I was so shocked by his words, I didn't know what to say. I pulled back and shared a look with Bandit. "Er, heck no," came my instant response. "I know you helped us, but I don't know you, and I trust no one. Nada."

Sully ignored me, warming to his decision.

"Those men are after me now too! You think they'll let me go if they catch me? There's nothing left here for me now, and Bandit needs my help. His wound will need to be regularly dressed. If it gets infected, which is likely out here, you won't have a clue how to fix it."

What he was saying wasn't unreasonable, but every nerve in my body was crying out NO! People had a way of screwing me over, and I really wasn't comfortable with the idea of us rolling on together. A girl and her dog didn't draw much attention, but add a man to the equation and it was all up for grabs.

"Look," he continued. "I've lost too much not to see this through. I want to know who those men are, and what they want with Bandit. I want to see the face of the person who took away the last link I have with Emma."

I didn't reply, brain in panic mode. He must have realized I wasn't caving any day soon, however, as he came at me with my biggest weakness.

"What about money? Do you have any? Because I do."

So then we were three.

30

THE MERCENARY

After the mutts had gone for him, The Mercenary had retreated into the operating theater. They'd trapped him into a corner, but The Mercenary had completed two tours in Iraq and wasn't about to be taken down by these fur on legs.

He'd tipped over the operating table and, using it for cover, he'd taken shots at the dogs with the tranq gun. Of course, he would've preferred a real gun, but the boss had commanded no casualties. Not out of the kindness of his heart, but to keep the clean-up down. Boss ran a near invisible operation, and that's how he liked to keep it.

The first row of dogs dropped fast, and once the others saw their fate, they scampered off in terror. Stupid animals. The Mercenary rounded up his men and sent half into the night to search for the dog while he and the rest ransacked the place. Among the things he found that could be of use was Sullivan's cell. While they searched, Sullivan's full background had been downloaded to his PDA. There was only one piece of information The Mercenary found of interest — Sullivan was a recent widower.

With this knowledge in mind, The Mercenary searched the apartment above with fresh eyes. This was a man clinging onto his dead wife; her things were everywhere. Since The Mercenary was a man who didn't like to lose — and yes, he had lost tonight — The Mercenary decided to have some fun and torched the clinic. Boss hadn't said anything about building casualties so, The Mercenary figured it was fair game. Besides, this Sullivan jerk deserved nothing less for giving him so much trouble.

Once the clinic had been set alight, he and his men had piled back into the vans and were off before a crowd had even gathered. Shadows in the night, that's what they were. The Mercenary took one last look at the blaze. It was quite the beaut, now spreading to the surrounding houses.

Good, The Mercenary thought, smiling. *If Sullivan ever returned, he'd have angry neighbors to contend with.*

Blackman, his guy with the scar on the right side of his face, suddenly handed him a phone, expression grim. "It's the boss," he said.

The smile was wiped instantly from The Mercenary's mouth.

31

CHASE

After we'd walked another two hours, we made our way to Scantic River State Park. Sully mentioned quietly that he used to come here with his wife. He figured we'd be safe here for the night, though when we passed a sign that revealed we were in one hundred and sixty-seven acres of open ground for deer and turkey hunting, I sincerely hoped no one would mistake us for dinner, not after all we'd already gone through tonight.

Sully checked Bandit's wound, said it was coping well under the conditions, fed him a pill, then redressed the dressing. He said he'd keep watch for the first few hours and if no one came, then he'd allow himself to rest. Since he was forcing himself on us, I'd asked what our plan was for tomorrow, but all he managed was to mumble he'd figure something out by the time the sun rose. I would've preferred to know what our next steps were right then and there — what if I didn't like what he was planning? Sully, however, wasn't forthcoming with any more information and seemed to shut right down. After instructing Bandit not to leave my side (you never know, some trigger-happy fool might think he was a deer), I found myself musing over the day's insane events.

It was strange. Most of the adults I'd met in my life weren't the responsible type. Heck, they were downright degenerates (especially my folks), and not surprisingly, I'd developed a healthy mistrust of them all. With Sully, I wasn't sure. Yeah, he really cared about his wife, but that didn't make him a good person. Judging by the constant flip-flopping in my stomach, my gut didn't know what to make of him as yet, so I'd be wary, just in case. People have a habit of turning on you when you least expected it. This I knew from experience.

Bandit curled up by my side and was asleep almost instantly. Poor guy, from being stabbed to escaping capture within minutes of his life-saving operation. I realized we had a lot in common. We were both survivors. It'd take a lot more than a few armed men to break us.

I stared across at Sully's profile. Outwardly he seemed calm, but his hands were clenched into fists, and his jaw set into a tense line. He was still staring into space when my eyes finally closed and I fell asleep.

32

SULLY

Morning light streamed in through tall oak trees, bathing us in a warm glow. Chase and Bandit were curled together, much as they had been the whole night.

I had barely slept. All night, my mind had raced with vivid flashbacks of the day before. From the moment of Chase's bloody arrival to my near brush with death. Military Man's sneering face regularly interrupted my flow of thoughts, causing me to wonder what kind of corporation he worked for that would condone such violence.

Obviously, one that didn't care one iota for the rules.

I'd told Chase I'd come up with a plan for them, and I had one, of sorts. Just not a very good one. I knew I was being irrational. This was crazy! A huge part of my brain was screaming at me: *go back! This won't end well!* But every time I considered leaving, a picture of Emma going up in flames entered my mind, and it made me madder than a wet hen. I wanted, no, *needed* to find the people who had done this to me. If I were honest, I also felt a flicker of excitement.

All year I had been a shadow of myself. Just motivating myself to do normal things, like cleaning up the house and taking a shower, had seemed monumentally hard. I felt nothing, only numb. Had been that way for so long now, I wondered if I'd ever feel anything again. Yet tonight, despite all logic, I was feeling a rush of emotions so intense, they threatened to overwhelm me. And that was before I considered the possibility of Bandit's super intellect. For sure, I was going to test that. As soon as I figured out how.

I looked at the sleeping girl and dog. I knew without a doubt that they needed me. As resourceful as she was, they wouldn't last long out here without help. Not that I felt beholden to them. It would take a while before I would get over how Chase had stolen from me. The defiance in her eyes when I'd caught her out!

I pulled out my wallet and counted out my money. Not much. Enough for food and some place to stay tomorrow, but they'd need more. I had a credit card, but I wasn't keen on the idea of surfacing for now. Better to stay out of sight until the heat had died down. Or at least until those soldier thugs weren't around.

Bandit stirred, waking. He got up, performed an all body shake, then padded over to greet me. I couldn't help smiling. As a boy, I had been one of those kids who couldn't get enough of animals. Soon as I could walk, I would chase after anything furry and on four legs. Sadly, neither parent was particularly into animals, so my early inter-actions only consisted of friends' pets. After I had met Emma (we were college sweethearts), we'd discussed getting a dog, but the timing was never right. And when the clinic opened, well, I had had plenty of animals to look after. We had decided to give the clinic time to establish itself, and maybe in a year or so, we would adopt a pet.

Well, Em, how d'you like me now? Instant father of two.

Chase woke, instantly alert. She gave me a wary look. "Morning," she said, as she dove into her bag before surfacing with several energy bars that she handed out to us. At least the girl had some manners.

"We're going to have to get him more appropriate food. That much sugar isn't good for him."

Stomach cramping from hunger, I nibbled on my own bar, though the sickly sweetness made me wince. I wasn't a breakfast guy normally, but I needed the energy. What I wouldn't have done for a cup of java.

"So what's the plan," Chase asked.

I forced the rest of the granola bar down my throat.

"We need to find a way to communicate with Bandit that's a little more than yes and no. Those men will probably be coming after us, and the more we know about them, the better off we'll be."

"But what can we use?" Chase wondered aloud.

"Something cheap. We don't have much." I replied.

At that, Chase grinned.

"Well, I'm kinda an expert on that." She stood up. "Come on."

33

THE MERCENARY

The Mercenary raged inside the empty van.

After they'd set fire to the clinic, The Mercenary's men had combed the streets until dawn, but the trio had disappeared. Vanished into thin air.

The Mercenary thumped the steering wheel with his fist. Pain shot through his hand, but he welcomed it with a twisted delight. *He had had them in his grasp! If only those damned dogs hadn't attacked!*

He knew for sure what had happened: Alpha had set those mutts on them. The worrying thought wormed through his brain, boring into the back of his eyes, making his head throb. In all the tests run at The Facility, nothing like this had ever happened. Could Alpha control other dogs, or had he simply asked? The Mercenary reported his findings to Dr. Robbins, but her reaction had disgusted him. She had been excited! She considered the dog an ever-evolving marvel, but The Mercenary knew the truth. Alpha was a freak who needed to be put down. And he was the man to do it.

The Mercenary flipped open his cell and dialed a number he kept for special occasions. The call was answered after a few rings by a curt male voice.

"Chicago PD?"

"Well, if it isn't Danny boy! How's pop?" he asked with something as close to enthusiasm as he could muster.

"Uncle? Hey, how are you, old man?"

"Less of the old, thank you," he retorted.

"We're all doing great. Dad caught a twenty-pound rock bass over the weekend. Hasn't shut up about it since."

The Mercenary smiled thinly, tapping his foot, impatient to get to the crux of the call. "But did he skin and cook it, or toss it back into the river?"

"What do you think?"

"Always the weakest link, my kid brother."

"So what can I do for you? Is this a social call?" Daniel asked.

Finally! "Afraid not, son. I need a favor. I'm on a case about a missing girl. Young Caucasian, around fourteen? First name's Chase, but that's all I got."

"No worries. I'll run it through the database, see what we can dig up."

The Mercenary smiled dangerously.

"Thanks, son. And when you've done that, I'm going to need another favor from you..."

34

CHASE

On a scale of one to crazy, this was definitely in the insane range. I felt like every person in the place was watching us.

We were in another generic mall. It was a Saturday, so the place was heaving with kids and families out to damage their wallets. Just like us. Me, my dad, and our guide dog. Only Sully's wallet was looking pretty empty, so our mission today? Get to a cashpoint and withdraw the hell outta it.

While Sully and I were on edge, constantly looking over our shoulders for any soldier types who might be after us, Bandit was having a dog of a time. This was only his second time in a place like this (the first being practically empty), but here, Bandit couldn't get enough of the noise, the bright lights, and smells. He was sniffing everything he could get his nose on. Including people. It was hugely embarrassing.

For his part, Sully tried to act like this was no big deal, but there was something in the way his shoulders slumped, how he dragged his feet. I would never admit it, but I was feeling kinda bad for him. I'm not really the touchy-feely type though, so I focused on the mall directory and located what we needed on the map with a finger.

"It's just down there," I pointed.

Sully looked at where my finger was.

"*That's* your big idea?" He didn't bother to hide his skepticism.

"Look, this is my area of expertize. I guess you wouldn't know that living where you lived, but this is what I know." I headed off before he could ask any more inane questions and looked down at Bandit. "What do you say, boy, want to go shopping?" I asked. He grinned at me and picked up the pace. Sully saw his reaction and patted his pockets worriedly.

"Let's keep it light, OK?"

Moments later we stepped into my favorite place in the whole world, The Dollar Store. Seriously, if you've never been in one, you don't know what you're missing. They have everything in this place. *E-very-thing.*

On my left was the cleaning section containing all kinds of amazing products that you've never heard of. From an eraser sponge to white vinegar spray — the most organic and best cleaner out there apparently, but whiffy I'd bet. Ahead of me stood the gardening section where tools were going for a dollar! And plastic nets for growing vegetables, and ooh, a red gnome! On the far side was the food aisle, where my feet naturally wanted to head, but that wasn't what we came here for. I silently commanded them to obey, and we — my feet and I — were about to move to the back of the store when Bandit took off down an aisle. Sully stopped me from following.

"I think I know where he's going. I'll go after him, you get the stuff."

Sensing there wasn't anything to fear in this place, I nodded and ambled to the back, following the signs until I found what I was looking for — books. But not thick, heavy tomes — who reads those, right? I grabbed bright and colorful children's books, ones suitable for a child just learning how to read. I wasn't sure what Bandit's reading age would be, so I grabbed one of each up until age six. After that, the books had fewer pictures and weighed a ton more.

I made my way to the cashier, but the quickest route there was to detour past the food. I took that as a sign from the Universe. Juices flooded my mouth as soon as I saw the breathtaking range on offer. It's just insane what you could get in here, especially when you compared it to other places. I once snuck into a Wholefoods just to see what the fuss was all about. The prices made my eyes water, no joke.

Almost of their own accord, my fingers plucked several heart attack-inducing cakes from the shelves, curling around the satisfying weight of them. *We had to eat,* I justified to myself and chocolate is good for energy. It's what rock climbers and survivalists carry for emergencies.

Within seconds, my arms were piled so high, I could barely see over them. You're probably wondering why I didn't just use one of those baskets? Well, I normally don't get to shop for more than a handful of things at a time, so it never crossed my mind. Rounding a corner, I almost crashed into the others. Bandit had the goofiest grin I'd ever seen on him, and in his mouth, he carried a bone so big, it looked like it could've been the leg of a horse or something. Sully's arms were loaded up too, with dog kibble, some other random stuff, and a backpack of his own. Despite everything he was going through, Sully's face was a picture of amazement.

"They have bags in here, for a few dollars! I've bought coffee that costs more than this!"

I couldn't help my grin. "Told ya."

Sully's eyes were wide, unable to comprehend it all.

"How do they make money at these prices?"

"I don't think they're doing badly," I replied, gesturing at the heaving store full of customers. We dumped everything in front of a cashier and she tallied up the items. Her hands moved so fast they were almost a blur.

"That's twenty-five dollars," she said. We looked at the four bags full of stuff we'd just packed. Sully couldn't keep the smile off his face as he handed the bills to her.

"First time in a dollar store. Won't be my last."

The cashier gave him a baleful look and kept silent. Clearly, she wasn't as excited by this place as we were. Fool. She forked over his change.

"Thanks for coming to your one stop family shop," she intoned emotionlessly, already reaching for the next customer's purchases.

Sully shoved everything into his new backpack, and we left the store.

35

CHASE

We'd gone a little way when Sully pointed across the mall at a Bank of America. I knew it was too risky for us to go inside, what with all the cameras banks usually had. We wanted to draw as little attention to ourselves as possible, so Bandit and I were back in "disguise."

Still, a blind kid with a dog gets noticed.

He handed me his backpack, and I decided to wait by the indoor water fountain while Sully made the withdrawal. Well, technically, Bandit decided this for us when he forgot our little charade for a moment and bounded towards the gushing display.

Luckily, a kindly woman helped "guide" me to him. I had to explain he was still young and in the process of being trained. Afterward, Bandit hung his head like I'd berated him when I really hadn't.

Who knew the dog would be so sensitive?

We sat by the fountain and watched as Sully slipped his card into an ATM. He keyed in his password, but something flashed across the screen that I couldn't make out. I could see the concerned expression on Sully's face though, all the way from over here. I stood up as a metallic taste flooded my mouth; I had bitten the inside of my cheek. Happens a lot when I get nervous.

Like now.

Sully tried his password again. This time the whole screen flashed red. Then a high-pitched alarm sounded from within the bank.

So much for not drawing attention.

Everyone in the mall was now looking in his direction. Sully backed away from the ATM, looking stunned. He turned, found my face in the crowd, and mouthed one word at me.

"RUN."

36

SULLY

I t all happened so fast, I hadn't had time to process it. I typed in the correct password, but the following message had flashed up on the screen:

Return the dog to us now and you and the girl will be spared.
We only want the dog.
Press #1 for our team to begin extraction.

The message stayed on the screen just long enough for me to take it all in, before it vanished, swallowing my card in the process. I could barely fathom it. They'd gotten into my account! The speed these people worked at, and how wide their net had been cast, was absolutely terrifying.

I had just begun to register the fact that we wouldn't get far without any cash when the alarm had sounded. It seemed every face in the mall turned to me. Even though I had done nothing wrong, I froze, and it was this moment of hesitation that undid me. A flurry of activity came from within the bank. Security guards raced towards me, guns raised.

I turned and searched frantically for Chase. Picking out her face from the crowd, I mouthed *RUN,* then bolted in the *opposite* direction, clear, even in the heat of the moment, that our best chance of not being caught would be if we split up.

I charged past startled shoppers and hurdled over a bench, but it had been some time since I'd participated in any school sports days. Technique all wrong, I came down heavy on one foot. A sharp pain shot through my ankle. I winced and pushed on, but at a slower pace, favoring my left leg. Seeing a guard approaching my flank, I swerved into a packed food hall.

"Hey, you! Stop right there!" The guard shouted.

I ignored him, weaving quickly through the shocked diners. Every step causing increasing pain, when I finally saw a way out, sequestered between the Chinese and Italian booths. I was three feet from the exit when a tattooed-covered cook swung a steel pan at me.

Pain EXPLODED in my stomach.

I crashed to the floor, hands over my stomach, gasping for breath.

37

SULLY

The pain ricocheted inside my stomach, tearing through my guts. I could do nothing but try to breathe through it all. The cook stood over me, holding the pan, grinning smugly.

"He's over here!" Applause broke out among the diners, enjoying the impromptu show. Boots thundered to my side, and I felt myself hoisted unceremoniously onto my feet. My arms were jerked behind me, and handcuffs slapped onto my wrists. The cool metal bit into me, threatening to cut off my circulation.

"Loosen up on the shackles," I growled, but my captor, an overweight rent-a-guard, only pulled tighter on my binds, enjoying the grimace this caused. Still winded from the chase, his cheeks were flushed an ugly red. Perspiration dripped from his forehead and ran in rivulets down his face. I noted the name sewn onto his uniform: "Sholtz, Henry".

Sholtz breathed into my face.

"Looky here, first catch of the day." It wasn't a pleasant experience since his breath reeked of smoke and coffee. Throw in a doughnut and we'd have ourselves every cop cliche under the sun, I thought. I leaned away from the other man.

"Someone could do with a mint."

Sholtz's cheeks turned even redder, if that was possible. All niceness disappeared from his eyes. "This way, scumbag."

He shoved me through the food hall, past the cheering diners, and into an elevator. With every step, my eyes roamed the area, searching for a blind girl and her dog, feeling relieved when I couldn't see them. Hopefully, they were long gone by now.

Sholtz punched B on the control panel and the elevator doors pinged closed. I watched the floor numbers descending. *Basement. Why does it have to be the basement?*

"Exactly what am I being detained for?" I asked.

My guard shot me a disgusted look.

"Like you don't know."

"Tell you what, let's assume I'm innocent until proven otherwise and oblivious to the crime. What exactly are the charges? Failure to retrieve money from my account?"

Sholtz shot me another look filled with loathing and spat out the words.

"Kidnapping of a minor."

38

THE MERCENARY

Like a spider who has spun his web and was now waiting patiently for his prey to land, The Mercenary sat in his van, drumming his fingers on the wheel.

A few hours ago, his ever reliable nephew, Daniel, had come good, sending through an email with information on the mystery girl. While it wasn't exactly a dossier, there was enough for The Mercenary to formulate a plan.

Her name was Chase Ryder. Fourteen years old, born in Holyoke, Hampden County to one Tracy Blueman. No father listed, Blueman was typical trailer trash, living off the state. Her employment history was as sporadic as her personal relationships; the woman couldn't hold down a job or a man it seemed, not until a few years ago when one Frank Tubble was added to the home rental agreement. There were two reports of domestic disturbances which hadn't led anywhere, but other than that, there was no more listed information until ten months ago, when Chase was reported as missing, a suspected runaway.

Local uniforms had interviewed the couple. Despite noting that they weren't particularly savory characters (the home was a wreck and there was evidence of alcohol abuse), they were not suspected of misconduct, and any questioning at Chase's school only revealed that the girl was a loner and seemed unhappy. Despite being described as bright from her teachers, Chase's grades were failing, and she seemed headed in a downward spiral.

The Mercenary didn't need to be a shrink to see the pattern. Desperate mom brings home a new stepdad who turns out to be less knight-in-shining-armor, and more abusive drunk. It was a story as old as time, though The Mercenary felt no sympathy; everyone had their cross to bear.

Blueman hadn't checked in on the progress to find her child in months now, something that pleased The Mercenary. *Good.* The last thing he needed was a busybody parent, nosing in on his plan. An absentee, uncaring parent was *exactly* what he wanted.

Having created a missing child report, The Mercenary had sent it to Daniel to distribute among the police stations across several states.

He had taken liberties with the report, describing Sullivan as a suspected kidnapper, painting him in a very bad light indeed since nothing was more abhorred than a predator of children.

When Sullivan and the kid eventually surfaced, it wouldn't be long before The Mercenary was informed...

39

CHASE

We watched the whole takedown in shock.

One minute Sully was at the ATM, the next he was being pursued by mall cops.

I signaled Bandit, and he came to my side immediately. Since everyone's attention was on the pursuit at hand, it wasn't hard for us to follow behind discreetly.

Sully sure could run fast! He put so much distance between himself and the out-of-shape cops that I thought he'd get well clear of them, but then he leaped over a bench and stumbled on the landing. I saw his ankle buckle — just a bit — but it was enough that he was in trouble. Still, he would've gotten away if it weren't for Slugger.

It was like I could feel the blow in my own stomach. I flinched as Sully went down. Hopefully, the guy hadn't cracked any ribs, or we'd be in serious trouble.

A hysterical laugh escaped my lips. *Like we weren't already.* Bandit tossed me a confused look. I didn't have time to reassure him of my sanity. I stood there, rooted to the spot, torn by my natural instinct to flee and my guilty conscience, which was shouting at me, telling me we couldn't leave Sully like this. Bandit must have realized what I was struggling with, as he barked twice, loudly, and stamped his paw in Sully's direction. I hesitated, then nodded. He was right, we couldn't leave him. We hurried after them.

A fat cop shackled Sully and marched him inside an elevator. I watched the numbers until they stopped at B, then we darted out of sight and into a stairwell. Taking the steps two at a time, we shot down them until we arrived outside a door marked "Basement". I grabbed the handle and twisted. As quietly as I could manage, I tugged the door opened, and we stole inside.

We found ourselves in a gray, windowless, stone security block. Cut off from the sunshine, the temperature down here plummeted, and I found myself shivering. I studied the reception desk up ahead. It was manned by a lone female cop. Behind her, there were a bunch of adjoining glass offices where I could see Sully being escorted into a holding cell.

I scanned the floor and located two cameras. One pointed at reception, the other overlooked the corridor that Sully had disappeared down. *So our problem was threefold. We needed to bust Sully out of there while avoiding both cops and cameras.* I was thinking the odds were majorly against us when I remembered I had a furry secret weapon on four legs.

As I stared at the cameras, a plan came together in my mind.

"Bandit..." I whispered. He pressed up against me and whined, waiting for my next command.

"How's your night vision?" I asked.

40

SULLY

I stared around my small cell.

With nothing to do and no possible means of escaping, I contemplated how my life had changed over the course of only a few days. From hero to zero.

At least that's what the cops around here thought of me. HPA, the organization behind this whole shebang — if that was even their real name — were prolific with their lies. As I was marched into my cell, the passing cops glared at me like the leper they thought I was. One guy almost spat in my face. I wasn't entirely sure whether he had missed on purpose or not.

As soon as I was shunted into the cell, Sholtz had reluctantly released my hands from the cuffs. Out of protocol, I knew, as opposed to the kindness of his heart. I was no longer considered a threat now that I was locked up in a 12x12 cell. A tiny barred window stood nine feet from the floor. Even if I could've gotten up there and somehow managed to tear the bars away, no amount of watching my diet and exercising would have made me fit through that small square. Other than the window, my prison contained a steel urinal that stank to high heaven and a flat bench that was wide enough to sleep on but not enough to be comfortable. If I managed to get out of this alive, I knew I would never complain about Motel 6 ever again.

I rubbed at the purple welts on my wrists, surprised they were all the injury I had sustained. Well, that, and the giant bruise that now covered my midsection. I poked gingerly at my side and inhaled a sharp intake of breath at the pain that caused, but happily, no ribs were cracked. I would take every small win right now.

Sholtz had warned me that the FBI had been notified of my capture, and several agents were now on route to extract me. I couldn't help the involuntary shudder the word "extract" had caused. Not knowing the real reason behind my reaction, Sholtz had grinned like the Cheshire Cat. Here was a man who enjoyed the suffering of others. The term "innocent until proven guilty" didn't seem to cross his mind. Then again, I didn't think Sholtz had much of a mind inside that gaping large head of his. I started pacing the small cell as panic set in.

HPA's men thought nothing of breaking into a person's home and attacking them. Hell, they'd burned my clinic down. Once they had me in their hands, what would they do to "extract" the information they wanted? I stopped pacing suddenly and hoped to God Chase had managed to escape. If they ever got a hold of that girl...

I shook myself, surprised by the level of my feelings. Since the day I had buried my wife, I had carefully cultivated a sense of detachment. Self-preservation really, so this new concern for the two's welfare came as quite the shock. As did the realization that, for the first time in eight months, the thought of Emma didn't bring a searing pain in my chest.

I was still marveling at this not-so-small miracle when the lights blew out, plunging the floor into darkness.

41

SULLY

I could hear shouts of alarm rising around me, though I knew it would only be moments before a backup generator kicked in. Even small-town mall cops have a contingency plan. I sat onto the cold bench, waiting for the commotion to die down, when I heard the sound of heavy breathing.

Wait, not breathing. Panting.

My nose caught an undeniable scent. *Dog breath.* In disbelief, I called out quietly.

"Bandit?"

My reply was a soft, "*Woof.*"

Something metallic clattered onto the floor. I dropped on all fours, moving towards the general direction of the sound, until my fingers brushed against a set of keys. Relief swam through me in waves. Feeling my way around, I found the lock and inserted a key. It wasn't the right one. Fingering a larger key, I tried that next.

"Come on, we don't have much time," came Chase's bodiless voice.

She had appeared like a ghost. I hadn't even heard her arrive. Someone not too far away shouted.

"We found the breaker!"

As power surged back into the building, I inserted the right key and twisted.

By the time the lights flickered back on, the cell was empty.

42

CHASE

Bandit couldn't contain his excitement as Sully snuck out of the cell and did several circuits around him, but if I was expecting gratitude, I had another thing coming.

"Of all the stupid... I told you to run," Sully hissed at me through the dark.

"Seriously?" I managed back. "I think the words you're looking for are, thank you!"

"This isn't a game, Chase! They could catch you both... I can't believe you came back..."

I was too concerned with our predicament to do this particular dance right now. "There's no time to argue, let's just get out of here," I instructed. My eyes had grown accustomed to the darkness, but even then, I could barely make out three steps ahead of me. I grabbed onto Bandit's makeshift collar with one hand and Sully with the other. "Hurry boy, get us out of here."

Bandit barked softly, then shot into action, weaving quickly and surely through the corridors. We'd been going maybe five seconds when the strip lights above us started to flicker.

"Duck!" Sully cried out.

We dropped into a crouch, flattening ourselves against the wall,

Bandit pressed up against me. Light flooded the room. In preparation for this, I had shielded my eyes. Consequently, my recovery time was fast. I blinked the haze away and took in our surroundings.

We were in one of the glass offices. Luckily, this one was empty. Unluckily, we were surrounded by four glass walls. If anyone came down either of the flanking corridors, we'd be seen. Sully pointed ahead of us.

"That's the reception desk. If we can make it there, the exit's just beyond."

I nodded. So now we had a plan.

"Bandit. You first. Head for the door."

Knowing stealth was of the utmost importance, he didn't bark, but pawed the ground at me. At my nod, he took off, a streak of brown across the floor. He was going so fast, he almost overshot the door. I saw him dig in his back heels and skid to a stop. He leaped up, grasped the fire exit door handle in his mouth, and tugged down. The door opened silently. He waited, propping the door ajar, head tilted towards us.

Sully gestured, and now it was my turn to make a run for it. I kept low, which wasn't hard for me since I'm pretty short, anyway. My sneakers squeaked on the linoleum floor, but I figured they wouldn't hear that over the noise the cops were generating: self congratulations and war stories if you can believe that. I made it to Bandit and slid past him into the stairwell.

Sully came after us. He was halfway across the floor when his injured ankle gave out. He dropped, and a cry escaped his lips, drawing the attention of the reception cop.

"What the… you! Stop right there!" she yelled.

Sully scrambled up and half ran, half hopped over to us. I lunged forward to help him, but he shook me off, pointing at the wall behind me.

"The fire axe!" he shouted.

I bolted to the cabinet housing the axe in question and smashed my elbow inside. Safety glass shattered into shards, raining harmlessly over my feet. I wrenched the axe from its moorings and rushed back to Sully. He grabbed it from my hands and wedged it between the handle of the door we'd just come through and the top step.

The cop came flying into the door just then, but the axe held. She threw herself at the door but wasn't able to get it open more than a foot. She pressed her face into the gap.

"You're in enough trouble as it is! We can do a deal if you stop running and turn yourselves in."

I stared her directly in the face. "Whatever they've told you about him, it's all lies. Sully hasn't done anything." Before she could respond, I slid under Sully's arm to ease some weight off of his injured ankle, and together, we hobbled up the stairs as more cops threw themselves at the door.

Moments later we burst onto the mall's main parade and headed quickly but discreetly to an exit. A few shoppers cast raised eyebrows our way, but no one intervened.

When we got outside, a bus was just pulling up. We didn't even see the destination sign, we just climbed on and hunkered down by the back. Only when the bus pulled away did we allow ourselves to breathe again. I couldn't believe we'd just engineered our first jail break.

Sadly, it wouldn't be our last.

43

THE MERCENARY

The Mercenary popped an aspirin and chased it down with a can of Red Bull that he downed in one gulp. He flexed his fingers until the can flattened into a metal disc, compressed in his gorilla-like hand.

He'd picked up news of Sullivan's capture on his police scanner and was heading to the mall when the blackout had happened. The Mercenary had been at this line of work almost his entire life and knew better than to believe in coincidences.

It was that damn dog again. He was sure of it.

He swung the unlicensed sedan into the parking lot and opened the glove compartment. Inside was a multitude of fake ID's. The Mercenary fished around until he found the one he was looking for. He stared down at his own face, only the one in the photo was neater and dressed, as he was now, in an all-black suit. The Mercenary checked his reflection in the rearview mirror. He wasn't a vain man, but took pride in pulling off a passable disguise. The face he saw smiling back at him was strong, with eyes that challenged anyone foolish enough to disagree with him. He nodded to himself, pleased. *A believable official.*

Sliding a government-issued firearm into his shoulder holster, The Mercenary emerged from the car and made his way inside.

A few minutes later he was standing by the reception desk. A frazzled young cop stared back at him. Seems she hadn't had a good day and was now taking it out on him. Or so she thought. The Mercenary wasn't anyone's punching bag. Unsmiling, The Mercenary flipped her his FBI badge, gestured at the cameras, and demanded to see the CCTV footage of their prisoner's escape.

She took offence at his tone but called her superior, a man named Sholtz. Sholtz was typical of these generic mall staff. Overweight and full of self-importance. The Mercenary would have fun taking him down a peg or two.

Sholtz reluctantly lead The Mercenary into the CCTV booth. A bank of monitors were already cued up with the requested footage. The Mercenary leaned forward and twisted the navigational cog. On the screens, the images sprang to life. The Mercenary recognized the corridor he had walked down only moments before, but as the camera panned left and settled on the reception desk, the screens fell black.

"We found a bunch of wires pulled from the breaker box. The kid, no doubt, but it doesn't make sense. If he kidnapped her, why would she sneak back to help him?"

The Mercenary stared down his nose at him. This fool hadn't noticed the girl or the dog, despite The Mercenary's fake police report. As far as he was concerned, Sholtz wasn't good enough to lick his shoes. "You haven't heard of Stockholm Syndrome, when a victim begins feeling trust and affection towards their captor? That's unfortunately what must be happening here." The Mercenary hoped that would be enough to shut him up, but Sholtz however, had no idea the repulsion he caused in The Mercenary and continued talking in his irritating voice.

"Not sure what you're hoping for unless you can see in the dark."

Without a word, The Mercenary retrieved a pair of glasses from his pocket. They had a retro wayfarer style, though the lenses were tinted red. If truth be told, they were far too hipster-looking for his taste, but since they weren't a vanity item, The Mercenary slipped them onto his face and triggered a barely perceivable switch on the right arm. Electricity hummed through the frame as the glasses powered up. He stared through the red lenses until the augmented imaging kicked in. Suddenly, he could clearly see the reception desk on the monitors. The glasses were a high-tech IED — Image Enhancement Device — designed and created by one of the Boss's many genius lackeys, and The Mercenary's favorite weapon of choice.

"Are those what I think they are?" the hapless cop asked.

"Yes," came The Mercenary's curt reply.

"Always wondered what they would be like to use."

In response, The Mercenary deliberately turned his back on him. "You may leave."

Sholtz bristled, finally comprehending the brush off. From the corner of his eye, The Mercenary could see Sholtz hesitating, wondering if he should retort back. He must have thought better of it, as he spun on his heel and left. The Mercenary turned his attention to the screen and proceeded to watch Sullivan breakout.

44

CHASE

We'd been riding silently on the bus for hours. Sully stared moodily out of the window, hands gripped into fists that only seemed to squeeze tighter the farther we got from his home.

He didn't say anything, but I knew his mind was on his wife and the life he'd left behind. While I still wasn't super keen on the idea of his tagging along, part of me was learning to deal with it. Like, what was I going to do? Send him away? The man could barely function. Besides, we had bigger problems to deal with, like how he didn't have a clue where we were heading. My mind wasn't much help either, drawing blanks as it was.

I shifted my position. Not for the first time, I wondered why the seats were designed to be so uncomfortable. It's like they didn't want you to ride the bus for a long journey. I looked down at Bandit, lying on the floor between my feet. He seemed more subdued than usual. I think something was bothering him, but he wasn't able to voice what.

Which reminded me.

I took out the easiest book we'd bought from the Dollar Store and laid it by his feet. The bus was pretty empty, and most passengers preferred to sit up front. I think actually because of Bandit. Seems the public don't like to be near a dog in a contained space. Made me wonder what kinds of dogs they were accustomed to. Bandit instantly perked up and pricked his ears forward. I bent down and whispered at him.

"We'll do a quiz later, OK?"

His tongue snaked out and licked my nose, making me regret being so nice to him.

The bus chugged through several New England neighborhoods. We passed a cheerful sign that said SCRANTON, Pennsylvania. WELCOME HOME! It looked like a nice enough place. The side-walks were free from litter, shopfronts were clean with fresh coats of paint. Any people I could see were busy moving to and from work or meeting up with friends. I only counted one homeless person, which is generally how I measure a town's success rate. I felt the bus slow down and craned my head around. We were turning into a bus terminal, where a small strip of sad looking businesses did trade.

"End of the line, folks," the bus driver called out.

Somewhere along our ride we'd lost most of the passengers, so there was only an elderly couple who made their way to the exit with us. I moved aside to let them pass first. The old woman smiled at me, then looked at Sully.

"What a polite daughter you have."

Sully's eyebrows shot up so high I worried they would shoot right off his face. He went to correct her, but I elbowed him silent.

"Thank you ma'am. I try." *Why draw more attention to ourselves, right?* Our motley "family" descended the bus and headed into the adjoining diner which was clean, if uninspiring. Tablecloths covered plastic furniture that was yellow with age. We found a table whose leg somebody had shoved a piece of cardboard coaster under to keep it steady. We sat down. I instantly grabbed a menu and pored over the offerings. That was the thing about being broke and homeless; food is a BIG deal. The biggest.

Sully signaled a nearby waitress. She was a big-chested woman, with even bigger red hair, all done up in a towering beehive. I couldn't stop staring. Must've been a whole can of hairspray up in there.

"I'm Rose, what can I do for ya?" she said, chewing a piece of gum noisily with her mouth open.

"Can I just get a bowl of water for the dog while we look at the menu?" Sully barely looked at her, but he seemed to have an immediate effect on Red. She stopped chewing her gum and batted fake eyelashes at him.

"Well, of course, Sugar. I'll be right back for your order." She headed for the kitchen, swinging her hips as she went. I was pretty sure it was all for Sully's benefit; shame he wasn't looking. He opened his wallet and took out the remaining cash. It was a pitiful supply. We'd have enough for a light meal here, but there wouldn't be much left after eating. He rubbed at his eyes, the weight of the world sitting on his shoulders.

"What day is it?" I asked.

Sully frowned. "Why?"

"Cos if it's Tuesday, kids eat free as long as they're accompanied by one paying adult," I said, pointing at an offer stuck to the window.

"It's Wednesday," he replied.

"Figures," I grumbled. I slid lower into my seat as Red came back with a bowl of water for Bandit, and also something else: a big plate. On it was a juicy red bone with lots of meat still clinging to it. Smelling it, Bandit shot up and begged, one paw raised. A whine escaped from the back of his throat as a long glob of drool dripped from his mouth. Red laughed.

"Here you go, pooch. Swiped this from our chef. He'd just throw it away."

Sully finally looked at her and gave her a genuine smile of thanks. "Thank you."

She winked at him. "Pleasure. Now, what about you? Know what you'd like yet?'

She pouted those red lips suggestively. I would've slid further down my seat if I could have. This was painful to watch. Sully, on the other hand, seemed oblivious to her mad flirting.

"You know when you've run into one bad thing after another?"

Red nodded, though she obviously didn't know where he was heading with this. Come to think of it, neither did I.

"I only get my kid one week out of the month. Planned on taking her for a nice meal, maybe a movie after, but damn machine ate my card and the bank can't get it back to me until tomorrow. I've only a twenty to last us until then."

"How unlucky," she said, totally buying his story.

I was amazed. Sully had some skills! Red glanced at the near empty diner, where only a few old age pensioners sat, sipping soup, including the ones who had gotten off the bus with us. Then she must have made up her mind as she looked at us conspiratorially.

"You know, Cook made up a batch of chilli earlier, but he'd left it on the stove too long. The bottom almost burned right through the pan. We can't sell it, but I could probably give that to you for free? It's going to be hela smokey, I ain't going to lie, but the offer's there if you want it?"

Sully reached across and squeezed her hand, causing her cheeks to flush bright pink. "You are an angel."

Reluctantly, she removed her hand and went to get us our freebie food. I looked at Sully, unable to hide my utter amazement. He stared back at me, a knowing glint in his eye.

"Still think I'm useless?" he asked. I snapped my mouth shut. *What, he was a mind reader too now?*

Red came back with two giant bowls of chilli. She'd also added some warm bread rolls, fresh out of the oven. I don't feel much affection for people in general, but I could've kissed her. She set the bowls in front of us. The smell of them caused my toes to curl. There were actual pieces of meat in there! Without waiting to see if I should, I shoved a heaped spoonful into my mouth. It was so good, I almost fainted. Red seemed pleased by my enthusiasm.

"Nice to see a girl who likes to eat," she said.

"Food is highly underrated," I replied. "This is so good, I could eat an entire pot of it."

Red laughed. "Well there's plenty more, so just let me know if you want seconds."

I didn't even mind when she reached out and ruffled my hair. I make exceptions for anyone who feeds me.

Sully had better manners than me, so he actually waited for Red to leave before eating. We dunked the rolls into the chilli, mopping up the sauce. Under the table, Bandit, too, was in ecstasy. He was licking and chewing that bone like it was the best thing he'd ever tasted.

When I finished my bowl, I leaned back and sighed happily. My belly, not accustomed to so much food, was distended and straining against the belt. Sully was still eating, so I took a second to examine the diner.

Red was serving the old couple from the bus. Sully's flirtation must have cheered her right up, as she was now friendly to all her customers. She chatted and flitted around the place, keeping everyone happy. I looked away from her, to a bookcase loaded with leaflets.

"I'll be back," I said to Sully. Bandit looked up at me in question but never stopped chewing his bone. I felt his eyes follow me, however, as I made my way to the bookcase.

As I'd thought, there were timetables of all the buses from the terminal. I scanned the destinations. Some names I recognized: Baltimore, Pittsburgh, Syracuse. None of them seemed interesting until my eyes landed on the one destination and I felt excitement brewing in me. Grabbing the timetable, I headed back to our booth, where I found two new bowls of chilli and rolls had been set onto the table. God bless that woman!

"What've you got there?" Sully looked at the leaflet clutched in my hand. I slid it across the table to him.

"Where we're going next."

Sully read the words on the paper. "Atlantic City?" he enquired.

"The whole reason I let you join us is because you had money, except now you don't. Can you think of a better place to make money?" I replied.

"Gambling's an art form, and one I'm not particularly good at."

"Well it's lucky we've a secret weapon here." I glanced down at Bandit, and Sully suddenly got my drift.

"Seriously?"

"Seriously."

And that was it. End of discussion.

45
——————

CHASE

I cleaned up in the bathroom, while Sully settled the bill. Well, there wasn't really a bill. We'd only drank tap water so Red hadn't charged us, but Sully gave her a tip anyway. I told him he shouldn't have as we needed every cent, but Sully said it wasn't right not to. Whatever. This is why I'd last longer on the streets than he would alone. He was clueless what it really took to survive.

Red seemed sad to see us go. I got the feeling she was a lonely girl. There wasn't a wedding ring on her finger, and judging by the clientele, it didn't seem like there were many eligible bachelors in this town. At least, none who were traveling by bus, anyway. I suppose anyone who was remotely successful would've been driving their own car, not using uncomfortable and tardy public transport like us losers.

Bandit — still chewing his bone — followed me outside. I found bus stop D and waited there for the bus to arrive. It wouldn't get here for another hour though, so I thought it was a good time to start Bandit's education. I fished out the book I'd decided on earlier. BRADLEY THE BUMBLE BEE, it announced in bright red letters. There was a drawing of a giant bee flitting from different things on the cover. Already, I had a pretty good inkling of how this story would go.

I found a seat on a wooden bench, and Bandit hopped up next to me. I looked across at the diner to see Sully had finally extracted himself from Red. I was amused to see him carrying a tub of what could only be more of the chilli. He sat down next to Bandit and quietly watched as I began to teach the dog how to read.

The first page had a picture of the Bee standing on a red apple. I spelled out each of the letters of "apple" to Bandit. He seemed to understand, but I wouldn't really be able to test him until we were alone.

Suddenly I noticed we had an audience. A man waiting by the next bus stop tossed us an interested look. A battered suitcase covered with travel stickers sat by his feet. He wore a shirt tucked into suit pants and had the air of a traveling salesman. I forced a heavy Russian accent into my voice and pointed at the picture book.

"Aaaa," I asked Sully hopefully, while flicking my eyes in the direction of our spectator.

"Good, now try the next letter. Paaaaa," he encouraged. He sure caught on fast. Dutifully, I copied his voice, exaggerating my pronunciation. Our act worked, as the salesman lost interest pretty soon after I reached "e", which I was thankful for. My mouth felt like it'd had a workout, and though we hadn't long finished eating, I found myself wanting a drink. I suddenly developed a newfound respect for actors. It wasn't as easy as it seemed.

I felt a wet nose on the side of my neck. It was Bandit's way of letting me know he was done with this word. It was pretty amazing how much he conveyed without a sound, but then, I guess that's what happens when you have a genius IQ dog. I turned the page. Bradley the Bumble Bee was now balancing precariously on a colorful beach ball. Three guesses on the word.

"Ball," I said quietly. "B...a...l...l." My finger moved along each letter as I pronounced them. Bandit's eyes followed closely. A bubble of excitement rose within me. This was really happening! Bandit was learning how to read! I could feel Sully all tensed up beside me. He was still struggling to believe that Bandit was special, even though to me it was pretty damn obvious. Something else was becoming apparent too, however; we were being hunted, and to stay one step ahead of them, we needed answers soon. And we would get them once we weren't quite so out in the open.

We sped through the book. We couldn't know for sure Bandit's reading age, but he was picking this up scarily fast. By the time we reached "S", our bus pulled up. The doors pinged open and our driver, a jolly man with a face lined with wrinkles from many summers spent behind the wheel, beamed at us.

"Howdy. Hop on up, folks. We'll be on our way in fifteen minutes" he said, gesturing into the vehicle. As Bandit climbed on, still carrying his bone, the driver reached down and gave him a giant scratch behind the ears. Bandit almost toppled over from happiness.

"Beautiful Collie, you got there. I've a German Shepherd myself. Best thing I ever did, getting a dog. Loyal to the bone and always happy to see you."

Bandit surprised us all next. He jumped up, placed a paw on either side of the driver's shoulders and vigorously sniffed at his neck. It wasn't a display of affection, as I first thought, but something else entirely. Sully was mortified and pulled Bandit down.

"No boy. We don't do that."

Bandit strained against Sully, scrabbling to get to the driver. For his part, the driver didn't seem concerned. He was quite liking all the attention, but Sully and I were worried. *What was he doing?*

Sully tugged — hard. I flinched, thinking of the pain this must be causing. Finally, Bandit whimpered and allowed Sully to drag him to the seats. Once more we sat at the back where we could have some privacy.

Sully bent his head close to Bandit's, his expression troubled.

"Why did you do that to the driver?"

Bandit dropped his bone, looked up at him, and licked his hand to reassure him that he was well. Still, there was something really bothering him. He circled the floor, agitated. An idea came to me. I fished out his learning book and asked if Bandit could show us anything in them that might help explain his concern. Bandit woofed. Using his paw, he began turning the pages of the book. When he got to "D" he stopped and placed his paw very deliberately on the center of the page.

We examined the picture. Bradley had been blown by a gust of strong wind and had hurt his wing. Luckily, a passing Doctor spotted him and helped bandage it up. In no time at all, Bradley was off flying again to "E".

I traded looks with Sully. He glanced over at the driver who was now chatting to another passenger as she ascended the steps.

"Is it the bee?" I asked.

Bandit chuffed twice, softly.

"If it's not him, then, the doctor? Is that it?"

Bandit chuffed once, but his whole body trembled. Whatever Doctor he had known had left him with some very bad memories. I rubbed his chin to reassure him.

"He's a driver, not a doctor, so why would you..." Sully trailed off suddenly. I looked at them both, no idea what was going on with them.

Bandit whined and shifted his paw slightly, so that the tip of one claw was now resting on top of Bradley's injured wing, like he was pointing to it.

Sully gave a sharp intake of breath and stared back at the driver.

"No way."

I couldn't take any more. "What? Are you going to tell me what's going on?"

Concern marred Sully's look of wonder. He continued staring at our driver as he explained. "We don't know how they do it, but some dogs can tell when a person is very sick. It's something to do with their extraordinary sense of smell. They're particularly good at spotting cancer."

I swallowed hard. Whatever I had expected, that wasn't it at all. "The driver has cancer? He's sick?"

"I think so."

And just to confirm what we'd already said, Bandit barked once. We turned back to our cheerful driver, welcoming more travelers onto the bus.

"Someone needs to tell him," came Sully's gentle reply.

46

SULLY

We drove leisurely along route 476. Our driver didn't seem in any real hurry to reach our destination, and the passengers, too, seemed to be enjoying the ride. I, however, was dreading the moment we would arrive at Atlantic City. After so many years working as a vet, I was used to giving bad news to a pet's owner, but telling a person he was sick with a potentially life-threatening disease? This was something new entirely.

Maybe the dog was wrong? The hopeful thought flitted through my mind but disappeared just as quickly. I'd read countless studies on canine cancer detection. The dogs are able to do this by detecting the very low concentrations of the alkanes and aromatic compounds generated by tumors. It was a remarkable but well-documented fact. Torn up inside, I squeezed my eyes closed and lay back against the headrest.

Now that Bandit's message had been conveyed, the restlessness had disappeared, but he kept his eyes focused on the driver at all times. I could feel the concern radiating from him. For the first time, the truth was sinking in... Chase had been right all along. Somehow, Bandit had an intelligence level far exceeding any dog of his species, and that virus warning was just a story manufactured to cover up

HPA's true intentions. I looked down at Bandit, cradling his bone between two paws but seemingly without an appetite any longer, and marveled at his ability to empathize. Intelligent or not, this was an ability some humans had not managed to master, so it was astonishing coming from a dog.

Just another thing to add to Bandit's list of talents.

We crossed into the heart of Philadelphia, the birthplace of the United States Marine Corps. I knew this little fact as I had considered running away to join it at twenty, when the difficulties at home had seemed unbearable. Staring at Chase, I felt ashamed now, realizing how good I had had it compared to her. Even during turbulent times, I had never known hunger, had never worried where I would be sleeping that night, or indeed, if I would ever wake again.

Oblivious to my musings, Chase sighed longingly at the many cheesesteak houses that passed by, drooling at the giant pictures of glistening, melted, yellow bites of heaven. Despite my dark thoughts, I couldn't stop my admiration; the kid could really eat.

The bus rolled past the eateries, down streets decorated with cheerful outdoor sculptures and murals, where small children played as their parents watched, chatting with friends and neighbors. In a moment of whimsy, I thought I might have liked to live here in another life. It was a sunny day, with the city blossoming under blue skies. We rode past several business blocks of polished black glass until a large green space came into view. Bandit tore his eyes from the driver to gape outside. We had reached Fairmont Park, a sign outside the park entrance announced. Seeing it, Chase's eyes lit up.

"That's the world's largest landscaped urban park."

"You learn that at school?" I asked.

"No. I read it somewhere once."

"Just once?" I raised my eyebrows, impressed. "And you've remembered it?"

Chase's thin shoulders lifted into a shrug. "I've got a photographic memory. Once something goes in, I can always find it again."

"That must come in useful," I said.

"Yeah. I usually ace my exams." She said it nonchalantly, like it was no big deal. While we were speaking, Bandit had pushed his nose as far out of the window as he could, gulping in big mouthfuls of air. It occurred to me that Bandit had probably never seen much of a natural environment before. I stroked Bandit's head.

"When all this is over, how about we take you to the countryside? There'll be rivers to swim in, mountains to climb, and animals to chase. First, we'll make some money, then we'll go on a trip."

Bandit grinned, pawing the ground. Liking the plan.

47

———

CHASE

The bus finally reached its last stop.

As the doors popped open, I could smell the salt in the air and see shimmering waves stretching out to the horizon. Gulls screeched overhead, soaring into the cloudless sky. Though we were officially here on business, I couldn't help but feel excited — this was only the second time I'd been to the sea!

When I was young, and before Tubs had entered our lives, my mom had taken me on a day trip to Provincetown in Cape Cod. I don't remember too much of that day. Just the red balloon a sidewalk performer had given me and the freedom I'd felt running barefoot along the beach. It was one of the few happy moments I had ever had with her. Not long after, Tubs had come along, and life had taken a downhill spiral to Crappytown.

This place reminded me of Provincetown, though it was way louder, like someone had ratcheted up the tacky counter to ten. Along the long boardwalk, brightly striped canopies shielded terraces packed with restaurant diners. Tourists took snapshot after snapshot, posing with cheesy smiles and peace signs.

Beside me, filled with excitement and desperate to leave, Bandit was darting up and down the length of the bus, bone still in his mouth, but first there was that conversation that needed to be had.

Sully waited until everyone else was off of the bus before approaching the driver.

The man smiled at us cheerfully, causing my stomach to twist in knots. It didn't feel right for us to be standing there while they spoke about something so personal, so I led Bandit off the bus and we waited outside.

I couldn't hear the words Sully spoke, but I had a clear line of sight to the driver's face. He went through a whole gamut of emotions. Sunny, then questioning, which changed to concern, and finally fear. His dark eyes roamed the sidewalk for Bandit. When he found him, there was a gratefulness I didn't expect to see. News delivered, Sully reached across and shook his hand. The driver, though shell-shocked, remained calm and resolute as he took it. Sully climbed down the stairs and joined us outside.

"Did he believe you?" I asked him.

"Yeah."

"Did he know already?"

"No, but he suspected something was wrong. Been feeling a lump in that same region for a while. Didn't get it checked out in case it was nothing. Said he couldn't afford to waste the examination fee since his company doesn't provide insurance."

He fell silent, his thoughts with the jovial driver whose day he had just crushed. "I told him the best cure is to take preventative measures."

We both fell silent; anything we might have said felt redundant.

Suddenly, Bandit walked back onto the bus, and very deliberately, laid his bone down by the driver's feet. Licking the man's hand, he nudged him with his nose — guess that was his way of saying "take care of yourself" — then returned to us. The driver stared at Bandit, open-mouthed. I was feeling pretty awed myself.

Sully looked down at Bandit. "You may have just saved a man's life there."

For once Bandit looked solemn.

48

CHASE

W e headed down the boardwalk, following the blinking lights of Caesar's Palace along the horizon. We'd been going a while when Sully stopped us outside a dive of a motel. I took in his choice of establishment, frowning. Of all the places on this street to choose... There was a much nicer bed-and-breakfast across the way, but Sully shook his head and pointed.

Of all the places here, this was the only one without CCTV cameras.

Rifling through his backpack, he fished out some items bought from the dollar store and handed a pair of scissors and hair dye to me. "Not sure how attached you are to being a blonde, but I think it's best if we alter our appearance."

I glanced at the box of dye and shrugged. "Brunette would make a nice change."

We headed to the reception desk, which was manned by a twenty-something guy with punk hair. Heavy metal blasted from his iPhone, which he didn't bother pausing to serve us. Just pointed at a sign, "$50 per night", got Sully to fill in a check-in form (he lied on just about everything), then handed us a key.

Sully took the key, and we moved past the reception desk and down the dark corridor. The decor was Icksville. Without thinking, I reached out and touched the raised wallpaper. It was a wine red color with an old-fashioned design, like something you'd see in an old Western movie. Made of some kind of brushed material, it felt greasy to touch, and I immediately regretted my decision to examine it without a pair of hazmat gloves. Yellow with age, wrought iron lamps flickered at us as dust collected on the rims. The floral carpet, which couldn't have seen a clean this side of the century, stuck to my sneakers as I walked over it. I waited until we were out of earshot before asking Sully the obvious question.

"How are we affording the room?"

Sully gave me a look that I think was meant to be confident, but he wasn't fooling anyone. "With our winnings."

I shot him a look. "You know that's the kind of thing a gambler-holic says, right?"

He shrugged. "I have every faith in Bandit."

Hearing his name, Bandit chuffed at us, though he still seemed a little down. I think he was feeling guilty about the driver. I made up my mind to cheer him up once we had some privacy.

Several identical doors passed by with faded brass numbers. When Sully reached twenty-eight, he stopped in front of it. "This is it."

He unlocked the door, and we stepped inside. Thankfully, the walls here were a lighter shade than the murder red in the hall. This was a pale green: I think the designers amongst you would consider it "mint". The carpet was the same as outside, but didn't look as sick-inducing with these walls. Two narrow single beds were separated by a dark wooden side table. On it lay a phone and a bible. Seeing the book, Bandit gave it an exploratory sniff.

"Don't think you're up to that yet," I said.

He shot me a questioning look but took my word for it as he padded off to investigate the adjoining bathroom. Sully had taken a seat on a battered armchair by the window. We had a nice view of a back alley, but at least there were no bars across the window. You get that a lot more in urban places like New York or Chicago. Guess

Atlantic City didn't see too much excitement. I was relieved by this since my claustrophobic self didn't like to feel locked in. A flash of memory darted across my mind.

I was younger and locked in a small closet, punishment for one of the many crimes Tubs regularly decided I was guilty of. The darkness was suffocating. I lay down on my stomach and pressed my face to the thin crack at the base of the door, desperate for a hit of air. I could hear the radio blasting in the next room, while Tubs and Ma argued. From experience, I knew they would be some time. Fighting to remain calm, I chanted the alphabet backwards in my head until eventually, I fell into an exhausted sleep.

I shook myself from the unwanted trip down memory lane. See how much fun life was before now? Made running away from mercenaries with shotguns a picnic. Almost.

I turned my attention to a small TV that was fixed to a bracket on the wall. It looked as ancient as the carpet. If I turned it on, would the whole thing explode? Feeling brave, I plucked the remote from one of the beds and hit "on".

The monitor flickered to life. Despite appearances, it was working fine. A woman with glowing skin was extolling the virtues of a 12 step detox system which looked exactly like green puke in a bottle. You too could have a complexion like hers if you drank a puke drink three times a day! Seriously, is this what people get up to when they have money?

I pushed the channel button, flicking through until Jeopardy came on. This wasn't my type of show, but at least it wasn't inane infomercial chatter either. I left the TV on and moved into the bathroom to inspect Sully's recent purchases. The hair dye looked strong; I hoped it wouldn't sting. I'd read somewhere that some people had these crazy allergic reactions to the dye where their scalps literally burned off. I seriously hoped that wouldn't be the case with me. I was kinda attached to my hair. Grease and all.

Bandit, who had found nothing of interest in here, wandered back into the main area. Seeing the television, he jumped onto a bed, before he settled down with his head on his paws, and proceeded to watch the quiz show.

I almost slapped my head when I realized.

Quiz show.

"Boy, you are gonna *love* this."

49

SULLY

The sound of television babble drowned out the ache that was intermittently attacking my heart. Seeing Chase's joy on the boardwalk, I had had to turn my face away so she wouldn't see my pain. Emma had loved the wildness of the ocean. Our first trip away had been to a seaside similar to this. The colorful balloons and sweet smell of the cotton candy brought on another onslaught of bitter-sweet memories.

Emma would never experience this again.

A woman laughed close by, her voice clear and jubilant. Full of life, and so like Emma's.

I felt a tightness in my chest when I realized that as time passed, I would forget what her laughter sounded like, how she smelled like freshly washed cotton. I squeezed my eyes together and pictured her now, laughing with her arms outstretched, twirling in circles in our bedroom. I made a mental note: twirling. I must never forget how she was.

But then the bedroom burst into flames.

I flinched, rapidly crashing back to the present. Emma's things, the items I had been saving, evidence of our life together — it was all gone in a puff of smoke. I swallowed and turned my attention to the dog, who hadn't taken his eyes from the television set since he had first discovered it. As the presenter asked a question, Bandit fidgeted, making a low whining sound. He knew the answer. As the contestant answered correctly, Bandit chuffed, pleased with himself, tongue lolling out goofily.

Despite my mood, I smiled.

50

CHASE

I t took close to two hours, but when I emerged from the
bathroom, I looked like a whole new person.

Gone was my shoulder length chestnut hair. In its place was a
choppy, shorter cut that barely covered my ears. And I had black hair
now. Surprisingly, this color and style made my eyes seem even
bluer. As part of my new disguise, I had ringed them with heavy
black kohl, but kept my cheeks and lips neutral (the goal was to look
different and not like a clown). Although the dark dye was a little
harsh on my skin and made me look paler than I actually am, I was
still a total babe! And bonus, I looked several years older.

Jeopardy had long finished and Bandit was now watching an
early episode of The Simpsons. When I appeared, he leaped off the
bed and pranced around me, whining. I looked at Sully, who hadn't
moved from his seat. He shook his head, no; he didn't know what was
eating at Bandit either.

Bandit spun around and pawed at the alphabet book, opening it.
His paw spun through the pages like lightning, so we could barely
keep up with him.

"He's memorized them," Sully's said, awed.

"What?"

"He's memorized them. See how he's barely glancing at the pages?"

I gave this some consideration. "Are you telling me, on top of being Einstein, he has super powers?"

Bandit stopped pawing the book, looked up at us, and gave two strong barks.

"Guess he's just your run-of-the-mill genius dog then," Sully deadpanned. I think Bandit appreciated the joke as his tongue lolled out of the side of his mouth again.

He found the page he was looking for and pawed it deliberately. We were at P. Bradley the Bumble Bee was hovering over a Princess who sang to him, causing the bee to swoon deliriously mid-flight. My brows furrowed into a frown.

"You want me to *sing*?" I couldn't hide the incredulous tone in my voice.

Sully laughed. "I think he's paying you a compliment, Chase."

I looked back at the picture before I finally got it. "I look like a princess? But I'm in jeans."

Sully and the dog both rolled their eyes like a comical duo. If I'd had a camera to record the moment, I guarantee it would've got a billion hits on YouTube.

"He thinks you look pretty," Sully spelled out. Bandit barked once, confirming the translation. With horror, I felt the beginnings of a blush on my cheeks.

"Whatever," was my gracious reply, but neither of them seemed bothered by it. Sully looked away, allowing me some time to recover, but the dog just grinned at me. Needing to change the subject, I fixed critical eyes on Sully. "Well, that's one down. One to go."

His confused brown eyes met mine.

"Time for your quick change."

Sully glanced nervously at the scissors in my hand. "You do know how to use those, right?"

I nodded. "Course. Don't be such a baby."

51

SULLY

The wind whistled through my newly shorn hair. It was a pleasant, if unfamiliar, feeling.

Chase, it turned out, wasn't bad with the scissors.

She'd mumbled something about cutting her mom's hair before she realized what she was saying and clammed up. One day, I was going to have to talk to her about where she came from. Holding onto bad things wasn't good for the soul. This was something I knew very well.

We'd left the motel and headed down the sunny promenade with only one goal in mind — to make money. The kids were reveling in the sights and sounds of the vacation town, forgetting for a moment the predicament we were in. They marveled at the colorful, toy-like buildings, played hide and seek inside a life-size model of a Monopoly board, and splurged on a bag of cotton candy. I, however, had tuned everything out.

An idea was milling around inside my head, an end goal of sorts, but for me, it would be a last resort. I knew we couldn't keep running forever. We needed a safe location, somewhere remote, where we could blend into the countryside and wait until the heat died down. I knew the perfect place, but I needed time to get used to the idea.

There was a reason the past stayed buried, but if we chose to go down that road, old wounds would be opened up.

The kids were now gaping at the flashy lights and tacky decor of the Taj Mahal Casino. Gold-etched domes battled against gaudy red lettering. I didn't need to look into my pockets to know how much money we had left. It was such a pittance, it wouldn't see us through another day. When we had first decided to come here, Chase had explained how Bandit had learned to play poker — and how they could use his special abilities to bend the rules. She was a resourceful and creative kid, and the idea certainly had merit, but since arriving here and doing a little reconnaissance, I knew it would never work. We wouldn't be able to cheat the system — not with all the guards and cameras in place, something we hadn't bargained on prior to hatching our plan. So now, it was onto Plan B... Despite how any attention drawn to us would be a bad thing; I knew we had to risk it. We would do this just once to see where it would get us.

Across the way was a convenience store, where a teenage boy exited, carrying a super-sized Big Gulp. Seeing him, I turned to the kids.

"Wait here."

I jogged over into the store, casually sauntered over to the soda fountain, and grabbed several paper cups. As I made my way to the exit, the store clerk yelled across to me.

"You can't take those unless you're buying a drink."

I waved and smiled. "My kid just bought one, but if I let him have the whole thing, we'll be stopping for restroom breaks every half hour. Better I share it with him."

The clerk stared at me, not buying the story. I pointed out the window, at the back of super-sized Big Gulp boy, who was now helpfully sitting outside on a bench, sipping his drink. Without waiting for another response, I left the store quickly and returned to Chase and Bandit, both watching me the whole time, full of questions.

My eyes searched the street until they landed on a corner that seemed perfect. No cameras, just a blocked off alley behind us. If we got into trouble, there would be plenty of time to see and get a head start. I gestured to the kids. "I have an idea how we can make some quick money, but it's risky."

Chase frowned at me, immediately concerned, while Bandit just looked at me, head tilted at an angle.

"Got the idea from you actually, Chase."

Her frown intensified. "OK, now I'm really worried," she said.

52

CHASE

Sully laid out his plan for us, but I was freaking out. We'd spent all this time keeping out of sight, and now he wanted us to solicit attention? How did that make sense?

"I'm not exactly comfortable with the idea myself, but we need cash and we need it now. What's the harm in trying?" He looked at me, not unreasonably, I hated to admit.

"Fine." It was anything but, however, he had a point. We sat on the ground, Bandit before us, as Sully handed me over two plastic cups that he'd lifted from the convenience store. He left one upturned on the ground before us, then took the remaining two cups for himself. I watched as he turned them upside down, then began hitting them on the ground in a catchy rhythm. His head nodded to the beat as he encouraged me to do the same. Seemed simple enough to do.

I fumbled a bit initially, but soon got the hang of it. When I had it down, Sully changed his own cupping to a beat that complemented my own. By this point, we had already caught the attention of a few passers-by. Sully cleared his throat, then started singing a well-known country song in a deep baritone. To my surprise, he was good — *really good*. The whole thing sounded great.

Then, our icing on the cake, our secret weapon, Bandit, began to sing.

He had impeccable timing and only howled when Sully nodded. The gathering audience who at first simply enjoyed the performance was now charmed by Bandit's antics. One by one, they dropped first coins, then bills into our cup.

Thrilled by our success, Bandit decided to crank it up a notch by adding dance moves to his repertoire, lifting opposite paws and prancing around. By now, folk were clapping and singing along. At the end of the performance, they gave us a huge round of applause. I was amazed! Some people moved on, but quite a few stayed for another track until the crowd grew even bigger.

Based on my reaction in the hotel room, you've probably gathered by now that singing isn't really a thing I do well, so hearing how naturally it came to Sully, I was a little jealous. I'd *love* to have a skill or talent that didn't involve just trying to stay alive.

Following Sully's lead, we blew through some twenty or so numbers. By the late afternoon, his voice was getting a little hoarse. Bandit too needed a break. He'd long stopped dancing, choosing just to howl along.

"I think that's a wrap," Sully said.

We crowded around the cup, which had been emptied a few times already and counted out the day's earnings. I couldn't believe my eyes.

"Two hundred bucks? All we did was sing?!"

Sully smiled, though he didn't seem quite as excited as I was.

"We're going to need more than that to get to where we need to go." He pocketed the cash, then threw the cups into a trash cash. My mouth fell open.

"What're you doing? We need those for tomorrow! Why would you throw them away?" I went to retrieve them, but Sully stopped me.

"We can't do it again. This was already a risky move. We need to move on. I have an idea where we can go, but two hundred bucks won't cover us getting there".

I frowned at him, while Bandit, picking up the concern between us, sneaked licks at our hands. "Well, how else are we going to make money, and more?"

He didn't respond right away, but there was clearly something on his mind. Something he wasn't particularly comfortable with, judging by the look that appeared on his face.

"You guys must be hungry."

Bandit barked "yes", wagging his tail with excitement. Sully probably thought he was pretty sneaky, using my biggest weakness against me as I did notice the rapid distraction technique he had just employed, however, the instant grumbling in my stomach wiped any objection clear out of my mind. Food first, questions later.

He led us to a cheap diner called NATE's. The flashing neon red sign was crusted over with dirt, and the N bulb had long blown, so the sign now read "ATE's", which kind of amused me. We sat at a vacant table to find that the menu was printed onto paper that covered the entire table. A sheet of scratched plastic sat on top, protecting it from spills. I couldn't read half of the descriptions due to the scratches, but that, it turns out, wouldn't be a problem.

"They have pictures of everything. Helpful."

"Yeah, I like how they've made a burrito look different by changing the sides that come with it." Sully joked, but it was half-hearted. Bandit laid his chin on Sully's hand, sighing loudly. Even the pooch was concerned. Absently, Sully reached over to scratch him behind the ears.

"You guys order. I've got something to attend to. I shouldn't be long."

He pushed back his chair and stood up to leave. I felt a moment of blind panic as the thought flashed across my mind that he wouldn't be coming back. I shot up from my seat as well, but too fast. My knee hit the table, knocking it. It screeched loudly across the floor a few inches, drawing a few perplexed glances our way. Sully must've sensed my fears then, as the distracted look that had been on his face went away.

"I'm just off to see about some money. I'll be back before you're done eating."

He patted Bandit once more, then took off across the street. I watched until he disappeared around the corner. My stomach gnawed at me, which wasn't unusual in and of itself, but I had a feeling this time that it wasn't from hunger. Bandit whined, liking Sully's absence about as much as me, which come to think of it, was weird. I hadn't wanted him to come along in the first place, so why was I acting all emo right now?

"He promised he'd be back, so let's just enjoy a meal. What do you fancy?"

Bandit looked down at the menu, nose so close to the plastic that his breath started fogging it up. Suddenly he stopped, lifted up his paw and very deliberately rested it on a picture. I slid his paw aside to see what it was.

"A burger. Good choice, buddy."

I signaled the waitress and focused on stroking Bandit, now sitting under the table. Sully said he'd be back. All I had to do was eat.

Simple, right?

53

SULLY

I knew Chase could take care of Bandit for an hour or two, but even then, it felt odd to be without them. I wasn't particularly sure I liked the feeling.

Motoring through the promenade at a rapid pace, my eyes scanned the lurid area for a certain establishment, as I tried not to think about what I was going to do. Instead, I mulled over how much my life had changed in the last forty-eight hours.

Aside from Florence and our animal patients, I had pretty much kept to myself this past year. Initially, when Emma had died, the sudden silence I had found myself in was crushing. Being at home was no longer relaxing. In fact, it induced outright panic. Thinking I didn't want to be alone, I had surrounded myself with family and friends. But pretty soon, the chatter, the constant battle to pretend I wasn't falling apart, exhausted me.

Without even realizing it, I began pushing people away. Just small things at first: not answering the phone; pretending I was asleep or wasn't home when well-wishers turned up at my door; to bailing out on last minute social functions until the invitations eventually stopped coming. Even Emma's family, reeling from their own loss and unable to deal with my standoffish behavior, began to avoid me.

Soon, I had no choice but to be alone since I had burned all bridges and no one wanted to be around me.

Except now I had two to protect.

I reached the end of another block when I saw the flashing sign across the road:

Pawn Shop. Instant Cash.

54

SULLY

I nside, the shop was dark and cramped.

The air tasted stale despite a row of opened windows. I assumed this was due to the sheer volume of items on display. Aisles of clothes, shoes and household objects dominated the front section. The back was filled with electronics, gaming consoles, and old television sets. Whoever was in charge of housekeeping could've done a better job as far as I was concerned — a fine layer of dust covered many of the items.

I worked through the maze until I reached the counter. A large, tattooed biker-type stood behind the counter. Around his thick neck rested a heavy gold chain with the name "Ed" on it.

"What have you got for me?" Ed mumbled. His tone wasn't rude, merely straight down to business. This wasn't a man who had time to fool around.

"You buy jewelry?" I asked.

Ed nodded. "Selling or pawning?"

"Selling," came my response. The word stuck in my throat.

"Let's see it." He stretched out a hand towards me, palm facing the ceiling. Waiting. I hesitated. As my mind raced, my eyes focused on the many lines and callouses on Ed's hand. This was it. No going backward.

I slipped the wedding ring off my finger.

The overhanging light bulb picked up the engraved writing on the inner band of the ring. I squinted to read the familiar words scorched into my heart: "Always and Forever." Her delicate voice sounded in my head, but it seemed far, far away, across an ocean of time. I waited until the last echo of her voice faded, then slid the ring across the counter.

Ed had been watching through my internal dialogue. He knew what I was going through. Though his expression never changed, Ed softened his voice when he spoke. "Nice piece. Shame the engraving knocks the price down."

I nodded, having guessed as much. "Just give me a ballpark."

The other man frowned, assessing the damage. "I know what it's worth, but no way can I match that. Best I can do today is three."

I couldn't hide my shock. "Three grand? That's a third what the ring's worth!" My fists tightened into balls as tension flooded through me.

Though Ed felt sympathy for me, he wasn't about to show it. Business was business after all, and there was a reason why Ed's had lasted long past the faddy shops he saw open, then close.

"It's my last and final offer. Take it or leave it."

55

CHASE

B andit and I had long demolished our burgers and fries, but that weird ache in my stomach was still there.

Bandit lay beneath the table with his head on my feet. Throughout my meal, I had been sneaking him food. When she had taken my order, the waitress warned that dogs weren't supposed to be in the diner, but I started freaking out, rocking back and forth with my arms wrapped around myself, chanting "dog stays with me, dog stays with me."

I was pretending I had a form of Aspergers and only my dog's company would calm me. I know some of you might find that distasteful, but separation wasn't an option, and you know, I had already committed to eating... After that, she gave me a wide berth except to give Bandit a bowl of water after the urging from her boss, the greasy-looking cook, who kept peering at us from inside the kitchen.

An old clock ticked slowly above the entrance. I kept looking at it, counting the minutes, until I nearly drove myself crazy. I sipped water from a chipped glass, trying to make it last as long as possible.

I wasn't sure what Sully's new money-making scheme was, but in the event, it didn't work, I made sure that I had only ordered one meal, and it was one of the cheapest available. I had already drunk three glasses and was busting for the restroom when I finally saw him walking towards the diner.

At my questioning gaze, he shot me a barely perceivable nod. If he was successful, why, then, did he look so damn miserable?

He had barely entered the diner when Bandit's tail started thumping. Pretty sure he couldn't have seen Sully from his position on the floor, so I'm guessing he must've caught Sully's scent. I remembered reading something about that this one time.

Did you know that to dogs, we're super stinky?

Not just our armpits, but our breath and genitals reek. Even our skin is covered in sweat and sebaceous glands (whatever those are) that churn out fluid and oils emitting our own particular scent.

As if that weren't icky enough, when we touch things, we leave a bit of ourselves on them, with our own bacteria steadily munching and excreting away. Next time your dog sniffs you, remember that.

Sully sat down next to me. "You done here?" he asked.

I nodded. "Don't worry, we didn't get much. Just enough to keep us here." Seeing his arrival, the waitress hurried over. I fell quickly silent.

"Are you her dad?" Off Sully's nod, she rushed to continue. "I'm sorry, but we might have had an incident here while you were gone. I didn't know about her... condition. I'm so sorry."

"Condition?"

Sully arched a brow, shooting looks at Bandit and I. I kept my gaze focused on the tabletop, saying nothing. Our waitress fussed over the table, picking up my plate, and cutlery as she shrugged apologetically.

"I tried to get her to remove the dog, which seemed to kick off some anxiety. My boss...," she gestured at the cook who made no pretense of watching us from inside his kitchen. "Said, as an apology, her meal is on us. He doesn't want no trouble."

Sully took the small win and nodded his thanks, though he was clearly burning with questions. Not unlike me, to be honest. He stood back up, offering me his hand. I was surprised until I realized he had no idea what my "condition" was and was hedging his bets.

Remembering that some people suffering from Aspergers hated to be touched, I recoiled and started making my way to the exit. Bandit followed immediately, not understanding what was happening, but game all the same. A few seconds later, Sully joined us outside.

"What was that all about?" he asked.

"I pretended I had Aspergers because she wanted Bandit to leave the diner."

He blinked at me. "Creative. Let me guess, you read about it once?"

"Yup."

I fidgeted on my feet. I had been patient all this time, but I couldn't wait any longer. "So, did your plan work? Did you get money?"

"I did."

I squealed and grabbed Bandit in a little dance. He chuffed happily at us. "How did you do it?"

A cloud of pain flashed over his eyes. As if he could feel it, Bandit stopped dancing immediately. "I don't want to talk about it."

So, of course, I wanted to plague him with a billion questions since his reply didn't tell me anything! But seeing his face, seeing how drained he looked, I shoved my curiosity down. I was pretty proud of myself, actually; I'm not known for my empathy. As we walked from the diner, a growl escaped from my stomach. Sully looked down, surprised.

"Are you kidding me? You just ate!"

"Not much, though. And I shared it with Bandit." I looked down. "I didn't know when you'd get back, and since I knew we didn't have much cash, I didn't want to risk ordering too much... in case we couldn't pay."

Sully looked at us both, eyes shining brightly. If I were a gambling girl (which from my disastrous previous attempt, we know

I'm clearly not), I'd say those were tears in his eyes. His voice turned gruff as he cleared his throat.

"Well, we've got a decent amount now. How about we do something special?"

My eyes turned wide. "Like a main *and* dessert?"

I don't know what I'd said, but he for sure looked emotional suddenly. So I have a big appetite. He already knew this about me. He didn't answer, just inclined his head to follow, as he cleared his throat from the frog that had suddenly appeared in it.

56

CHASE

When Sully told me his idea of special, I couldn't believe it! This is what dreams are made of! Having seen numerous glorious ads for Caesar's restaurant, we headed straight there. We were sold before we'd even tasted a thing.

Their famous Bacchanal Buffet (*seriously, who comes up with these names?*) is apparently the best in the city, winning awards and everything. We walked into a massive hall of food. My eyes nearly popped out of my head when I saw the spread before me.

There were some nine restaurants in the one hall, each specializing in a different food, with a team of chefs preparing food right in front of us! My mouth salivated at the rows upon rows of dishes set out onto the tables: prime ribs, roasted South Carolina shrimp and grits, oak-grilled lamb chops, handmade dim sum and baked-to-order souffles (OK, I'm reading off labels now, and don't know what half of these things are. Still, they sound nice!).

One section contained only meat: both full sized and mini burgers, steak skewers (STEAK at a buffet!), sausages dripping with fat, stuffed and sliced roast chicken done in a million different ways, plus wings, ribs, and legs of every possible variety you could think of. Next was the seafood table where crustaceans were arranged artfully on mountains of ice and lemon slices. My taste buds are pretty simple though, and this was a little too fancy for me, if not outright gross. Don't you think king crabs look like giant alien spiders? Inside my mouth is the last place I'd want them to go.

Beside the seafood was a carb table filled with trays of mac and cheese, mashed potatoes, pasta, and freshly baked bread. There was even a section just for fries! Curly fries, thick cut fries, Southern fries, Steakhouse fries, wavy fries, and what I'd decided would be my favorite: tornado fries (basically a spiral cut fry on a stick). The thing was *huge*!

But then I realized, although I love my carbs, I couldn't possibly fill up on what was essentially the cheapest item there. I would eat what I usually couldn't afford on the street... and that meant *meat*.

And so it was that I loaded my plate with meat of every kind, taking care to source some for Bandit, who was doing a great job at being Sully's guide dog. His nose was going a hundred miles a minute, and he was practically swooning, but he was so good. His tongue didn't sneak a lick, not once.

Seems the other diners were also impressed with his restraint. I soon saw that they were "accidentally" dropping food on the ground, which Bandit dutifully hoovered up. He was having the best time, but then again, so was I, and I hadn't tasted a thing yet!

When there was a mountain of food on my plate, I gestured to Bandit, who guided Sully to an empty table. I dived into my meal, eating with my hands since I hadn't thought to bring cutlery. I must have looked like an animal, but I just didn't care. Sully used a fork to eat, but even he seemed to be enjoying himself, though he showed a ton more restraint than me.

I shared everything on my plate with Bandit and found that when he liked a food in particular, he would place his paw on my foot, applying gentle pressure. It was amazing, really, how we were learning our own sign language. Just think what we could do if we had the proper tools.

In no time, we devoured the first plate, and I went back for more, this time around allowing myself some of that amazingly gloopy looking mac and cheese. I even remembered a fork. And napkins, but mostly because my hands were sticky, and the servers were shuddering at the sight of them. I picked all of Bandit's favorites and sat back down to share, being careful to be stealthy all the while. There were so many diners, it was easy to get away with, really. Occasionally, someone caught on, but the fact that Bandit was a guide dog meant no one said a thing.

When we'd polished off four plates of food, I gave a loud belch and admitted defeat. No more food. I was fit to burst.

But then I saw the desserts.

Three cheesecakes, two pies, and one chocolate mint sundae later, I was done. Even Bandit — who could seriously compete in a food competition — had given up and was now lying contently on the ground. Sully had long stopped before either of us and had spent the rest of his time trying not to ogle at the amount of food I was shoveling down. *He was blind after all, remember?*

Sully's hands were wrapped around a mug of coffee that he sipped slowly from. He seemed to be savoring the flavor. He must be one of those caffeine addicts as the very act of drinking it soothed him. He put the mug down and focused at a distant point over my shoulder.

"Well, that is money well spent, even if I do say so myself."

I was just about to ask if this amazing meal had bankrupted us when Bandit suddenly tensed up. As I froze, worried at what he might have seen, he began frothing at the mouth. His eyes rolled into the back of his head as he fell onto his side, his body shaking with convulsions.

"What's happening?!" I screamed at Sully.

Forgetting all pretense of being blind, Sully leaped out of his chair. Pulling Bandit away from the wall, Sully shrugged out of his jacket and wrapped Bandit securely inside. He then slipped his hand under Bandit's face so that he wasn't slamming it against the hard ground, but other than that, he did nothing else.

"Why are you just sitting there? Do something!" I screamed at him again. By now, the other diners had stopped eating, some had gathered around to watch. Murmurs rose like a mumbled chorus. Most were concerned for Bandit, though a few wore confused expressions when they saw Sully didn't have a problem seeing with his eyes. I saw one kid filming everything on his phone but shoved the thought to one side.

"There's nothing else to do until the convulsion stops. The most important thing is to make sure he doesn't damage himself during the seizure." Seeing the panic in my eyes, he softened his voice. "It looks much worse than it is."

"Why is this happening to him? Is he... sick?" I meant to demand this of him, but I barely managed to whisper the words. Sully kept his face impassive, but I felt the concern rising from him in waves.

"I don't know. We need to see what's going on inside his head to find the cause of the seizure. It could be something as common as epilepsy..."

"Or it might have to do with the experiments they performed on him," I finished grimly.

He gave a curt nod. That was his guess.

I ran my fingers along Bandit's nose, hoping he wasn't in any pain. I hated that he was unconscious and unresponsive and possibly in pain, and willed him to look at me with his intelligent eyes again.

I heard a noise across the room and glanced over to find hotel staff coming our way. By the set of their shoulders, I knew we were about to be hit with more bad news. And I was right. Having discovered Sully wasn't blind, the staff reprimanded us for bringing Bandit inside. I ignored them and focused on my furry friend, who had finally stopped convulsing and was blinking sluggishly. After a few quivering breaths, he found me with his eyes. I ached at the fear and confusion I saw there.

"It's OK, boy. You were sick, but you're good now." For what seemed the longest moment of my life, Bandit stared at me without any hint of the intelligence I had grown to know and love in him. The awful truth hit me like a ton of bricks.

He didn't recognize me.

Had the seizure done something to his brain? As I was running these terrifying scenarios in my head, Bandit forced himself to his feet and pressed against me. Feeling my anxiety, he had very deliberately trod on my foot. The relief flooding through me was palpable.

I tugged on Sully's sleeve — he was arguing with the security guards, refusing to move Bandit until he recovered — and let him know Bandit was good to go. Relief flashed over his face, echoing my own.

Though Bandit could walk, Sully decided to carry him. He didn't want Bandit to be any more taxed than he already was.

With the security guards at our backs, we hurried back to the motel.

57

CHASE

Sully was burning a path into the carpet. Since we'd arrived back, he hadn't stopped pacing the small room. I was getting whiplash just watching him.

"If I had my clinic, I could run the scans, find out what's wrong with Bandit."

"Can't we just take him to another vet?" I asked.

"And risk another attack by those thugs? No. We can't trust anyone."

I wrung my hands. Bandit had calmed since the convulsion and seemed back to himself, but there was a darkness in his eyes. A new awareness. He wanted to know what was wrong with him. "We can't keep running. We need a base, somewhere safe where they won't find us. Don't you have someplace we can go?"

Sully finally stopped pacing and tossed a look in my direction. Sighing, he hung his head low. "Yeah, but it's a last resort."

I snorted. "Think that train left a long while ago..." Sully didn't reply. I let out an exasperated breath. "What else is more important than saving Bandit? Whatever your problem is, get over it! We need a safe place, and we need it now!"

Sully shot me a look. I worried maybe I'd gone too far. My mouth shooting off again before my brain could catch up.

But then he began to pack our things. I jumped up to help. Since we didn't have much, we were pretty much done after a few minutes. He checked Bandit's wound and redressed it. It'd need to be bandaged for a few more days, but he seemed pleased by the progress.

I was relieved.

We needed all the wins we could get.

58

SULLY

An hour after we'd left the motel, we arrived at the Amtrak station. Tension caused my head to throb. On a scale of bad to worse, this idea was off the chart and yet, there really was no other choice. Not if we were to have a chance of saving the dog.

Chase stared at me, burning with questions, but knew enough not to ask. I appreciated her understanding. I'd get to the explanations in due course. I marched wearily to the ticket office where an agent waited with barely concealed boredom.

"How can I help, sir?"

"Two tickets to Montpelier."

The agent hit a few buttons on a screen and a price flashed up. "That'll be $156.75."

I was counting out the bills when the agent glanced behind me, noticing Chase retying Bandit's "collar".

"Is she under thirteen?"

I froze mid count and gave the guy an incredulous stare. "She's not my girlfriend if that's what you're asking."

The agent's mouth snapped shut, his cheeks flaming red.

"No, sir. I just meant... if she is, she can go for a child ticket.

I felt shame spreading through me. Poor guy was trying to help and here I was, ready to rip out his throat. "Right. Sorry. It's been that kind of day."

The agent nodded understandingly but didn't make any more eye contact. Once the tickets were printed, he quickly slid them under the counter.

"When's the next train?" I asked.

The agent glanced down at a timetable. "Four-thirty."

I looked at the clock behind me. "That's not for two hours."

The agent nodded. "We have a small waiting area, or if you prefer, there's a strip of shops one block away."

I took the tickets and change, nodded my thanks, and we went to kill time.

59
___

SULLY

We'd been wandering around aimlessly for what seemed like ten hours when Chase suddenly stopped dead in front of the Walmart window. Eyes wide, she took in the poster which advertised the week's best deals. She turned to Bandit and me, barely able to hide her excitement.

"I need some cash. I've got a great idea for something!"

I opened my wallet. "How much?"

Chase looked at the advertisement. "Four hundred and fifty."

I snapped the wallet shut. "Are you kidding me? What could we possibly need that would cost that much?"

"Please, Sully. I, of all people, know the value of money. You've got to trust me. It's a surprise."

She looked so honest, so excited, that I found myself forking over the bills despite my good sense. *What was the girl up to?*

"One sec..."

She disappeared inside, leaving me staring in bemusement at the dog. "Now I know what those dads with teenage daughters feel like. A chump."

Bandit woofed, though I knew he hadn't really understood my comment. He circled the sidewalk as if trying to find some clarity.

We waited for close to fifteen minutes, but still, there was no sign of Chase. Just as I was beginning to feel a hint of concern, Chase reappeared with a shopping bag full of things. At my questioning face, Chase shook her head.

"Nope, not yet. Patience" was all she'd say.

I shrugged, fine. Far be it for me to pry. We did a slow lap around the shops, then headed back to the station, where our train was just pulling in.

Bandit's tail wagged from side to side. He'd read about a train in his book, but this was his first real life encounter. What with the engine sounds and seeing passengers climbing on and off the train, it was about all the excitement he could take. He pranced eagerly, anxiously waiting for our turn. Chase had to lay a restraining hand on his neck, in case the moment was too much for him. I had decided it would be pointless to warn them that too much excitement or stress could potentially cause another fit. There was nothing we could do if it happened. Better the two got to enjoy themselves while they could.

When it was finally time for them to board, Bandit shot off. Despite my reservations on our destination, I couldn't help but smile at Bandit's child-like enthusiasm. I traded a grin with Chase as we followed him onto the train.

60

THE MERCENARY

The Mercenary tugged at the designer suit he was wearing — a far cry from his usual combat gear. The soft fabric made him uncomfortable, offering no protection whatsoever.

Clutching a leather suitcase, he blended into the sea of suits that spilled onto the sidewalks of Wall Street, eagle eyes focused on the revolving door of one particular building. Patiently, he waited for the face he'd spent the last eight hours studying.

He ran through the details he'd memorized in his mind.

Suspect was born and raised in The Bronx to alcoholic parents who relied on the state. In spite of his troubling family life, suspect excelled at school and had an affinity with numbers. It was this skill that landed him a scholarship to college. After which, suspect joined one of Wall Street's top financial firms, where he spent his twenties billing the most hours of his peers.

He made his first million by twenty-five and now worked three days a week for an extortionate consultant fee. He played as hard as he worked and changed dates more frequently than his underwear. He was also Sullivan's longest-known friend and confidante.

The Mercenary's spine tingled, a sure sign that his prey was in sight. Spotting Mark's face in the crowd, The Mercenary smiled and skillfully navigated his way towards him. When he was inches from Mark, The Mercenary reached out a hand and clamped it onto the other man's shoulder.

"Well, I'll be a son of a gun, Mark? Mark Armstrong?"

Mark spun around, a questioning expression on his face.

"Yeah, who's asking?"

"Joel. Joel Miller. We have a mutual friend."

Mark smiled, his initial wariness vanishing. "Which friend is that?"

"Sully." Mark's smile wavered, the only outward sign of a problem. The Mercenary filed this away, knowing it would come in use later.

"How do you know him?"

"He helped out a dog, I know."

"That's Sully," Mark said, shaking his head. The Mercenary could see he wasn't going to get much out of him this way. He swapped tactics.

"Terrible news about Emma. She was so young, so full of life."

Pain flared in Mark's eyes. "Sully hasn't been the same since. It's like he's been gutted."

The Mercenary features softened sympathetically.

"Can't be easy on you either. Wouldn't know how to cope if our positions were reversed."

"Don't know how well I'm doing on that front either." Mark looked down, filled with worry. The Mercenary gave a moment's pause.

"Hey, I'm just on lunch break. You want to go grab a sandwich together?" Seeing the hesitation, The Mercenary's eye's twinkled kindly. "Man's gotta eat, and it's a lot more fun with company."

After a moment's pause, Mark nodded. The Mercenary hid his triumphant smile by gesturing across the way.

"I know this great little place..."

61

THE CEO

The CEO placed his hand on the reader. A quick scan and an automated voice welcomed him inside the secretive area known as the Genesis lab. A foot wide steel door swung inward, and he was immediately met with a sea of white.

Ceilings, counters, and lab coats; everything was blindingly white and sterile. The atmosphere was kept at an even temperature, and only select personnel were ever allowed inside. The CEO himself was not a frequent visitor, not wanting a constant reminder of The Facility's reason for being. His eyes searched the room until they found what they were looking for.

She was an attractive woman. Of average height and build with alabaster skin that barely saw the sun and dark, wavy, almost black hair that she kept tied back in a neat ponytail. Her brown eyes shone with intelligence from the rimless glasses she wore. Right now, they flicked over to him and tried to quell the anxiety that his appearance always brought.

Dr. Elora Robins. Who would know such a brain existed beneath that lovely facade?

She set down the clipboard in her hands and hurried across to him.

"Good afternoon, sir. I wasn't expecting you today."

The CEO merely smiled but did not offer an explanation. As lovely as she was, he enjoyed watching her squirm. Enjoyed wielding the power his wealth brought.

"Any news on Alpha?" She tried, but couldn't hide the concern that clouded her eyes. She loved Alpha. Had cared for him since he was a pup, hand rearing him from the minute he was "born" until the escape. She was the only mother he had ever known, and his disappearance hurt her almost as much as it had cost him.

"My man is on the hunt. Seems Alpha has made some friends, and they've all gone on the run."

62

ELORA

Pride surged inside of Elora before she quickly bolted it back down. Alpha wasn't alone! And if he'd revealed his intellect, he might be safe after all.

Since his escape, Elora had fretted like any mother whose child had run away. She worried how vulnerable the dog was. Worried he would get run over by a car, or worse, captured by unruly characters who might use him as a fighting dog (she had recently watched a documentary about just this horrifying subject). But now that he wasn't alone, Elora knew he was protected. She hoped he knew what to do, hoped she'd taught him enough.

The CEO's steely blue eyes focused on her face, trying to read her feelings. Elora kept her expression impassive. "At least he has more chance of survival now."

"Not if he's been talking to them." He waited several beats before speaking again. "Any news your end?"

Elora shook her head. "There was some movement with F-12, but no birth as yet." At her words, The CEO felt an unfamiliar emotion take hold. Something he had not felt since he was a penniless child living in the slums of Brooklyn.

Fear.

His hands shook. He tried to hide the action by clenching them into fists. "What's your ETA?"

"Three, maybe four days? It's hard to tell. This isn't an exact science."

A wave of exhaustion suddenly hit him. He took a step back to steady himself and hoped Elora hadn't seen. She hadn't, busy checking the figures on one of her endless charts. "If we don't find Alpha in time, this will all be for nothing."

"He never fails you." She was referring to The Mercenary. Her tone was placating, though not warm. The two had never gotten along.

"He knows what will happen if he did." The threat hovered in the air between them. Elora turned away to hide her distasteful expression.

"He won't fail. He'll find Alpha and bring him back."

He wanted to reach out to her. Wanted nothing more at that moment than to touch her hair and feel the silky skin of her face. Instead, he spun on his feet and stalked stiffly from the lab.

Elora let out a relieved breath. She knew he had feelings for her, but they weren't reciprocated. Elora could never love a man so coldly driven, even if she knew he had very good reasons for being the way he was.

She moved past the nameless scientists to the glass screen that separated her lab from their experiments, wincing inwardly at that word. Experiments. She looked into a room where thousands of test-tubes abounded. Inside each were embryos, all at different stages. Some were nothing more than a few combined cells, but others - such as F-15 - she could already make out their features. The long line of the jaw, the black snout, the curve of a tiny tail.

The light was low and a throbbing, vibrational sound played out via inset speakers - all to emulate the inside of a womb. Elora had hired a world-famous composer, who had worked many months to get the ambiance right. It all had to be perfect.

Elora pressed her hand to the glass and lovingly waited for her children to be born.

63

CHASE

The train rocketed us along at a hundred miles an hour. Having never been on one before, it wasn't just Muttface who was having a blast; I was enjoying every minute of the ride too.

Fields of green blurred into one. I reached up and pulled open the window, letting the air lash against my face. It brought tears to my eyes, but I didn't mind. Somehow, it made me feel more alive. I turned to Bandit, perched on the seat next to me, and grinned.

"You're supposed to be hanging *your* head out of the window."

In reply, Bandit cocked his head in question, then moved to join me. As soon as the wind was on his face, Bandit's eyes went wide with delight and his tongue fell out. I grinned and gestured to Sully to join us, but he only rolled his eyes at our antics. Killjoy.

Our tickets had already been checked, so I knew we wouldn't be disturbed for a while now, if not for the rest of our journey (we'd been on the train for an hour, so there was still another ten and a half to go). Deciding now was the time, I reached for the Walmart bag.

"Guys, I've got a present for Bandit."

At his name, Bandit tore himself from the window and bounded over to me, his face filled with expectation.

"What've you got? More books?" Sully asked.

At the word "books" Bandit jumped up at me and licked my face. His tail wagged so vigorously, I worried it would whip my face into shreds. I laughed and pushed him down. "No. Better."

Unable to wait for an unveiling, Bandit all but climbed into the bag. He emerged seconds later with a box clutched gingerly between his teeth. Sully gasped when he recognized the logo.

"An iPad? How rich do you think we are?"

I ignored his comment, refusing to let him spoil the moment. "Not the newest version, but I figured that wouldn't matter." I was practically buzzing with anticipation. Bandit didn't have a clue what was going on, but he seemed extraordinarily happy just to have been bought a present. I took the box from Bandit and slid the gleaming device out of the box.

"Figured Bandit would use up any and all books we could buy him in seconds, but with an iPad, we'll never run out. Plus there are the games and quizzes we can download." Bandit barked, and I pretty much got the gist of his excitement. *Books and quizzes, oh boy, oh boy!*

I turned on the iPad and tapped some pre-loaded icons. "But best of all, there's this little program..." and placed the device on the ground by Bandit's feet. Sully crowded around us for a better look.

An app had been opened, called Speak, Spell and Read. I tapped a tab, and a chart of common words appeared next to a diagram illustrating the word. I pressed one word, and the iPad said "hello" in a friendly male voice. I hit some more, and we heard "how are you today?" Bandit was so excited he couldn't keep still. His whole body shook, and he had pretty much slobbered all over me by this point.

"When you want to read, you hit the 'books' tab here and choose an age group for the correct reading level. Going by what you've read already, I'd say you're what, five or six years?"

Sully nodded in fascinated agreement.

"So we tap five, and look, hundreds and hundreds of books appear for you to read. Then later, when you're a little more advanced, there's stuff like Peter Pan, Charlotte's Web, Paddington

Bear. Any word you don't understand, you just have to input it like so and…" Chase touched the word "robot".

The male voice explained, "Artificial life. A machine capable of carrying out a series of complicated commands automatically. In science fiction, it is a machine resembling a human being who is able to replicate certain human movements and functions automatically."

"Wow." Sully was blown away by the thing. "This is exactly what he needs to communicate with us."

"I know, right?" I practically beamed. "We can even pick the voice that suits him best." I pulled up a menu and started going through the options. The first was too clipped. The second, too mature. Another too corny. We went through what must have been twenty before the perfect voice materialized. It had a joyful tone, full of life, and sounded young and excitable. Exactly how we thought of Bandit. He seemed to think it was right too as he laid his paw on my hand to stop me from moving to the next sample.

"But wait." Sully suddenly had a thought. "How will he be able to touch those buttons? Have you seen the size of his paws?" Bandit moved his paw away as if embarrassed by the enormity of it.

"Aha!" I dived into the bag once more, reappearing with a box of plastic styluses. "Like the ones they use with the Nintendo game thingies," I explained. But these things were tiny, something I had also given some thought to. I took out some cheap pens and some tape and taped the stylus onto the pen. I then offered the stylus pen to Bandit, who gripped it between his teeth.

Bandit lowered his head and tapped some buttons. "Hello. My name is…" There was a pause as Bandit tried to find his name, but it wasn't on the most common words list. I reached down and toggled a few menus.

"You press this button — learn — then type in the word. B-A-N-D-I-T. Hit save and look, there it is!" At this, Sully looked almost as excited as Bandit.

Bandit snuck another great big lick at my face, dropping his stylus in the excitement of the moment. He picked it back up daintily and tried again. "Hello. My name is Bandit and I love you."

Let's not lie; I practically melted at this, but he wasn't done. He looked pointedly at me, then down at the screen. Then back up to me. I understood immediately what he wanted, even though neither he nor the iPad had voiced his thoughts.

Bandit pressed learn. Then when the blank window appeared for my input, I spelled out my name. Bandit hit save, then his borrowed voice told me, "Chase. You are my best friend."

"And you mine, Muttface."

I threw my arms around him and buried my face in his fur.

64

SULLY

It was ironic.

Here we were on the run, heading to the one place I had tried to escape from so many years ago, and yet I hadn't felt this good since, well, since the day I'd married Emma.

The "kids" (as I was coming round to calling them) were lying on the floor having real conversations. In no time at all, Bandit's vocabulary had shot up. I estimated he was now reading and conversing at the level of a ten-year-old. It was all too easy to forget he was a dog.

"Hold up, I need a minute."

They looked up at me with such complete trust, I felt a pang in my chest. I lowered down to Bandit's side and peeled back the bandage. The skin was beginning to knit together around the stitches. I was relieved to find there wasn't a rotten smell — which would have indicated an infection. The wound was healing as well as it could under the circumstances. I would've preferred for Bandit to be resting in my clinic, not straining himself, but that wasn't an option anymore. I changed the bandage quickly, meaning to let the kids continue, but I noticed Bandit's eyes drooping. I sat back onto my seat and motioned to Chase.

"I think someone has had enough excitement and needs sixty winks."

Chase immediately rose. "You sleep," she told the dog. "We'll talk later."

"But I am not tired..." Bandit managed to get out before his chin sank onto the iPad and he closed his eyes.

65

CHASE

Grinning, I removed the stylus, tucked it into the iPad's case, and took a seat opposite Sully. Moments passed in companionable silence before I caught Sully staring at me. When I didn't say anything, Sully bit the bullet and asked, "Do you have any siblings?"

I knew we would eventually get around to this, but even this simple question caused tension to flood my body. I stared out at the trees blurring past, hoping he wouldn't pick up on it. "No. I'm an only child."

"No other family?"

"None that I know. We weren't exactly what you'd call close."

Sensing Sully wanted to ask more but was too polite to push, I let out a deep breath, my face finally expressing the sadness I'd been holding onto all this time.

"When I was little, I used to love Christmas. Not for the food, or the decorations, or even the toys — I never really had many toys — but for the movies. I loved watching happy families gathering together, being together. Even liked it when they argued 'cause that made them seem real, you know?" I took a breath before continuing.

"They were always such a unit. A real family. So different from my mom and me. I mean, we were OK. We never had enough money, and I was always hungry, but we were doing OK. Until she met Tubs."

Saying his name brought tension to my shoulders. Sully moved as if he wanted to reach out to me, but he didn't want to break the spell. He stayed in his seat, saying nothing, but encouraging me to continue with his eyes.

"He was a trucker. She met him at the diner she was working at part-time. Said he swept her off her feet, but all he did was pay her a little compliment. Mom was so starved of attention, she lapped it up like a dog." Bandit's ears pricked up at the word "dog", but his eyes stayed shut.

"Within a month he'd moved into our home. Mom doted on him, hand and foot. She loved that she now had a man paying the bills. I tried to have some kind of relationship with him, but Tubs was never interested in me. Far as I knew, he hated kids, and I was just one big annoyance. But then annoyance turned into out-and-out hate, especially when he was drunk — which he was becoming more and more frequent. Seemed I couldn't do anything right, and everything I did wrong would send him into a rage. Got so that I cut my hair just so he couldn't drag me by it anymore."

Sully's breath hissed out, and I saw him bite his lip. I turned back to the window and shrugged. "Anyway, things stayed like that a while, until one day, I realized Tubs was paying a bit *too* much attention to me. He was always watching, always leering. I tried telling mom, but she wasn't interested in hearing anything bad about him. I knew I wasn't safe there anymore, so I stole their savings — which wasn't much — and got outta there. Made do until I met Bandit. That's my story, really. Not very exciting."

By now Bandit was softly snoring and had missed my tale. I was glad. I didn't want him to lose the sweet naivety he had.

When Sully finally spoke, it was terse. "Some people just don't deserve to have kids."

"No, they don't," I agreed. I looked at him questioningly. "What about you and Emma? Did you guys ever want kids?"

Sully seemed to flinch at the question. "Yeah," he managed to get out. "We did."

"I'm sorry," I blurted out suddenly. "If I hadn't come to you, they wouldn't have destroyed your home. This is all my fault."

Sully shook his head. "You wanted to save Bandit. You weren't the thugs who burned my place down. You didn't start this. They did."

"But they wouldn't have done that if I hadn't chosen you."

"But you did choose me, and… I'm grateful for that."

My eyes were misting over with tears, but I felt hopeful now too. "You are?"

Sully smiled. "I've been living a lie, Chase. The last year, I've barely managed to survive, but now, I'm beginning to feel alive again. So no, I don't blame you for what happened."

"So you're not mad at me?" I had to get clarification, not being good at reading people at times.

Surprise broke over his face. "If I was, don't you think I'd have said something by now?"

"Tubs didn't," I said. "He'd stew over things until they boiled over."

Sully's features hardened. "Yeah, well, don't ever mistake me for that coward."

He fell silent for a moment, thinking. "The only thing I'm angry about is that I don't have anything left of Emma's. I was hoarding her things, holding on to them as if that kept her alive, and now there's nothing but my memories of us. Everything's gone."

I bit the side of my lip as I studied him, torn. Then, silently, I opened my backpack and reached inside. "You should have this." I handed a framed photograph to Sully. He stared down at the picture, overwhelmed to see Emma's smiling face looking back up at him. In the picture, he had his arm around her and they were strolling down a beach. A captured moment of normality, but one that now meant the world to him.

Tears erupted, tears he didn't even bother to hide. He ran a finger over Emma's face. "Why did you take it?"

I could feel myself squirming, uncomfortable. "I don't know. You both looked so happy."

Sully looked like he didn't know what he could say, so he kept it simple.

"Thank you, Chase. Thank you."

66

THE MERCENARY

The Mercenary wasn't pleased.

After spending two hours listening to Armstrong drown his sorrows — the man really liked the sound of his own voice — one thing was clear: he had no idea where Sullivan had gone, and Sullivan himself was a ghost. No contacts listed under family outside of his wife, no mention of where he grew up. Digging through the national birth registry revealed some three hundred listings for a Jake Sullivan. The Mercenary was hitting a wall, and he didn't like it one bit.

After he paid for lunch, an act that felt alien to The Mercenary who wasn't known for his generosity but would be something his "character" would do, The Mercenary retreated back into his van, where his men were scanning airwaves and the internet for signs of any activity that would match their perpetrators.

As per standard operating procedure, The Mercenary had put eyes and ears on Armstrong and the annoying old woman who had worked at the clinic. The busybody spent her entire time on the phone, calling everyone she knew, telling them of her concern over Sullivan. So far, they had tallied up twenty hours of recordings.

Thank God The Mercenary wouldn't need to listen to them himself. There wasn't enough money in the world to make him endure that torture.

All he could do now was wait.

And that was the worst part of his job.

67

CHASE

I'd never told anyone my sorry story before. It wasn't something I liked to think about. I'm not one of those "woe is me" people, you know? I just deal with it and move on with my life. Besides, if I spent my time mulling over the past, I'd be a seriously depressed person... or a drunk. And neither of those were possibilities for me. You see, I had long decided that I'd prove mom and Tubs wrong. I *was* someone special. I *was* worthwhile. And if they didn't want me, someone out there would.

Bandit snuck his head onto my lap, finally waking from his nap. A tuft of brown fur stood up messily on the top of his head, giving him a very human and comical look. Trust him to have bed head. I reached over and smoothed it down. His nose searched my pockets and fished out the stylus of his own accord. I watched him crawl eagerly to the charging iPad and turn it on. Don't think I'd ever not get a thrill watching him use it. Judging by the sappy expression woon Sully's face, he was thinking the same thing. He always looked at the dog like it was Christmas morning. Like the kids on those heart-warming holiday movies.

Bandit tapped a few words. "Hello again friends! I am hungry." I rubbed my stomach, feeling sympathy pangs.

"Do we have anything left?"

Sully rummaged around inside his bag but came up empty-handed. He shook his head. "We've got juice, water, and a few nuts, but that's it. There's a dining car on the train, though. We could give that a try."

I stood up and held out my hand for some cash. Sully opened up his wallet and forked over some more bills. I totally dug that. Getting money had never been this easy before.

Bandit nudged against my leg, wanting to come with me, but I figured we should keep a low profile. "No boy. Stay here. Keep out of sight." He whined, unhappy to leave me alone, but said "OK." I smiled. I would never get enough of this talking thing.

68

CHASE

I stepped out of our cabin and closed the door behind me.

Though I wasn't anticipating any problems, it didn't hurt to be safe. Gorgeous scenery flew past the window, so beautiful that even *I* had to stop and admire.

Horses grazed on grassy fields beneath towering maple trees that arched over pockets of water. Every so often a quaint church or cluster of buildings interrupted the picturesque view, a reminder that even out here, in the most remote countryside, people could thrive. I wondered if we would find a place like this at the end of our travels. I wouldn't mind spending the rest of my life lounging under a tree, playing fetch with Bandit.

Briefly, I wondered if Sully would be there.

I wrapped my arms around myself and realized that for the first time since Tubs had appeared in my life; I felt hopeful. A smile snuck over my face.

Humming to myself, I made my way to the dining car, which, it turns out, sounds a lot more exciting than it actually is.

Plastic tables and molded seats lined one side of the carriage, where an elderly couple sat, nursing cups of coffee and slabs of a pasty-looking cake. The other half of the carriage contained a kiosk housing vending machines, a grill, and a display of ready-made deli-like dishes. The elderly couple looked up on my approach. Seeing my smile, they smiled back, which was a whole new thing for me too. Usually, they just grimaced, wrinkling their nose in disgust when they caught a whiff of me.

I arrived at the display cabinet and surveyed the contents inside. There were tubs of potato salad, slaw, and salad, and platters lined with slices of chicken and ham, with a mound of pickles decorating the center.

The bored service girl looked up from the National Enquirer she was reading. "Let me know when you've decided," she said, noisily popping a piece of gum. She didn't wait for a response and went right back to reading.

"I've decided."

She put the magazine down and came over. "That was quick."

"I don't mess around when it comes to food."

"Apparently not. So what're you having?"

I pointed at the tray of meat slices. "I'll take those, some turkey and lettuce sandwiches. Those brownies and juice boxes. Four. Might as well throw in a bag of Cheetos too. The extra large."

She looked at me, a pair of metal tongs in her gloved hand. "How many slices of the chicken and ham?"

"All of them."

She blinked, pausing a beat. "Like, *all* all?"

I nodded. "Just put them in saran wrap. That'll be great." She didn't respond but looked at me like she thought this was all some kind of sorority stunt. I figured some clarification was in order. "They're for my dog. We forgot to bring food for him."

At that, she unfroze. "I thought you were joking, but that makes sense now. I've got some nuggets in the fridge too. You think he'd want them?"

"Heck, I'd take 'em just for me, but yeah, nuggets would be great too. He's got a big appetite."

She grabbed the platter, tipped it on one end, and slid the meat into a plastic baggie. "They all do. We have a tiny terrier at home;

she's smaller than a cat, but she can eat like a horse. Don't know where they put it all."

So we were sharing now. This was nice. I tried not to fidget, anxious to get back to Sully and Bandit. "So how much does that come to?"

She packed the rest of the items I'd ordered into a paper bag and rang up the total on a cash register. "Fourteen eighty-nine."

I counted out three fives and handed them over. "Keep the change." Although it gave me a bit of a thrill to say that, part of me already questioned my generosity. It wasn't that long ago when my only source of food was from a dumpster.

She nodded thanks, then immediately went back to her tabloid rag. I'm guessing she gets tipped a lot and eleven cents wasn't much of a big deal. Arms loaded up with supplies, I made my way back.

I caught a few curious stares. One lady commented, "you must have big appetites in your family." I faked a laugh and nodded but didn't stop or elaborate. She turned back to deal with her two kids, fighting over a PS Vita.

I was pretty thrilled by her response.

No suspicious stares, no worry that a cop was going to come along with questions. I was finally passing as a normal kid. I practically skipped back to our car, letting myself in with a clever use of my elbows since my hands were full.

"Well, I hope you're really hungry, 'cause I pretty much got us one of everything." My hip bumped the door closed, and I turned to face the seats, expecting everything to be the same as I'd left it.

Only it wasn't.

Sully was crouched on the floor, Bandit's head in his lap. His hands held Bandit securely as the last of the shaking eased from his body. White froth spilled out of his mouth, covering his jaw line. I looked at Bandit's eyes, but they were unfocused, glazed. The food tumbled out of my hands, crashing to the floor.

Sully tried to reassure me with a weak smile. "He had another seizure, but it's mostly done with now."

I fell onto my knees, wanting to comfort my furry friend, but worried that I would hurt him somehow, I only allowed myself to take hold of a paw, fearful that he would break if I applied even the faintest pressure.

"But this is so soon after the last one."

Sully nodded but kept silent, his brow knotted with tension. I could almost see the cogs in his mind turning over as he tried to make sense of it all. I knew if I asked, he wouldn't keep the truth from me.

"Why is this happening to him? Is he sick?"

"I don't know, but I'm sure as hell going to find out."

69

CHASE

It was a full ten minutes later when Bandit finally came to. In the back of my mind, I noted his recovery time was much longer than the first convulsion. I mentioned this to Sully, but he just nodded and pursed his lips. Judging by his expression, this wasn't a good thing. Though my stomach and heart were twisted up inside, I put on a bright smile.

"Hey, so I got tons of food. Anything you want to try first?"

Bandit blinked up at me as the fogged cleared. Sluggishly, he typed into the iPad. "It happened again?"

My first instinct was to lie. I wanted so badly to protect him, but Sully got there before me.

"Yeah. Sorry, fella."

Bandit thought for a while. "Will it happen more?"

Sully steeled himself. "More and more frequently, I'm afraid. Once we arrive at our destination, you should get those scans we need. Until then, there's nothing else I can tell you for sure."

Bandit's little body shook. Sully and I tensed, each preparing for the worst when Bandit spoke again. "I am scared."

I wrapped my arms around him and squeezed tight, ignoring my instinct to treat him like a glass doll. "Me too."

It was a while before any of us could eat.

70

THE CEO

Lush lawns crunched underfoot as The CEO strolled through the grounds, carrying a bouquet of timeless white flowers. The cloudless sky was a vivid shade of blue, and the shining sun kept away the chill of the fall morning. He took in the familiar swaying oaks and immaculately tended rose beds. To the unobservant eye, this seemed like nothing more than a delightful park, one of those privately maintained ones that seemed to pop up in elite neighborhoods.

But he knew better.

He'd come here weekly for years now, always on Monday mornings, right after breakfast. He couldn't remember how this routine had started, but it was instinctual now. Like checking his stocks over his morning bowl of oatmeal, or the whiskey nightcap that he drank from a diamond shot glass, presented to him from Arab royalty after he had sold him the world's largest hotel chain. Yes, The CEO was a creature of habit, and he was fine with that.

An elderly man stared blankly as his caretaker engaged him in mindless chatter. They were feeding a flock of Eastern Bluebirds, a colorful bird with bright blue plumage and a red chest. The CEO only knew what they were as he had captured twenty or so of the birds once, keeping them in a cage at home to admire, but he had soon tired of their constant chirping...

He turned away, blocking out the sight of the man and his caretaker. He never looked here, never really wanted to know. The truth was already too much to bear without this constant reminder. He quickened his step, anxious to reach his destination, the wing named "Nightingale" after the historical figure. The sign loomed up ahead now. Discreet, like the rest of the place. Along with their reputation, it was the reason he had chosen this establishment. He approached the red-bricked building, noticing the ivy that covered the roof.

Reaching the door, he pushed it open and stepped inside, momentarily disoriented from the dark corridor ahead. Numbered rooms lead off from both sides of the corridor. The CEO didn't need to look to know what they said; he knew them all by heart. He counted in his head now as he moved past the rooms: *three... nine... thirteen...* At fourteen he stopped. The door was wide open.

He stepped inside. Light flooded the quaintly decorated room. Patterned curtains hung on the windows and inviting sofa's and armchairs were arranged into a seating area facing a large flat screen television. A bookshelf packed with framed photographs and mementos covered an entire wall, all featuring a woman lovingly embracing her child, a young boy, while a king-sized bed swamped in matching cushions stood opposite. Yet, despite all this effort, there was no denying that this was a hospital room.

And sitting up in the bed was an elderly woman.

Her gray hair was curled neatly, makeup dabbed carefully onto her face. Dressed in a pastel matching twinset — one of many The CEO had provided for her — she was hunched over the latest Nora Roberts' book when he stepped in. At his appearance, she stopped reading and looked up.

"Hello, mother. How are you today?" The CEO asked.

His mother, Irene, stared at him, confusion and fear in her eyes.

"Who are you, and what are you doing in my room?"

71

THE CEO

T he CEO moved over to his mother, taking a seat next to her.

"It's me, Ma. Your son," he said, but she just frowned at him.

"Don't be ridiculous. My boy's only ten, and he's at school!"

He leaned closer, wanting to take her hands, but resisted the urge, knowing it might frighten her as it had so many times before. "I'm all grown now. And successful. I'm the wealthiest man in America. It's what you always wanted for me." He hated the way his voice sounded. Whiney and pleading. Weak. But then, outside of his empire, she was the only thing — and certainly the only person — he had ever cared about.

She looked at him, those violet eyes that used to shine so bright now dull from years of mindlessness. Sighing, he stopped trying to talk to her in the present. "Tell me about your boy."

It was like a light came on inside her. Her face turned animated, and she sat up a little taller. "He's so clever. Why, just the other day, his teacher told me he was functioning five times higher than his classmates. Five times! I'm just fit to burst. All these years juggling multiple jobs, it's been worth it to see how my boy is progressing."

Bitterness swept through him like a wave. This woman was his life: she was alive, and yet she might as well as be dead for all the good it did him. She would never know him as he was now.

Footsteps sounded in the corridor outside as a cheerful Nurse appeared, carrying a tray with several covered plates of delicious-smelling food. Seeing him, she shot him a big smile. "Back again. How're you today?"

The CEO managed a smile back at Ellie. At only thirty-something, she was already beginning to turn gray, but the endless care and devotion with which she took care of her patient was one of the reasons he kept her on staff. Ellie was a private nurse who he'd hired solely to look after his mother. "I'm well. How has she been?"

Ellie set the tray on a wheeled table, maneuvering it so that it sat in front of Irene. "Good. We played checkers yesterday, and she enjoyed her aqua workout. Didn't you, dear?" She said this to Irene, who nodded, even though she clearly couldn't remember. Ellie leaned forward to help her to sit higher. Fluffing up a pillow, she slipped it behind the older woman to support her back. Lifting the lids off the plates, Ellie described what the menu had to offer today: "French onion soup to start, followed by honey and mustard chicken with seasonal vegetables, and an apple pie for dessert."

Irene focused on the food, delighted. "Onion soup, my favorite! How did you know?" Ellie sneaked a wink at him, clearly her co-conspirator. Prior to enrolling his mother here, The CEO had given detailed instructions on what to feed her. Having made a list of some fifty of her favorite foods, her personal cook — another employee on The CEO's payroll — prepared these meals on rotation. The soup sat in a handcrafted bowl while the chicken was artfully arranged on top of the roasted vegetables. The pie too was elevated, sitting on a crumbed cookie bed with what looked like ice-cream foam on top. It was high-end, restaurant-quality, and a far cry from the meals typically served in such an establishment. Seeing how delectable the meals looked, he made a mental note to pay the cook more.

Irene reached for a spoon and scooped up a spoonful of soup, but as she raised it to her mouth, her eyes glazed over, and she blinked, startled. Lowering her hand, she looked across at him, suddenly angry. "Who are you and what are you doing in my room?!"

Unperturbed, Ellie took the spoon from her. "Here, let me help you with that." With patience and care, Ellie began feeding Irene, wiping her mouth with a napkin when the odd bit of liquid dribbled down her chin. The CEO turned away, pain stabbing at his heart.

It was unbearable to see his mother, the strong woman who had raised him, an invalid like this.

Ellie must have seen his reaction as she smiled at him reassuringly. "If it's any consolation, she doesn't remember any of this."

He knew her words were meant to comfort, but they had the opposite of the intended effect. He stood up, unable to bear anymore, and moved to the sink where he filled a vase full of water before setting the flowers he had brought with him inside. He placed the vase on the window beside Irene, letting it catch the sunlight. She looked up over her soup to admire them with delight.

"Oriental lilies, my favorites! How did you know?"

The CEO dropped a kiss on her forehead and left without another word.

72

SULLY

The sky shone midnight blue when the train finally pulled into our destination.

On the train ride here, Chase had done a little research on my hometown, which she'd been keen to relay. Montpelier was the capital state of Vermont, best known for being the least populated state capital in the United States. Named after its cousin in France, for every one hundred women, there were only eighty-two men, which kind of sucked for those eighteen other women, Chase had thought. Unless they were gay. Which, come to think of it, how did they know the men surveyed were into women? What started off as a simple fact-finding mission soon turned into an epic debate which I was extremely reluctant to enter into. These were dangerous territories, and I wasn't primed for them yet.

Montpelier Station was an old-worldly place. Rickety benches lined the short platform. A vending machine, the only concession to the twentieth century, stood full and unused. Baskets hung from the rafters, exploding with bright flowers. I fixated on one, a bright red clover, the state flower. Seeing the familiar blossom, memories came flooding back to me.

As a six-year-old, I had loved surprising my mom with gifts. She delighted in simple pleasures, and I was only too happy to oblige. As far as I was concerned, mom was the center of my world and the greatest thing in the universe.

This particular afternoon, mom was baking my favorite dessert, a key lime pie. With the scent of the sweet pie teasing my taste buds, I had decided to gather the biggest bunch of wildflowers I could find. Plan created, I fidgeted on my feet, anticipating her delight.

I took my mission very seriously as I scoured the length and breadth of the land that I called home. I picked Wild Columbine, Milkweed, and Mountain Mint, saying each of the names out loud as I gathered them, proud that I remembered them all. Mom liked to try new things, and currently, she was working on some natural home remedies. It was she who had taught me about the plants.

When I thought I was done, I scrutinized my selection with a critical eye. It wasn't quite right; something was clearly missing. I walked around until I found what it was I wanted. Red Clover — but they were inside a dense cluster of bushes. Setting my bounty down, I squeezed myself through the bushes until I arrived at the bed of clovers. Grinning, I plopped myself onto a raised area on the ground and proceeded to pluck the best flowers.

It was while I was reaching for the biggest clover I felt something crawl across my thigh. Looking down, I saw a large black ant. I flicked it away with a finger and continued, but moments another ant found its way on me. Then another. And another. Within seconds, I looked down to see hundreds of them on me. I was sitting on an ant's nest!

Their legs tickled on my bare skin as the ants got under my clothing. As I swatted them away, they started to bite. And suddenly it wasn't ticklish any longer. Fire burst over my skin as the ant's jaws found soft flesh. Screaming with pain, I raced out of the clearing and ran for home.

That was how Mom found me. Screaming and sobbing as the ants tore into my young body. Later, after Mom had soothed my pain with hydrocortisone cream (she had tried one of her remedies first, but it had done nothing), Dad had laughed about my antics, though Mom was touched by my actions. When I had fully recovered, I went back to collecting flowers for Mom, though I was careful not to sit on an ant's nest again.

To this day, I didn't like those bright Red Clovers and gave them a wide berth.

I helped Bandit and Chase off the train and looked around. Aside from our traveling companions, only two other passengers descended onto the platform. Senses honed from the attack at the clinic, I shot the two passengers a cautious look. They were a middle-aged couple wheeling two large suitcases. As I watched, an elderly couple greeted them excitedly. "You finally made it home! How was London? You must tell us all about your trip!"

The coast was clear. We'd made it here without any issues. I allowed myself a brief moment of respite.

"Where to now?" Chase asked. Since Bandit's second seizure, she had kept one hand on the dog, as if she could keep the attacks at bay by doing so. I wished it were that simple.

"We've still some ways to go."

Rubbing shoulders stiff from the eleven-hour ride, Chase didn't seem thrilled by my reply.

"So, now what?"

"You had your fun. Now it's my turn to shop."

73

SULLY

The car dealership was two miles south of the station. I had driven past it on many occasions as a child, and I had admired the shining new paint jobs on the lot. Since we'd lived well off the beaten track, it was impossible to know what color our 4x4 had originally been, hidden, as it usually was, beneath a thick layer of dried mud. With their busy careers, my parents never cared much for simple chores like housekeeping. They had a cleaner for that, though the car never came under her remit.

I remembered the dealership's flashing neon sign, which used to blare out of the darkness. OPEN TWENTY-FOUR HOURS! It had announced cheerfully. I had often wondered what kind of people would need to buy a car in the middle of the night, never expecting for a moment that it would be me.

The roads here were quiet, with only the odd car passing by. Still, I made them walk single file down the edge of the road. As we were relatively near the train station, street lamps lit our path, but they would soon disappear, plunging us into darkness. I hoped we would reach the dealership before the lights ran out.

Crickets chirped into the night. An occasional bat swooped overhead, but otherwise, all was silent bar our own footsteps. Chase seemed unnerved by the stillness. She kept her shoulders hunched, expecting trouble with every sound.

"It's actually much safer out in the sticks than it is in town. Nowhere near as much crime," I offered.

"But everyone carries guns out here."

I couldn't deny that she was right. I shot a quick glance at Bandit, who seemed to have fully recovered from the early seizure. Sensing my concern, Bandit looked up at me and sneaked a quick lick of my fingers.

The silhouette of a building appeared on the horizon. I squinted and made out the open expanse of the car lot. Grinning, I upped my pace, only to fall to a crushing stop moments later at our destination.

The neon sign was still there, but now it hung at an angle, its moorings having rusted and fallen off from time. And it was dark, unlit. I took in the empty car lot. The only vehicle that remained was a rust bucket not fit for use, even if it could be started. I swore under my breath, massaging the back of my neck.

"Doesn't look like anyone's been here for a long time," Chase noted.

"I should've checked instead of assuming." I would've kicked myself if it were physically possible.

"Can we take a taxi?"

"Maybe if we had a number, but I doubt anyone's still working this hour."

Chase looked at Bandit. "Can I borrow your iPad?"

He woofed then stood still, head raised so she could pull it out of its case. Chase called up a website and Googled "taxis". Several hits turned up. She went to each one, looking at their hours of business, but sighed. "You're right. All closed. Plus they're in the next town over."

With nothing else for it, I led them back onto the road, where we continued walking. I tried to make light of our situation.

"It's nice to stretch our legs after being cooped up on the train so long."

"Yeah. Exercise. Woo." Chase's feigned enthusiasm raised a few brows.

"Well, we know one thing for sure. You can't lie worth a damn."

We walked for several hours until our legs felt fit to drop. I was about to announce that we camp down for the night when a vehicle approached from behind. Ignoring my earlier road safety lecture, I leaped into the road and started waving my arms. The vehicle kept approaching without altering its speed. Worried the driver might not see me, Chase flashed the iPad screen in their direction. That did the trick. The vehicle — a truck — slowed and an unruly head stuck out of the window.

"You folks broke down?"

She was around thirty, with the bluest eyes I had ever seen and a friendly smile the size of Texas. Freckles lined her nose, and the sun had lightened her already blonde hair. I didn't read any malicious intent in her eyes, but more than that, Bandit had already made his way below the window and was trying to lick her fingers.

"Wow, you are a gorgeous thing aren't you?"

Bandit woofed, which caused Chase and I to share a smile. The driver was too busy playing with him to notice.

"We're stranded, more like. Got off the train and was hoping to buy a car." I trailed off and gestured at the disused car lot.

"Old man Stanton closed that down when he retired some eight years ago now." She frowned, studying my face. "You from around here?"

I stiffened, weary about giving my information away to a complete stranger. Guess the years of living in a city had taught me some things after all. I smiled and said, "No, but I visited as a kid. We have family nearby."

She kept smiling, though a knowing look appeared in her eyes. Wherever we were from, we weren't up for swapping life stories. "My name's Sam, Sam Dubeau. I'm heading up to Middlesex. Can I offer you folks a ride?"

I hesitated, but Bandit answered for them with another loud woof. Before the humans could respond, he went around to the passenger side and scratched at the door until Sam opened it. Bandit leaped inside and settled next to Sam, who grinned and stroked the wacky dog. "Your pet seems to like me."

Chase clearly didn't like to see the other woman's hands on Bandit or him sitting in the car alone with her. She ran around the vehicle and leaped in after Bandit, leaving me standing alone on the road.

"Can I pick up a car there?" I asked.

"There isn't a dealership for another twenty miles, but I know someone who's selling a truck if that'll do you? I could drop you there."

I hesitated, unsure.

"It's on my way."

I finally smiled. "That'll be great. We'd appreciate it." I climbed in after Chase, and as she offered a hand to Sam.

"My name's Bella, and this is my dad, Charlie. The furball here is Ed." I shot her a look but otherwise kept up the pretense.

"It's nice to meet y'all. Where have you come from?"

Sam spoke to them both but aimed the question at Chase. Chase glanced at me and hesitated for a split second before answering.

"Washington, DC."

"You folks aren't in politics, are you? Cause I gotta say, I'm not terribly fond of politicians."

I offered my first genuine smile. "No. Not a suit among us."

"Well, that's a relief. So, you're here visiting family?"

"Sort of." I wanted to keep this as brief as possible. I also wanted to dissuade this whole line of questioning. Options flew through my mind until the perfect solution came to me.

"My father passed away. I'm here to settle up the estate and deal with the funeral."

Sam's eyes widened in sympathy. The joviality left her face and took on a respectful expression. "Sure am sad to hear that. My thoughts are with you and yours."

I glanced down as if to hide a tear. Surprising me, Chase leaned across and took my hand.

"It's alright, Dad. Pops wouldn't want you upset."

So I was wrong about her ability to act. She seemed to have the perfect mixture of empathy and sadness. Even Bandit joined in, blasting a sigh out of his nose and lowering his head onto our clasped hands.

If it wasn't in bad taste, I would have laughed.

74

SULLY

We drove in relative silence for the next hour — relative in that there was no talking. Sam, however, sang along to each song that played on the country radio. She was a hearty singer and kept a good melody with an impressive memory for song lyrics. I had to stop myself from joining in a few times because I felt this was an intimate thing to do. More importantly, Emma was the only woman I had previously sung for.

We drove past a small town with barely four shops on Main Street. All were closed up for the night. Out here in the sticks, it was a complete contrast to the bright lights and sounds of New York. There were no overnight food joints here, no late opening bars where one could drink themselves into a stupor only to stumble home at first light.

At last, we pulled up to a long and winding drive. The name on the mailbox read "Warrington." Sam switched off the ignition and climbed out.

"You guys wait here. I'll fetch Warrey."

Moments later, she returned with a man built like a brick house. With a checked shirt and ripped jeans, he wouldn't have looked amiss on the cover of GQ — if GQ were doing a blue collar special. I didn't know why, but Warrington's good looks made me anxious.

The other man's hands were covered in oil. He wiped them onto his clothes but managed to smear a line of black over his face. I elbowed Chase even as I began to feel her smirk. Warrey eyed the group suspiciously.

"Sam tells me you're on the lookout for transport?"

I nodded, then reached out to take Warrington's hand. We shook, but Warrington held on a moment longer than necessary, sizing me up. I extracted my hand and had to force myself not to wipe away the grime that now covered it.

"Well, let's not waste time." He gestured for us to follow him to where a truck waited. The paint job was peeling, and a few dents covered the body, but the defects seemed superficial.

"Had it six years, but since business is booming, I treated myself to a present."

I looked over Warrington's shoulder to see a brand new Chevrolet. At least it wasn't the convertible I was expecting.

"That's a nice looking ride. How much you want for this?"

"Two grand," came Warrington's instant response. Sam's reaction reflected what I was feeling. She simply dug her elbow into his ribs. Hard. Warrington flinched and stepped out of arm's reach. "What's your problem?"

"Two grand and he can have my truck!" Sam exclaimed. "Are you crazy? This isn't how you do business. These are good, honest folk."

I cringed inwardly at her blind faith in us and halted her defense with a hand on her shoulder. "My offer's 800, take it or leave it."

Warrington narrowed his eyes at them. "As I understand it, you don't have any other options. 1500."

Not to be outdone, I stared him down. "How bout I just pay Sam to drive us." I turned to Sam. "What do you say? I'll give you 200 just to get us there."

Before Sam could reply, Warrington stepped in and stopped her. "Fine! 1000 and you get off my land."

I grinned at Warrey, who didn't bother to hide the glower he was sending my way. "Nice doing business with you." Forking over the cash, I climbed into the truck to examine my new ride. Inside, the vehicle fared better. The upholstery was fine and everything seemed to be in working order. This wasn't a bad deal, not a bad deal at all. When Bandit and Chase settled beside me, Sam leaned in through the window.

"Guess I'll be seeing you then?" She gazed at me a split second too long to deny the interest simmering in her eyes. I could feel a jolt run through me. No one had looked at me like that since Emma, but I quickly pushed the feeling down. Now was not the time even if I could see her again. It was too soon.

"I doubt it, but it was great to meet you. Thanks for your help with the truck." To her credit, she didn't seem fazed by the rejection, though I couldn't understand the sudden disappointment I felt. Sam gave Bandit one last pet, shot Chase a smile, and nodded at me.

"You folks take care now." She turned and walked back to her own vehicle. I watched until Chase issued an impatient sigh.

"Are we going or are you just going to stare at her butt until it's gone?"

Cheeks flushing bright red, I started the engine and peeled out of there.

75

THE MERCENARY

Looking down at his tablet, The Mercenary watched the video clip for the hundredth time.

Shaky footage started playing (the filmer wasn't much of a cameraman), as a busy food hall came into view. Mountains of delicious looking platters were attacked by greedy tourists, heaping food onto their already overflowing plates as the filmer, "xxGetGud420xx" judging by his handle, droned on in the background, explaining what he had already eaten and what he would be tackling next. The Mercenary found it a disturbing sign of the times that someone so clearly lacking in brain cells, with zero charisma, could have a YouTube following of thousands.

Frankly, he would pay just to shut the kid up so he wouldn't have to hear that monotonous voice again.

The kid was deliberating over the hot wings and whether he should go for BBQ instead, while The Mercenary was wondering if the Boss would object to an unauthorized hit when cries of alarm rose up from the crowd. The camera swung 180 degrees, the footage blurring until it auto-focused on the scene ahead.

There, on the ground, convulsing violently... Alpha.

The Mercenary watched as Sullivan administered aid while that skinny street kid screamed at him. She had dyed her hair and cut it, but he saw straight through the disguise. The Mercenary froze the footage on the girl's face: her mouth was open in a perpetual scream, eyes wide with fear. This wasn't the emotion of a kid who was just worried about a normal dog. No, this was the terror of someone who had already bonded with Alpha and knew how special he was.

It was enough to make The Mercenary scream, himself.

Thanks to Getgud, The Mercenary was able to determine where the action was taking place. Caesar's Palace. And not even the flag-ship casino, but its lesser-known, smaller cousin in Atlantic City. A part of him was impressed with their ingenuity - The Mercenary had cut them off from Sullivan's funds after all - though his team had already confirmed the trio hadn't had much luck scoring cash, as a hack into the hotel's security feed showed, they hadn't tried their luck on the tables or slots. Probably worried that a kid and her dog would be too conspicuous. Sensible really, but unluckily for them, The Mercenary's high-tech network of eagle-eyed IT geeks had spotted Getgud's video within minutes of it being uploaded.

One short flight later, and The Mercenary was stabbing his fork unenthusiastically into his own plate of food at the buffet. Wearing a new disguise as a Mexican tourist, The Mercenary had questioned the hotel staff and customers discreetly, as protocol required, but he already knew Sullivan & co would be long gone.

The last twenty-four hours had been spent fruitlessly searching bus garages and train stations for any sign of them. He had exhausted every possible lead bar one, which is how The Mercenary found himself now standing inside 30th Street Station in Phil-adelphia. It was a long shot, and a ways away from Atlantic City (for that, he was grateful). He glared at the bronze statue of an angel in front of him. The embossed plaque beneath it read: *Angel of the Resurrection by Walker Hancock.* Created to commemorate the 1,307 Pennsylvania Railroad employees who died in World War II, it was apparently the artist's favorite piece of work. The Mercenary thought it overwrought and distasteful.

He stormed through the Art déco styled hall, ignoring screaming children with their harassed parents. Their screams seemed to echo in the grand hall, something which displeased The Mercenary no end. Why did architects never consider these things before they designed their buildings?

Reaching the bank of ticket booths, The Mercenary made his way to each one, catching his reflection on a wall of glass. This afternoon he was dressed in a police uniform. It offered some benefits; the crowds parted like a wave, the public obeyed and never questioned his authority. In short, it made work like this far easier.

He took out a wanted poster his people had created using Sullivan's driving license, a recent photo Dr. Robins had supplied of Alpha, and a mockup of what the girl now looked like. With this, The Mercenary began questioning each ticket operator. It wasn't until he reached the sixth one that he caught a lead. The guy, a spotty, nerdy type who barely left his basement room by the looks of things, remembered Sullivan. Something about him being edgy and jumping to conclusions over a standard fare inquiry. He also remembered the girl. Said she was cute but seemed way too young for him.

The Mercenary wanted to know what train they had gotten onto, but the useless operator couldn't remember and made excuses about the amount of traffic that came his way. He did remember that they had some time to kill and had taken off to mosey around the nearby shops.

The Mercenary took a seat on a bench and made a phone call.

"Control, HS 031290 requesting assistance".

Within moments, the log of the operator's ticket sales over the last two days was downloaded onto his phone...

76

THE MERCENARY

Black as night and just as stealthy, the pilot steered the black-ops helicopter, not onto a helipad as one might expect, but into a retail car park.

A stunned late-night shopper loaded with bags froze mid-step, staring as the alien aircraft landed beside her car. Surprised, she lost her grip on the shopping. The bags dropped by her feet, spilling their contents. Oranges rolled across the tarmac in all directions. She watched in fascinated horror as one bright orange bumped into the military boots that had descended from the helicopter.

Boots which now flattened the fruit, leaving a sticky mess of pulp and juice on the ground.

The shopper's mouth snapped closed in shock, but she said nothing. Lowering her gaze to avoid eye contact, she scrambled around for her groceries but made sure she kept the black-clad man in her line of sight.

Single-minded, The Mercenary marched towards the supermarket entrance, caring nothing for the stunned glances cast his way. This particular part of his mission wasn't of a classified nature. The Mercenary glanced at a Swiss Army watch on his wrist. Time was of the essence, and too much of it had already been wasted.

A family of five exited the store just as The Mercenary arrived at the doors. Their chatter faded instantly. Except for the youngest, a three-year-old with sticky fingers and cheeks smudged with chocolate, too young to recognize danger when it was before him.

"Copter!" he shouted.

His Mom shushed him, instantly sensing the coldness emanating from The Mercenary. "Hush baby. Let's just get to the car and clean those hands of yours."

"But I wanna see 'copter!" He squirmed and tried to get down, but Mom clung to him tightly. Dad patted his son's shoulder, steering the shopping cart away.

"Last in the car doesn't get any ice cream!" At that, the two other kids made a mad dash away. The Mercenary tossed a disdainful glance their way as he stepped beneath the glowing Walmart sign.

77

THE MERCENARY

It was a good thing Walmart had security cameras that his geeks could hack into, or The Mercenary might have missed this very important stop.

After he'd located the salesboy who had advised the girl on her recent purchase, The Mercenary left the store with his own bag of goodies. Once again, he ignored the incredulous looks thrown his way, striding back to the waiting bird. Jumping in, he slid the door closed, banging on it two times to signal the pilot. The two had worked together on many missions and developed a streamlined method of communication.

The blades quickly whipped to life, and within seconds, they were airborne. The Mercenary leaned back and allowed the tiniest of smiles. While others hated the rocky motion of the aircraft, The Mercenary thrilled in it. He loved anything that resembled danger and had since he was a child. He remembered it was something his mother had worried about, this constant attraction to danger, but his father, a strict and successful corporate lawyer, had praised what he had considered his son's edge. Of course, this very edge would turn out to be their family downfall. The Mercenary frowned, snapping back to the present, surprised at the visit down memory lane.

Somewhat angrily, he removed the iPad from the shopping bag and turned it on. Cross-referencing a handwritten list of apps that the salesboy had scrawled down for him, The Mercenary began down-loading the listed apps. It took only minutes to install them all. When the first app opened, he felt his stomach plummet as the welcome greeting flashed onto the screen.

Hello! Welcome to Speak, Spell, and Read, your one-stop app to teach your child how to speak, read, and write in two easy steps!

The Mercenary's breath hissed out of his lips. They were teaching the dog to communicate.

78

CHASE

Open green expanses passed by as the truck rolled past with a comforting motion. We'd been going for a couple of hours now, and Sully hadn't spoken a word. Suppose I shouldn't have teased him about Sam, but honestly, if you'd seen the way he was ogling her. He was like the drooling cat in those cartoons, watching and waiting until the oblivious mouse went scrambling past.

Bandit lay next to me, snoring softly, the iPad nestled under his chin like some kind of high-tech security blanket. Earlier, he had told me how he's waited a very long time for people to understand him. Now that we had a system going, he didn't want to leave anything to chance and made sure the iPad was always in reach — just in case. The smooth rocking suddenly made way for a bumpier ride as Sully swung a left. I looked out across the dense forest around us and frowned.

"Er, you sure I shouldn't consult a map or something? Pretty sure, if it came down to it, we're not going to win a fight with a giant tree." Sully gave a snort which I took for his shortened version of "trust me". *Honestly, is it so hard to speak the words?*

He expertly maneuvered the truck onto a muddy path which I could only just see now that we were on it. We hit several bumps, one big enough to jolt Bandit from sleep. He raised sleepy eyes at me and yawned. I got a big hit of dog breath and tried not to gag (he is so sensitive after all).

Suddenly, the trees cleared, and we were at the edge of a ranch. It was a one-story building with a wraparound porch to one side. A stable stood to the far left of it that must house a couple of horses as I could hear a whinny in the distance. Just in front of the porch, a large plot of land had been turned into a thriving vegetable garden.

Sully stopped the truck, and we got out. Bandit and I were both taken aback by the lush fruits and vegetables being grown. A strawberry patch stood next to pears and apple trees. Thick vines, sagging from the weight of plump purple grapes, wove around a pergola. Vegetables of all shapes and colors decorated the area, including exotic-sounding ones like Kohlrabi and Daikon (thanks to my photographic memory and a school project on homegrown produce, I knew the names of most, though I had hardly tasted any of them). All I could think about was how one of these plots would have fed me for life on the streets. *Mental note to self: in the future, if still homeless, live on open land and learn how to farm.*

Bandit was sniffing around a tomato when a GUN SHOT thundered by, so close, it must have narrowly missed our heads. Sully immediately threw himself on top of us, sheltering us with his body. Bandit whined, scared and confused, but kept still.

"Who the heck's firing at us?" I hissed.

Sully's eyes swept the place quickly before finding their mark standing on the porch. I followed his eye-line to see a guy, a little older than me, pointing a lethal looking shotgun at us. He had shoulder length hair that would be girly if it wasn't for the square cut of his jaw. He was dressed in jeans and a flannel shirt, but even from here I could tell he was all muscle. Ridiculously, though we were in a pretty dangerous predicament, I found myself wondering what his eyes looked like close up. Apparently, I was about to get my wish as he called out to us.

"I'm going to count to three, and if you don't state what it is you're doing, my friend here (he gestured to his gun) will be only too happy to see you off."

Sully stuck both hands in the air. "I'm here to see my dad."

The boy lowered his gun. "You're Jake?" Amazingly, he managed to make this sound loaded with accusation. Sully didn't have a clue what his problem was, but his priority was to not get killed.

Sully nodded. "Is he here?"

The boy inclined his head *inside,* then disappeared into the ranch. I found the whole encounter weird. "Is this how they normally greet strangers in these parts?"

Sully helped me up to my feet. "Not usually, no."

"So we're really going into the house after the mad boy with the gun who just shot at us?"

Sully didn't reply but started walking in after him. I shared a perplexed look with Bandit before we followed hesitantly after him.

"Well, I hope your dad's going to be happier to see us."

79

SULLY

I stepped through the double doors and into the house.

Several rooms led off from the large entryway. To the left, there was a large, open-plan living area. Through the right doorway stood a well-stocked library and home office. I caught a glimpse of the kitchen where Zeb's prized moonshine rack stood. Ever since I was a kid, Zeb had been distilling his own moonshine using a still he'd found antiquing in New England. It was a dangerous hobby, and as a young boy, I had been warned to keep a wide berth. Not that I was ever curious enough to investigate — the white whiskey stank as far as I was concerned, and I never knew how anyone could stand to be near it, much less drink it. Zeb himself only ever drank them on special occasions, which were few and far between. The sight of them was at once familiar yet painful — there wasn't much happiness that I could remember, only anger and crushing disappointment.

Though this wasn't my childhood home — I had grown up in Burlington — I was familiar with the ranch as we had spent many a summer here when Zeb's friend, Roberts, had owned it. The last eight years or so hadn't been kind to the ranch though, which was finally showing its age. Paint peeled from the windows and worm-like threads dangled from curtains that hadn't been washed in what must have been a decade.   I was surprised. When had the man turned into such a slob?

I stepped through into the lounge and gazed down at the floor where a myriad of scratches were now gouged into the floorboards. *Strange.* I didn't remember those.

Chase stared at me, frowning. *What's up with you,* her eyes all but said. I shook my head, *nothing. Everything's fine. Even though my insides are flip flopping around.*

As I began to wonder when Zeb would make an appearance, there came the unmistakable sound of powered wheels. Even before the old man in the wheelchair approached, I had found the answer to the scratches.

I looked down at my father and spoke one word in greeting. "Zebediah."

80

CHASE

The old man in the wheelchair was the spitting image of Sully — if Sully were *old*.

Instead of brown, Sully's dad's hair was a shocking white. He had a beard too, but I don't think he'd ever be mistaken for Santa — his eyes lacked the twinkle. Those gray eyes pinned on Sully with an unreadable expression. There was a pregnant pause as both men stared each other down. Finally, when Sully's dad spoke, his voice was loaded with an unexpected hardness. "I was wondering when you would show your face."

Of all the things I had expected him to say, that wasn't one of them. Sully seemed to take it in his stride however, and didn't react to his less-than-welcoming tone.

"You knew I was coming?"

Zeb stared up at him, managing to look stern and disapproving in one go. "Insurance company called with some story about your clinic burning down, and you having pulled a runner. Told them the truth: that I hadn't seen you in almost ten years." He stopped, assessing Sully with those knowing eyes. "So it's bad then, whatever you've gotten yourself into?"

Sully's silence was answer enough. Zeb shook his head, as if he should be surprised by this, but wasn't. Watching him, watching his treatment of Sully, I felt an indignant rage building up inside me. *What was this guy's problem? How could he talk to Sully like this?!* As my mouth was about to shoot off with something I knew I'd regret later, Zeb's posture suddenly relaxed as some rigidness left his back.

"Sorry to hear about your loss. She seemed like a nice girl."

As Sully stared back, I saw his expression harden. "She was, which you would've known if you'd bothered to come to the wedding."

The sympathy in Sully's dad's eyes faded then, like a switch had been thrown. One minute he seemed kind, the next, I found myself taking a step back from the force of his anger.

"You threw your life away, turned your back on your mother and me, God rest her soul. After everything we had done for you, that was how you repaid us."

Sully's shoulders tensed, and he took a big breath before replying. "Everything you had done? You were my parents! You didn't do anything special. Far from it, in fact."

As Sully's Dad glared, a twitch formed in one of his eyes. "I got you into the best medical school in the country, but you wanted to toss away a career as a promising surgeon to cut into animals!"

I felt Bandit flinch then. He whined unhappily, not liking this turn of events. Couldn't say I blamed him, this was not my idea of a successful reunion. Standing behind Zeb, shooter boy seemed uneasy too.

"That's what I wanted to do, and I'm good at it," Sully seethed, hands clenched into fists by his side. "But you didn't care about that. All you cared about was your own reputation and carrying the family line".

"Your mother and I would've given anything to have half the talent you had, Jake! We never made it as surgeons, but you could have made something of yourself! Your decision didn't just make us a laughingstock, it was a criminal waste of your ability."

"It's not a waste to the families of the animals I save every day.

Just because my patients can't say the words doesn't mean they're any less thankful for their lives."

At this, Bandit woofed. I guess, like me, he couldn't bear seeing Sully being taken down like this. The old man caught himself, suddenly remembering our existence.

"Who are they?"

"Chase and Bandit. They need our help."

Sully's dad laughed humorlessly. "So that's why you came back."

I'd been standing here, trying to pretend it wasn't awkward as all hell (which I think shooter boy was doing also, judging by the weird shuffle he'd been doing with his feet), but enough was enough. This wasn't going to get us anywhere. I took out Bandit's iPad. Before I continued with my plan, however, I needed to know one thing. I pointed at shooter boy.

"Who is he and can he be trusted?"

The boy snorted, insulted, but I didn't care. Clearly, the time for niceties had long gone. He looked me straight in the face.

"I live here with Zeb. Help him run the ranch."

Is this a weird time to notice his eyes were a frosty blue? Though they currently exuded hostility, I couldn't help but think how pretty they were. Zeb, Sully's dad, glared at me.

"Gideon is like my son. The son I never had."

The last sentence was said for Sully's benefit and it did the job; he looked like he had been punched in the gut. To his credit, he recovered quickly. He turned to stare Gideon down.

"This isn't a game. They burned down my home, we barely made it out alive. If you don't want to be a part of this, you're free to leave now."

Hearing the words, the antagonism left Zeb's face. He took in our haggard state, Bandit's wound, and the light way we were traveling. His expression turned serious.

"What's going on?"

"It's easier if we show you."

81

CHASE

The small group relocated into the parlor where a fire was already burning. Out here in the sticks, despite the sunshine outside, there was a chill that ran through my bones. Not used to the cold, I wasn't able to hide my shivering. I watched as Bandit walked over to the fireplace and sat, tongue hanging out with pleasure. He stared into the dancing flames, watching them with a childlike delight. I kneeled on the floor next to him, placing the iPad between his paws.

Gideon wheeled Zeb into the room, positioning him opposite Bandit. From his impatient expression, I could see he didn't care for all the theatrics. He wasn't happy with Sully's return, and he certainly didn't care for me, but, out of respect for Zeb, he was keeping a lid on his feelings. At least, I was hoping he would. I'm not a girl who likes confrontations, and we'd already had a few today.

Sully looked at us. "How about you guys show them why you're so special." Bandit turned from the fire to gaze at Sully. I handed him the stylus, and Bandit bent down and started to type...

"Hello. I am Bandit. Chase and Sully are my best friends."

The words were spoken from the app, but Bandit had clearly chosen them. Zeb and Gideon couldn't hide their shock. I was kinda amused, having gone through this exact moment myself, though obviously these were nicer surroundings. *Take it all in fellas.*

Zeb cleared his throat. "That's some trick."

In answer, Bandit typed anther sentence. *"No trick. I am special."* And there was that tongue again, lolling out in a grin. I wrapped my arms around him, resting my chin on his head.

"Yes, you are."

Gideon snapped his mouth closed. "How is he doing that?"

"*I read,*" came the reply. *"Chase got iPad. Now I can speak."*

Somewhat skeptical, Zeb wheeled close to the dog. "Can you do anything else?"

Bandit tilted his head to one side, considering the question in such a human gesture, I thought there'd be no question whether we were telling the truth or not.

"I am smart."

Zeb raised his eyes to Sully, frowning as his scientific mind struggled to comprehend what he was witnessing. "But how is this even possible?"

At that, Bandit lowered his chin to his paws, exhaling gravely.

"They made me like this."

82

———

CHASE

Sully and his dad had been talking for some time now.

Well, some of it was talking.

Some was outright shouting as one or the other brought up past grievances. Bandit, Gideon, and I were in the kitchen where we'd moved to give them privacy, as it really was awkward having to watch them fight it out, but even here, we could hear their raised voices.

Zeb had a ton of questions; some of which I actually understood, but most contained words far too scientific for even my photographic brain to have come across. I sat with Bandit by the table, while the boy, Gideon, kept watching us from across the room. Always with those eyes. I'm not sure what it was about him, but he made me so nervous, my hands kept getting sweaty. Bandit must have noticed (he probably smelled the sweat), as his tongue kept snaking out to lick them. I moved them away from him and wiped them on my jeans, hoping he wouldn't notice. After a while, he came over from his position by the door and sat by us.

"Is he friendly to strangers?" he asked.

Bandit barked once, but it only caused him to flinch back. "One bark for yes, two for no," I explained. "And you can speak to him directly, you know. I mean, he's right there."

Gideon gave me a look but didn't reply. It was funny: he seemed to care so much about Zeb, but that concern stopped right there. There was an air of disdain around him, a deep mistrust for anyone else... and that included dogs, intelligent or otherwise.

He stared over at Bandit, frowning, as he wrestled with some thought or another. Finally, he must have decided that Bandit wasn't a threat after all, as he moved closer to him.

Tentatively, he reached out a hand, leaned across, and stroked him. Bandit sighed happily and nuzzled him with his nose. At this very normal response, Gideon couldn't help but smile... and my breath caught in my throat.

Turns out, his face was quite nice. Especially when he wasn't threatening anyone with a shotgun. There were dimples on his cheeks that made him look suddenly younger. Briefly, the thought flashed across my mind that he must have been a cute baby, before I shoved it aside, annoyed. *Why was I acting like some swooning teenage girl?* The kind of girl I'd seen at the mall, giggling and batting their lashes at some guy always made me want to hurl.

"When I was young, I always wanted a dog," he finally volunteered. I was so deep in my mental examination of his face that his voice startled me.

"Yeah? Your folks didn't let you get one?" Figured I'd make an effort at conversation since that's what we were apparently doing now. If I was honest, I didn't really mind.

"They weren't the giving type," he replied. His expression never changed, but I could hear the bitterness in his voice.

"Well, guess we have that in common," I responded before I could help myself. I'm usually very good at keeping things to myself, so this was unusual. It must've been those dimples. They were bizarrely distracting. "How did you come to live with Zeb? Are you related?"

He shook his head. "He took me in after my folks threw me out. Never liked them much anyway, so it wasn't a big deal. I moved around until I came across the ranch. I'd steal from Zeb's vegetable garden and sleep in the barn. Didn't think he knew, 'cept one day I woke to find a plate of hot food next to me." His eyes took on a faraway look. "I took the plate back to him after I had washed it. He told me I could stay so long as I helped around the ranch. I've been doing that since." He focused on me then. "How did you come to be on the streets?"

He asked so easily, so matter of fact, but I still wouldn't, *couldn't*, talk about it in any great detail. "Similar story, not very interesting." His eyes turned knowing, and he nodded, accepting this small explanation. I was grateful he wasn't going to pry. *There are some things a girl needs to keep to herself.*

Bandit laid down suddenly and lifted his leg, baring his stomach. Without thinking, I reached down to stroke the soft fur on his tummy, like every other time I did this, only this time, Gideon did exactly the same. Our hands touched, and I felt a brief shock of electricity before we both snatched our hands away. To my horror, I felt my cheeks redden.

"I need food," he said suddenly, shrinking back from me like I had the plague. Now, an ordinary girl might've had some issue with this, but me? My thoughts had already settled elsewhere.

"I could eat," I answered quickly, while my stomach had already begun a dance in anticipation. Bandit woofed once too, equally keen for provisions.

He stood up, somewhat peeved by how we had hijacked the situation and made his way to the fridge.

And with that, we hurried after Gideon, whether he wanted us to or not.

83

SULLY

I'd been talking to Zeb some three hours now, yet the old man showed no sign of fatigue. Fact was, he seemed more energetic than ever.

It took a while, but I had brought him up to date. During the long train ride, while Chase was fooling around with Bandit, I had worried how I would be able to recruit Zeb's help. A researcher in the medical field, Zeb was a smart man, but he hadn't had the acumen necessary to become a surgeon. What he lacked in physicality, however, he more than made up for in knowledge. More importantly, along with general antiquing, Zeb was a collector of old medical equipment, and amongst the odd assortment of machines and fixtures, I knew Zeb had in his possession, a refurbished 2004 CT scanner. Exactly what I needed to see into Bandit's body.

If it wasn't for this, I wouldn't have come back, tail between my legs. While I had expected my old man's hostility, what I hadn't counted on was how much frailer he now looked. And it wasn't just the wheelchair — something that had happened after I left. He just seemed *old*. A decade could really change a person.

The room fell silent as both of us contemplated our thoughts. I asked the question, pressing on my mind since I first arrived.

"What happened?" I gestured at the wheelchair.

The old man's face tensed. "An accident."

I waited for more, but it seemed nothing else would be forthcoming. I tried again. "But what caused it?"

A hiss of annoyance escaped Zeb's lips. He wheeled away, turning to face the window that looked out over the green fields beyond.

"That was always your problem, Jake. Never knew when to leave the past in the past." He wasn't referring to Emma, I knew, but I couldn't stop the raw ache that appeared in my heart at his words, nonetheless.

Taking a breath, I spoke. "You don't want to talk about it, fine, but let's set up some ground rules here. I don't ask about your accident, and you never bring up Emma. Agreed?"

If Zeb was surprised by the ultimatum, he didn't show it. Without blinking, Zeb issued a curt nod. "Now the dog. He needs a full workup: x-rays, blood tests, the works, right?"

I nodded in agreement.

"Tell me you still have the scanner?"

84

SULLY

I followed behind as Zeb took me through the ranch. Gideon and Chase appeared alongside, wolfing down the remnants of a sandwich. A few crumbs clung to Bandit's fur, the only sign of his own recent snack. I made a mental note to get Bandit more dog food, unhappy with the amount of human food the dog was consuming.

As we passed by the rooms, I was struck by the familiarity I felt, though I had never lived here myself. I recognized odd bits of furniture, and the patterned curtains my mom had struggled for an age to make.

Zeb arrived at the back of the ranch and proceeded to go outside. A path had been cleared on the lawn, laid over with smoothed out timber so that the wheelchair could glide over it without issue. I followed as my father lead me towards the barn out back. The building had changed some since I was last here. A fresh coat of paint covered the building, and old siding had been replaced with new. Even the roof had been renovated.

Reaching a double height set of sliding doors, Zeb gestured at Gideon to open them. I watched as Gideon wrapped his hands around the door handle — an iron lever — and tugged it down. The doors slid open effortlessly as strip lights flashed on inside. I gasped.

Instead of the messy, hay-filled barn I expected, all manner of scientific apparatus lay neatly before me, separated into types: there were medical monitors designed to measure vital signs; physical therapy machines to help rehabilitate injured patients; and life support equipment, like the defibrillator, commonly seen on every medical show known to man. I, however, was only interested in the diagnostic section of gear. Striding quickly across the room, I zeroed in on a large donut shaped contraption in a corner of the barn.

"That GE Lightspeed 16. You've had it what, twelve years now? Does it still work?"

Zeb looked at me.

"Guess it's time we find out."

85

CHASE

Bandit whined unhappily.

Though Sully had explained what he wanted to do, just walking into the barn with all that medical equipment had made him anxious. He couldn't stop himself from panting, and I saw him walking behind me on shaking legs.

I kept turning to look at him, speaking encouragingly the whole time, but Bandit could sense my fear; it was impossible to miss, being almost as great as his. My concern only made Bandit's worse. He pressed close to me for reassurance.

I looked up at Sully, standing by the strange machine. "You're sure this won't hurt him?" I asked. My voice wobbled on the last word, and I hated myself for it. I wanted to be strong for Bandit.

"It's just an X-Ray machine, Chase. He won't feel a thing, but this will give us an insight into what's going on inside. With this, we should be able to see what might be causing the fits..." He trailed off, stopping himself from saying what was on his mind.

Bandit tugged on my sleeve to get my attention. When I looked down, Bandit pressed the home button on the iPad.

"What will it do?"

Activating the machine, Zeb looked straight at him. "You will lie here as several harmless beams will come from the machine. They will scan you and form several two-dimensional images that are then put into this," he pointed at another machine, a few feet away. "Once the images are inside the computer, the computer will layer them together to make a three-dimensional image that will clearly show us what is going on inside you. Does that make sense?"

Bandit barked twice. *No.* "*What is number die-men-son-all?*"

Sully grabbed a sheet of paper from the counter and drew onto it before showing it to him. "Do you see this test tube I just drew?"

One bark.

"This is two dimensional, as it is a flat picture, an image of the actual test tube." Bandit watched solemnly as Sully then picked up an actual test tube from the counter. "See this test tube, however, it's real. I can hold it in my hand. This is three dimensional. A three-dimensional picture, would be a picture that is made in such a way that it seems real. That's all that means."

"By doing this, we'll get a good image of your insides."

Bandit chuffed, but none of us understood his response. Seeing our confusion, he typed into the iPad.

"*OK.*"

Moments later, Bandit lay under the machine as Zeb nodded to Gideon, who flipped a switch. The CT scanner powered into life. Feeling the hum of electricity, Bandit's body shook with terror and unbidden, a yelp escaped. Having not left his side, I immediately touched him.

"What's wrong boy?"

Bandit whimpered and then seemed to calm. Laying his head down, he focused on a spotlight on the machine...

86

SULLY

I saw the way Bandit's body tensed as soon as the scanner switched on.

Chase immediately offered what comfort she could, but it hurt me, all the same, to think what was done to him that simply turning on a machine could cause fear to grip him so entirely. I knew the scans wouldn't hurt him, though convincing the dog of this was another matter. At least the scanner looked like it was working. *If we had come all this way to find it wasn't...*

"Stand back," came Zeb's command.

Chase looked as if she were going to argue. "Just for a second, Chase. Just while the rays get to work," I said.

Chewing anxiously on her lip, Chase took a few steps back, but her eyes never left the dog. Wheeling back, Zeb settled a few feet away before picking up a remote switch lying on his lap. Giving one last look around the group to make sure the table was clear, he pressed the button.

Bars of light danced across Bandit's body as radiographic images began to appear on the computer by Zeb. While it was an old system, having come off the line somewhere around 2002, it had been refurbished to a good standard, and though it could only provide a 16-slice measurement (top-of-the-line ones could now manage 320), it should — provided it still worked properly — give us a decent look inside Bandit's body.

I watched as the cross-sectional images came together to form a three-dimensional map of Bandit's body. Even though I had seen CT scans throughout my career, I never stopped marveling at the technology being displayed before me. This simple but miraculous machine had saved countless lives.

"Almost there," Zeb spoke reassuringly. To Bandit or Chase, I wasn't sure, but the kindness in his voice surprised me. I couldn't remember a time when Zeb had addressed me in such a manner.

Bandit was proving to be a trooper. Aside from his initial discomfort, he lay there calmly, but I could tell the dog was still anxious. Bandit was trying to steel his nerves but couldn't quite control his panting. His chest was rising and falling a little too fast. I kept this information to myself. No point stressing the girl or dog out further.

Within a few moments, the scanner fell silent and Bandit was pulled out. He immediately leaped off the gurney and shook himself as if to rid himself of that unpleasant experience and made his way to Chase's side.

"Good boy. You did so well," she said as she stroked the sweet spot behind his ears. I moved over to the computer and stood by my father, already reviewing the information on the screen.

"You see that?" Zeb asked solemnly.

He pointed at a mass, around the size of a quarter, that was growing on Bandit's brain. I nodded, unable to stop the sudden sinking feeling in my stomach.

"Yeah."

Chase came over, shoving me aside.

"What is it? What've you found?"

87

CHASE

The black-and-white image didn't make much sense to me, but I knew it wasn't good news. Sully's eyes looked haunted.

"What is it?" I asked again. More urgently this time.

When Sully's answer came, it was small. Defeated. "He has a tumor growing on his brain."

Somewhere in the back of my mind, I distantly remembered that that was what had killed Emma. A part of me felt deep sorrow for him that he would have to go through this again with someone else he cared about. Then I caught myself. *Wasn't tumor another word for cancer? My Muttface had cancer?*

"But it's fixable, right? You can get rid of it?" My voice came out a lot more panicked than I intended. Neither man spoke, just looked down at Bandit and me. "You're a vet, Sully! You must be able to help!"

Sully looked at me, concern radiating from him. "It isn't as simple as that. The tumor is aggressive; see how it's pressing on the normal brain tissue? It looks as if it's been there for some time, which doesn't make much sense. If Bandit escaped from a lab, there's no way a mass that size would have gone unnoticed. Frankly, it's a miracle he is able to function as well as he has."

"That's just science talk for you're not going to help him, isn't it?" I couldn't keep the accusatory tone from my voice, and *frankly*, I didn't care.

"It means I'm not sure I know how to. If I go in blind, I could do irreparable damage. This isn't my area of expertize. It's not something I've done or even know how to do."

I breathed in sharply. "Look, your dad's an expert researcher, and you're a vet. Putting the two together, surely that means you'll be able to help him?"

Sully and Zeb stared at each other. Sully looked aghast, but Zeb seemed to be considering my words. "It's incredibly risky."

I looked him straight in the eye. "If you don't help him, he's going to die, anyway." At this, Bandit's whole body shook. I hated myself for scaring him like that, but the others needed a push. Zeb paused, considering my words. When he finally spoke, his tone was reluctant.

"I need to think. Let's all rest and talk about this tomorrow."

I opened my mouth to argue, but Gideon shot me a look. "Enough already. He said he'll talk about this tomorrow." Without another word, he steered Zeb out of the barn and back into the ranch. I turned to Sully, faking a confidence that wasn't there.

"This is going to work. I know it."

He didn't reply.

CHASE

Sully showed me to a guest room overlooking the vegetable garden.

The room was basic, containing only a double bed, a chest of drawers, and a side table, but to me, it was heaven and a serious step up from Motel Gross in Atlantic City. It made me wonder what Sully's room was like growing up. Even though he and Zeb didn't seem like they had had a great relationship, I'd bet the house that it's still better than what mine was like. Bet Sully had more than a bug-ridden mattress on the floor.

An old patchwork quilt lay over the bed. I sat down on it and ran my hand over the stitched squares. The handiwork was a little rough: some threads could've been better trimmed, and if I looked closely, I could see the squares weren't all the exact same size, but whatever; it was clean and comforting.

Seeing me studying the quilt, Sully stopped beside me. "My mom made that," he said. "Had a period where she tried to be crafty. Some mom's at school kept giving her grief because she was a career woman, and I guess they were threatened by that. One summer she decided to give them a run for their money. Didn't last long, though. She wasn't very good."

"Still, nice that she tried. The only thing my mom made was me and look how that turned out." I meant it flippantly, but Sully seemed upset by my words. I really have to watch this mouth of mine. Not everyone wants to hear my tale of woe. I looked to change the subject. "You haven't spoken about your mom before. What happened to her?"

Sully's eyes took on a distant look as he turned to stare out of the window at the vegetable garden. "She had the same line of work as my dad. They were both workaholics. She was more patient, though, and kind. When I was young, she was my world, but when I got older and told them I wasn't going into the family business, they didn't take kindly to that. Things got worse when they learned I wanted to be a vet. Neither of them cared much for animals; they both considered it a waste, especially considering my pedigree. Far as they were concerned, I was a disappointment."

His voice broke a little at that word. He stopped, clearing his throat before continuing. "Ten years ago, out of nowhere, she suffered a heart attack and died. Just like that. No warning, no sign anything was wrong. Two world-class medical researchers living in the same house and neither of them had a clue."

Bandit left my side to press against Sully, offering his support. Sully gave him a grateful smile, bending down to stroke him. "After that, things changed. My dad, while never soft and cuddly, turned into an outright jerk. He retired, left the city and moved to the ranch here. I got a job in town working at the local garage. Saved every cent I earned, then went off to study. I met Emma at college. Knew from day one she would be my wife. We were happy and in love, but my dad refused to come to the wedding. Blamed her for not talking me out of this lowly career. After that, I decided he wasn't worth having in my life."

He tried to sound pragmatic, but I could see he was still hurting. It made me uncomfortable. This kind of raw emotion, I didn't know how to handle it. It actually made me regret ever asking, so I stayed silent. Sully must have picked up on my unease, as after a few moments, he asked, "What do you make of Gideon?"

To my horror, I felt my cheeks flush again. "Nothing," I managed to mumble.

He stared at me funny. "You spent a good while with him; you must have an opinion?"

"I don't know. He's just normal, I guess." I shrugged, hoping the ground would open up and swallow me whole.

"You think he can be trusted?"

My only answer was another shrug. By now Sully's brow was furrowed in an expression I can only describe as "perplexed". Probably wondering where the mouthy girl he'd gotten to know had disappeared to. I was wondering that myself. He must've finally sensed my discomfort as he headed to the door.

"Get some rest. I'll be in the room down the hall."

With that, he was gone.

89

SULLY

Something was clearly up with Chase.

While I knew she was stressed about Bandit's condition, what I hadn't bargained on was this bizarre crush she had obviously just developed on the boy, Gideon. Teenage hormones. I remembered them with the fondness of a rash I couldn't scratch.

I headed down the hall to the second guest bedroom. The sun had set by now, and my room on the East side of the ranch was pitch black. Flipping the lights on, I saw it had almost the same layout as Chase's room. There was a double bed in the center of the room, a closet, and a desk by the window. This bed was also covered with one of my mom's quilts; one of her earlier efforts. It had a marine theme with pictures of sailboats and seashells. I remembered how I had loved it as a kid.

Somehow, seeing that quilt brought her to the forefront of my mind. Whatever my issues with my dad, Zeb had truly loved my mother. Despite never having lived in this house, her little touches were everywhere. Feeling a deep ache, I turned away, shrugging out of my jacket, when footsteps sounded outside. I looked at the door to find Gideon standing with a tray of food in his hands. There was a sandwich, some vegetables freshly dug from the garden, and a glass of water.

"That for me? Thanks." I reached for the tray, but Gideon didn't move. Just stood there staring at me.

"Zeb asked me to put this together for you. If it were up to me, I'd tell you to do it yourself."

It was impossible to miss the hostility in his voice. With plenty on my mind already, I really didn't need an angry teenager to contend with, so I decided to tackle the issue head on. "You don't like me much, do you?"

"Why whatever gave you that idea?" came Gideon's snarky reply.

"I don't know what he's told you, but I can almost guarantee it's revisionist history." I didn't know why I was explaining myself, especially since I didn't care what this kid thought of me. His attitude galled me all the same.

Gideon came into the room, crossed over to the desk and dropped the tray onto it with enough violence that half the water spilled out of the glass. "That's where you're wrong, *Jake*." The way he said my name made it sound like a dirty word. "He hasn't said anything. What I know about you, I figured out myself."

I knew I could correct him if I wanted to, but I was over my daily limit of teenage angst. Seeing my dad was causing enough negative emotions, and that was without venturing into the minefield that was the brain tumor territory — which alone was enough to drain my energy. I just wanted to lie down and sleep.

So instead of correcting him, I said nothing. I sat on the bed and very deliberately pulled my boots off, preparing to sleep. As I had hoped, Gideon took this as a sign to leave, though he couldn't hide his disappointment. This kid was giddy for a fight.

Spinning on his heel, he marched out of the room. I wondered what Chase saw in him.

Kids.

90

CHASE

B andit had already jumped onto the bed, iPad on and waiting to communicate when I heard footsteps stomping outside. Tiptoeing to the door, I peeked through the keyhole to see who it was.

It was Gideon. And he looked furious.

He was coming back from Sully's room. By the looks of things, whatever had gone on between them hadn't ended well. *What exactly was Gideon's problem with Sully? The two had never met before now, so what was with his salty attitude?*

He stormed past my room, disappearing down the hall. Even angered, there was something about the way he looked that drew me. I watched until he was gone.

Bandit woofed softly at me.

"What? I'm not doing anything." Caught, I answered automatically. In hindsight, he probably wasn't asking why I was staring after Gideon, but that's the first thing that crossed my mind. Moving guiltily from the door, I climbed onto the bed beside him where he was already busy typing.

"What is tumor?"

The official explanation was "a swelling of a part of the body, generally without inflammation, caused by an abnormal growth of tissue, whether benign or malignant." I knew this as I'd come across the explanation in a scientific journal once, back when I was studying and tossing around the idea of being a doctor (yes, I had dreams too - though I did also consider being a space cadet when I was young, so...). There was no way Bandit would understand *that* though, so we searched YouTube for videos that might make it clearer.

We watched a couple of videos put out by the American Cancer Society, followed by clips of past sufferers who were now cancer free. They had happy demeanors, but their eyes looked haunted. By the end of our research, I had almost convinced myself of a positive outcome.

God wouldn't make Bandit special just to kill him off.

That would make no sense whatsoever. Then again, I used to wonder why I was created if this miserable existence was going to be my life.

Clearly, God didn't exist.

We were screwed.

91

SULLY

An owl hooted outside my window. As it was an unseasonably warm night, I'd flung the window open to let the breeze in, but I now couldn't sleep due to the cacophony of sounds outside. In addition to the owl, a choir of crickets chirped incessantly as the occasional bat swooped across the dark sky. It had been so long since I had heard this much nature that, despite my fatigue, I was having a hard time sleeping.

Then again, I could only ever sleep next to Emma.

There was an old radio alarm clock plugged into the wall. Probably one of Zeb's "collectibles," as the red digits were stuck at 12:03 and had been that way since I'd first come into the room. I had no idea what time it really was, but it was long past midnight.

Sighing, I rolled out of bed and headed out into the night wearing just my shorts. The air was cooler out here, and a blessed relief from the cloying stuffiness of my room. Zeb was old school and had never believed in air conditioning. Said a man wasn't a man unless he could brave the climate naturally. I used to argue that his logic was asinine since we relied very much on heating during the long and brutal Vermont winters, but all that had done was to enrage my old man to the point my mom would have to step in to diffuse the situation.

The owl hooted again. I looked up into a cluster of trees to find him silhouetted against the round moon. He blinked at me, wide yellow eyes alert and watchful but showing no fear. Folk around here tended to leave the animals alone, so unlike in the city, they had not grown to fear man.

The moon shone over the ranch, granting enough light for me to see some distance ahead. Enjoying the moment, I started walking when a whinny caught my attention. I smiled, suddenly excited, and made my way to the stables.

Sliding the door open, my eyes picked out a group of thoroughbred horses. The gray, Derby, was a two-time state champion of Vermont. She'd ran for most of her life until skeletal fractures had cut her career short. Her owners — a pair of mercenary scumbags I had wanted banned from owning any animal — hadn't wanted to stump up the small fortune it would take to fix her injuries, so Derby was heading for the butcher's block when eight-year-old me had stepped in.

My mom and I had been visiting a local food market when I overheard Derby's owners haggling with the butcher. Appalled that this magnificent animal would see such a sorry end, I had pleaded with my mom to save her. My tears and compassion had moved her into action. Within a few hours, Zeb had come home to find himself the surprised owner of a retired racehorse. My philanthropist ways didn't stop there. Over the next ten or so years, I saved several more horses from the slaughterhouse. The ones I could rehabilitate were given to families to live out their days on green pastures and sunshine. The ones who couldn't were sent to Roberts' ranch, as there wasn't space for them in our townhouse in Burlington. I had spent every school vacation caring for my horse. Derby was my first rescue and my fondest.

I made a clicking sound in my throat. Derby looked up and snickered back a greeting, prancing on her legs. She remembered who I was. With a few strides, I reached her and threw my arms around her neck. Derby lowered her mouth to my shoulder and nibbled my shirt in that comforting way she did when I was just a kid.

"Hey old girl, how've you been?" She whinnied, pawing the ground. "I know, it's been a while. A lot's happened, but I've never forgotten you. You've always been my favorite girl." The horse seemed to calm at my words. She blew into my face, sniffing at me. As I stroked her I took in the other horses. There was one other familiar face, but I was surprised to see new inhabitants in the stables.

Leaving Derby was the hardest thing I had had to do, but there was just no way my new life in New York would allow for a horse. Before I had left, I only asked one thing of Zeb; that he care for Derby with the grace and compassion she was owed. While Zeb had never been an animal person, he still respected their right to a happy and safe life. I was inordinately grateful now to see how well Derby looked. In my absence, she had been well cared for. Having spent years resting, even her fractures had healed.

Two brushes still hung on the wall where I had left them: a curry comb and a hard brush, designed for use after the curry comb. I took the comb and started grooming the horse using circular motions, beginning from her neck, then to the barrel and all the way down to her rump, removing any loose hair, dirt, and mud. Derby's tail flicked from side to side, enjoying the pampering. When I was done with both sides, I took the hard bristle brush and went over Derby's coat again until it was gleaming and free of dirt. She was a whole new filly by the time I was done with her.

Hanging up my tools, I promised to see her again and was heading back to the ranch when I saw a crack of light spilling out from the barn.

Frowning at the lateness of the hour, I headed toward it. When I reached the door, I found Zeb inside, typing busily on the computer. Scans littered the counters around me as the printer hummed loudly, spouting reams of information.

"You're working late?" I said.

Zeb looked over at me, surprised by the visit, rubbing his red-rimmed eyes. "There's so much to consider. We can't miss anything."

I walked over to him, taking in the charts and diagrams, only some of which made any sense to me. "You honestly think we can do this?"

Zeb peered at me over the top of his glasses. "What choice do we have? That dog is a miracle, a scientific breakthrough." He laughed suddenly, at something only he could hear.

"Care to share the joke?" I asked.

"Your mother and I spent thirty years studying and learning, but here you are with the kind of breakthrough we always hoped to find."

It was meant as a compliment, but the way he said the word "breakthrough" had me on edge. "Bandit's family; he's not an experiment to us."

Zeb had the decency to look embarrassed. "I didn't mean it the way it sounded."

I nodded that I understood, though I couldn't find the words to say it. Like so many times before, when I had entered into Zeb's work zone uninvited, Zeb turned his attention back to the work at hand. As far as he was concerned, the conversation was over. However, unlike all those other times, I wasn't a kid, and I didn't accept the dismissal. Instead, I picked up a sheet of Zeb's findings, frowning as I tried to make sense of it.

"This tumor isn't like any I've seen."

Zeb looked up again, surprised I was still there. As if he suddenly realized I could be an asset, he opened up. "It's almost as if it's man made. Look at the placement. It's perfect."

A chill ran through me that had nothing to do with the night air. "You think they gave Bandit a tumor intentionally? Why would anyone do that?"

"I don't know. Maybe his intelligence has something to do with it."

"I know there have been cases where people were seeing things or became smarter than they were originally due to a tumor growing on the brain in just the right place, but this would be crazy. How would they know where to put it, for a start?"

We both looked at each other as the same thought crossed our minds.

"How many more dogs have they done this to?"

92

THE MERCENARY

It was a bright and beautiful fall morning. Green fields flashed by in a blur as the train thundered down the tracks.

The Mercenary ignored them, having no interest in the scenery, pushing past passengers as he made his way to a specific carriage. He checked the log on his phone: Carriage C. Finally locating it, he moved inside, only to find a middle-aged couple in "his" seats. At The Mercenary's approach, the husband, a balding man in his forties with a protruding stomach, looked up from a half-completed cross-word puzzle.

Though he was no longer dressed in police uniform, there was no denying The Mercenary's commanding presence. He leaned over them, letting his shadow fall over their faces.

"Sir, Ma'am, I'd greatly appreciate if you would move to a different carriage." He flashed open his wallet. The fake ID showed his unsmiling face and the logo of the FBI. "I'm investigating a possible crime that took place where you are sitting right now."

The woman recoiled with horror, clutching at her husband, who was already gathering up their things. "What happened? Did someone *die*?"

The Mercenary kept his face impassive. "I'm not at liberty to disclose that, Ma'am."

She sighed, shocked, reading into his reply. By now, the husband had their things loaded in his arms and was tugging her towards the door. "Margaret, come," he hissed, eager to get away. To The Mercenary, he said, "No problem Officer, we'll be moving right along."

The Mercenary watched impatiently. As soon as they had gone, he leaped into action. Sliding on a pair of glasses, The Mercenary waited and watched. An ordinary person wouldn't have spotted the difference between these and his image enhancement glasses, but The Mercenary could tell. These held a thicker lens and weighed more to accommodate the extra tech.

Within a few moments, a hum sounded between his ears as the glasses powered on. Suddenly, the carriage looked very different as the marks and lint, invisible to the naked eye, appeared. Staring at the multitude of sweat stains that now covered the seats, The Mercenary restrained a grimace. This was one of the reasons he preferred to travel in his own vehicles. People were nasty creatures.

Code flashed on the lens as the glasses filtered through their findings, listing every recognized item and discarding them as anything of note. The Mercenary scanned the room slowly, giving them a chance to work their magic. Eventually, they hit the jackpot as cross hairs zeroed in on a tiny speck. The Mercenary lowered into a crouch, moving his face in close.

It was a hair.

The fiber was tough and short. And brown. The Mercenary waited impatiently for the glasses to confirm their findings. Finally, a single word flashed up.

** MATCH **

It was Alpha's fur.

93

THE MERCENARY

Within seconds, the findings had been uploaded to the Facilities computers, with Dr. Robins, hard at work, examining the fur. The Mercenary didn't know what it was she was doing — he never knew the ins and outs of her work. He was a simple man with a simple job and operated on a need-to-know basis. And what she did with those animals, what she did *to* them? Some things were better left unsaid.

Finding nothing else of interest, The Mercenary left the carriage and moved along the rest of the train. It was a warm day, and The Mercenary had dressed accordingly, though the muggy air clung uncomfortably close. A trickle of sweat formed at the base of his neck. He ignored it, focusing on surveying his immediate surroundings. Passengers were dotted around the carriage. Most, he noted, were elderly or poorly dressed. He assumed anyone with the means would prefer to drive rather than travel in this suffocating hellhole.

A sign ahead caught his eye. The Mercenary already knew Sullivan's destination — it was stamped across his ticket. That meant a seven-hour train ride. It was doubtful they had the foresight to purchase provisions ahead of the journey. The Mercenary was hoping to find more information up ahead.

With that in mind, he entered the catering car.

THE MERCENARY

Seconds later, The Mercenary strolled up to the counter where a twenty-something guy leaned against the refrigerator with an expression of utter boredom. Going by the droop of his shoulders, The Mercenary didn't think he'd be lasting long in this job. He glanced up at his approach. "Can I help you?" he asked.

"I need to know who was working this carriage yesterday, on this same train," The Mercenary said.

The server's face grew guarded. "Why? Did she do something?"

The Mercenary smiled reassuringly. "No, she's not in any trouble. I just need to speak to her."

He could see he wasn't getting anywhere, however, as the server just grew more suspicious. Seeing the Paranoia magazine peeking out from his bag on the floor, a publication read by conspiracy theorists, The Mercenary — an expert at profiling — made a snap decision.

"Look, I shouldn't be telling you this, but I'm with the FBI. We're looking for a criminal who we believe traveled on this very train yesterday. It's a long journey. I expect our suspect wouldn't have had the foresight to bring provisions, in which case they would have visited the catering car. I only want to speak to her, see if she can confirm a sighting." The Mercenary flashed his trusted FBI badge at the guy who leaned closer to The Mercenary, eyes wide with interest, though he still seemed reluctant to part with any information.

"I could get fired for giving out personal information..." He said, hesitantly.

The Mercenary nodded. "And I'm not asking you for any. You obviously know the girl who worked here yesterday." The Server nodded. "Can you just call her and let me speak to her now?" he asked. The Server hesitated, worried over any possible work ramifications. Suddenly, he shrugged. He wasn't doing anything wrong. Taking a phone out of his pocket, he tapped through several screens. Within seconds, the words "Calling Janet Home" flashed up and was answered after a few rings. The Server quickly explained why he was calling, then handed the phone to The Mercenary.

"I'm looking for some people who were on this train yesterday. A thirty-something guy traveling with a teenage girl and a dog. I think you might've seen them."

An excited female voice came on the line. The Mercenary guessed she was somewhere in her early twenties. "Haven't seen any guys with that description. People traveling on the train are usually older than that. I did serve a young girl yesterday, though. Come to think of it, she said she was buying food for her dog!" Janet said.

The Mercenary kept his face calm, though he was starting to feel a surge of excitement race through him. "Did she talk about it at all?"

The girl sounded confused. "Who, the dog? Not really. Just said she was buying some food for him."

The Mercenary took note of her use of the word "him." "Can you remember what she bought?"

Again, a confused silence came on the line. "Just some sandwiches and she took a whole tray of meats. Said I didn't need to bother wrapping them, just to dump them in a bag since they were for her dog."

The Mercenary nodding, mentally filing the information away. "We're almost done here. Can you give me a detailed description of what she looked like?"

The girl hesitated then. The Mercenary could almost see the questions racing through her mind before she voiced them. "Well, if you're looking for her, shouldn't you know what she looks like?"

The Mercenary smiled, though it didn't quite reach his eyes. "I need to establish whether we are talking about the same person, and any information I give out to you could sway your memory. It's better if you speak freely without any interference from me."

Her voice softened. The Mercenary could hear the moment she accepted his response. Even the Server bought his story, hanging onto every word.

"She was around five foot four. Short dark hair, kind of messy cut actually, but it suited her. She was pretty, but a bit heavy-handed with the eyeliner if you know what I mean?" He didn't, but let her continue. "Think she was wearing a hoodie and jeans. They could've done with a wash. I remember thinking for a pretty girl, she sure didn't know how to dress to her advantage. And that's about it."

Nodding, The Mercenary slipped a business card onto the counter. "Thank you. You've both been a great help. If you think of anything else that might be useful, please contact my office."

With that, The Mercenary left. He'd gotten what he needed and didn't want to spend a second longer talking with these two idiots.

CHASE

A bright stream of sunlight landed on my face, waking me.
I yawned, stretching before noticing how *comfortable* I was. Suddenly, my eyes flew open as I remembered where I was. Bandit — who had still been sleeping — snapped his eyes open. He chuffed softly, which I took as his morning greeting. I scratched him under the chin.

"Morning Muttface."

He grinned at me; I guess he got the joke. I lay there for a blissful second, Bandit curled up by my side. Other than Motel Horror, it had been almost a year since I'd slept in a bed, and I'd totally forgotten how nice they were. Honestly, just wait until you've been sleeping on the sidewalk with nothing other than a newspaper to cushion you against the cold. Then you'll know what discomfort is.

BANG! A thundering crack sounded from outside.

"STAY DOWN," I yelled to Bandit. Rolling out of bed, I crouch-walked to the window, keeping my head as low as I could. My heart was racing so much I thought it would leap out of my chest. Rising slowly, I peeked out, sure I would see one of those SWAT-like guys who attacked Sully's clinic. But instead of the mass of black-clad figures I expected, there was only one. And he wore jeans and a tight shirt that showed off even tighter abs. Gideon.

He was aiming a pistol at a row of cans perched on a fence some distance away. As I watched, he pulled on the trigger. BOOM! A can danced off the fence and fell to the ground. He paused for the slightest second before letting off another shot. A second can tumbled down. Then another and another until all the cans lay on the ground. I was impressed but didn't want to show it. Instead, I opened the window and stuck my head outside.

"You can't use an alarm like normal people? What's with the gunshots so early in the morning?"

He spun around and found me framed in the window. "There's two things wrong with that sentence: one, it's after twelve, so morning has long gone, and two, what makes you think I want to be like normal people?"

I frowned. "Well, what time is it?"

"Time you made yourself useful. This isn't a hotel, it's a working ranch." He turned back to the fence and walked away from me, apparently done with me right now.

I'll be honest. The guy might be cute, but he sure lacked in the affability department. I looked at Bandit, who was staring at me, head tilted questioningly.

"Yeah. I don't know what I see in him either."

96

CHASE

Moments later, we were invading the kitchen.

The fridge had a bunch of meats and cheeses in it. I grabbed some of each and a jug of juice and was heading to the dining table before I saw a neatly stacked mound of canned dog food and biscuits. Someone had already been up and shopping that morning.

Grinning, I grabbed a can that was flavored with turkey apparently and dished it onto one of the two brand new metal bowls that was lying on the counter. Bandit couldn't keep still. He was literally doing circles around me. I'm guessing the smell of the food was driving him mad.

He whined, nuzzling my side impatiently.

"OK, OK, hold your horses, dog."

A confused sound came out of him, a cross between a moan and a sigh.

"It's just a saying. No need to get all literal," I explained as I placed the bowl onto the ground. He dived into the bowl, chomping and slurping with gusto. Remember how daintily he took that fritter from me back when we first met? Yeah, that dog was long gone. Apparently, he totally dug the food choice.

Smiling, I slapped some meat and pre-sliced cheese between two slices of bread and was chomping away at it when Sully appeared in the doorway. He was dressed in clothes I hadn't seen before. Zeb must have loaned them from his own collection, judging by the faded flannel shirt he was wearing.

"I was coming to wake you, but I see you already found the food," Sully said wryly.

I nodded, mouth too full to speak.

Bandit barked once, happily, his bowl already empty. He was licking it so much, the bowl was being pushed across the floor. I tore open the large bag of doggy biscuits and started pouring some into the bowl for him. Bandit didn't even wait for me to finish, just stuck his snout in there and started woofing down chow at a rate that was akin to the speed of light.

Sully grabbed a glass from the cupboard and poured himself a glass of OJ. Sipping it, he lifted Bandit's bandage and inspected the wound.

"A scab is forming. That's good news; it's healing nicely."

"That's one down," I said. It was meant to sound optimistic, but somehow came out a little desperate. Sully must've been able to hear it in my voice but chose to ignore it.

"I'll take it. I'll take anything I can get right now," he replied. He sounded weary. It was only when I took a closer look at him that I saw the dark rings under his eyes.

"You didn't sleep?"

"I was up most of the night. Zeb and I were trying to see what we could do."

He spoke without thinking, I don't think he realized he called his father by name, but I caught the use. Sully's issues with Zeb must run deep if he can't even call him "dad."

"And? What did you find?"

"Not much yet. We need to keep looking." He reached down to stroke Bandit, who had long finished his food and was now sitting there, watching us solemnly. I could feel myself wanting to ask if he could look a little faster, but another look at the bags under his eyes and I bit my tongue. Sully was trying his best. No need to beat him over the head with it. He gulped down the juice and took his glass over to the sink where he rinsed it before setting it upside down on a dish rack. He did this in one quick motion, like he'd done it a million times before, which I guess he probably had. I wondered whether this was something Emma had drilled into him. Somehow, I couldn't picture Sully being this domesticated without help.

"Will you guys be OK while I get to work in the barn?"

"Sure. We'll find something to do to occupy ourselves," I said. He nodded, eyes distant, thoughts already drifting away to the enormous task at hand. Within a few beats, the doorway was empty. I turned to Bandit.

"So... What do you fancy doing?"

97

CHASE

Turns out, Bandit just wanted to play outside in the sun.

He was running around, chasing and barking at anything that moved — being a goofball, basically. I was kinda surprised he didn't want to watch YouTube or read, but he'd said something about loving the smell of grass. I think where he was from, they probably didn't let him out much. If at all.

A brightly colored orange and black butterfly flew by. A Monarch. Bandit barked at it then chased it until it disappeared into the sky. He watched from below, tongue hanging out to one side, having the time of his life.

"He doesn't look *that* bright," came Gideon's voice from behind me. I forced myself not to turn, despite all my senses screaming at me to look at him. *Be cool.*

"He might be clever, but he's still a dog." I gave myself an internal pat on the back. Gideon stopped beside me, and we watched Bandit play. As the silence grew, I could feel myself tensing up. What was it about him that made me feel so awkward? I cleared my throat and gestured across the grass to Gideon's gun range.

"Where did you learn to shoot like that?"

"Here. Zeb thinks it's important to be able to protect your own."

"This doesn't look like the kind of place that needs protecting," I said. He turned to face me. The sun was behind him, casting his face in shadow. I tried not to focus on his chiseled cheekbones.

"It's not like we're back in New York. Can't imagine crime gets any tougher than a rabbit stealing from the vegetable garden."

He looked at me curiously. It was probably the first time I'd seen his brow unfurled. "That where you're from? New York?"

I nodded. "Not originally. But I've been living on the streets a year now. It's tough, but at least I'm my own person, you know? No one tells me what I can or can't do. And if anyone touches me, they get a taste of my fist."

Oh wow, I was mortified. I'd turned into Chatty McChatty. Flinching, I mentally chided myself for my behavior, hoping he couldn't hear my inner dialogue. All the while, he kept watching me with those intense blue eyes. I had to look away, worried they would see straight into my soul. "Bandit's the only friend I had until Sully came along."

Gideon kicked at a blade of grass. "That's like me and Zeb. He helped me out when I was in a bind."

Looks like neither of us wanted to mention our family or parents, and I was totally fine with that.

"So you're good in a fight?" he asked.

I stood taller. "I can hold my own. I've been learning the Israeli self-defense form of martial arts."

"You know Krav Maga?" He couldn't hide his surprise.

"You know what that is?" I couldn't hide mine either. Most people had never heard of it.

"I've seen Taken. We're not all complete hicks out here." His voice was empty of humor. There was the very real possibility that I had insulted him.

"I didn't mean you were. It's just not a common thing to know is all." I went to bite my tongue again before I caught the glint in his eyes. He was teasing me! A warm feeling flooded my body. I hoped to God my cheeks weren't as red as they felt. Luckily, he gave me the out I needed.

"You ever wanted to shoot a gun?" he asked.

98

CHASE

I watched as Gideon balanced five cans along the fence. The labels on the cans were bleached by the sun and riddled with bullet holes, but I could see enough to make out the pictures of coffee beans and peas. He scanned the ground quickly and found Bandit a few meters away.

"Hey," he called out tentatively to him, still not used to addressing a super intelligent dog. Immediately, Bandit stopped playing and trotted over to him. "This is dangerous work we're about to do. Can you go on back up to the ranch and wait by the porch?"

"*WOOF*," came the reply, then Bandit was off, running back to the ranch, tail in the air. Gideon waited until Bandit was a safe distance behind us before walking over to me. He held a small gun in each hand, which he showed me now.

"There are two types of handguns, a revolver and a semi-automatic pistol. Typically, the ones you see in cowboy movies are revolvers — they're the ones with a cylinder in the middle of the frame of the gun that's loaded with cartridges. Usually, these hold six bullets, but some hold five: those are made for smaller hands, like yours."

He showed me the revolver and gestured at my apparently small hands (I'd never given much thought to their size before, so it was news to me that they fell in the petite range).

"Revolvers have a revolving cylinder for holding ammo. You load it up and it's ready to go. As the trigger is pulled, the cylinder rotates, and the hammer pulls back. Like this, see?" He aimed into the distance and fired off a shot. Once again, a can danced on the fence before tumbling to the ground. "See how the cylinder rotates and lines up the next cartridge? When the trigger is pulled back far enough, that releases and strikes the round, firing the bullet. When all five shots are fired, you remove the empty casings and reload the cylinder." Done with the revolver demo, he slid it into his belt.

"Now, the other gun, a semi-automatic pistol, has a sliding mechanism at the top and a mag of pre-loaded ammo in the handle. When you pull the slide, a semi advances the cartridge into the chamber from the mag. As the first round is fired, part of the force of the shot pushes back on the side, ejecting the casing and chambering the next round in a fraction of a second. This makes for a faster and deadlier weapon." He held the semi closer to me to inspect. "That's pretty much it. There's the safety here. I've had it locked in place so we can't accidentally fire it. To turn it off, flip it up. There's a bit more to it than that, but that's probably all you need to know."

I raised a brow at him. "Why, because I'm a silly girl?"

He shot me a level stare. "Because I can't think of a situation where you'd need to know anymore."

"Oh." I did my best not to sound chastised, but failed miserably. I held out my hand. "Can I try the semi?"

He tried to restrain a smile. "Going for the heavy artillery. I like it." He handed it to me, muzzle down. "Take it from me gently, be careful not to touch the trigger until I say so."

I took the gun into my hands. The metal was cold and hard and heavy. My hands shook when I thought of how this was a weapon designed for killing. Weirdly, I found myself breaking out into a sweat. I felt slightly nauseous, and I was pretty sure it wasn't Gideon who was causing this reaction in me.

Gideon moved behind me so that his face was over my left shoulder. "Hold the gun, keeping your trigger finger outside the trigger guard."

I did as he instructed, trying to block out the strange feeling inside me.

"That's good. Now, keep the barrel pointed straight downrange, never up. A bullet fired up by accident will come down at some point and could hurt someone." He leaned in close until I could feel his breath on my shoulder. "Hold the gun in the firing-ready position."

He showed me what he meant with the revolver. I matched his finger work perfectly, so why did I still feel like throwing up?

"Good, steady the gun with the other hand like so."

Again, I matched him, move for move.

"Now stand in the proper firing stance. Your feet shoulder-width apart, one foot slightly in front of the other for balance." When he was happy with my form, he continued. "Line up the front sight on a can, and center it with the back sight."

"OK." As I said the words, they seemed to stick in my throat. I focused on the first can, keeping my hand as steady as I could.

"When you're ready, pull the trigger," he said.

I slowed my breathing then held it. Counting in my head. *One... two...* On *three* I pulled the trigger, but flinched as I did it. The bullet shot out of the gun, its recoil slamming down my arm and knocking me back a full step. The world slowed to a crawl as the bullet flew way past the target, impaling itself harmlessly into the trunk of a tree. Lowering the gun "downrange," I turned to Gideon, feeling sheepish. "Sorry. I didn't realize it would feel like that."

He shrugged, fine. "It's not as easy as it looks. You'd have more luck hitting the can if you don't flinch when you pull the trigger."

"Yeah. I know," I said. Ignoring the sick feeling in my stomach, I positioned myself to try again. *Ready... aim... and FIRE!* Again, I felt myself flinch when the bullet shot out of the chamber. This time, the bullet swerved left, missing the cans by an even wider margin. He frowned at me.

"Try again."

We went several more rounds. Each time, I kept flinching and kept missing my mark. Gideon grew more and more impatient until he snapped at me. "Look, you'll never hit anyone if you're scared of using a gun!"

I was already berating myself internally, so I really didn't need him to do the same. I felt stupid and weak enough as it was. He obviously didn't read the signs though as he continued. "These men coming after you are dangerous. The only chance you'll have against them is if you can use a gun."

"You think I don't know that?! I've already gone up against them! I saw what they can do, so I don't need you telling me!" I snapped back.

He glared at me, suddenly angry himself. "I'm just trying to help you!"

"Well don't!" I shouted back. Handing him the gun, I spun around and stomped back into the ranch, fuming.

99

CHASE

A few snacks later, and even food wasn't soothing my bristling self.

Poor Bandit had been trying to comfort me, nudging me with his nose and trying to engage me in conversation, but I was *mad*. For some reason, Gideon had rubbed me up the wrong way, and try as I might, I hadn't been able to shake my anger.

Sully and Zeb were locked in the barn researching. Luckily, Gideon had taken off somewhere in the truck, so I didn't have to deal with him again for now. Bandit and I had been wandering aimlessly through the house when we had stumbled upon a computer in the den. I fired it up, and we fooled around on a few quiz sites. Even though my heart wasn't in it, I wanted to keep up the pretense for Bandit's sake.

It was while we were messing around on the internet that I realized maybe I could help with the research. While we were doing the last quiz, pop-up windows advertising VPN's had flooded the screen. A VPN, in case you didn't know, stood for Virtual Private Network. Every computer that connects online has an IP address, basically a unique chain of numbers that identifies every computer. Of course, sometimes you might not want people to know where you are, like when you're doing things for nefarious reasons, or in my case, when you're trying to find out where Bandit came from, and that was where the VPN came in.

Accessing one was easy. You can literally subscribe to a service for a few bucks. Still, I hadn't lasted so long out here by using my money when I didn't have to. I signed up to a service that offered a free one month trial. Then I created an anonymous email address that wouldn't be traceable. Using the VPN was as simple as downloading the application and turning it on. So now we were in stealth mode, I took a big gamble.

I went to the national missing animals database and input the numbers tattooed into Bandit's ear. Yes, I know this is probably what caused the SWAT team to arrive at the clinic, but they wouldn't be able to trace us this time, especially since I wasn't going to be dumb enough to call them on a landline.

Sorry, Sul, but that wasn't the smartest move you could've made.

The missing animal database seemed normal enough. It was a pretty active site, with some several thousand animals being reported every day. I figured it must be legit, though I wasn't about to take any risks. I set up a profile, calling myself Jane Doe who lived at 0800 Bite-Me Lane, Neverland, California. Luckily, it wasn't one of those sites that cross-checked your address against real data, so it accepted my details just fine.

A tingle of apprehension went through me as I called up the window to input the serial number from Bandit's ear. I typed the numbers in carefully, but I stopped short of hitting enter as a wave of doubt flooded over me.

What if I was wrong?

What if they could trace this?

I stared at Bandit, looking up at me with those soulful blue eyes. Then, in my mind, his eyes rolled back into his head as I watched him suffering through his first convulsion at the buffet.

My mouth filled with bitterness. So this is what fear tastes like.

Remembering what I'd said to Sully last night, that Bandit would die if we didn't try...

I hit enter.

100

CHASE

I don't know what I was expecting. Maybe an explosion across the screen. Or for those black-clad SWAT guys to burst through the roof. None of these things happened. Instead, another window flashed up with a warning. This said the dog had escaped from a research lab. The dog was carrying a virus, but they made sure to state that it wasn't contagious. It made several mentions not to approach or communicate with the dog.

That's how it kept referring to Bandit. The dog. Jerks couldn't even give him a name. I studied the window, careful not to press anything that would make it go away, but there was no identifying information. Disappointed, I sat there, stumped, when a ping sounded — the alert that usually accompanied a new email. Clicking off the window, I went into the tab that still had my email mailbox loaded. There was one new message.

> SENDER: Sunshine Research Laboratory.
> SUBJECT: WARNING!
> VIRUS CARRYING DOG ALERT!

I read the sender name and snorted.

Sunshine Research.

Who did they think they were kidding with that name? Might as well call themselves KILLERS R US!

The message of the email was pretty much a repeat of the warning. I couldn't see anything useful. When I hit reply however, the To: subject line automatically replied with the sender's email address, and something else... A series of numbers separated by dots inside two rectangular brackets. I wouldn't normally have known what that was, except for the samples I was shown while setting up the VPN.

I grinned, thrilled by the finding — an IP address — and felt a moment of smugness. Googling the numbers, it gave me the location of Maryland, but nothing else. Still, determined to give Sherlock Holmes a run for his money, I input the same location into Google Maps.

Bingo.

I was in satellite view, so the building that appeared could easily be seen. It was long and low with a connecting maze of wings. The only windows were high up, presumably so prying people wouldn't get much of an eyeful. A discreet sign was mounted by the entrance.

I hit zoom to read the words inscribed there.

PLATINUM INDUSTRIES.

101

CHASE

I had a real lead!

I turned to Bandit and pointed at the sign.

"Does this mean anything to you, Boy?"

He woofed twice. *No.*

I was disappointed, but I should've guessed that would be the case. They probably never referred to the name of the company that was keeping him prisoner. Wouldn't make sense for them to be using personalized stationery or something. I spent a while more Googling before I finally hit pay-dirt.

Platinum Industries was the name of a group of commercial companies owned by billionaire Sebastien Forbes. A self-made millionaire by the time he turned twenty, Forbes was considered one of the world's wealthiest businessmen. Literally everything he touched turned to gold.

Apparently he was raised by a single mom working three jobs and never knew his dad. Wanting to help his mom, who was suffering from some kind of illness (I couldn't find any reference as to what it was), Forbes won his first job working in the mailroom of a prestigious real estate firm. Within a year he was promoted to office assistant.

Another year and he had his own office. By the time he'd been at the company five years, he'd become the majority shareholder. After this, he bought company after company, for such obscene sums of money that it made my eyes water. How was it possible for someone to have this much, when others — like me — had so little? It was insane.

I tried to find useful details on the actual building, but information wasn't forthcoming. It was listed as a lab, but that was about it. Looks like Forbes didn't want anyone to know what kind of experiments might be going on inside.

I pulled up a picture of the man. As soon as his face flashed on screen, Bandit whimpered, his whole body shaking from fear. There was no need to ask if he knew who he was. The answer was clear. Seeing his terror only made me more determined.

"He won't hurt you anymore, boy, I promise. He won't get away with this."

I made the promise before I even knew what to do. But it didn't matter. I would stop this man, billionaire or not. He wouldn't hurt Bandit ever again.

Cross my heart and hope to die.

102

SULLY

I rubbed tired eyes, blinking when I realized how dry they were. I had been staring at the scans for so long that their images were seared into my brain.

A man-made tumor.

It was impossible to fathom what twisted mind would create something as horrific as this, and I should know. I'd been trying all day only to keep coming up empty-handed.

Surrounded by papers himself, Zeb sighed, coming up for air. "I don't know what to tell you."

I tried not to let despair wash over me. "I know. It was a stupid idea. We can't go into his head like this. We'll kill him."

Zeb started organizing his papers into a neat file when Chase and Bandit burst into the barn. She held a printout in her hands and was out of breath from sprinting there.

"Sully! I know who's after Bandit! Look!" She thrust the piece of paper at me. It was a profile on secretive billionaire Sebastien Forbes. I was aware of him due to the man owning half of New York. It was one of the reasons the rent was so high that Emma and I were driven out of the housing market and had to settle outside.

I frowned. "Why would it be him?"

Chase gave an exasperated breath. "I did some detective work OK. I used a VPN, then put Bandit's serial number into that missing animal database." Seeing my alarmed expression, she raised a hand in my face. "It's fine, don't worry. The VPN hides our location. I'm not stupid OK? Anyway, I didn't get anything on the database, but they sent an email to the anonymous account I set up. And the identifying information lead me to Platinum Industries, which is owned by Sebastien Forbes." She pointed at the printout where Forbes's unsmiling face looked back at me. "It's him, Sully. Just ask Bandit."

I looked over at Bandit, who pawed the ground, agitated, as Chase set up the iPad.

"Bad man. Bad man. Bad man."

Chase threw her arms around him, holding him tight. I was about to ask some questions when Bandit's eyes rolled into the back of his head. His little body tensed as I sprinted forward, hoping to catch him before he fell, but I wasn't fast enough.

Bandit dropped to the ground as his body shook violently.

103

CHASE

Oh God, not again.

That was the only thing running through my mind as I held Bandit's face in my hands. A loud buzz sounded between my ears. Somewhere, in the distance, I could hear Sully calling out instructions, but my mind couldn't make sense of his words. Terror was taking over, and all I could do was watch my best friend, hurting.

Bandit's tongue hung out. But what I usually found endearing now filled me with fear. Were the edges of his tongue turning black? I couldn't be sure, but in the weird monochrome that the world had suddenly faded to, it seemed like the color was draining from him.

Someone appeared behind me.

It must have been Zeb. He was talking heatedly with Sully. The two were trying to figure out how to help Bandit. An alarming keening sound rose from the ground. Like a banshee wailing in the wind.

It was a few moments before I realized it was coming from me.

I rocked back and forth on my knees, focused on Bandit. "Please... please... please..."

The words came out of my mouth but failed to form a sentence. My mind was blank. Unable to make sense of anything.

Suddenly, the door to the barn slid open. Gideon had returned, a large bag of groceries in his arms. Hearing the commotion, he had come straight to the barn instead of the house. He stood there now, framed in the doorway, mouth agape, face reflecting the shock all of us were feeling. He took a step towards us when the bag in his arms EXPLODED.

White liquid spurted out in a thick stream, soaking his boots, as the remnants of a milk carton drifted slowly to the ground. Gideon looked down, confused. Everyone else froze. *What had just happened?* It was Sully who realized it first.

"GET DOWN! WE'RE UNDER FIRE!" he screamed.

Gideon dropped the groceries and dived behind a steel cabinet as Zeb wheeled into a corner. Sully just had time to fly on top of me, shielding Bandit and me with his own body, before the room erupted in gunfire.

104

——————

CHASE

Bullets tore through the barn, riddling the walls with holes, eating everything in their path.

Gone were the strip lights that were previously suspended from the ceiling. Cables severed by the incoming shots, the bulbs smashed down, plunging the room into near darkness. The light-box containing Bandit's scans exploded as shards of glass and metal flew every which way. A particularly nasty looking spear of steel whistled past my ear, impaling the ground inches from my head like it was nothing more than a marshmallow. My eyes went wide. That was way too close for comfort. Sully pressed down on us.

"Don't move!"

More bullets sprayed into the barn, devouring everything in their wake. Beams of light shone through the bullet holes, illuminating just enough of Zeb's barn to show it now resembled a set from an apocalyptic Hollywood movie production. I doubted that the remaining pieces would still work.

The onslaught had shaken me out of my daze. Heart racing, I could feel the adrenaline pumping. Every one of my senses were on fire, ready for action. One wrong move and we could be dead. I quickly checked on Bandit; he had stopped convulsing but was still unconscious. His breathing labored. *Why would they risk killing Bandit if they wanted him so badly?*

As if they knew what I was thinking, the gun fire ceased. Silence blanketed the room. We waited, but after several more seconds of inaction, Sully rolled cautiously onto his feet. Gesturing for the rest of us to stay down, he crept over to the wall and peeked out of a bullet hole.

"What do you see?" I whispered hoarsely.

"Those same SWAT guys who destroyed my clinic. But there are more of them. Three dozen or so."

Taking advantage of the moment's calm, Gideon hurried to Zeb, while I took stock of the damage done to the barn and noticed that the holes in the walls were a lot higher up than I had first realized.

"They're not trying to kill us."

Sully snorted, "Could've fooled me."

But I pointed at the walls. "Look. That's at least several feet over any of us. They're just trying to scare us. Bandit is too valuable for them to risk anything happening to him."

Knowing this, I felt a little safer. Not much, but enough to make my own way to Sully. Staring outside, I got my first look at the killers who were after us.

They littered the scenery, an abomination of nature. Each of the men was dressed the same: black pants and a tight fitting top that showed off how lethally fit they all were. Over their sweaters, they wore some kind of rubbery-looking vest; three guesses they were going to be bulletproof. Their faces were hidden under helmets with shiny visors. That figures.

Of course, this kind of scum wouldn't want to show their faces.

Each of the men held some kind of weapon. I knew enough from Gideon's lesson to know those weren't handguns, more likely some kind of automatic rifle. They probably weren't even legal. *But that's the great thing about America, our constitutional right to bear arms, right?*

Some distance away, a helicopter waited. I blinked, not believing my eyes. How could one have landed so close without any of us hearing it?

Like the men, it was black, with tinted windows that obscured the interior. It didn't look like any I had seen in movies before, which might go some way to explaining its stealthy capabilities. This must be a toy Forbes had bought for clandestine operations. The more I knew about that guy, the more I knew he was never getting on my Christmas card list.

The blades of the helicopter were spinning and showed no sign of slowing down. Guess they didn't think they'd be here long. Sully pulled back the lids on Bandit's eyes. There were beginning to focus. "He'll come to soon."

Checking that Zeb was fine, Gideon glanced over at him. "Yeah, then what?"

Sully looked at me. There was no question in my mind — we would fight to the death. But before I could reply, a voice called out from outside.

"Mr. Sullivan and friends. We're not here for you. We just want the dog, so if you would be so kind as to step aside, you will not be harmed."

I looked outside again. Standing in front of the men was the leader, the guy Sully called Military Man. His skin was tanned, and aviator glasses wrapped around his face — not the face-obscuring helmet the others wore, but hiding all the same. He spoke through the helicopter's loudspeaker, his voice blaring out into the wind. He couldn't have looked shadier if he had tried. There was no way we could trust him.

Sully must have thought the same, as he yelled out, "Get lost!"

Military Man frowned, not liking his response. His army advanced several more feet, but at a signal from him, they stopped as one. Like eerie stone statues, they didn't move a whisker. Strangely, this frightened me more than the weapons in their hands. Anyone who could stop dead like that meant business.

"The dog will die if you don't listen to me!" said Military Man. "He's having fits, yes? Increasing in frequency? That's because he needs weekly medication that he can only get from the lab."

Sully and I exchanged looks, the same question mirrored in our eyes. *If he wasn't telling the truth, how would he know about the fits? There was no way he could see into the barn.*

"The dog escaped two months ago. That's two months he hasn't had his meds. I'm not a doctor, but we have one in our lab. She raised him and knows what he needs. If he doesn't get his meds soon, the next fit could kill him."

Everything he was saying sounded plausible, but I also knew there was no way Bandit would be safe if we just handed him over.

"Gideon and I can draw their attention. Buy you enough time to escape from here," Zeb offered. Sully looked surprised. I don't think he was used to seeing this side of his father. Zeb gave him a small smile. "I haven't been here much for you, but this I can do." Gideon obviously didn't agree with his decision though, going by the frown he failed to mask.

"I appreciate the sentiment, but they must have the place surrounded," Sully said.

"Whatever you decide, we can't stay here. There's next to no cover in this barn," Gideon was quick to point out. "We need to get back inside the ranch."

Zeb pointed to the tarp that had been covering the CT scanner. "Here. We'll use that as a stretcher to carry Bandit inside." Sully and Gideon hurried in the direction he pointed while I continued checking on Bandit. He lifted his head gingerly, slowly coming to, but he was weak and groggy and confused. I stroked his nose.

"Don't move, Bandit. You had another attack, but you'll be fine in a minute. We're just getting you back inside the house."

He laid his head back down in relief. He must've understood me, even if he was unable to respond. Sully kicked at the glass and metal now covering the ground, clearing a space while Gideon laid the tarp beside Bandit.

"Get his back end. Careful now," Sully instructed as he gently slid his hands beneath Bandit's head. Gideon took hold of Bandit's flank, and together they half lifted, half slid him onto the tarp.

"Good. Now grab the ends and stretch them taut. We want to

make it as flat as possible," Sully said. They pulled in unison until the tarp stretched tight.

Zeb gestured to the west side of the barn, at a door I hadn't noticed before. "Quickly, there's a smaller exit on that side. It's closer to the ranch." He went ahead, the rest of us following close behind.

"On three... ready?" Sully asked. We all nodded. "*One... two... three!*"

On three, Gideon ripped open the door and the three of us bolted outside.

105

CHASE

Bright sunlight blinded me for a moment, my eyes having gotten used to the dimness of the barn. I must have stopped as someone kicked my ankle.

"Get moving!" came Gideon's voice.

I snapped to it, sprinting into the house as fast as my legs would carry me. Sully and Gideon came next, carrying Bandit between them. Zeb took up the rear, his wheelchair slow on the dirt path. I watched, gesturing crazily. "Hurry up, Zeb!"

He was moving as fast as he could when a wheel got caught in the gap between planks. Zeb tugged on the wheels, but the chair wasn't shifting.

Sully didn't think twice. He raced out into the open, reaching Zeb in seconds. Grabbing the handlebars, he shoved *hard* until the wheel came free. Pushing Zeb, Sully was running the last few feet to safety when shots blasted through the air. Sully hesitated only a second as the surrounding flowerbeds exploded before charging into the house with Zeb.

I slammed the door shut and bolted it, then turned to find Sully sliding down the wall to the ground. His face was pale. A dark red stain blossomed on his pant leg.

"You've been shot!" I gasped.

Zeb spun around, shocked, not having realized Sully had been hit. Sully examined his own leg, grimacing through the pain.

"I'll be fine, there's an exit wound," he said. His voice was relieved.

Gideon raced into the next room. I was so shell-shocked by Sully's injury, I didn't react. All I could think was that he was running away, and I couldn't really blame him. But seconds later, Gideon returned, the two handguns tucked into his belt and a shotgun in either hand. He gave me the semi, then handed a shotgun to Zeb. Seeing the gun in my shaking hands and my less than confidence stance, Sully shook his head in protest.

"She can't use that."

"She can, and she will," came Gideon's terse response.

Gideon raced to a window and drew the curtains across it. Zeb wheeled to the remaining window and did the same. I grabbed a tea towel from the counter and pressed it against Sully's leg.

"Press tight," I said. Sully grunted but did as instructed. Sweat beaded across his brow. It was horrible to think how much pain he must be in. By now, Bandit was on his feet. He must have gotten the lay of the land as he moved over to Sully and kept licking the hand that wasn't pressed against his leg.

Zeb peeked out from his window, immediately ducking back. "Here they come."

I knocked a table over and shoved it in front of us. It wasn't much, but it would give some cover so we weren't just sitting ducks.

And suddenly the door blew inward, splintering into a thousand pieces.

Gideon and Zeb opened fire.

106

CHASE

Shots rang out, ringing my ears.

I was expecting the horde of men to swarm inside, but there was only a robotic mechanism with a metal battering ram for a face. It had smashed the door with enough force that the entire thing imploded. Now it retreated as the black-clad men advanced.

Bandit whined, terrified, as Gideon and Zeb let off more shots. Bullets rocketed towards them but ricocheted harmlessly off their vests. Even Gideon, who I knew had great aim, wasn't making much of a dent against them. Having played enough The Last of Us at a friend's house, I screamed at them from behind the table.

"Shoot their legs!" They adjusted their aim and let off another round. Suddenly, screams filled the air as the men started falling, one by one. Reacting on pure instinct, they started firing back. Zeb wheeled out of the way as Gideon dived behind the fridge, opening it so the door could give more cover. Outside, the guy in charge yelled at his men.

"Cease fire! Cease fire!" But they were trained killers and our guys had shot at them. No longer holding back, they let rip with the full force of their arsenal.

I watched as Gideon and Zeb fought back. Sully was still bleeding, his color fading with every second. And I realized something then. These men, they would all die fighting for us. For Bandit and I. Unless I did something.

And just like that, the answer came to me.

I leaned in close to Sully and whispered in his ear. "I'm so sorry. I'll make this right."

He looked at me, confused.

"What're you talking about?"

I didn't answer, instead placing a hand on Bandit's neck. "Can you run?" I asked him.

Bandit's woof was drowned out by the gunfire, but I saw his jaws moving.

"Come. Heel, Boy!"

And with that, we took off through the house as I tried to drown out Sully's voice, calling out after me.

107

CHASE

We ran, ducking and weaving beneath the windows, keeping out of sight.

Bandit was still a little wobbly on his feet, but he was doing better than I was. I had a plan. It filled me with terror, but it was the only one I could think of that would stop the others from getting killed, and it would give Bandit the best chance of survival.

We ran to the far side of the house, but even here, there were a few men blocking our escape. I felt the world spin as my breath caught in my throat and panic started setting in. *How would we get out of here without them seeing?* Suddenly, Bandit barked. And just like the first time we met, he ran off a few feet in front, stopped, then turned back to look at me.

So, of course, I followed.

Bandit ran through the ranch, towards the west wing. Reaching a door, he jumped up, grasping the handle with his teeth, turning his head until I heard an audible click and the door opened to reveal a flight of steps leading into darkness.

"A basement! How did you know this was here?!" I asked.

Bandit woofed then pawed his nose. I got his drift immediately. *He had smelled it. Didn't I say what amazing senses they had?*

With Bandit leading the way, I followed him down the stairs. Light shone through several small egress windows. I zeroed in on one in particular where a cabinet and chairs were already stacked in front of it.

"Over here," I called to Bandit. We hurried to the window where I scrambled onto the chair, then the cabinet. I had to keep my head down so I wouldn't hit it on the ceiling. With Bandit watching from the ground, I quietly opened the window. At a gesture from me, Bandit climbed up beside me and we both crawled outside.

A wall of ground greeted us, but it was only a few feet high, and there were staggered inset foot holdings in place — I'm guessing this was in case of fire. I climbed the steps quickly and took an 180-degree review of our surroundings where, as I'd hoped, it was clear. All the action was taking place by the kitchen. They weren't paying attention to this section.

Bandit ran up beside me, and together we stole across the grass, thankful it hadn't been cut in quite some time. The helicopter sat ahead of us. Aside from the pilot, there was only one other man guarding it. I gestured for Bandit to be quiet now. We would only get one chance at this.

Hunkered down, we crept towards the guard. When I got close to him, I didn't stop to think about what I was doing, just swung the gun on the guard's head, but a branch snapped underfoot, and he spun around to face me at the last moment. Startled, I flinched and only managed to hit him lightly. It wasn't enough to knock him out as I was intending, but he lost his balance, tumbling backward where he smacked his head hard against the helicopter. He dropped to the ground, out cold with barely a sound.

Well, that works too, I thought to myself.

Creeping to the back of the helicopter, I opened the door and had the gun touching the pilot's head before he even saw me.

"Don't do anything stupid. The gun's loaded." I hoped I sounded confident because I sure as heck didn't feel it.

"Don't shoot. I'm just a hired pilot. I'm not a soldier," came his fast reply.

"So don't do anything stupid, and I won't have to." That was actually a line from a movie I saw once, and if we ever get out of this alive, remind me to thank the screenwriter.

I checked out the interior of the aircraft, but the weapons were stored on the passenger side. The pilot had nothing on him; he was unarmed. Hopefully, he was telling the truth, but I wasn't taking any chances. Bandit and I climbed on board. I kept the gun trained on him the entire time.

"What do you want?" he asked.

I gestured at the controls with the gun. "What you're paid to do. Start flying."

"Where to?" he said.

I took a deep breath before answering.

"Platinum Industries. We're going to pay your boss a visit."

108

SULLY

It was a war zone.

Shots rang out in every direction. I was painfully aware that I was injured, that Chase had probably gone off to do something stupid, and that we would all die if I didn't think of something quick. We were fast running out of ammo and options.

Gideon popped out from cover and fired at Military Man. With unnervingly good aim, he caught the jerk on the shoulder. I took immense pleasure watching the guy stagger back, blood pouring from a wound, but that feeling was short-lived, as three men came within fifteen yards of the house.

The two fell back as I scanned the kitchen, frantic for ideas, trying to blot out the screaming in my mind that I had to go after Chase when my eyes fell on Zeb's prized moonshine rack. Suddenly, inspiration hit. I half crawled, half dragged my way to the kitchen counter, calling out to Gideon, "Gideon! The moonshine!"

Gideon glanced over, confused, "What?" he said, as he fired another shot.

I pointed. "The moonshine rack! Get me the rack!" I yelled.

Seeing me fumbling in a drawer for a lighter, Gideon suddenly got it. Keeping low, he darted for the rack, carrying it back, where he plopped it down with a thud in front of me. Quickly, Gideon found a corkscrew and started unscrewing the bottle, but I frowned.

"That'll take all day! We don't have time!" I yelled. Snatching a bottle from him, I smashed the head of the bottle against the counter. It came away, raining glass onto the ground. Some clear white moonshine spilled out, filling my nostrils with its strong alcoholic scent. I set the opened bottle onto the ground, as Gideon hurriedly copied my messy, but fast technique. Grabbing a dish towel from the cabinet handle it was slung across, I used a knife from the drawer to slash the fabric, tearing it into strips as Zeb called over from his position by the door.

"The two of you need to hurry that up! I'm almost out!"

Nodding, I stuffed the end of a fabric strip into the first bottle of moonshine. Gideon and I worked frantically, adding more strips to more bottles until a row of the bottles sat waiting. Glancing outside, Zeb saw that the men were just three yards away now. I pushed myself onto my feet and in complete agony, hopped over to flank the other side of the door.

Gideon snatched two bottles and ran to my side as I sparked up the lighter. Gideon dangled a bottle over the flame.

"Come on, come on," I said impatiently, waiting for the flame to catch on the strip of fabric as Zeb continued shooting at our attackers.

Suddenly, with a fizzle, the strip caught fire. I grabbed the bottle from Gideon and HURLED the Molotov cocktail into the crowd of fast-approaching men. The bottle hit the ground, showering the men in liquid. A wall of flame ignited, engulfing the men in fire. Their anguished screams pealed out. I didn't wait to listen.

As Gideon handed a second lit bottle to me, I threw it at another group. More flames danced along the ground, followed by more cries. By now, Gideon had fetched two more lit bottles and was passing them to me, wordlessly. I threw missile after missile until the grounds were a cauldron of fire. What men survived were running for their lives as their vests melted into their skin. Only Military Man stood firm, a black shadow in the distance, just beyond the reach of the flames.

He would not run.

109

THE MERCENARY

The Mercenary was filled with an icy fury.

His cowardly men had taken off, running blindly through the flames in a mad panic and ignoring his command. The Mercenary glowered at their retreating backs, his eyes narrowing into thin slits. Imbeciles. If any of them survived this, they'd have him to contend with, and he was far more lethal than any fire.

Through the orange wall of flame, The Mercenary could make out Sullivan watching him from the door. He'd stopped throwing Molotovs. The Mercenary assumed they must be out. The two faced each other in a two-man stand-off. Then the boy started raising his handgun at The Mercenary. The Mercenary ducked, but the shot never came. Sullivan had stopped him.

What was this?

The Mercenary had his own weapon aimed at them and wasn't concerned that they would hit him first. He'd trained with the best and hadn't missed a headshot in over a decade. He watched as Sullivan took the handgun from the boy and gestured for him to take cover before he faced The Mercenary head on. His injured leg was giving him trouble. Even from here, The Mercenary could see

Sullivan favored his left leg. He smiled to himself. *This fool thought he would outshoot him? Well, he was game.*

The Mercenary pulled the trigger of his semi.

It clicked, but nothing happened. *It was out of bullets.* Sullivan must have realized this, as he suddenly looked confident, while The Mercenary himself was filled with an awful apprehension. A million possible escape notions ran through his mind, but The Mercenary was rooted to the spot.

He would not run.

It was while he was thinking this that Sullivan took aim and fired.

The shot flew from the barrel and flew into his body. Pain exploded in his chest. The Mercenary staggered back, stunned, as he touched a hand to his now bloody chest. He looked across at Sullivan with unblinking, unbelievable eyes.

Then suddenly, the ground came rushing up to meet him.

And all was silent.

110

CHASE

The helicopter lifted into the air.

As soon as we took off, Bandit darted between my legs. Poor guy. I had tried to explain to him what was about to happen, but I guess I didn't do a good job of it. He sat there, huddled against me, nose shoved under my armpit. If we weren't about to do the most insane, most dangerous, there's-no-turning-back-from-here thing we'd ever done in our lives, I'd probably find that funny. As it was, I wished I had someone's armpit to stick my own face into.

Scratch that. That didn't sound right *at all*.

As the helicopter rose, and the ranch came into full view, I felt a sinking feeling in my stomach at the devastation before me. The barn was now punctured with so many holes; it was a miracle the entire thing didn't collapse in on itself. As I had experienced more times in the last half an hour than in my whole life, another wave of fear shot through me. Sully and the others were in danger, yet here I was running away. *What if they couldn't defend themselves? What if it was all too late?*

I shook my head to clear away the doubts. Only fools play the what-if game. I'd learned that the hard way when I was just a kid, wondering what if she wasn't my real mom? What if, somewhere out there, my real mom was a wonderful woman who loved to bake cookies and was desperately searching for me, her darling baby who was snatched from her during Christmas Mass? See? Even as a kid, I had a vivid imagination.

I stuck my face to the window, craning my neck to see below. The black-clad figures were advancing, but just when it seemed all was lost, a burst of flame engulfed the men! Sully was tossing some kind of homemade fireball at the attackers and it was stopping them dead! Go, Sully!

I watched as more and more rows of flame appeared on the ground. The men started running. It was hard to make out every-thing from up here, but it seemed Sully had won the fight. I sagged back against my seat as the relief poured through me. They were safe. Now it was just me and Bandit.

I kept my eyes and gun trained on the pilot. Now and then, he'd peer at me through a strategically placed mirror, but I met his gaze each time. If he even stared at me a little too long, I waved the gun at him. I think he got the message.

Fields of green passed below us as we hurtled toward Forbes and the place Bandit had originally called home. I stroked Bandit contin-uously, blocking out the negative thoughts that flittered at the edge of my mind. The ones that devilishly whispered things like *keep stroking. After all, you may not get to do that for much longer.*

You know, unhelpful stuff like that.

They must be related to the *what-ifs*.

Bandit trembled in my arms, and I found myself making soothing sounds of comfort. "It'll be OK," I told him. "We'll find a way to heal you. Nothing will happen to you."

I was really hoping it wasn't a lie.

111

THE CEO

His head was pounding.

Forbes rubbed at his temple and swallowed some aspirin. The headaches were getting worse. Last night, he could barely sleep due to the throbbing in his head, and the stress of Alpha's escape certainly wasn't helping matters.

He looked away from the computer screen in his office. The numbers he so loved watching rise blurred into each other today. Well, it was time for a break; The Mercenary was due to check in any moment now. In anticipation of good news, Forbes pressed the intercom.

"Yes, sir?" came the voice of his assistant over the line.

"I'd like a tea," he instructed.

"I'll bring your usual, sir," she responded. Moments later, his assistant entered carrying a delicate jade teapot and a matching cup. A pair of dragons were engraved onto the jade, swimming through the air, talons engaged. The powerful fabled creatures were something Forbes had taken a liking to as a young child.

His assistant, a neat brunette who wore the same uniform of shirt and skirt every day, picked up the pot and poured. Dark oolong tea swirled into the cup. Forbes breathed in the exotic aroma, feeling the tension leave his body.

Da Hong Pao was a rock tea grown in the Wuyi Mountains of China. A heavily oxidized oolong tea, according to legend, the mother of a Ming dynasty emperor was cured of an illness by it. Only six of the bushes where the tea originated were thought to remain. Ridiculously expensive, the tea cost more than gold and could sell for up to US\$1,025,000 per kilogram.

Forbes had developed a taste for it after a business visit to China. The tea — traditionally only given to honored guests — had been used as a symbol to seal the deal.

Picking up the cup, Forbes took a sip, letting the warm liquid slide down his throat. His assistant left quietly. She knew the drill, knew he didn't like anyone to hover, particularly during this daily, sacred tea time.

The telephone rang, cutting into his moment of calm. Forbes reached over and pressed the answer button. "Yes?"

The voice that came on the line wasn't one he recognized. "I'm afraid I have some bad news."

Forbes closed his eyes, already predicting what the caller would say next. "The dog escaped."

"Yes, sir."

It took every ounce of willpower not to scream at the caller. He was lucky his head was pounding so much.

"Um, sir? There's something else. Hector's dead. They killed him."

A tidal wave of fury coursed through him. Unable to restrain himself any further, Forbes hurled the cup of tea against the wall where it smashed to smithereens. His head threatened to explode from the sound, but he was beyond caring now.

He shot up to his feet, grabbed the teapot and flung that too. Next came the computer, then the phone, whose cable he ripped out of the socket. All went flying against the wall.

The door opened a crack. His assistant, hearing the commotion, was back again to check up on him. Seeing his rage, she waited.

Forbes searched for more items to destroy, but there was nothing. His desk was minimally decorated as he abhorred clutter.

Suddenly deflated, he sank back into his chair. Immediately, his assistant entered, a dustpan and brush in her hands as she went to work cleaning up the mess he had made.

Within minutes, a new phone was installed, and a new computer on his desk. His people knew the drill.

"I'll bring you more tea, sir," his assistant said.

Forbes didn't reply.

112

SULLY

With that one bullet, the man who had destroyed my home and cherished memories of Emma was dead.

I had thought that killing him would magically make me feel better. Instead, the hollowness inside stubbornly refused to fill. It seemed nothing would heal me but time.

As the initial madness subsided, I froze, a cold feeling in the pit of my stomach. "Chase! She's gone!"

Zeb, who had been tending to my wound by tying a towel around it, looked up. "What do you mean, she's gone?"

I took a deep breath. "She said she was sorry for everything, but she would fix this." I shook my head, barely able to comprehend my words.

"But how could they have gone?"

From my position, I had a clear view of the grounds. I could clearly see the vehicles belonging to the ranch and my own recently purchased truck. They were all accounted for. It was as I turned to stare at Military Man's downed body that the answer came to me.

"The helicopter. She must have hijacked the helicopter!"

"She did what?!" came Gideon's shocked question as he returned to the room.

I could punch myself for my stupidity. "He said Bandit needed meds, or he'd die. Oh, God."

Gideon couldn't take it in. "She wouldn't risk her life on a foolish thought like that."

I whirled on him, heart in my throat. "She wouldn't? You've known her two days! That dog was the only friend, the only family she has. Sure, she talks tough, but Chase is just a girl who has grown up without anyone caring for her. Do you know what that does to a person? Bandit is the only one who has shown her any love, so yeah, she would do exactly something as foolish as this."

Silence fell on the room, my outburst causing us all to take stock. Surprising us all, Zeb spoke.

"Then we'll go after her."

Of all the things I had expected my father to say, that was not it. I shook my head, but when I spoke again, there was a gruffness in my voice.

"We can't."

I didn't elaborate. Zeb opened his mouth, preparing to argue, but Gideon jumped in to finish what I hadn't been able to. "Your wheelchair, Zeb. You would only slow him down."

Zeb didn't like it, but he knew the truth when it was smacking him in the face. Another unwanted truth surfaced, however. "I hate to be the bearer of bad news, but you can't go after her either, Jake. Not with your leg like that. You can barely walk."

My mouth fell open in shock. My concern for Chase and Bandit were so great, I hadn't even considered my own injury.

It was Gideon who finally came up with a solution. "He can if I go with him. Zeb, you'll be OK on your own?"

Zeb nodded, even as I started to protest. He held up his hand, stopping any further objection from me. "Gid already called the cavalry, and they're on their way. There's no more danger for me here, so the two of you can keep wasting time, or you can go after that girl and bring them home."

And with that simple truth, our minds were made up. There was just one problem.

"Well, we know they've gone to... what was that name again?" I racked my brain, trying to think through the pain. *What had she said yesterday?* I pictured Chase flying into the room, waving her computer printout. Finally, it came to me.

"Platinum Industries! That was it, that's what she said!"

My euphoria was quickly dashed as Gideon looked at me, frowning.

"But where the hell is it?"

113

SULLY

While Gideon did his best to help, I — under my own father's insistence — was currently in the office, hoping to find a trace of Chase's whereabouts. I knew where she had gone — the lab Bandit escaped from — but nothing about its actual whereabouts. Scratching at the day's growth on my chin, I perched onto the edge of the chair in front of the computer. Moving the mouse, the screen blinked on. Pulling up the search bar history, I moved through it quickly, hoping to find some information here.

I got more than I bargained for.

The last search was the Wiki entry for one Sebastien Forbes. I scanned through the billionaire's biography, hoping for something to leap out at me. The man was richer than God — and had an ego to match — judging by the way he bought and sold companies on a whim.

Going backward through the results, I read through Chase's previous search on Platinum Industries. There wasn't much information on the business, just a building listed out in Rochester, which, if memory serves, was East of Niagara Falls. I could find nothing on what "industry" the company dabbled in.

So far, so nothing.

It wasn't until I got to Chase's email — and thank God she was still logged on — that everything fell into place.

And Chase was rushing into the Lion's den armed with only a sick dog and a gun.

114

SULLY

Time was of the essence.

Every second we wasted, the likelihood of saving both Chase and Bandit grew sparser. Those men hadn't hesitated to shoot. Once Bandit set foot on their premises, Chase's usefulness — and her life — were as good as gone. I tried not to let that terrifying thought debilitate me.

It was Gideon who came up with the idea.

The kid seemed to have gotten over his initial hatred of me, and for that, I was grateful. The last thing I needed was an angry teenager riding shotgun. We set up Zeb in the living room so he could see down the hill. If there was any sign of trouble, more unwanted visitors, he would notice them right away. I left him with food, water, and the phone within arm's reach.

Despite our history, I hesitated to leave. So much was left unsaid between us. So many years of resentment. As if he knew what I was thinking, Zeb laid a rough hand on my arm and uttered one simple word. "Go."

I nodded gruffly and turned to Gideon. "You have everything?"

He handed me a rucksack. Inside were the remnants of any ammo we could salvage. The shotguns were out completely, so there was no point in taking them. All we had was Gideon's trusty revolver, a swiss army knife Zeb once found at an antique fair, and a few thousand bucks that Zeb had stashed in the safe for a rainy day. In the cold light of day, our arsenal didn't look like much, and we both knew it.

"Maybe we'll get lucky and find a wine cellar there," Gideon grinned suddenly. "I brought a lighter, just in case."

My opinion of the kid rose up a notch after that. Despite the life or death situation we had on our hands, here was this kid quipping like he was from a Marvel movie. Gideon moved over to Zeb. "The Sheriff said they'd be here in less than ten minutes. It's been eight already."

Zeb nodded. "I'll be fine. I was just thinking life had been a little dull lately. This excitement came in the nick of time."

With a nod, I turned away from my father, forcing down the lump that suddenly appeared in my throat. I was surprised to feel tears pricking at the corners of my eyes. Not since Emma was diagnosed with terminal cancer had I felt this level of fear. Not only for Chase and Bandit, but as I realized now, for my father too.

"Don't die," I said to him.

Zeb snorted. "It'll take more than bullets to dispose of me."

Despite the gravity of the situation, a small smile broke out over my face as Gideon slid himself under my arm, taking the weight off of my injured leg.

Together, we hurried from the ranch.

115

SULLY

Moments later, however, we hadn't gone anywhere.

We stood, staring in shock at the sight before us. My truck, while it had been some time since it had come off the line, was now riddled with bullets. Oil spilled out from a gaping hole in the gas tank. I looked at Gideon. "What about the 4x4?"

Gideon was already moving, running to the side of the ranch.

"Well, damn," were the only words he uttered when he saw Zeb's car. All four wheels were punctured, and the hood popped up. He went to look under it when I stopped him. "Don't bother. They made sure we wouldn't be going anywhere."

"Well, what're we going to do? It's not like there are any taxis around here." Gideon said. I thought for a moment, lost, then looked towards the stables. Following my gaze, Gideon shook his head incredulously.

"Are you crazy? Those horses haven't been ridden in years! How do you know they still work?"

I stared at him evenly. "Horses don't lose the ability to run unless they're injured, and that bunch has had years to recover. Come on, help me there."

Moments later, we were each perched on top of a horse. I stroked

Derby, my mount. She trotted friskily, seemingly excited by being taken out. I studied Gideon's ride critically; his horse was less eager for the exercise ahead but was otherwise fine. The short journey wouldn't do any damage to the two of them. Having ridden since I was a kid, I felt entirely comfortable up there, though I could see the same couldn't be said of Gideon, whose horse pranced nervously, feeling the boy's tension.

"He can feel your uncertainty. You need to take control."

"Well, it's a little hard to fake that when the thing weighs nine thousand pounds more than me," Gideon complained, tugging on the reins.

"Yeah, but *he* doesn't know that," I replied. "Use your legs."

With that, I kicked at my horse with my good leg and took off, galloping across the field, a trail of dust in my wake. Determined not to be left behind, Gideon yelled, "Giddy up," like he'd seen in the Westerns. His horse, Spirit, shot after me, leaving Gideon holding onto the reins for dear life.

116

SULLY

After we'd left the ranch, we rode some eight miles over several fields of corn, with Gideon calling out directions as we went. I was relieved that the area around here was flat, and from my position on the horse, I could see for miles. Several times, I glanced behind me to see if Gideon was keeping up, and he was, though his riding skills could do with some finesse. If these weren't such desperate times, and if my leg didn't have a bullet-sized hole in it, I would be enjoying this ride. I'd forgotten how great it could feel to be on top of a horse, wind whipping against a man's face.

Within some ten or so miles, the fields turned into a gravel drive. "Take the turn here," Gideon instructed.

I swung my horse around as a runway appeared before us. Situated at the end of it was an airplane with the slogan "I love a good crop dusting" sprayed onto its side. The plane was rusty and small and made me — not the greatest flyer in the first place — feel sick to my stomach.

"That's the plane? That rust bucket? Does it even fly?" I asked, an incredulous look on my face. Gideon seemed amused by my question. Probably payback for me dismissing the boy's horse-riding fear earlier, but I was saved from answering, as a bald man covered in grease stains approached, eyes bulging out at the sight of us.

"Someone shooting a Western I don't know about?" the man asked. I climbed awkwardly off Derby, my leg hampering progress, and landed on my feet much harder than I expected. Pain shot up my leg, leaving me momentarily breathless.

"We suffered some transportation hiccups," came my only explanation.

The man studied my wound where the blood was already seeping through the makeshift bandage. "What happened to your leg?" he asked.

I replied instantly. "Caught it on a sharp edge."

The man waited for more of an explanation, but I stayed silent until he finally took the hint and turned to Gideon, nodding at him. "Gideon. How's Zeb?"

Without missing a beat, Gideon responded. "Fine, Frank. He's staying home today. We have need of your services, however."

"Yeah, you want I should spray the lawn again? I keep telling you to chop some of those trees down, they're drowning the property in shadow." Frank said.

I stepped forward. "The lawn's fine. We need a ride."

Frank looked more interested in the conversation suddenly. He must've seen dollar signs in his near future. "Where to?"

I showed him a map where I'd circled our destination. Frank covered his eyes, shielding them from the sun, and looked down at his marker. "Rochester. That's some two, three hours flight from here."

I gestured at the plane. "Can it make it?"

Frank's face twisted into annoyance that he didn't bother to hide. "Of course it can. But I can't do it for a day or two. Mrs. Deloris wants me to spray her cornfields. Been having a problem with pests lately, so I told her—"

I held up my hand, interrupting. "It has to be now."

Frank stared at me bug-eyed. "But, Mrs. Deloris..." He never finished saying what Mrs. Deloris wanted, however, as I took a wad of bills out of my bag.

"Well… that's some nice change you got there, not enough for me to drop a regular client, however," said Frank, hedging his bets.

"I'll throw in some horses. Thoroughbreds," I replied.

Frank looked over my shoulders, at Derby and Spirit, and frowned. "That gray one doesn't look like there's much life in her."

"She's not for sale, but you can have your pick from Zeb's stables," I countered.

Frank studied me with a calculating eye. "And why would Zeb agree to that?"

I stared right on back. "Because he's my dad." Behind him, Gideon nodded confirmation.

A smile broke out over Frank's face. "Well, why don't you hop on in and we'll be on our way."

With that, Frank hurried to the plane, seemingly having forgotten Mrs. Deloris altogether.

117

CHASE

J ust as I was beginning to doubt whether our pilot was actually
taking me to Platinum Industries and not the ends of the Earth
(it felt like we'd been in the helicopter some three weeks
already), a building appeared, nestled amongst the green.

It wasn't a tall building, just two stories high, but what it lacked in
height it made up for in length. The place must've been two city
blocks wide. A modern (read: ugly) structure, blending steel and
brick. The first thing I noticed was all those high-up windows we'd
seen in satellite view earlier.

Can you say suspicious?

The pilot nudged the joystick (at least that's what it looked like),
and the aircraft responded by tilting forward as we started our
descent, but I tapped him on the shoulder with the gun.

"No. Don't land here," I said. I pointed to a field close by where a
cluster of overgrown trees and bushes lived. "There."

He didn't respond, but shifted the controls accordingly. A few
moments later, we landed neatly behind the trees, where I was
hoping the helicopter would be shielded from sight. The pilot killed
the engine. The sudden silence hung heavy in the air.

"We're here. What now?" he asked, challenging me with a glare. I got the distinct feeling he didn't like being bossed around by a kid. Well, tough.

"Get out, slowly," I said. I paid attention to his body language, bracing myself should he suddenly decide to do something stupid like run away. He climbed out, and I followed behind, close enough to do damage but not close enough for him to take me down if he chose to go that route. Then I walked around to face him.

"Good. Now get down on your knees."

He glared at me but sank to his knees. I looked over the top of his head, back into the helicopter, hoping to find something I could tie him up with, but other than a few headsets whose cords weren't even a foot long, there were just some seat belts, which if I had a knife on me, I could do something with, but of course, I didn't, which left me with only one option. Despite not liking the pilot, I gave him an apologetic smile as I swung the gun at the side of his head. This time, my technique was better. The gun connected with his head. He fell onto his side, out for the count.

"Is he really unconscious?" I asked. Bandit tilted his head at him, sniffed, then woofed. *Great.* I slid my hands into his pockets and came up with a leather wallet, a phone, and some keys. Tossing the phone on the ground, I stamped on it, HARD, until I felt the metal give way and heard the distinct *snap* of breakage. I've seen the movies, I know how cell phones are basically personal tracking devices and I wasn't about to take any further risks. Besides, look where my VPN trick had gotten us.

Flipping open the wallet, I saw a photograph of our pilot with his wife and two kids. They were smiling into the camera, looking like any other happy American family.

Wonder if his wife knew what line of work her husband was really into?

I scanned through the bills, some three hundred or so, resisting the urge to take them, and finally came upon a strange-looking swipe card.

It was strange in that other the name "Joe Kramer," who I guessed was our pilot, there was only a barcode beneath and a discreet logo on the top right corner.

I stared at that logo, recognizing it from my Google research.

Platinum Industries.

Bulls-eye.

118

CHASE

Bandit and I were outside Platinum Industries.

We were crouched beside a van in the busy parking lot. I kept my eyes peeled for security cameras, but unless they were camouflaged, I didn't see any.

From our position, I could see the main entrance, where a set of double doors separated us from the secrets within. Occasionally, a person passed by behind the doors, but it was relatively quiet — which was bad news for us. If we walked straight in through the entrance, they'd spot us immediately. We had to find another way in.

As I was contemplating our options, a car pulled into the parking lot. Some kind of weirdo pop music in another language played from the radio. As the engine died, an Asian lady got out. She wore white shoes and the overalls of a cleaner. Locking her car, she started walking towards the building, but instead of the main entrance, she steered left, taking a discrete path set into the manicured lawn that I had missed before.

Feeling a tingle all over, I whispered to Bandit, "Follow her."

We kept low as we followed the cleaner to the side of the building where she came upon a door. This one wasn't glass, and it wasn't see-through, but it was locked. The cleaner took out a card and swiped it on the door. I heard a few beeps before the door swung open and she stepped inside as the door swung automatically closed behind her.

Bandit looked at me and whined. He knew what was coming next.

We hurried to the door, then, before I could second guess myself, I took out Pilot Kramer's card and swiped it.

The door swung open, revealing a long, dark corridor ahead. Swallowing my fear, I looked down at Bandit.

"Stay behind me at all times."

And with that simple instruction, I stepped inside.

119

CHASE

We'd been swallowed up by the corridor.

Or at least that's how it seemed.

Light fell in slants through those weird upper windows, leaving the bottom half of the corridor covered with shadows. I was filled with a sense of foreboding so great; it took all my willpower not to turn and run back outside. Hysteria was bubbling under the surface, and I had to bite down on my lip to keep from giving in to it.

I looked to Bandit for strength and saw that he was sticking to those shadows, blending in like a ninja. I was surprised at how good he was at this, then remembered that this was the dog who had broken out of here not that long ago. He had experience with this place.

The cleaner was nowhere in sight, apparently in a hurry to do her job. And who could blame her? This place was so damn jolly. We followed the corridor, past closed doors and offices — all blessedly empty — and down to a main hall. Discrete signs hung from the ceiling announcing boring departments like HR, Admin, and Research.

Nowhere was there a sign with "Unethical Secret Lab That Tortures Dogs." Hitting a dead end, I frowned.

What to do? It wasn't like we could just ask someone?

The answer that came was unexpected.

Bandit, who had been standing by my side while I studied the signs, suddenly shook with fear. His mouth opened and his tongue fell out, panting loudly before whining, a high-pitched, pathetic sound that stabbed at my heart.

Then, shockingly, he peed himself.

Right there in the middle of the hall. I grabbed him and we ducked behind a giant cheese plant, seemingly growing out of the marble ground.

"What is it?" I asked quietly, holding up the iPad. Bandit tapped quickly.

"I smell him. The Bad Man."

I hated myself for what I was going to do next, but I knew there was no other choice. "Take me to him, Bandit. It's the only way."

He whined again, circling in agitation. I stroked him, trying desperately to calm him down. It took several counts before the panting died down, but the trembling continued.

On shaky legs, Bandit started leading me towards the department labeled "Research."

120

CHASE

We headed down more corridors, all gloomily lit like they couldn't afford the electricity here, which, very clearly, they could. I wouldn't be surprised if Forbes owned all the electricity in America. Judging by what I had read of him, he seemed the type.

We went past a door. Closed, with only a small window containing glass that couldn't have been bigger than a ten-inch square to see through. They were all like this, the doors. All hiding the experiments that must be being conducted on the other side. I would never have thought I'd be thankful for this, but as it was, it made being stealthy a whole lot easier.

We were approaching a doorway up ahead now. Beyond this, the corridor divided into two. I couldn't see past it, but I trusted Bandit, and right now he was my eyes. But as we crossed through the doorway, disaster struck.

An alarm SCREAMED overhead.

Too late, I looked up to discover we had just walked under a security camera. As we hadn't seen any before now, I had gotten complacent, and it was our downfall. I guess Forbes only put cameras in the ultra-secret areas.

We froze.

As I tried frantically to figure out an escape plan, a guard rounded the corner at a sprint.

"You there, STOP!" he called out.

Of course we didn't. We spun around and started sprinting back the way we had come, only to find one — make that — TWO guards flanking us from behind. Bandit barked loudly in warning. I was pretty sure he was telling them to back up, but either the guards didn't speak dog or they just weren't scared.

They advanced in unison. The guard who had spoken marched up to me.

"Hands up," he commanded.

Bandit bared his teeth at the guy, growling fiercely in response. I'd never seen him look so feral before. I totally bought his act, if that's what it was. The guard didn't consider either of us a risk, however, as he went to grab my shoulder. And that's when I didn't even think. Just reacted.

I jabbed him hard in the Adam's Apple. He choked, staggering back at his suddenly crushed windpipe. Feeling a sense of power, I spun around to face the remaining two guards. One kept his focus on Bandit, but the other's attention was on me. Roaring, I charged forward, meaning to destabilize him. My foot lashed out, and I kicked behind his knee.

Nothing happened.

He didn't fall like those YouTube videos had shown. Undaunted, I went for him again, but he was ready for me. At the exact moment my foot should have sent him tumbling, he bent his knee and caught my foot in it, vice-like. I was left hopping on one foot, trying frantically to disengage, but he wasn't letting go. He laughed at me.

"Someone's been learning self-defense, I see," he taunted.

I've gotta say, that was the last thing I expected or wanted him to say. Not wanting to show he had the upper hand, my mouth ran off as per usual. "Amazing what you learn on YouTube," I snapped back.

In hindsight, that probably wasn't a smart move.

He smiled menacingly, then punched me in the stomach. It

happened so fast I wasn't prepared for it. Pain EXPLODED in my stomach, bringing tears to my eyes. I doubled over. I was fully focused on breathing, so my mind didn't make the connection of what was about to happen. In a very deliberate move, he round-housed kicked the back of my knee and that was it.

I went tumbling to the ground.

Bandit LAUNCHED himself at the guy but was tasered with a baton-like stick. Electricity sparked and hummed as Bandit hit the ground, unconscious. I screamed, crawling towards him. Before I could touch him, the other two guards hauled me onto my feet.

The guard who had struck me laughed again.

"Now that's how you do a Krav Maga takedown, girlie."

121

CHASE

The next few minutes passed by in a blur.

Holding my throbbing stomach, I could only watch help-lessly as Bandit was laid onto a stretcher and carried beside us through the building. In the back of my mind, I knew I should be paying attention to our surroundings, that I should be memorizing the route so we knew how to break out, but the only thing running through my mind were the words, *please don't die, please don't die...*

The guards ushered me to the second floor and into an office. At least, it was adorned like one, with a giant glass desk and black couches arranged artfully around a coffee table. It was furnished like an office, but one entire wall was made out of glass, and this glass wall looked down over the entire building. From where I was stand-ing, I could see just how gigantic this place was.

Hundreds of white lab-coated minions toiled away at stations, working on scientific equipment I had never seen before. In one direction, I caught a glimpse of a room that was dark, with what looked like thousands of cages in it. I couldn't see what was inside them from here, but I had an inkling. Everywhere, as far as the eye could see, experiments were being conducted. The scope of the operation took my breath away and caused my heart to thump wildly in my chest.

How would we have any chance of beating this? The man owned an entire universe!

And as that thought entered my mind, the man in question strolled in.

"So you're the girl who's been giving me so much trouble?"

I looked over at the sharply dressed man standing in front of me. He wore an immaculate suit of steel gray. Everything about it was precise, including the purple handkerchief folded into the upper left pocket. He had a commanding presence and walked like he owned the world, which probably wasn't too far from the truth. I was surprised to see he was bald and younger than I imagined him to be. He didn't look much older than Sully. But then I noticed how his cheeks were too smooth, how his forehead was empty of lines. Forbes wasn't averse to cosmetic enhancements, it seemed. His voice was soft, cloyingly gentle, and there was something about it that set my teeth on edge. I glared at him defiantly.

"And you're the jerk who put a tumor in Bandit's brain."

I wasn't sure what I was hoping for by antagonizing him like that, but it wasn't the small arch of his brow.

"Bandit? How quaint." He managed to make it sound like the worse insult in the world. "But, cute as your display of bravado is, it's time for you to leave. Alpha — my apologies — *Bandit*, is back where he belongs, in the lab that created him."

While Forbes was talking (*don't the bad guys always have to spout some spiel?*), I had been reaching my right hand behind my back. It was a slow movement. I was counting on the fact that neither Forbes nor his men would notice, their attention, as it was, drawn to Forbes and his rant.

Feeling my fingers tighten around the base of the gun I had taken from the ranch, I swung my hand in front of me now. Before any of them could move, Forbes found himself staring down the barrel of a Beretta 92. His men froze, not expecting this. Forbes's eyebrow twitched, the only outward sign of his disapproval. He looked at his men like they were something he had just scraped from the bottom of his designer shoes.

"Why does she have a gun?" he asked, his voice unnervingly soft.

The guard who had taken me down flinched, embarrassed... but there was something else in his expression... fear. "We didn't think to search her. She's just a girl after all..."

"A girl who has traveled across the country and broken into my building," Forbes replied, still softly, but now with a chill in his voice.

From the corner of my eye, I saw one guy try a flanking move. "Freeze, or your boss is going to eat a bullet."

He stopped immediately. My eyes darted from guard to guard, hyper aware of their positions. My finger was tensed on the trigger. I was prepared to use it and they knew it. What they didn't know, was how utterly terrified I was, and I was desperate not to show it. Willing my hand not to shake, I started backing towards the door.

"Let go of Bandit," I ordered.

The two men holding him in place released their grip on him. Bandit started moving over to me. Hope was beginning to rise up in me. *We can do this! I can get him safe!* Bandit was three steps from me and freedom when he dropped to the ground, shaking violently, head knocking against the floor.

It happened way faster than his other fits and was ten times as fierce. Losing it completely, I screamed, "Help him!"

The men didn't move, waiting for Forbes to respond. Forbes merely smiled at me before pressing a button on the intercom. "Please ask Dr. Robins to step in with Alpha's meds."

I ran towards Bandit, heedless of my own safety. Gathering his head in my lap the way Sully had shown me, I tried to stop him from hurting himself, all as I kept the gun trained on Forbes.

After what seemed an eternity, but was, in fact, only seconds, a woman rushed in holding a syringe. She wore one of the same white lab coats I had seen others wearing, but unlike the emotionless robots working for Forbes, there was panic all over her face.

"Alpha?!" she cried. Seeing him convulsing, her eyes flared open in alarm, and she darted towards us with the needle.

"Stop Elora." Forbes's command was chilling in its authority.

The woman, Elora, looked over at him, confused. "But he needs his meds. I've never seen a convulsion as strong as this. He was never supposed to survive this long without them. He might have only seconds before irreparable damage is done to his brain," she cried.

Forbes looked down at me. "Well, that depends on our young friend here. Kick over the gun and Dr. Robins will save Alpha. Or you can watch your friend die."

Every nerve in my body was screaming at me to do as he said, but I knew this was the only bargaining chip I had. I had to try one last time. "After everything you've done to get him back, you wouldn't risk his life any more than I would," I said.

Forbes just looked at me, a half-smile playing on his lips as if this whole thing were just a slight inconvenience. "What I need from him I can get whether he is alive or not. Can you say the same?"

I'd called his bluff, but he'd called mine, and as we all know, I'm a terrible gambler. Laying the gun down, I slid it over to him. One of his guards picked up the gun as Forbes nodded to Dr. Robins. She ran over and injected the contents of the syringe into Bandit's flank. I found myself counting in my head as I watched his small body convulse. *One, two, three, four...* by the time I reached five, the fit had stopped. Bandit's chest was rising and falling at its regular speed. Another two seconds and he opened his eyes. This time, there wasn't any of the confusion that had preceded his previous episodes.

Dr. Robins let out a relieved breath. I was surprised that she actually seemed to care for Bandit. It made her decision to work for Forbes even more baffling. I shot her a grateful look, regardless. She had just saved my best friend, after all.

"Thanks."

She took me in, blinking behind her glasses. I guess she hadn't really noticed me until now. Since her arrival, her attention was only on Bandit. Now, she saw the way we cuddled, how Bandit pressed up against me. Her eyes softened.

"Alpha, you made a friend," she said.

Bandit *woofed* in response. "One bark for yes, two for no," I explained. At this, her eyes teared up. So she wasn't a monster. Maybe Forbes wasn't either? Could I try appealing to his nice side? I looked back at him.

"I'm sorry I pointed the gun at you, but I was desperate. Bandit's not just my friend, he's family. He's all I've got. Can we figure out a way for you to get what you want while keeping him safe? Then we'll get out of your hair and you'll never have to see us again. We just want to live a normal life."

My voice cracked with emotion. I was on the verge of tears, but for the first time, I didn't care who saw it. I meant every word I said. Bandit's tongue snaked over and licked me across the face.

Forbes watched us emotionlessly.

"That was a lovely speech, and I truly feel your pain, but unfortunately, the answer is no. I will never let Alpha go."

122

SULLY

While I didn't think much of Frank's integrity, I had to hand it to the man; the guy could fly a plane. We landed an hour later in a field near Platinum Industries, a good hour ahead of his initial estimation. We were still a good football field away, but I figured this was far enough that we shouldn't be spotted unless someone was looking out for us, in which case, nowhere would be far enough.

As Gideon helped me off the plane, Frank tipped an invisible cap. "Good doing business with you."

"Give me a day or two. We'll be by to pick up Derby and Spirit, and we'll arrange the rest of your payment then," I said.

Frank nodded. "Fine. The Missus will take care of your horses until you return." And with that, he took off.

Gideon pulled a face at me. "Shouldn't we have kept him here for our escape?"

"We could have asked, though he didn't seem all that trustworthy, and I wasn't inclined to explain what it is we're doing here."

Gideon shielded his eyes and stared across to the building on the horizon. "It's still a ways away. We'd better get started."

Ordinarily, I would have run the distance in a minute flat, no sweat. As it was, all we could manage was a slow, limping shuffle. I've always hated having to depend on someone else, particularly someone who had had an issue with me, so I was grateful for Gideon's matter-of-fact help and attitude.

Especially as on the inside, I felt like I was falling apart all over again.

123

SULLY

S ome ten minutes later, having crossed the fields, as I was approaching Platinum Industries, a glint of sunlight bouncing off of metal caught my eye. I stopped, staring into a dense crop of trees.

There was something behind them.

Going on nothing but gut instinct, I motioned to Gideon and reeled at our discovery when we got there. A jet-black, military-looking helicopter sat before me, a man on the ground next to it. He was wearing the dark uniform of the men who had attacked the ranch. I would bet the house that he was the pilot, and that this was the helicopter Chase had hijacked for a ride. *Clever girl*, I thought, smiling grimly. The man on the ground moaned, trying to sit up. Seeing us (and clearly not recognizing us), he touched the back of his head gingerly.

I took the moment to take stock of the situation. "Is Chase OK? The girl?"

The pilot blinked at me, confused, as his thoughts tried to collect themselves. "That goddamn brat. She hit me on the head."

"Yes. But is she OK?" I had no sympathy for him. Suddenly, the pilot must have realized who he was talking to, as his face turned spiteful. "You killed our men."

I glared down at the man, heaping as much heat into the look as I could muster. "You shouldn't have attacked us first. We won't go down without a fight."

The pilot smiled unpleasantly. "If she's still alive, she won't be for much longer. She's as good as dead."

I wasn't sure if it was the pilot's smug face or his words that did it. All I knew was that a deep rage was building inside. Seemingly of its own accord, my hand formed into a tight fist that swung at the pilot's face, full throttle. On connection, the pilot's head snapped back, smashing into the side of the helicopter with such force that his cheek would be fractured for sure. He fell back, unconscious again. I glowered down at him.

"No one talks trash about my family. No one."

124

CHASE

It was all starting to sink in. Forbes had no intention of letting Bandit go. Ever. And I had just walked him straight into his arms.

I could kill myself.

How stupid could I be that I trusted they would help? Didn't I know better by now? How many more times did the universe need to show me that PEOPLE WERE BAD?

I looked into Bandit's intelligent blue eyes, the world crashing down around me.

"Take them away," Forbes instructed his men. And just like that, he was done with us. His men advanced towards us, all eyes focused on Bandit. I was merely an irritation, a fly to be swatted away. I didn't even merit any thought from these men. Forbes turned away, about to leave, when the rage, pain, and confusion burst out from me.

"But why?!" I yelled after him. Forbes and his men stopped in their tracks. It seemed they had already forgotten about me. Forbes turned to look at me, confusion etched across his features.

"Why what?" he said.

"Why are you doing this? You can't take Bandit away from me without even telling me what this is all for?!" I cried. "That's not fair!" I knew my last comment sounded like a whiney kid, but that's all I had right now. I needed to know and wasn't thinking about my language. Forbes considered my question, then waved at his men to stop. He walked back to me.

"I've spent a lot of money and effort on Alpha. I can't just give him to you," he said, sounding almost reasonable. I wanted to kill him.

"How much money? If you just give us time, Bandit and I can make your money back, I know we can." I was willing to try anything. Pride was a long, distant memory.

Forbes hesitated as if reconsidering. "I've not seen this level of devotion before. It's really quite touching. Unfortunately, my life is worth more than this dog's."

I frowned, not understanding. "What do you mean, your life?"

Forbes opened his mouth to reply, but suddenly his eyes glazed over. One minute, they shone cold and calculating, the next they softened. He blinked in confusion, staring around the room as if he was seeing us for the first time.

"Do you know where my mom is? She's supposed to take me to school, but I haven't seen her? She told me to wait right here."

Forbes' voice came out like a child. The change was so startling, so sudden, that I found the whole thing super eerie. Then the moment was over. He shook his head as if mentally clearing away a fog.

"I've not seen this level of devotion before. It's really quite touching. Unfortunately, my life is worth more than this dog's," he said. Again.

"You said that already. Literally word for word. It's pretty disgusting that you're going to mock me when you've won already. I mean, who does that?" My mouth shot off before I could stop it. I steeled myself, waiting for the slap I could feel was coming. Except it never came. Forbes looked to Dr. Robins.

"It happened again?" he asked her, quietly — and something else I didn't expect to hear in his voice — resigned. She nodded. He turned back to me then.

"Well, yes. I do believe you deserve an explanation. You see, I am sick. A particularly nasty strain of Alzheimer's runs in my family. You know the disease? It is a progressive mental deterioration that can occur in middle or old age, due to generalized degeneration of the brain, and it is the most common cause of premature senility," Forbes said. He gestured out of the wrap-around window at the experiments below. "Everything I have built, all the billions I have earned, it is because of my mind. I clawed my way up from the bottom, from humble beginnings, but at the moment of my greatest success, I was informed of my condition. Since then, I have dedicated my enormous wealth to finding a cure. Everything you see here, this lab? It was created solely for this purpose."

As he spoke, pieces started falling into place. "And Bandit? How is he involved with this?" I asked. Although I was terrified by what the answer could be, I had to know.

"Alpha is the key. Within his brain lies the potential for a cure... except he ran away."

Dr. Robins had been listening quietly, but now stepped forward. "There are many, many cases throughout history of people having suffered head trauma who suddenly became incredibly gifted. Such was the case of one Texan man, who hit his head while diving, and subsequently lost thirty percent of his hearing. However, he also became an astonishing piano player overnight — when he had never even touched one before or learned to read music. It seems the head trauma caused his brain to reorganize itself in such a way that it could now do — at a mastery level — what it had never been able to do before."

She gestured with her hands while speaking. This was something she believed in absolutely. Seemingly not picking up any of my wariness, she continued.

"Another case study involved a high-school dropout brutally beaten by muggers that left him in a coma. When he awoke, he became the only known person in the world able to draw complex geometric patterns called fractals, which is, in layman terms, a never-ending pattern."

"I don't understand how any of this helps your situation." I directed my question at Forbes.

"Current treatment for Alzheimer's involves drugs that may help with both cognitive and behavioral symptoms. Researchers have spent years looking for new treatments to alter the course of the disease, but *what if it is the brain itself that should be altered?*" he said, eyes feverish with conviction.

You see how *What-If* questions are bad, bad, bad?

I stared at them both. "So this tumor Bandit has you gave it to him to simulate brain trauma?" Even as the words left my mouth, I understood the insanity of them.

"Yes," said Forbes. "We believe that once the brain suffers from trauma — that we control — it will reorganize itself and ultimately defeat Alzheimer's." His voice was triumphant, as if just stating this point meant it was a success. I realized in that moment that the man was completely and utterly insane.

"But that's crazy! You have no way of knowing this will work, and in the meantime, you're torturing all those poor animals!" I said, unable to stop myself.

Forbes's eyes narrowed into slits at the word "crazy." Thinking about it, I must've touched a nerve.

"I know a simpleton like you won't understand, however, what I do, I do for the good of all mankind."

I ignored the slur he directed at me, desperately hoping that if I could keep him talking, I would be buying Bandit time for a miracle.

"Well, why can't you wait a while, make sure that this will actually work?" I pleaded.

Forbes said, "I have begun to experience the latter effects that my mother experienced, prior to her losing her mind completely. We can't delay this any longer. We must operate now."

"*Operate?*" The word stuck in my throat, along with the fear. Forbes was already losing interest in me, keen to move things along, so I turned to the Doc for help. For someone who was on the brink of a medical breakthrough, she didn't look too happy.

"Mr. Forbes, I can't guarantee this will work, and operating on

Alpha will most likely cause him to lose his intelligence. At worst, it could kill him," she warned, wringing her hands.

Forbes sighed. "That is something I will have to live with." At that, his men started towards us again. Bandit bared his teeth, growling fiercely, ears flattened to his head. He pressed urgently at my side, determined to protect me. But it wasn't me they were after. There were only three feet away from us now and approaching fast.

Suddenly, Bandit FLEW at one of the guards, savagely sinking his teeth into his arm. The guard screamed, flinging his arm about, trying to loosen Bandit's jaws from his flesh. Taking his cue, I launched myself at another guard, plunging my fingers into his eyes. He shrieked, staggering back. The tiniest flicker of hope rose in me. Maybe, just maybe, we could get out of this alive...

But then the guards trained tranquilizer guns at Bandit and fired. Darts stabbed into his flank. He yelped and dropped to the ground. Shaking his head to clear the fast rising fog, he tried to get up onto his paws, but whatever was in the darts was already taking effect. Within seconds, Bandit blacked out. I watched, helpless, as he was carried out, struggling against the guards who now held me captive.

Forbes frowned at me. "Despite what you may think, I am not a complete monster. I will allow you to watch Alpha's last moments." He left, and I found myself escorted into a viewing room overlooking an operating theater.

The guards shoved me against the window, and then I was suddenly alone. I ran to the door and tugged at the handle, but it was locked. I pounded my fists on the door, banging and screaming until my hands were throbbing with pain, but it was no use.

The hopelessness of it all overwhelmed me.

I sank to the floor, hugging my knees to my chest, and cried as I waited for them to kill my best friend.

SULLY

We finally arrived at the infamous building.

Seeing the glass-fronted entrance, I knew we couldn't just walk in, not without consequences, so we performed a quick reconnaissance around the building. It was Gideon who had spotted the staff entrance, which, hiding behind a dumpster, we were scrutinizing right then. An old man in blue overalls, a janitor, was leaning against the wall, smoking a cigarette. He must have been pushing seventy; what hair he had left was thin and gray, and skin sagged from his arms. Judging by the butt, which was almost done, he'd already been out there awhile. I knew if we were going to act, it would have to be fast.

"When he goes back in, we need to follow quickly behind. As soon as he turns, we move, got it?" I said. "We've got to be quiet. We can't give him cause for concern."

Gideon nodded, unfazed, which I suddenly realized was a curious thing. How was this kid so cool about breaking into this place? I was about to question the boy on it when the janitor threw the cigarette to the ground, stamping it out.

"As soon as he turns... now!" Gideon darted forward lightly on his feet, sticking close to the janitor, but I had momentarily forgotten about my injury, which slowed me down something awful. Thankfully, the janitor moved slowly with age. We were standing behind him when the janitor swiped his card, but when he looked up from swiping the device, my reflection appeared on the glass in the door. Startled, the janitor stopped short of fully stepping inside, the door held open in his hands. He turned to me, wary of seeing someone so close to him. I didn't think, but reacted instinctively. Leaning forward, I held the door open for the janitor, smiling in a friendly manner.

"Here, let me get that for you."

The janitor was pleasantly surprised. He smiled at us both, showing large gaps in his crooked, yellow teeth. "Not many youngsters with manners nowadays. Thank you, young man." He shuffled inside, not the least bit concerned he had allowed two strangers into the building. Even I was taken aback at how easy it was to break in. *Just goes to show, a little courtesy goes a long way in this world,* I thought to myself.

We followed the janitor inside, watching as the old man disappeared obliviously down a long corridor. I took in my immediate surroundings. No cameras. That was good. No guards either. Either Forbes wasn't concerned with break-ins or he wasn't hiding anything. Knowing the answer to that, I almost snorted out loud. Astonished by the arrogance of a man who would conduct unethical experiments out in the relative open like this, I limped along the corridor, keeping my eyes peeled for anything that might help.

We hadn't gone far when Gideon whispered to me. "Sully, quick, over here." I turned to find him standing in front of a closed door. A discreet sign on it said "changing room." Gideon opened the door cautiously. Once he was sure the way was clear, we snuck inside.

We were in a large changing room. A row of lockers took up an entire wall. Shower cubicles stood side by side, their glass still fogged from recent use. Beyond those, I could see spotless restrooms. These janitors really earned their keep. Gideon sprinted up to the lockers, tugging on several of their handles, but all were locked.

"What're you doing?" I asked.

Gideon slipped a hand into his pocket, retrieving a lock pick set. "I'm going to help us go incognito," came Gideon's reply. I watched in fascination as Gideon slipped the tools into a padlock, twisting them confidently until the lock suddenly dropped open — like my mouth.

"How the hell did you do that?" I demanded to know.

Gideon opened the locker. Inside, there was a pile of magazines, some pairs of socks, and a few granola bars. Nothing of interest really, so he moved to the next.

"Before I lived with Zeb, I, er... learned a few things."

"I see," came my response. I stared at the boy anew, seeing him with different eyes. Feeling my stare, Gideon sighed.

"Oh, come on, like Chase hasn't done worse living on the streets? Not everyone had a home like yours, OK? You should count yourself lucky." Gideon continued breaking open the lockers, so he didn't see my face reflect the shame I now felt. I had never considered myself lucky, not with the way my relationship with Zeb had deteriorated after mom's death, but seeing how Chase was living, what she had to put up with, and now hearing from Gideon a similar tale, I vowed never to feel sorry for myself again. From here on, I would be grateful for all I received.

"Bingo," Gideon said suddenly, having found what he was looking for — two white lab coats complete with ID's clipped onto their pockets. He handed the larger of the coats to me. My eyes fell on the ID now pinned to my lapel.

"So we'll be fine as long as no one looks down at the thing and sees I'm not Chinese," I said. I flashed the card at Gideon, who glanced down at the picture of an Asian man in his forties, a Dr. Lim.

"If anyone gets close enough to read them, we'll be toast anyway, so I wouldn't worry about that," was Gideon's only reply.

I had to hand it to him. The kid had a way with words.

We left the changing room and headed down the same path as the janitor. Rooms veered off now and then. I caught glimpses of expensive lab gear, steel tables, and high-tech computers. Everywhere I looked, my surroundings reeked of money. Forbes had spent a small fortune on this place. *He must mean business*, I thought to myself. The thought wasn't very reassuring.

We hurried through twisting corridors, going more on instinct than anything else. Every now and then, we would pass a PI employee. It took every ounce of willpower in those moments not to dart away. Forcing myself to continue as if it were my right to be here, I carried on, Gideon by my side. The staff seemed oblivious, focused on their own jobs at hand.

After some fruitless searching, I was beginning to panic when a sign caught my eye. It wasn't much, but the single word caused a chill to race down my spine. I pointed at the sign.

GENESIS.

126

SULLY

G ideon looked at me funny. "What about it?"

"Genesis. You know what that means? The origin of something. In the Bible, it literally means "In the beginning.""

Apparently not feeling any of the apprehension that had suddenly flooded my body, Gideon marched towards the door. "Then what are we waiting for?" And with that, he opened it and stepped through.

I was so unprepared for the move, I froze. When I finally recovered, I limped after him. "Of all the stupid..."

... And stepped into a giant room.

There were cages, seemingly hundreds of them. Inside each was a young dog. The dogs consisted of all breeds and sizes, nothing connecting them except their species. A tablet was attached to each cage with information on it, but I couldn't see what it said from here. I moved closer to one cage.

The dog inside, a German Shepherd, was spinning round and round without stopping. An outsider might think this was a trick or cute behavior, but I knew better. It was a sign that the dog was suffering from a compulsive disorder, most probably caused by living in such a confined space. This was a condition most often seen in shelter animals who had been stuck there for some time and was essentially a sign of severe distress. A wave of compassion swept over me. I clicked at the dog, making soothing sounds.

"Hey fella, you OK in there? It's going to be alright." The dog didn't react at all. It was as if he couldn't hear me. He just continued spinning, round and round and round. It hurt to watch him, so I turned my focus across to the next cage only to find that the Terrier in there wasn't faring much better. He sat in the corner, staring blankly at the wall. It was his way of tuning out his fears. If he couldn't see the scary things, then they weren't really happening. The Terrier was behaving like a terrified young child. Pain stabbed in my chest. *These poor animals, what were they doing to them?*

Across from me, Gideon was staring into the cage of a Bull Mastiff who had licked his paw so much, it had caused an open wound. "What's wrong with him? Why is he doing that?" he asked me.

But I couldn't speak for fear I would explode with rage. I looked at the information on the tablet of the German Shepherd's cage. There was a video file. I hit play.

Video footage flashed up on the tablet. The German Shepherd was chained up in a room. There was no give to his chain, so he couldn't move and was forced to stare at a screen. In front of the screen were five large numbers. As I watched, the number 4 appeared on the screen. The German Shepherd was panting, showing clear agitation. He whined, but couldn't get free. Suddenly, a jolt of electricity shot up from the chain to hit the dog. He yelped and pressed a paw onto a button, button two. The screen made an "error" sound, and a jolt of electricity zapped into the dog again. As the dog stood quaking in terror, the screen reset and the number one appeared. The dog got it wrong again and was punished for his mistake. I stopped the video, unable to watch anymore, but to my horror, I noted the clip was thirty minutes long.

Why were they torturing these poor dogs?

Closing the video, I was automatically taken to a live scan of the dog's brain, but there was something wrong with it. There was a mass, a tumor growing on it.

Just like Bandit.

"No..." Trying to curb the rising horror in me, I sprinted to the next cage and examined the tablet for the Terrier. There was more footage of the torture experiments that I had to click through before I located the live scan. It was the same, though the Terrier's tumor was in a different position. Gideon watched me, confused and concerned.

"What is it?" he asked again.

I went past several more cages, each time finding the same results. Finally, unable to take any more, I stopped at the sixth cage, shock radiating from me. "The dogs have all been given tumors in their brains."

"But why?" Gideon asked, utterly baffled.

Seeing an office across the way, my eyes hardened.

"I don't know, but we're going to find out."

127

ELORA

The mask on her face was irritating her today.

Elora looked down at Alpha's brain, which now lay open before her, like a work of biological art. She checked his vitals, liking what she could see. He was doing better than expected, which was something she had learned to expect of him.

Although she had voiced her concerns to Forbes, as usual, he hadn't been willing to listen. The thought that Alpha would lose his intelligence pained her more than she was able to admit. He was always her favorite, and after seeing him with the girl, she felt awful that she was going to sever their relationship with one cut of the scalpel, however, as always, Forbes was watching, and if she didn't do this, didn't do what he commanded, her family would be in danger. He had made that threat clear enough.

She glanced over at the girl, Chase, secured in the viewing room. She was sobbing and banging her fists on the glass. Elora wished she could reassure her, let her know that if nothing else, once the tumor was removed, Alpha could have a chance at living a long and normal life, even if he lost the personality that she had obviously fallen in love with.

She refocused on the brain now. Missing all those weeks of meds had taken a huge toll. Had they waited any longer to remove the tumor, Alpha's next seizure would most likely have killed him. Despite how she might feel about the situation by bringing him home, Chase had saved him. Elora worked swiftly, nimble fingers skimming across the brain.

With one final cut, the tumor was free, and with it, Elora was finally able to pinpoint the exact placement and position of the tumor that had caused Alpha's intelligence. This was the missing key they had been searching for. Elora shot a silent prayer of thanks to Alpha. If she were able to use this knowledge to help Forbes, maybe they would all be free of him.

Elora placed the tumor into a steel tray and moved to seal Alpha's brain when Forbes's voice came over the loudspeaker.

"There's no time for that."

She stopped, shocked. *What did he mean?* Her unspoken question was answered as Forbes entered the operating theater.

"Stop! His head is open. You can't just come in like that. Do you know how many germs you could infect him with right now?" She leaned over Alpha, hoping to protect him, but Forbes merely took hold of her arm.

"You are going to put his tumor into my brain," he said, eyes gleaming with madness. "This tumor, pressing in such a way on the dog's brain, caused his intelligence. Don't you understand, Elora? *It caused his brain to reorganize itself.* This is what you've been working for!"

Elora gaped at him in astonishment. "But there's no guarantee it will work. There are too many unknowns..."

Forbes glared at her suddenly. Elora could feel his infamous rage simmering at the edges. "Is that a refusal, Elora? Are you saying no?"

She snapped her mouth shut, not trusting herself to speak. She just stood there, scared, shaking her head mutely.

"Good," he said simply, calmly, as his voice dropped back into its normal, soft tone. As he marched her from the room, Elora only had time to glance at Alpha, head lying open on the operating table, before he was out of sight.

128

SULLY

The office was neat and tidy — and unlocked, which surprised me. Then again, I imagined everyone who worked here already knew what experiments they were conducting and mostly likely condoned them, so there was no need for secrecy.

A small plaque on the neat desk said this was the office of one Dr. Elora Robins. Aside from a computer, there were a few medical journals stacked neatly on the desk and a pot of identical pens. Dr. Robins wasn't one for collecting, it seemed. Only dogs.

I pulled open a filing cabinet. Inside were hundreds of suspension files, labeled with a mixture of letters and numbers. Some sort of reference system. I ground the back of my teeth, overwhelmed by feeling. The dogs meant nothing to these people. They didn't even deserve a name. I opened a file and took out the paperwork. There was a picture on the front page, a Golden Retriever. Her stats were listed beside the headshot: weight, height, size — the usual. There was nothing of interest until the next page, which detailed her tumor extensively.

While I read, Gideon turned on the computer. He launched the mailbox, sifting through emails, looking for anything that might point them to Bandit and Chase's whereabouts. There were plenty to go through, and I could tell Gideon was beginning to feel the fruitlessness of our search.

Eye's skimming across the file, I suddenly found the answer I had been looking for.

"They're not trying to make super intelligent dogs! Forbes has Alzheimer's, and he's throwing all his billions into finding a cure!"

Gideon looked at him, not understanding. "But Bandit's intelligence, how does that factor into anything?"

"It doesn't. It's a miracle, a once-in-a-million side effect," I answered.

Thoughts raced through Gideon's mind, one in particular, something he had read. "But, I'm sure I've read that there are other animals that are a better genetic match to us than dogs."

"Yeah. Monkeys and pigs are typically closer to humans, but they require more care, and are harder to source, unlike stray dogs they could literally snatch off the streets." I waved the file at Gideon. "There were plans to roll the experiments out to other animals, but Forbes started deteriorating much faster than expected."

Still searching the mailbox, one suddenly caught Gideon's eye. He clicked it open. "Oh no," was all he could manage to say.

Dropping the file, I leaned over the boy's shoulder. The message on the screen was short.

Alpha is back in the building. Extraction will commence. Report to the Nursery.

I GLANCED down at my watch. "Dammit! This email was sent an hour ago! We've got to find this Nursery."

Gideon moved the mouse offscreen, bringing up a 3D image of the entire complex with every section helpfully labeled. He pointed to the one marked "Nursery." I blinked, not sure what just happened.

"How did you do that?"
Gideon grinned.
"The map is her desktop wallpaper."

129

CHASE

I couldn't believe it!

After everything he had gone through to get Bandit back, all the people and buildings he had destroyed, he was going to leave him there to die?! I felt a fury so strong; I thought I would explode!

Throughout the whole operation, I was helpless to do anything. I just sat and watched as she cut into his head. I will never forget the sound of that blade sawing into his skull for as long as I live. It felt like it was hammering into my own head.

At first, when Forbes explained what this was about, all I could think was how devastating it would be if Bandit lost his intelligence — if he couldn't talk to me anymore, or answer any pop quizzes. Then I realized I loved him. He was my family, and if that meant he was "just" a normal dog, he would be *my* normal dog.

The screens monitoring Bandit's vitals continued to beep, but I could see a clear decline in the figures. I didn't know what they meant exactly, but I was pretty sure a drop was BAD news. I had no idea how I would save him, I just knew I had to be in there with him. I couldn't stay locked in here apart from him any longer.

There was nothing in the room with me except for a desk and a couple of chairs. I grabbed hold of a chair now, and with all my might, I SWUNG it at the glass. The chair hit the window with a gigantic THUD, and the glass cracked but held. I backed up another step and took another swing, this one harder than the first. The glass started spider webbing as cracks began forming everywhere. Pumped by my progress, I hit the window.

Bang, bang, bang...

And suddenly, glass erupted everywhere. As Bandit was some ways away, no shards landed on him. I jumped through the hole I had created and scrambled to his side, fully expecting guards to stop me at any moment.

Seeing his head open like that, being able to see his actual brain, was *terrifying*. And the *smell*. I can't even begin to describe it. But even more frightening was the thought he might die. I looked for a phone, hoping to call someone for help, even though in the back of my mind, I knew it was hopeless. Who would I call? A newspaper? How would that help him? But in that moment of utter panic, fear, and desperation, I couldn't get my head to think straight. I needn't have bothered, however. There was no phone.

No help was coming.

He was doomed.

130

CHASE

I wasn't in the theater long when I heard some kind of a scuffle outside. I figured I had only seconds before the guards busted in and finished us off. I took hold of Bandit's paw, defiant to the end. So be it. If this was it, at least we'd be together.

Briefly, I wondered how Sully and the others were doing. Now that the end was near, I felt enormous guilt at the pain I had caused him. First, he lost everything he had of his wife and the clinic. Now his father's home was also destroyed, and who knew if Sully's gunshot was fatal or not. I wasn't normally a praying girl, but even I was willing to give it a go now.

Please God, please save Sully. Don't let him die too.

The noise from outside intensified. Something smashed. I stood in front of Bandit and planted my feet, determined to buy him more time.

Suddenly, the door crashed open, and in ran Sully and Gideon! I was so stunned I didn't move, just stood there, gaping stupidly at them. Was this a mirage? Was this wishful thinking?

Or was I just dead already?

Sully took in the scene before him and uttered one word, "Jesus."

It was that one word, spoken in typical Sully fashion, that cut through my shock. I ran over to him and threw my arms around him.

"You're here?! You're really here?!" I sobbed into his chest, not the least bit ashamed of how happy I was to see him. I felt his arms tighten securely around me. "You've got to help him Sully! Forbes made the doc leave before she could close him up!"

Sully quickly detangled himself from me. "Block that door," he instructed Gideon. "They'll probably try to come through once they know we're here. I need you to buy me as much time as possible."

Gideon nodded and grabbed an unused metal stand in the corner. I'd seen those on TV before, they were usually used to hang IV's or blood packs. Gideon slid the pole under the door handle, wedging it in place. Then he ran for some steel cabinets, pushing them towards the hole in the window I had created. Realizing what he was doing, I sprang forward to help.

Sully rolled up his sleeves and rinsed his hands in a sink. Tossing us some facemasks, he told us to put them on, then took position by Bandit. Even though half of his face was obscured by the mask, I could see the tension there. Remembering what he had said back at the ranch, about how brain surgery wasn't exactly his thing, I knew he must be doubting himself. So I spoke.

"Sully, you've got this. She's already taken the tumor. You just need to close him up. You've got this."

He glanced over at me, grateful for the encouragement.

Then, with Gideon and I watching out for Forbes's men, Sully operated.

131

ELORA

Elora watched as Forbes laid the tray containing the tumor next to the operating table. This room was smaller than the one Alpha was in and more private. There was no window, no viewing room overlooking this. She noticed that everything was already in place for the operation. Forbes must have planned this all along to have it ready, which made her feel like an idiot. She should have known.

Forbes laid down on the table and waited impatiently for Elora to start. Elora glanced at the two armed guards who had marched her in and were now standing before her.

"I can't work with them here like this. It's too much pressure, not to mention, unsanitary."

Forbes scrutinized her face as if to assess her honesty. He must've decided she was telling the truth, however, as he nodded for the guards to leave. Elora moved to his side and began fastening the arm restraints around him when he stopped her.

"What are you doing?" he demanded.

"Securing your arms. It's standard procedure," she replied. His eyes narrowed suspiciously. Elora stopped, but went on to explain patiently. "In the event, the drugs wear off, which can happen one in five hundred thousand cases, any movement from you could have devastating consequences while I am operating. You know it's a delicate procedure. We can't afford to have anything go wrong."

She stood there, waiting for his answer. Finally, after what seemed like hours, he nodded. Elora reached over and secured the restraints around him. Then she picked up a syringe, depressing the needle until the air was squeezed out. As she approached, Forbes frowned. "Aren't you going to anesthetize me?"

"This will do the job," Elora explained, already sinking the needle into his arm. Forbes's brow creased with worry. "That isn't procedure. What is it?" he asked, trying unsuccessfully to mask his fast rising fear.

Elora smiled. "Ketamine. We usually use it on the dogs. I thought this would be apt."

Forbes' eyes flared open with alarm as he realized she wasn't abiding by protocol. He made a move to shout for help, but Elora was one step ahead of him. Covering his mouth with her hand, she spoke.

"I'm sorry, Mr. Forbes. This brings me no joy, but you have clearly lost your mind, and I can't stand idly by as you destroy any more lives."

Feeling a calm she didn't know she possessed, Elora watched the clock and started counting the strokes of the needle. When she reached nine, Forbes was out for the count.

132

CHASE

I watched Sully like a hawk.

His hands moved quickly and surely. They didn't show the doubt he had felt just minutes ago when I had to cheer him on, but he was having obvious trouble standing. He kept stopping, kept shifting his weight. The whole thing was mesmerizing, yet terrifying. He moved the flaps of Bandit's skull, repositioning them, ready to close him up when there came a pounding on the door.

Gideon shot towards it, gun held in his hands, aimed in case the people outside somehow got through. He looked to Sully for guidance, but Sully kept his focus on Bandit. I grabbed a metal clamp in my hands and went to wait beside Gideon. I figured I could get at least one good hit with the thing before I went down. I was hoping I would get someone's soft head with it. I was getting really good at that.

"Let me in, I need to save Alpha," came a frantic female voice from the other side of the door. Sully was so surprised, he stopped working.

"Who's there?" he called out.

"Dr. Robins," came the reply. "Forbes forced me away before I could finish closing him up, but he needs my help or he'll die!" she called. Sully and I looked at each other. Her voice sounded desperate enough, she *seemed* sincere, but what if it was a trick? In the end, I went with what my gut was telling me.

"It's true," I said. "She wanted to help him, but Forbes wouldn't let her."

Sully listened to my words and made a snap decision. "Open the door carefully. If anyone other than the doc comes in, Gideon, you shoot."

"Got it," Gideon said grimly. I took hold of the metal stand and pulled it away. Grabbing the door handle, I cranked it open a tiny notch. The doc's fearful face filled the gap.

"Hurry, let me in before the guards know what I've done," she said. I opened the door, steeling myself for something to go wrong. Beside me, I saw Gideon's whole body tense as he also prepared to fight, but the Doc darted inside and quickly shoved the door back closed. I jammed the rod beneath the handle again, locking us in.

The doc took in Sully's actions with horror. "Get away from him, you don't know what you're doing!" she cried.

Sully's voice was calm but firm. Professional. "I'm a vet, but I could do with your help. This is more than I'm used to." Reassured by his manner, the Doc rushed over, pulled on a pair of gloves and proceeded to help. Safe for now, I made my way back to Gideon's side. He looked at me, frowning as if he were struggling to find the right words to say to me.

"You think Bandit will be OK?" he finally asked.

I could feel the tears welling in my eyes again and fought to keep them down.

"He has to be."

133

SULLY

I couldn't begin to describe the relief I had felt when the good doctor stormed inside. Craniology wasn't my area of specialty, and though I didn't want Chase to know, the entire time I was working on Bandit, my heart wasn't just in my throat but dancing a fandango.

With Dr. Robins on the scene, I was able to take a backseat and assist with the closing. It was a marvel really, the way her fingers stitched so quickly yet neatly. The needle darted in, then out, with seemingly no effort at all. From the moment she took over, things went so fast, it wasn't long before we were done. The second she made the final cut of the stitches, Chase hustled over, fists gripped tightly by her side.

"Is he OK?" She had obviously been waiting this whole time just to ask.

Robins answered. "We won't know until he wakes up."

I had already rinsed my hands and was now wiping them on my jeans. "We need to get out of here pronto before Forbes comes back."

"I bought you some time, but he'll be discovered soon," Dr. Robins said. Off my questioning look, she explained, "I shot him up with ketamine. He'll be down for a while, though the guards might check up on him."

Remembering how the SWAT team had first arrived at my clinic with tranquilizers armed with that very drug, I felt a faint sense of justice. *Good, let's see how he likes it.* Chase shot a grateful look at her.

"Thank you," she said simply, but with meaning.

The Doctor flushed with something like shame, hanging her head low. "I'm so sorry about all this. Alpha was always special. I should've stopped Forbes sooner, but he'd made threats to my family…"

Seeing how distressed she was, I reached out and squeezed her shoulder, offering what little comfort I could. "When push came to shove, you helped. That's what counts."

She straightened up, resolved. "In the basement, there is a network of corridors. They're only ever used by my team. You can sneak out that way," she said.

Chase frowned. "Won't the guards know about them too?"

Robins shook her head. "No. My team are the only ones. We… use them to sneak in dogs for testing." As soon as she said the words, her eyes filled with tears. I was torn. On one hand, I wanted to alleviate her guilt. On the other, well, she had been torturing those poor animals for years. As if she knew what I was thinking, Robins straightened up suddenly. Probably realizing her feelings weren't important when there was so much more at stake.

"You'll show us the way out?" Gideon asked.

Robins looked at us. "Yes, but I need you to do something for me first."

I looked at her, suddenly apprehensive. "What?"

"I need you to help me free all the other dogs."

134

CHASE

My first instinct was to run.

Bandit was stable, and I knew the guards and Forbes would soon be hunting us down. It was on the tip of my tongue to say no when an image of thousands of Bandits trapped in cages flashed across my mind. I looked down at his unconscious face, at the ugly vivid scar on his head, which only minutes ago had been opened because of the experiments they conduct here. And I knew, without a doubt, they had to be saved.

Every last one of them.

"Sully... you take care of Bandit. I'll go with her and help the dogs." If Sully were surprised by my decision, he didn't show it. Instead, a look of pride came over his face. Then Gideon spoke.

"Me too. They're not keeping another one in those cages." He sounded real mad. The Doc smiled at us, grateful, then looked at Sully.

"Follow me, hurry," she said, already darting away. Sully grabbed hold of the gurney Bandit lay on, steering it after her. Gideon and I took up the rear. We hurried through winding corridors as the Doc led us to the west side of the building. I knew it was west, as the sun was beginning to set, casting a golden hue all around us. I kept an eye out for those cameras that had caught me out before, but the Doc knew her way and avoided anything that would alert them to our presence. Finally, we arrived outside a door marked "Genesis." Sully and Gideon looked grim.

"We're here," Sully said. It was clear by the expressions on their faces that they must have already been through here on the way to save Bandit. The Doc came to the same conclusion, I think as she didn't bother to ask how he knew. She opened the door, then propped it open with a chair.

"Any sign of them, you shout and we'll go," she said.

Sully nodded. "Just be quick." To my and Sully's surprise, Gideon handed him his gun. Sully didn't make a big deal of it, but he knew this was a big move on Gideon's part; it wasn't that long ago that Sully was Public Enemy Number One. Gideon must've known that Sully hadn't forgotten his early treatment of him, as his cheeks were starting to flush with embarrassment.

In typical Sully fashion, however, he simply stated, "Thanks."

I snuck Bandit one last look, then followed Gideon into Genesis... and was immediately, painfully, struck by how many trapped dogs there were. I saw the tablets attached to each cage, but there wasn't time for me to explore. Gideon and the Doc were already sprinting to the far end of the room. I guess we were starting there first.

I reached a cage where a tiny Pomeranian was trembling. It ran to the back of the cage, obviously terrified of human contact. I had to grit my teeth to stop the wave of rage building in me. The cage had a simple bolt on it. No lock. I drew the bolt back and flung open the door. The dog whimpered, staring at me with fear-filled eyes, trying desperately to back herself further into the cage.

"It's OK pup, I'm here to save you," I said. It still wouldn't leave, not used to being offered freedom. I reached my hand in, meaning to take her by the scruff of her neck, but something amazing happened. As my hand came near her nose, she sniffed and suddenly, she licked my hand as the fear vanished. At first, I couldn't understand it, but then I realized what it was - she could smell Bandit on it! She could smell a happy dog and knew I couldn't be bad! I called out to her again.

"Come, heel." Hearing the encouragement in my voice, the dog ran out of the cage. Triumphant, I started on the next cage where a giant Doberman sat. This time when I went to persuade him to leave, I had assistance. The Pomeranian barked short, clipped barks at him. He pricked up his ears, listening, then came out without any urging from me. I was amazed but had no time to marvel at this display of communication, having already made my way to the next cage. From the corner of my eye, I could see Gideon and the Doc frantically doing the same.

"It's taking too long," Sully called suddenly from the hallway. I could hear the frustration in his voice. It must have been awful, him standing there watching us but not able to help. Abruptly, he wheeled the gurney into the room — but only just past the door, in case he needed to leave quickly — and limped into the room with us. By now there were some thirty dogs running loose as Sully started flinging open the cages. It was total chaos.

I was breathless, my lungs taking a pounding from the franticness of it all. My fingers were starting to feel sore where they were being rubbed by the metal of the locks, but I soldiered on — thinking of the dogs, yes, but if I were honest, mostly of Bandit. The longer we took in here, the more danger he was in. We had to do this quickly so we could get out of there.

We worked fast as a team. In no time at all, I glanced up to see we already had most of the cages opened. There were dogs EVERY-WHERE, but noticeably, after their initial communication, they were now silent. It was like they knew we needed to be quiet. I wondered if any of these dogs were as intelligent as Bandit, but then I remembered they couldn't be, otherwise, Forbes would have cut their heads open too.

That one thought gave me a second wind. I worked faster.

As we were reaching the finish line, alarms suddenly peeled overhead. The Doc called out, panicked.

"They found Forbes! Hurry!" she yelled.

Instinctively, I started running for Bandit while the others continued freeing the last of the dogs. Grabbing the gurney, I started steering him back into the hallway, but suddenly guards appeared, blocking my path!

"SULLY!" I screamed.

135

CHASE

The guards rushed towards me. All eight of them.

The others looked over and froze across the room from me. Sully had the gun, but he couldn't take out all of them at once, and stupidly, I was so panicked, I couldn't think straight. There was nothing I could do to stop them.

Then something miraculous happened.

The freed dogs bounded over, forming a barrier between the guards, Bandit, and me. Baring their teeth, the dogs — who were previously so scared, they wouldn't leave their cages — now turned into vicious animals. Snarling, saliva dripped from their jaws as they growled at the guards warningly. The guards stopped dead in their tracks. Though each had a weapon, there were far too many dogs for them to take on. They were at a complete standstill.

Not so, us. "Chase, this way!" The good doc called. I spun the gurney around and sprinted for her. She was standing by another door, Gideon beside her. Sully rushed up to greet me and took over the handling of the gurney. Together we ran for the door the Doc now held open. Seeing us escaping, however, one of the guards took aim at us.

SSSSSSssnap.

A bullet shot towards me, whistling through the air, narrowly missing the top of my head to impale itself into the wall which exploded behind me. Before I had time to react, the dogs flew at the guards. Round after round of panicked shots were fired. A dog whined, then fell down, blood pouring from a gaping wound, but was immediately replaced by another dog, now savagely attacking the guard who had killed his fellow canine. It was carnage. I wanted to help, but there was nothing much I could do.

But then I saw the gas canisters. They were dotted around the room, used for some horrible purpose or another.

I pointed at them. Sully caught my gesture. It didn't take him any time to know what I was thinking. He nodded.

"Gideon," he called out. "Take over Bandit!"

Gideon shot him a questioning look but ran to replace Sully all the same. We split up to gather as many of the canisters as we could. Sully pointed to a point in the center of the room and dumped his canisters there. I followed suit as Sully threw the lab coat he was still wearing on top of the mound.

By now, the dogs had torn their way through several of the guards. Only two were still standing, still fighting, but it was a losing battle. The second from last guard was suddenly overcome by dogs, disappearing beneath them. Seeing this, the last guard turned abruptly and ran away. I took a grim comfort in this small victory.

"Dogs!" I called out, "Well done. This way!" I urged them through the door where Gideon and the Doc were waiting on the other side.

Sully found a bottle of isopropyl alcohol, which he poured onto the material. I remembered from chem class that isopropyl alcohol was flammable and could be used as an accelerant.

Holding the bottle, he ran through the room, making his way to the fire alarm, where he smashed the safety glass and pulled the lever. I was momentarily confused by his actions. Why was he warning them what we were about to do? As if he heard my unasked question, he explained. "They don't all deserve to die..."

As alarms shrieked overhead, I saw them now. Hundreds of people. Lab coats and cleaners and office staff, all racing for safety.

Sully removed a lighter from his pocket and spoke fast.

"When I light this thing, we may have only seconds before it blows," he said. "The three of you need to leave now to get a head start. I'll catch up with you."

I shook my head at him. "But Sully, you can't."

"I'm the fastest runner, Chase. Go, I'll be fine," he said. His expression was soft, but I could see resignation there too. Somewhere in the back of his mind, he knew the odds weren't good.

"No, you're not. Not with that leg." I pointed to his gunshot wound, which he had obviously forgotten about. He blinked at me, uncomprehending. "You can barely walk without help, much less run."

Sully opened his mouth, but couldn't come up with a logical argument. I spoke quickly before he could stop me. "You have to stay alive. Bandit still needs your help. And Zeb needs Gideon. And the dogs need the doc. I'm the only one who's dispensable." Even as I said the words, a gnawing hole opened up in my stomach when I realized the truth of them.

But Sully took me by the shoulders suddenly. "No, you're not Chase! Don't you ever say that again!" As if to prove how much he meant it, he crushed me to his chest. I could feel another sob rise up in my throat and had to pull myself away before I gave in to it completely.

"Guys... we need to move!" came Gideon's panicked voice. He looked equally unhappy by this new plan, but there wasn't any other choice. It made no sense for us all to risk our lives. Reluctantly, Sully handed me the lighter.

"You don't stop for anyone, understand? Once you light this, you run like the wind," Sully commanded. "I mean it, Chase. I've lost enough family this year, I'm not losing another one."

I nodded, not trusting myself to speak. Sully dropped a kiss on the top of my head and tore himself away. I swore there were tears in his eyes.

Then, despite the fact that my heart felt like it was being broken in two, I watched as they all left me behind.

136

SULLY

The Doc took us down into a basement where rusty pipes lined a maze of corridors.

The place was dark and dingy, lit only by aged lamps spaced at three-foot intervals. All the money Forbes spent didn't reach down here it seemed. We hurried after the Doc, running for what seemed like days but was probably only seconds. I couldn't stop seeing Chase in my head.

We shouldn't have left her!

The thought screamed in my mind until my ears pounded. There was a crushing tightness in my chest that had been there since the second I'd had to force myself to leave Chase. She'd looked so lost, so small, standing there.

It was a ridiculous plan. Why did they ever think it would work?! A few times, I turned to go back, but as if sensing my turmoil, Gideon had grabbed me by the arm and dragged me away.

I lost all sense of time. I shuffled after the others with only the pain in my leg keeping me grounded. After what seemed an eternity in the darkness, I saw a dim opening of light up ahead. We burst through into the fresh air with renewed rigor where I was struck by how dark it had gotten. The tip of the sun was barely visible on the horizon, the encroaching night approaching fast.

We had made it.

But no time to celebrate. We ran with the dogs to a safe distance away and waited.

Why hadn't Chase set the thing off yet?

What if something had gone wrong?

What if that last guard had brought more thugs back with him? What if Chase was lying dead and I would never see her again...

It felt like I was in the midst of a heart attack. Gideon paced as the Doc checked on Bandit, who still hadn't woken up. She pressed a finger high on the inner side of his thigh and felt for a pulse, nodding, happy with whatever she found. I felt a small fraction of my tension lessen. At least that was something. I was just wondering what the hold up was, when an almighty explosion went off, shaking the very ground we were standing on.

That was it. Chase had set the canisters off. A bright orange plume of fire sprang up into the night, illuminating the area for what seemed like miles. Windows shattered, destroyed by the soaring heat. I stared into the dark tunnel, straining my eyes, willing with every ounce of my being for Chase to appear.

"Come on, come on..." I mumbled.

After the longest time, something moved in the tunnel. A dark shape. It was so slight, I thought my eyes were deceiving me. But then a figure appeared, lurching forward, coughing up lungfuls of smoke. The face was blackened with soot, but I recognized her anyway. Sprinting forward, ignoring the pain that shot up my leg, I crossed the distance between us and hugged Chase tight.

"What, you wait for a bus to get here?" I said.

She coughed again in answer but grinned at me. "Just keeping you on your toes."

"What now?" Gideon asked. The Doc hesitated, thinking fast.

"We can't take my car, they'll have it surrounded by now," she said.

"Is there anything else around here?" Chase asked, gulping in large mouthfuls of air. The Doc nodded and pointed.

"There's a gas station and a drive-in burger place around two blocks away. There should be cars you can acquire."

I wasn't the only one who noticed the way she said "you". We turned to her, concerned.

"You're not coming with us?" I asked.

She shook her head, eyes shining with regret. "I need to see these dogs are safe. They can't go with you, so I'll have to lead them away."

"But where will you go?" Chase asked.

"I have friends, organizations I can contact who will help. I'll see to it that these dogs are rounded up and adopted into good families. It's the least I owe them." She stopped, her voice cracking. "Thank you for your help. I hope... I hope Bandit is OK."

Chase and I both took in her use of the name Bandit. With a small smile, she spun on her heel and ran the opposite way to them, calling out to the dogs. Some of them followed her, but others cocked their heads at us as if confused.

Chase pointed after her.

"Go with her. She'll keep you safe," she told them.

I didn't know if they really understood her or not, but they ran after her.

And then, for the third time that day, we found ourselves running for our lives.

137

CHASE

My lungs felt like they were drowning in smoke, but otherwise, I felt pretty great. Platinum Industries was burning to the ground, the dogs were free, and we were on our way home. Not a bad day's work.

The gas station and drive-in Dr. Robins mentioned loomed up ahead. I spotted it easily since there wasn't much around these parts. Sully was weary, sure that the drive-in and gas station served PI staff more than anyone else. We had to be careful. It wouldn't do to get caught now when we were so close to freedom.

Approaching the parking lot, Sully scanned the area until his eyes fell upon an old — and to my eyes — barely standing Range Rover. It was empty. Its owner probably inside, feasting on a happy meal.

"That one," Sully pointed at the car.

I frowned at his choice. "You don't think maybe something more new and comfortable?"

But Sully shook his head. "Too conspicuous. Besides, the owner is likely to care less about a rust bucket like this."

Gideon and I nodded and followed him there. Sully tried the doors — locked. He started searching the ground for a rock to smash the window with when Gideon stopped him.

"I've still got my lock picks," he said. I was confused, not understanding this exchange, but Sully stepped back to let him do his thing. He slipped the tools inside the lock, twisting it in a series of directions, feeling for the right moment. The lock sprung open, much to my astonishment.

"You have got to teach me that," I said.

Sully knew, as the adult, he really should dissuade them from such criminal activities, but the usefulness of the skill couldn't be denied. And truth be known, he wanted to learn how to do it too. Only for emergencies, though, of course.

Gideon opened the door and climbed inside. A jacket had been dumped carelessly on the backseat and there were a few cans of coke in the footwell, but the car was otherwise empty. In the trunk, Gideon came up with a toolbox, blankets, and the usual car maintenance items one found in a vehicle. But what he couldn't find were the keys.

I folded a blanket and laid it over the backseat. Sully carefully lifted Bandit from the gurney and set him on top of the blanket.

"So, you know how to hot-wire the thing too?" Sully asked hopefully. Gideon shook his head, however.

"I just broke into vehicles, I never stole them," came his reply. My ears pricked up at this bit of information, a fact Sully seemed to notice with some discomfort. I was searching the car for something, anything that would help, when opening the glove compartment, I suddenly grinned.

"Jackpot." I sat back, a cell phone in my hand.

"What're you going to do, call AAA for help? Couldn't we just use Bandit's iPad for that?" said Gideon.

I was already busy pressing buttons.

"No stupid, it's out of charge."

"So what're you doing with the phone?" he asked again.

"I'm going to show you how this is done," I replied, confident. Moments later, I held up the phone.

"Look, here's a video showing you exactly how to hot-wire an old car."

Sully looked down at the phone's screen and goddamn if I wasn't right.

YouTube.

What an invention.

138

CHASE

We drove through the night.

I kept watch by Bandit's side, hoping he would wake, but Sully had said it was a big operation and he needed rest. He said I shouldn't worry. The length of time he was sleeping meant nothing.

I wasn't sure I believed him.

Gideon drove while Sully sat shotgun. It wasn't until we got into the car that Sully had collapsed, unable to move. He'd been forcing himself to continue despite his injury, but now that we were safe, he just sat, keeping watch in case our stolen vehicle was flagged up. There didn't seem to be much crime in these parts to generate any concern, however, or the cops were all asleep. Either way, our drive passed in relative calm. I, however, had had two cans of coke on an empty stomach, so I was on a nervous buzz from the caffeine high.

Sully kept the radio tuned to a news station. We figured if there was an arrest warrant out for our motley crew, we'd soon be hearing about it over the airwaves. I was starting to feel the beginnings of my sugar crash when we finally arrived back in Montpelier. And with a pang of deep shame, I remembered about Sully's dad. I'd been so consumed with fear for Bandit that I'd completely forgotten about his dad and the condition we'd left his house in.

We drove up to the ranch. Police tape formed the morbid outline of deceased people on the ground, though the bodies themselves had been moved. The bullet-riddled vehicles had been towed, and a tent now enshrouded the barn to contain DNA and forensics. Gideon parked the car and turned off the ignition. Sully took one end of the blanket, and Gideon the other. Stretching it taunt, they lifted Bandit out of the car. I hurried on ahead.

"Zeb? Are you here?!" I called out without thinking.

"Chase?" came his relieved voice, answering from his bedroom.

I ran in to find him propped up in bed. And he wasn't alone. Sam, our singing, hitch-hike driver, sat next to him wearing a Sheriff's outfit. Seeing me, her mouth fell open.

"Why, Bella. Hello again."

139

SULLY

Hearing voices, I hurried to my father's room, but the last thing I expected to see was Sam again. I blinked at her stupidly, gaping at the outfit she now wore.

"You're a Sheriff?" I asked.

Sam nodded, tipping an invisible hat. Seeing Bandit held between them, Sam rose out of her chair.

"Why do I get the feeling I haven't been given the whole story?" she said. Zeb stared at the two of them, frowning.

"You know each other?"

"I gave them a ride on their way here." She looked at me. "You're Zeb's son?"

Gently, I laid Bandit onto a couch, throwing cushions to the ground in front of him in case the dog rolled off in his sleep.

"Yeah." I didn't trust myself to speak further, unsure what was happening right now, of what Zeb might have told her.

"So your father isn't dead after all," she said this wryly, with an arch of an eyebrow. I had the decency to look embarrassed off Zeb's glare.

"Zeb here explained about the attack, but he hasn't said who they were or why they came after you. Apparently, he doesn't know. I'm inclined to believe differently."

"You hear that, Jake? She's calling me a liar to my face." Zeb's words were fighting, but there was a sparkle in his eyes. He liked her, I could tell. Still unsure what to reveal, I tried for distraction.

"What happened to the men who attacked us?"

"Dead. All of them. Damndest thing too, none of them carrying any ID. It's gonna be awhile till we can find out who they were." She studied our faces, one by one, trying to get to the truth, but neither I nor the kids would cave. Eventually, Sam settled her gaze on Chase.

"So what's your real name when you're not plagiarizing Twilight characters?" she asked. Chase flushed, called out. Sam went on, "I have nieces. They've made me watch that trash some six or seven times."

Chase hesitated as if wanting to lie, but must have sensed it wouldn't do any good. "Chase," she finally answered.

Sam nodded thanks and turned her attention to Bandit. "What happened there? That's a real nasty wound on his head."

As Chase plugged in the depleted iPad, preparing for a possible test of Bandit's skills, I was trying to think of a believable explanation, when two things happened simultaneously.

One, Bandit stirred, waking up.

And two, Forbes appeared in the doorway.

140

CHASE

I didn't know where to look first.

Bandit was finally waking up, but there was Forbes, pointing some kind of a military rifle at us, eyes bright with madness.

"You escaped," was all I managed to say.

Forbes glared at me, triumphant.

"You thought your little fire would kill me? Think again," he said.

Sully made a move towards him, but Forbes immediately swung his gun at him.

"Do not move, Mr. Sullivan. One more step and it will be your last," he warned.

Throughout the exchange, Sam had been watching the whole time, keen eyes assessing the situation. Her hand moved slowly towards the gun clipped onto her belt, but Forbes must have seen the motion.

"I wouldn't do that, Sheriff. Not unless you are prepared for the aftermath," he warned.

Sam stopped immediately, raising both hands over her head. "Sir, I don't know what any of this is about, but if you lower your weapon, we can discuss whatever it is that's bothering you." Her voice was calm, almost pleasant, though I heard the underlying steel there.

Forbes looked at her, expression scathing.

"Oh stop. Your tactics won't work with me. These people destroyed my life's work and stole my future! Now I'm going to take back what's mine, and there's nothing any of you can do to stop it." As he spoke, he waved the rifle around, not a care in the world that it could go off. Like he was playing eeny, meenie, he pointed the gun at each of us, finally settling the sights back on Sam. "Very slowly now Sheriff, I would like you to kick your gun away from you."

Sam nodded and slowly removed the gun from her belt. Bending down, she set the gun on the ground, then kicked it away from her, into the center of the room.

Forbes swung the gun very deliberately to Bandit, who sat up now, shaking his head groggily. I don't know if he meant him any harm or was just getting used to aiming with that gun, but I didn't think at all. I dived for Bandit, shielding his body with my own.

"Bandit, get down!" I cried.

But Bandit didn't move. I landed beside him, fully expecting my insides to be blown apart any minute. However, Forbes didn't shoot, focused intently instead on Bandit's face. He was waiting for his reaction. I rose onto my knees, staring into his eyes.

"Boy. Do you know who I am?" I asked, unable to stop the tremor in my voice. He stared at me blankly. There was no sign of intelligence in those eyes. No hint at all that he recognized me.

With horror, I realized that the Bandit I knew and loved was gone.

141

CHASE

My heart exploded painfully in my chest. At least, that's what it felt like. Bandit looked at me, but there was nothing there that showed he was the same dog I had gone through so much with.

"Bandit?" I cried, broken. He didn't even look at me, gazing around the room in confusion, then at Forbes. Directly at Forbes. It hit me like a sucker punch right then - Bandit wasn't afraid of Forbes. Forbes noticed the same thing as he suddenly started to laugh.

"All that wasted effort, when it seems he's nothing but a dumb dog after all," he guffawed, lowering his gun. Sam was staring at him hard, unmoving, trying to piece everything together, but there wasn't a single one of us who were able to explain. We were all too busy grieving. I reached out gently and took Bandit's face in my hands.

"Hey, fella. It's OK. All that's important is now that the tumor's gone, you won't get sick again. I love you. You're my best friend."

Realizing he had won, that there was nothing worse he could do to us, Forbes turned away, leaving, uninterested in us any longer.

Bandit barked once.

I froze as that simple sound caused hope to flare inside. By the door, Forbes stopped dead. He turned slowly around, a frown beginning to appear over his features.

My bag was lying beside me, I took out the stylus and handed it to Bandit who took it gently in his mouth. Then, as we all watched, he very deliberately typed out the words *I LOVE YOU CHASE.*

Overwhelmed with relief and love, I flung my arms around him as Sam looked on, shocked. Gideon was grinning stupidly, Sully had tears in his eyes. Even Zeb was smiling. The only one not happy was Forbes. He stood there, shaking his head. "No... how can this be?"

Sully looked at him, triumphant.

"I'm guessing even without the tumor, his brain re-organized itself so he could stay intelligent. Nature is nothing but prolific when it comes to adapting. Funny how a simple dog can do what you can't, not even with all the billions you own."

"*WOOF!*" Came Bandit's timely response. His tongue was hanging out goofily again, and he couldn't stop licking my face. Having twisted in the knife, Sully turned his back on Forbes to fuss Bandit... which is how he didn't see the other man looking suddenly enraged. He didn't see Forbes raise his gun and point it at Sully's back.

But I did.

The world slowed to a crawl as adrenaline kicked in. I saw his fingers close in on the trigger. Without thinking, I dived for Sam's gun - on the floor in front of me - took aim, and fired. The recoil almost snapped my arm off. I was flung backward, but as I hit my head on the floor, I saw the muzzle flash tear out of the chamber as the bullet tore into Forbes' chest. A look of astonishment appeared on his face. He staggered back, blinking in disbelief, as blood blossomed over his shirt. Falling against the wall, he touched his chest. Seeing the blood on his fingertips, he slid down, unable to breathe, unable to take it all in.

Sam jumped into action, bounding over to snatch his rifle, which had clattered to the ground. She pressed her hand onto his chest.

"Don't you dare die. I want to see you do time for your crimes," she said grimly, but it was a losing fight. The color had already drained from his face, now encased in a sheen of sweat.

At the sound of the gunshot, Sully had looked over at me, at the gun in my trembling hands, still pointed at Forbes. It took a moment, but then it must have sunk in, how close he had come to meeting the reaper. He rushed over to me, holding me tight.

"It's alright now baby girl, everything is alright now."

I dropped the gun and wrapped my arms around him, bawling like a baby.

142

SULLY

The following hours passed by in a blur.

After Chase had saved my life, Sam had called in the cavalry, who arrived just in time to witness Forbes's demise. I didn't have faith in the system like Sam did and was mightily relieved when the paramedics announced his time of death.

Justice had prevailed.

Sam assured us that Chase would not be facing any charges. There were five allowable witnesses to testify that it was self-defense.

The coroner removed Forbes's body, and we were left to recover while Sam personally oversaw our statements. Still, it took a while to corroborate our reports, seeing as the words "super-intelligent dog" couldn't make it onto the document.

So much had happened in the last few hours, but one thing was startling: I was surprised how happy I was to see Sam again. As she worked at collating our reports, as she was told the whole story, I was taken by her confident yet compassionate attitude. She was a trooper too. After Bandit's initial words, he came right up to her and introduced himself. Bandit shocked us by telling her he liked her as she was *a good person*. Sam had seemed tickled pink by this.

I found myself in the kitchen next, setting the table while Gideon cooked, assisted by Sam. People were hungry, and it seemed natural for us to eat together. Chase sat with Bandit on the floor. She hadn't left his side since his return, and I couldn't really blame her. The two had been conversing furiously since Forbes's death as Chase explained everything that had happened following his capture.

Sam's laughter suddenly cut through my thoughts. It was warm and bubbly, and I wanted to hear that sound over and over.

"Soup's up," Gideon called out, carrying a pan of meatballs in tomato sauce to the table. I headed to the cooker where Sam lifted the lid off a pot of spaghetti.

"Here, let me," I offered and drained the water into the sink as Sam held back the spaghetti with a wooden fork.

"It's all about the teamwork," she said as she winked. I found myself noticing her dimples for the first time. *Cute*, I thought to myself. *Very cute.*

As we sat around the table, I saw how happy Chase looked. Surrounded by people who cared about her, Chase looked like the kid who'd woken up on Christmas morning and found the tree surrounded by presents. It brought a lump to my throat when I realized she'd likely never experienced that before.

I made a mental note to get the biggest Christmas tree I could find that year and to flood it with presents.

143

CHASE

S itting around that table, stuffing our faces with the best spaghetti and meatballs I'd ever tasted in my life, I was feeling pretty amazing. Everyone was laughing and joking, and I noticed the way Sully kept sneaking looks at Sam. It made me feel warm inside. He'd been in such a bad way over Emma when I'd met him, but now it looked like he was finally coming out of it. And you know, Bandit's just the best judge of character, and he liked her a whole ton.

I had a feeling we'd be seeing a lot more of Sam in the future.

Since we'd arrived back, Gideon seemed different too. He wasn't argumentative or angry anymore. In fact, it seemed like he had something he wanted to say to me because I kept catching him watching me with this serious look on his face. Course, it could've been the way I was stuffing those meatballs into my face, but I'm telling you, they were so good!

When we were done eating, Zeb took off for a nap. His body had gone through a war and he needed rest in order to recover. Sully's leg had been patched up by the paramedics. Apparently, he'd been lucky as no major damage was done. It would hurt like crazy for a while, though. And he'd likely need further checkups and maybe some rehabilitation.

Sully and Sam went outside for a beer on the porch while Gideon and I cleaned up the kitchen. I didn't mind in the least. Here's a little-known secret: I like housework. I know that's not exactly exciting, is it? But housework is calming, and you get to see instant results. I don't know, guess I'm just weird.

I was washing up while Gideon took up drying duty since he knew where everything lived (although the place was still pretty shot up, so it'd need a heap more work to get it resembling anything like normal again). I caught Gideon looking at me strangely again, but this time I decided to call him out on it.

"What?" I demanded, throwing the sponge into the sink. "Why do you keep looking at me funny?"

He blinked, taken aback by my question, then a slow flush crept onto his cheeks and down his neck. It was quite adorable, to be honest, not that I'd ever admit it.

"I just er... wanted to apologize. For my behavior before," he began. I don't know what I expected him to say, but that wasn't it. I stared at him blankly as he continued.

"When you first got here, I was pretty rude. And then the thing with the shooting. I'd put two and two together about Sully and came up with five. You were just collateral damage."

"Collateral damage?" I said. "Wow, you sure know how to make a girl feel special." It was a few beats before my words sank in. I sighed, exasperated. "I already knew all of that on account of me not being brain-damaged, but thanks for the apology."

He shrugged awkwardly, shuffling on his feet. I could see his embarrassment as clearly as if he had a neon sign flashing over his head.

"I'm not a jerk, that's all," he finished.

Two barks sounded below us.

We both looked down to find Bandit at our feet, watching us. We burst out laughing as Bandit asked, *"What is so funny?"*

144

CHASE

The days following Forbes's death went past in a blur.

Using her influence, Sam had spun the truth until it became a simple story of how one billionaire, who had lost his mind to dementia, had attacked an innocent family in their home. She kept my name out of it (to protect the child witnesses), and of course, there was no mention of super-intelligent dogs, which suited us just fine.

The report also detailed how Forbes had burned down his own building in an effort to hide the cruel experiments he had been performing on animals. That last bit of information had hit a little too close for comfort, but Sam had said it was there to dissuade any of Forbes's former employees from continuing with the work if they should decide to do so.

While he recovered, Sully had received word from Doc Robins, who had managed to round up the escaped dogs, but now needed help to remove the tumors. The Doc turned up with a team of people who fixed up the barn overnight, converting it into a giant operating theater. They did such a great job that it looked better now than it had originally. With Sully's help, they worked tirelessly to remove the tumors as the dogs were then ferried away to a secret location where they could rehabilitate.

Apparently, the Doc had found many loving families willing to adopt the dogs. I was thrilled for them.

When they'd worked their magic on the last dog, Sully and the Doc came out of the barn. They found us on the porch swing, watching the sunset. This had become a ritual for Bandit and me. He loved the peace and quiet while I just loved being with my best friend. At their approach, we looked up at them.

"All done?" I asked.

Sully nodded, rubbing red-rimmed eyes, tired, but happy.

"That's it. That's the last one," Sully said.

Bandit jumped off the swing onto the ground, tail wagging, as he licked Sully's hand. The Doc bent down to look Bandit in the eyes. Sensing she wanted to speak with him, Bandit forced himself to sit, waiting.

"I'm so sorry for everything you went through. I never wanted that for you. I should've done something sooner. I hope you can forgive me," she said tearfully. Bandit stared at her solemnly, then barked once. *"Woof."* Her face broke into a smile as she stroked him on the head.

"Now that we're done here, what's next for you, Elora?" Sully asked.

She straightened up, turning to face him.

"I'm going traveling. Somewhere I can do some actual good for a change. I'm thinking Africa. They need all the help they can get with the crisis over there," she replied. "Of course, it won't be the same. I'll miss this little guy here, for one."

"He'll be fine," I said. "He has us now."

The Doc smiled. "Yes, he does."

145

SULLY

I saw Elora off, wishing her well on her future travels, and went to talk to Zeb. I'd been doing this for several days now, working on the dogs then popping in to spend time with the old man.

Entering his room, I found Zeb in a recliner, engrossed in the latest James Patterson thriller. My brow raised of its own accord.

"Never thought I'd catch you reading something so mainstream."

"There's only so much Shakespeare one can stomach. Besides, this is good, solid fun," Zeb replied as he stared at me critically.

"How's the wound today?" he asked, already leaning forward to examine it. I turned to give him better access, knowing from experience any refusal would just be ignored.

"Itchy, but it doesn't hurt much anymore."

"Good. That means it's healing," Zeb leaned back, satisfied with my progress. Folding my arms across my chest, I went to study the titles on a stocked bookshelf. "Wow. You've certainly gotten through a lot of his books. Must be what, several hundred of them here?"

"I was stuck in bed for a while after the accident. Amazing how literary one can get when they can't move from their bed," came Zeb's reply. There wasn't a hint of bitterness in his voice, only sadness. I caught it, and for the first time, braved the question that had been playing on my mind now for a while.

"What happened, Dad? How did you end up in a wheelchair?"

Zeb stared out of the window, mind deep in his thoughts. I thought the old coot would ignore the subject as he had so many times before, but then Zeb continued.

"I was drunk. I was furious and broken, and one night, I drowned myself in my sorrows. It was shortly after you left, back in our old townhouse, after many heated words were said. I was so angry at you, but I was also crushed. When I came to my senses, I decided to come after you, but a bottle of vodka and two rums later... Funny how I'd been running up and down those stairs with no trouble at all for some twenty years, except that one night. I missed the top few steps and fell. When I woke up, I was paralyzed."

I was stunned, having never imagined I was the cause of Zeb's accident. And now things fell into place.

"This is why Gideon hated me. He blamed me," I said.

Zeb nodded. "I told him it wasn't your fault, but he never saw it that way. Kid's loyal to the bone. He didn't mean nothing by it."

A thousand thoughts flashed through my mind. All that time I'd spent hating my father when the truth was, we were both as stubborn as each other.

"I'm just glad you're home now, son," Zeb said finally.

I smiled. "I'm glad to be back."

146

SULLY

The sky shone like a dark sapphire.

I lay on my bed, staring out at the sky, thoughts tumbling through my head but at long last, feeling the peace.

Hearing nothing but crickets, I thought about how much my life had changed this past year. Yes, losing Emma was the most bitter blow and something that would probably take years to fully recover from, but being here now, back under my father's roof, knowing both Chase and Bandit were safe, I felt a calm that I hadn't felt since Emma was lying by my side.

I pictured her now, twirling in our yellow living room, paint splattered on her nose and laughing as she chased me with the loaded brush. And for the first time since her death, instead of gnawing grief, I felt only a deep sense of love.

I was still feeling this love when I fell asleep.

147

CHASE

It was a bright and sunny fall day.

Zeb sat on the porch swing, a blanket covering his lap, playing chess with Sully. It looked serious, both of them focused with furrowed foreheads. They'd been at it an hour already. Sully had promised he'd teach me how to play in due course, but seeing how much concentration was needed, I wasn't sure it was something I wanted to try. I'd had just about all the excitement I could take.

Earlier, I overheard Sully make a phone call. And before you say anything, I wasn't snooping. I was getting something from my room when I heard his voice. He was talking to a buddy named Mark. Sounded like they'd had a falling out, but they were patching things up. I was relieved. Sully couldn't have had that many friends to begin with or he wouldn't have thrown everything away for us. Sully had told his friend that he was happy now that he was with his *family*. Isn't it funny how one small word can make you feel so many things? He promised Mark he'd get to meet us all one day. I didn't hear the rest of the conversation, as I'd already headed back outside, feeling guilty at what I'd overheard.

Gideon was tossing a frisbee with Bandit, whose wounds were healing nicely. Ever since our chat, Bandit had taken Gideon under his wing, so to speak. It was like he was waiting for Gideon to come to his senses about me before he would be his friend. It wasn't the same as us, however — Bandit and I were inseparable — but the two were definitely buddies. I appeared on the porch carrying a tray of cookies I'd just baked. The delicious smell of chocolaty goodness wafted over to them as they all turned to stare at me, astonished.

Annoyingly, I could feel my cheeks turning pink.

"What? They're just cookies. No need to make a big deal out of it," I said, embarrassed. Gideon jogged over and grabbed one off the plate. Sniffing it suspiciously, he took a tentative bite.

"It's good. Really good," he confirmed, and suddenly Sully and Zeb wanted one. *Men, right? Jeez.*

"Not you, Fella," I said to Bandit, sniffing around me hopefully. "You get these special non-chocolate ones," I said, sliding a plate of plain cookies under his nose.

Note to reader: in case you didn't know, chocolate is super poisonous to dogs, so don't ever give them any.

Bandit took one delicately into his mouth, reminding me again of that fateful first day when we met. I sat on the floor beside him, munching away, admiring my own baking skills.

"So buddy, now that we can do anything we want, what do you want to do next? We have the whole world in front of us, so go crazy," I asked him.

He cocked his head at me and typed into the iPad.

"A quiz!!! Oh boy, oh boy, oh boy!"

Anything in the world and *that's* what he wanted to do?

Stupid Muttface.

Thank you for reading WANTED.

If you loved this book, then please leave a review to help keep a roof over Jo's head, and also so other readers know to check out Jo's work!

If you know others who might enjoy the series, let them know! You could even tell your local library to get the books so that those on a low or fixed income can enjoy them too.

The more reviews she gets for a book, the faster she prioritises writing more books in that series.

Keep reading for a look at HAUNTED,
the Chase Ryder series Book 2
AND
a special preview of her new series which also features an adorable dog!

HAUNTED, THE CHASE RYDER SERIES
BOOK 2

"What do you do when the past refuses to stay dead and buried?"

Six months have passed since the explosion at Platinum Industries.

For the first time in our lives, Bandit and I knew what it felt like to be with a loving family, and it was a lot like getting to eat a main *and* dessert every day, for every meal (and having starved on the streets for so long, everyone knows how much I like my food).

Things were going great and we were about to celebrate some joyful news when the inexplicable happened: Sully received an impossible message from his past, then my own demons caught up to me. Even Bandit wasn't happy, unable to get the stray we recently rescued to like him. For whatever reason, the two dogs could not get along.

In no time at all, our close unit fragmented as we were each faced with our very worst nightmares until I finally found myself alone and stranded, with Sully nowhere in sight. And Bandit? He'd been dognapped. Taken by someone with evil intentions.

The thought that Bandit could be stuck in a cage again filled my heart with fury, but with my family on the brink of implosion, and our enemy seemingly invisible and one step ahead of us at all times, just how was I going to save him?

Continue the thrilling adventure HERE!

WE'RE NOT DONE YET!

Jo has another series that you might like!
Continue reading for a sneak peek of her new romantic suspense series.

There is love, laughter, suspense, danger, a hot yet tender man, a complicated woman in need of help, and a super adorable dog in every book!

Perfect for fans of Nora Roberts, heartwarming romantic suspense, and dog lovers

(Available as ebook, paperback.
Audiobooks and large print coming soon!)

UNTIL THE STARS DON'T SHINE

SILVER SCREEN SECRETS BOOK 1

A heart-warming Suspenseful Romance for Dog Lovers!

When an ex-marine and his highly trained dog are hired to protect the daughter of a Hollywood star, love was the furthest thing from their minds. But when it becomes clear that she is in danger, how far will he go to save her?

Kane Turner is a simple man who cares nothing for riches. Scarred both physically and mentally from his tours as a marine, all Kane cares about is his bike, beer and dog Bud – and not necessarily in that order. He lives in a trailer on the beach, working security detail for his friend's company, protecting some of the wealthiest (and most super-ficial) people in the world with loyal Bud at his side.

Ask anyone and they'd tell you that Lexi Gray-Rockefeller has it all. The daughter of Hollywood royalty, she's rich, one of the most stunning women in the world with parents who dote on her. Yet Lexi is lonely. All she wants is to work with animals. She doesn't care for the LA lifestyle having struggled to make any lasting relationships:

people are generally too in awe of her family or befriend her only for what they can get.

Following a series of threats, Kane is hired to protect Lexi, yet despite their world of differences the two of them find themselves falling in love. In Kane (and his dog Bud), Lexi has found an authentic soul who doesn't care who her parents are or how wealthy she is, while Lexi is the one person who can seemingly heal Kane's wounds.

When Lexi is kidnapped, Kane only has a short time to save her. Can he find her before time runs out?

Heat level: a hint of steam - nothing graphic.
This book also covers billionaire and military themes.
This is a standalone book with no cliffhangers though you'll get the best experience by reading the series in order.

★★★★★ – *"Charming romance but the dog nearly stole the show! This is one of the best new romances I've read in awhile. I enjoyed it so much I read it through in one-sitting."* - **D. Wise**

★★★★★ – *"How will she and Kane deal with each other? You will HAVE to read this wonderful book to see what happens. As always Jo writes with passion and is so descriptive and thorough you can see everything as it happens. What a wonderful book. AN ABSOLUTE MUST READ!!!"* - **Candy**

★★★★★ – *"There is suspense, drama, danger, kidnapping, a villain... and romance. Great story."* - **Babs**

★★★★★ – *"A well written story that's captivating and pulls you in. The characters are wonderful and the chemistry between them is realistic. You'll be glued to the pages until you finish the book."* - **buzymomof2**

★★★★★ – *"Marvellous romantic suspense with a K-9. I adored the characters in this story. The [dog] Bud does steal many scenes! It is a fast paced suspense that will keep you glued to the end."* - **Amazon Customer**

★★★★★ – *"Fantastic. This is the 1st book I've read written by Joanne Ho; she has done a great job at writing a good book; I can't wait to read more of her books."* - **Jeanne Richardson**

★★★★★ – *"Wow! A captivating and well-written book with an intriguing plot and awesome characters. Love the chemistry between Kane and Lexi."* - **Kindle Customer**

Read the first two chapters of this heart-warming series —>

CHAPTER 1

He pored over the grainy photographs that covered the length of one wall.

Rubbed his eyes that were stinging from hours of staring, hours of working in the airless, dark, and dank room.

Stuck in a haphazard fashion, the photographs overlapped one another, blocking out much of the shot though that was of no importance.

Whether it was the row of snooty shops on Rodeo Drive that he wasn't brave enough to go into, or the grounds of the luxury estate that she called home, he didn't care what was in the background.

Only the person who had been carefully framed in the center of each photograph mattered.

He waited in the near blackness, breath held as he slid the exposed sheet into the tray of developer solution. Picking up the end of the tray, he agitated it, letting the chemical wash over every inch of the sheet.

The acrid smell of the solution stung his nose and often gave him a headache, but there was no other choice: he couldn't have these photographs developed at a store — not if he didn't want to raise alarm bells.

It was a small price to pay for the miracle at hand.

He waited, calmly watching the liquid squish back and forth, knowing that patience was a virtue. It had been a hard lesson to learn as a young boy, but he could see now that he had benefited from it, and while he didn't cherish the memories, he had begrudgingly learned from them.

A picture of himself came into his mind, of a skinny, starving, small-even-for-his-age four-year-old, sucking his thumb and sobbing into his mother's chest.

He hadn't eaten since the night before. When would food be coming? *Patience child,* had always been the answer. *We're all hungry. As soon as we have some money, we'll get food.*

He needed to study, but the lights wouldn't work, why weren't they turning on? *Patience child, we just need the electricity to switch back on... once we've paid the bill.*

After walking hours to get home from school in the pouring rain with shoes whose soles had eroded away, he'd pleaded for a new pair only to be told: *patience child, one day we'll have enough money that you won't ever have to worry about holes in your shoes.*

How well that patience was serving him now.

He stared at the print, his mind playing over those desperately unhappy periods of his childhood as again, he wondered how life could be so unfair to some yet overload others with so many blessings that they couldn't even count them.

He ruminated over his lot, until, after some time had passed, the magic began.

The outline of her hair appeared first.

Thin gray lines that would go on to form the darkest part of the image. Then the skimpy brown bikini she had worn on the day that only just covered her parts. Line by line, section by section, she appeared on the print.

He recalled the moment he had captured her in his lens as if it were yesterday.

It had been a stifling Californian summer's day. Throughout the city, its citizens had taken refuge from the sun's relentless heat however they could. She, of course, utilized her family's spectacular infinity pool that overlooked the ocean.

As usual, she had been on her own.

In all the time he had watched her, outside of her family and two failed short-lived relationships, she never seemed to have many friends. Then again, it wasn't *that* surprising: you only had to dig a little under the surface to uncover what lay beneath.

Despite how often he stared at her, the sight of her beautiful face with that wanton body still caused an unwelcome reaction in him. Feeling the heat surging through, he had to close his eyes and force himself to remember the truth.

Beneath that angelic face lay a monster.

He had studied her for hours as she'd first swam, then sunbathed while reading a screenplay beneath a wide-brimmed straw hat. He'd zoomed in with his camera, hoping to see what had captured her attention so fully. It would have been fortuitous if it was something he could use to expose just how two-faced she was, but the lens on his camera hadn't been up to the job.

The one he'd wanted to use was far too expensive for him to afford.

His stomach clenched at the thought, at how unfair it was that she had everything handed to her on a silver platter — not even silver... gold — while he'd had to struggle quite so much.

She had never starved or worried about what she could and couldn't afford. He doubted she'd ever even considered the price of a purchase, not with the kind of wealth her parents commanded. He didn't know the exact number that they were worth, but Entertainment Tonight had listed it in the region of nine figures.

And their *home*?

It was outrageously opulent, dripping in riches. There was even a two-story outbuilding that was bigger than the biggest dwelling in his neighborhood, a spare building that he knew the family never used.

It was especially heinous when you took into account that only three of them actually lived there. The state of California commanded one of the highest rates of homelessness, yet three people lived on a property that could have easily housed several hundred if not *thousands* on its grounds.

Life was terribly unfair, but made even worse with people like her.

Dragging himself out of his thoughts, he stared down at the fully developed image in the tray.

Using a pair of rubber-ended tongs, he lifted the print carefully, rinsed it under water, then submerged it into the stop bath. This step would stop the image from developing any further. Then it went into a tray of fixer. One more much longer rinse and it was done.

Squeegeeing off the remaining water on the surface of the print, he hung it up to dry beside the dozen of other prints he'd already developed that day. They moved gently in the breeze caused by the fan he had brought in to speed up the process.

Wiping his hands on his pants until they were dry, he sat on the stool by the bench he'd crudely made using pieces of driftwood he'd found and bound together.

A large brown envelope waited for his attention in front of a line of wooden figures that he'd painstakingly carved by hand. He liked that they seemed to be watching him as he worked, his little silent friends. *They* never had a bad word to say about him.

They never said a word at all.

Carefully opening the mouth of the envelope, he shook its contents onto the bench. Black alphabetical letters that he'd pre-cut from magazines and newspapers floated out, stockpiled for just this purpose.

This would be the third note he was sending to them. With each one, he was becoming better and better at making them.

A jolt of excitement shot through him as he thought of how his plan was coming together.

Using his whittling knife, he arranged the letters onto a sheet of white paper, gluing them down until the two sentences were formed. Leaning back from the bench, he held up the sheet of paper to the red light that was suspended from the ceiling and read over his work.

You act like you're so nice, but I know the truth. And I'm going to make you sorry. I'm going to make you ALL sorry.

His mouth curled into a sneer.

Turning back to the wall of photographs, he glared at her many oblivious faces, from all the times he had watched her without her knowing.

Soon...

Soon he would make her pay.

CHAPTER 2

He had just come off a trying assignment and was looking forward to some R&R when the call had come, smack in the middle of what constituted packing.

A few shorts, his trusty camo shirts, briefs, and cargo pants as beat up and put through the ringer as he was, were being shoved into a canvas backpack when his phone had buzzed.

The melodic rap by D'angelo that had been blasting from the old school sound deck that provided his one luxury in life stopped playing, replaced by that annoying ringtone that seemed to reverberate around the tin walls of the Airstream Travel Trailer he called home.

Though it was only thirty feet long, the trailer had everything he needed for full-time living: a bedroom with a double bed that connected to a small but serviceable living room that also doubled as his kitchen and office, with a shower room and laundry at the other end of the trailer. And it came with one of the most glorious views of the Malibu ocean that he would never be able to afford in his lifetime if he wasn't living in a mobile home.

Truly, it offered the best of both worlds. And the icing on the cake? When he inevitably felt that siren call to move, he could simply shift his home and his life by attaching it to his truck and hauling it off to the next place.

The ringing continued its insistent call, interrupting his thoughts. Lips turning down with disapproval, he looked for the phone but couldn't locate it anywhere near him.

"Bud," he called out. "Fetch my phone."

The German Shepherd who had been snoozing by the bed sprang up and raced into the lounge, letting the rings guide him. When he padded back, the phone was gripped carefully between those two strong jaws of his. Intelligence shone from his brown eyes as he looked up at his owner for approval.

"Thanks, Boy."

He took the phone from him and ran a hand over his dog's smooth head in the way that he liked. Bud chuffed happily, lifting first one paw, then the other before returning to his position by the foot of the bed, circling round in the way that dogs do before lying back down.

The man stared down at his phone, at the name of the lowlife who dared to interrupt this most holy of times — that of vacation.

He'd worked long and hard, and this downtime was due him. People knew better than to bother him when he could almost taste the grit in his teeth and feel the desert air whistling through his hair.

It was going to be him, his bike, his trusty dog and the unforgiving outback of the desert.

Which was just how he liked it.

His eyes slid over a shelf of framed photographs and knick-knacks collected from a lifetime of experiences. Landed on the only picture he had kept from high school, back when he hadn't been half as tough or rugged as he was now.

The two teens in the picture were skinny things, all arms and legs with glasses and unfortunate zits that were the cause of many a beating from the jocks that'd had their run of the school.

After a pretty miserable childhood being bullied and living under the roof with a drunk for a father, and a drug addict for a mom, when

Kane Turner suddenly grew two feet — seemingly each way — he'd fled to the marines as soon as was feasibly possible.

Disciplined, driven, and relieved to be getting out of his crummy home situation, he advanced up the ranks quickly due to formidable physical skills and an almost sixth sense for danger.

Didn't matter if he was in the sketchier parts of downtown or conducting a dawn patrol in Afghanistan, Kane always knew moments before contact with a hostile was initiated. It was this uncanny ability that had kept him alive throughout each of his tours when so many of his brothers had fallen by the wayside.

Despite being so good at his job, he never enjoyed it.

It was in his blood to protect and serve, but he didn't like fighting people, didn't like hurting them, however misguided they were. Still, he would have stayed a marine if it wasn't for the devastating loss that occurred in Operation Condor.

It was supposed to have been a routine expedition.

A simple patrol in a small town in the middle of nowhere where only a handful of people lived. They were to show their faces, let the locals see that the US controlled the region when an IED went off as they neared.

The car ahead had flipped over, though luckily, Kane had felt that tingle in the back of his neck, that flutter in his stomach that had warned him something was amiss.

Slowing down his vehicle as he scouted the area, he had been far enough back that the bomb only did surface damage. The wounds he sustained would leave a few wicked scars, though they were nothing compared to the devastation his marine brothers faced.

Suffering through weeks of agony, their injuries finally proved too great as a number of them died one after the other. Those who clung to survival did so by a thread: tormented by PTSD, they only made it through the day by medicating themselves with whatever was available.

And those were the lucky ones.

Unable to work or return to normal civilian life, a few became homeless, sleeping on the streets before vanishing off the face of the earth completely.

Kane hadn't wanted that for himself.

He hadn't survived his childhood to let that be the end of his story. He knew he had to quit before his number came up.

After he returned to civilian life, Kane flitted around from city to city, working various manual jobs from construction to bartender to a stint as an Uber driver, until his high school buddy Wilson had called, offering to employ him.

The class nerd, Wilson had gone on to make a major success of himself and now ran one of the most sought-after VIP security services. Having heard that Kane was struggling, he wanted to help the one person who hadn't made his life a misery at school.

The money was decent, and it was fun to mix with the Hollywood elite who were as eccentric, as out of control as a person would expect. From well-organized "sleepovers" featuring some of the country's best-known faces to basement S&M dungeons, Kane had seen it all.

Despite some of the crazy things he'd witnessed and how he could likely fund the rest of his life if he would only pen a book detailing the madness he'd been privy to, Kane was a consummate professional and would never betray his employer's trust.

This kind of integrity was a quality often missing in LA, and so he found his services in constant demand, particularly when the employer happened to be a bored and lonely housewife.

Many fell for his brooding good looks, while others simply loved the challenge.

Kane frequently found himself in uncomfortable situations where he would catch his client walking around in nothing more than a thong and a smile.

He never took advantage of the moment.

The women who threw themselves at him? He never found them attractive. He didn't like their too-tight facial features so often caused by surgery, or the voluminous breasts that never moved. The fake tans made him think of overcooked frankfurters on a grill. In fact, he hated fakeness in general, which was why, although he was seen as a catch, he still hadn't found The One.

Not that he believed in that kind of thing.

Having seen what a loveless marriage could do to two people, he had sworn off the idea. This was just as well, as none of his previous relationships had been at all successful with an average lifespan of only a few months — if that.

He knew he was far from perfect, but he'd considered himself above average in many respects and most of the women he came across tended to agree... until they came home with him for the first time.

Apparently, his tiny tin home didn't hold quite the same appeal for them as it did him.

After the first night, many didn't bother returning while the ones who hung in there he would inevitably find fault with.

What was it about the women in this town that made them all so focused on fame and money?

He'd lost count of how many celebrity parties he'd worked at where women initiated conversations with potential "love" interests by asking them what job they had or how much square footage their house contained.

It all left a bad taste in his mouth.

Having finished a trying job with a diva pop star who'd acted very badly when Kane had rejected her drunken advances, he had packed a bag and was ready to take off on his Harley for a week in the mountains. Now, the one person in the world he couldn't ignore was calling.

"Wilson," Kane answered his phone. "I'm literally walking out the door so this had better be good..."

"I know, but this just came through," Wilson responded with uncustomary excitement.

Mack "Stonewall" Rockefeller, the well-known movie mogul who owned Pinnacle studios, was receiving death threats. This wasn't unusual in and of itself — the rich and famous were always being targeted by money grabbers and weirdos. However Wilson was particularly concerned as the threats were coming from the same source...

And they seemed to be escalating.

The Rockefellers had a daughter who they had managed to keep out of the limelight for most of her life. Not much was publicly known about her other than she was about to turn twenty-five and an enormous yet "private" party was being thrown to celebrate the occasion.

Wilson explained how bad an idea that would be: Stonewall would essentially be opening his home to thousands of strangers. If anyone wanted to do something to them, there wouldn't be a more perfect opportunity.

Stonewall and his movie star wife Mandy were resisting, however, and were in the process of finalizing the firm they would go with for the job. In particular, they were looking for a bodyguard for their daughter. The literal King and Queen of Hollywood, Wilson had fought for their business for years. If he was able to win this contract, it would set up the company for life.

"So what's the problem?" Having had all this explained to him, Kane wasn't sure the point of his call.

"I'm stuck on this detail in DC right now and none of my usual men are cutting it. I need someone different, someone who might shake things up."

Kane ran through what he'd been told about the family in his head. "They sound high maintenance and I just got done with a job like that."

"Just meet them. Talk to them like you would any other client. If they don't go for you, fair enough. But I'm telling you, every firm I know is fighting to land this gig. It would mean a tremendous amount if we could win the account."

Kane glanced over at Bud. His ears were pricked high as he listened keenly, picking up on his reluctance.

"I already told Bud we were going. You know I hate disappointing him."

As if he understood, Bud sighed, staring at him with sad,

accusatory eyes designed to pull at his heart. He tossed a rubber bone at him that Bud snatched out of the air with his jaws.

"Tell him there's a giant marrow bone in it for him if he'll wait just a little longer." Wilson sounded hopeful, knowing his pleas were working.

"Tell him yourself," Kane grumbled, shaking his head. He looked longingly out of a window at the faint outline of the mountains that seemed to be moving further away into the distance.

"Thanks man. Appreciate it. Get the job and you can have a long break after. As long as you want."

"Don't forget the marrow bones," Kane reminded him, determined that Bud would not lose out.

"I'll have a box shipped over," Wilson laughed. "You'll need to get there this afternoon. Go flash them some of the Kane charm. Clara will collate a file and send it over to you ASAP."

Clara was Wilson's assistant. She'd worked with him for close to five years now. She wasn't the quickest, but Wilson swore she was loyal and could be trusted with anything.

Kane hung up the call and sent Bud an apologetic look.

"So... it looks like we're going to have to put a pin on that vacation I promised you..."

Bud responded by groaning and covering his eyes with a paw.

"Don't be such a drama queen. At least you've got bones coming."

At that, Bud perked right up. His tail thumped against the laminate floor tiles.

"Let's grab a walk before we head over there. I've got a feeling this job is going to be rough."

Barking with the kind of excitement that would make a person think he had never been out on a walk before *in his life*, Bud raced to the door, jumped up to the handle and tugged on it with his mouth. The door swung open. Light and sea air flooded into the trailer that had his mouth opening to capture it all, but he stopped short of going outside.

He was too well trained for that.

Kane nodded, giving a hand signal. "You can go."

At that, Bud bounded outside, yapping and barking like he was a puppy again and not the grown-up three-year-old that he was.

Rolling his eyes at his dog's antics, Kane joined him outside.

You've reached the end of your free preview.

To continue reading, get the book HERE!

ALSO BY JO HO

ROMANCE

Silver Screen Secrets Series

A heart-warming suspenseful romance series for dog lovers!

If you like Nora Roberts and our four-legged friends, then you will love this series!

Until The Stars Don't Shine, Book 1

Until The Sea Runs Dry, Book 2

Until The Last Leaf Falls, Book 3 (June 2020)

Until Color Fades Away, Book 4 (Fall 2020)

YOUNG ADULT

The Chase Ryder Series

Read this heart-warming thriller trilogy to learn the story of a mysterious dog who has escaped from a sinister lab, a lonely homeless girl surviving on wits alone, and a grieving veterinarian still haunted by a past that he can't let go of.

Can they keep their new family together while fleeing from the army of a ruthless billionaire? Will they even survive?

Gold Medal Winner of a Readers Favourite International Book Award

Wanted, Book 1

Haunted, Book 2

Hunted, Book 3

Twisted Series

Between her bizarre roommate, standoffish new friends, and overbearing father who's followed her to campus, Marley's first year at Blackville University is off to a rocky start. But when a strange night out leaves her with magical powers, college starts to look a lot more exciting...

What Doesn't Kill You, Book 1

Beware The Signs (Book 2)

See No Evil (Book 3)

The Blood That Binds (Book 4)

When Trouble Comes (Book 5)

Bad Habits (Book 6)

Left Behind (Book 7)

Hell Hath No Fury (Book 8)

In Her Skin (Book 9)

First Date Jitters (Book 10)

Grave Matters (Book 11)

Plus more to come!

Standalone Books

Who is the boy next door? A thrilling mystery that will keep you guessing until the very last page!

The Boy Next Door

See them all including her special discounted boxset deals at:

www.johoscribe.com

ABOUT THE AUTHOR

A proud geek and video gamer, and champion of complex female protagonists, Jo brings her page-turning screenwriting style to books to weave well-crafted, suspenseful stories with twists you don't see coming. She writes YA books under Jo Ho and heartwarming suspenseful romance under Joanne Ho - most of them featuring dogs!

A self-taught screenwriter, Jo's writing life began when she created the groundbreaking, critically acclaimed CBBC action fantasy television series, "Spirit Warriors," which introduced leading actress, Jessica Henwick ("Game of Thrones," "Star Wars: The Force Awakes") to the screen. Granted the biggest budget ever given to a CBBC show at the time, it was nominated for "Best Children's Programme" at the 2011 Broadcast Awards, with Jo herself, going on to win the Women in Film & Television's "New Talent" Award in 2010. Jo even made history for being the first East Asian person - man or woman - to have created a British television drama series.

Since then, Jo has worked with some of the most acclaimed producers in the world with several television shows and movies currently in development, she also writes for games. When she isn't working on her own stories, Jo helps others with their work - she is one of the BFI's (British Film Institute) recommended script consultants.

Jo suffers from MCS (Multiple Chemical Sensitivities), a debilitating condition she has developed over the last few years which has left her mostly housebound. Unfortunately, it is still not officially recognized in the UK despite the World Health Organisation listing it as a physical disability. There is currently no help for sufferers of MCS in the UK. Unable to travel or attend meetings and writersrooms, she has lost many screenwriting opportunities but has refused to allow the condition to rule her life. Despite the wrench life has thrown at her, Jo started to write and publish books.

Her debut novel WANTED, Book 1 of the Chase Ryder series has been a bestseller in 15 YA categories. It also won top prize in the YA Sci-Fi category for the 2018 Readers' Favorite Book Awards. It is her dream to bring all of her book series to screen and she believes she can make it happen with her readers' help!

Jo lives in London and hopes to travel across America one day in a super kitted out, MCS-friendly, Zombie-apocalypse-ready RV with her lovely fella Matt, and three equally lovely kitties.

Don't forget to SIGN UP to her mailing list for updates, book release details, gifts and exclusive offers at www.johoscribe.com

Check out her romance books here: https://www.amazon.com/Joanne-Ho/e/B081QVSCH5

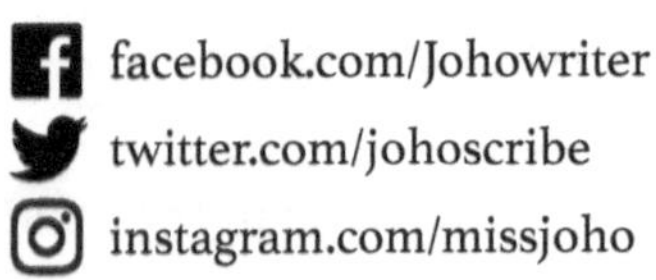

DON'T MISS ANOTHER RELEASE!

SIGN UP

to Jo's mailing list and be the first to her about her news, book
releases, gifts, competitions, and exclusive offers at
www.johoscribe.com